PASSING JUDGMENT

PASSING
JUDGMENT

Keith Ferrell

A TOM DOHERTY ASSOCIATES BOOK

NEW YORK

PASSING JUDGMENT

A Forge Book
Published by Tom Doherty Associates, Inc.
175 Fifth Avenue
New York, NY 10010

Forge® is a registered trademark of Tom Doherty Associates, Inc.

Design by Ann Gold

Library of Congress Cataloging-in-Publication Data

Ferrell, Keith.
    Passing judgment / Keith Ferrell.—1st ed.
       p.   cm.
    "A Tom Doherty Associates book."
    ISBN 0-312-86173-7
    1. Religious fundamentalism—Southern States—Fiction.
2. Politicians—Southern States—Fiction. 3. Retirees—Southern
States—Fiction. I. Title.
PS3556.E72574P3   1996
813'.54—dc20   95-52687
                                          CIP

First Edition: August 1996

Printed in the United States of America

0 9 8 7 6 5 4 3 2 1

FOR MARTHA

PART
ONE

CHAPTER 1

I AM NOT THE ONLY member of my high school class to have become rich and famous, but I was the first and that, along with the profession I pursued for several years, has earned for me a certain notoriety among those with whom I shared adolescence. They send me cards and letters. They ask for help, they ask for money, they ask for encouragement, they ask for autographs. More than one of them asked me to get them started in Hollywood. They know they have what it takes—they are positive—and would I please nudge the door open for them just a little bit? They can take it from there. I still receive such requests from time to time, although each of them must know by now that I have been through with the Industry for several years.

Roy Duncan never once asked for help. He did not need it. Roy became wealthy and well-known in his own way, moving up quickly as an attorney and even more rapidly as a member of the state legislature. A lot of people think he will be governor one day soon and that could well be the case. His career was as much a rocket as my own, and his was still climbing. Roy Duncan was practicing law at twenty-three, a legislator two years later. Last year this boy wonder made national headlines as coordinator of a special task force that broke up several drug conduits in our state. The governor appointed Roy to the position and he made the most of it. Roy stumbled onto some good information and the dealers tumbled like dominoes. It was a ripple which grew into a wave whose crest was ridden by federal officials and lawmen in other states. The wave did not recede until a dozen major arrests were made on the West Coast. Roy arranged to be present for some of those arrests. He looked very good in the papers and he handled himself well on television. You could see the fire in his eyes. He had started something from North Carolina which they had failed to do from Washington. It did not take long before the demand for Roy Duncan as an after-dinner speaker began to exceed even his energy. He must have given a speech a night. His reputation as a decent and honest young man was established. A crusader, a homegrown hero. A young man of virtue.

This young man of virtue had aligned himself very solidly with the New Spirit for American Morality movement, that group of nonpolitical politicians proclaiming moral rebirth as the only and necessary cure for all the nation's ills. When the newspapers weren't running pictures of Roy Duncan drug-buster, they were running pictures of Roy with New Spirit's leader and founder, the Reverend Frederick Prescott. Roy had been with Prescott a long time, since barely after we left high school, and Prescott never missed an opportunity to praise Roy and enhance his celebrity. When *Time* did its cover story on Prescott and New Spirit, there was decent Roy Duncan getting a healthy column-inch of coverage at the head of a sidebar.

I suppose I thought of Roy Duncan once or twice a month, more often if he was making headlines. But I was not thinking of him the day he arrived at my home, and certainly I was not expecting him. I was not even there.

I was down at the lowest of my three ponds, going after bass. I had been there since early morning. I'd landed nothing, but was enjoying a duel with a large one. I would drag a lure and he would reject it. From his occasional tug I could tell he was large enough to be smart enough to be beyond easy temptation. He would be hooked only if I could fool him with a good trick, but I had no good tricks.

The sun climbed quickly, the air was still and dry. I shucked off my shirt and let the heat raise a film of perspiration on my back. I was not going to catch this fish, and as the heat of the morning arrived I called it quits. I carried my rod and tackle box back through the tall itchy grass, a slow stroll back to my home. The sky was bright blue, high, without a hint of rain. It had not rained in weeks, but that bothered me less than most of my neighbors. I owned a farm but was no farmer. My crop of weeds flourished in drought or downpour.

When I turned onto the long, unpaved and dusty driveway that led to my front porch, I saw an unfamiliar car parked beside my little truck. There was a sudden sour taste in my mouth and I stopped short. I didn't care for visitors; I always wondered what bad news they brought.

I stepped closer. He was sitting on my porch and as I approached he stood up. It had been years but of course I recognized Roy Duncan, and would have if he had never appeared on the news. I would have known him anywhere. After high school we'd gone on to the same university. He married Ellen Jennings, a girl I once dated, the first love of my life.

Roy always told people he was my friend. He was wrong.

CHAPTER 2

ROY BOUNDED DOWN MY STEPS, hand outstretched, big smile creasing his adorable babyfat face. "Baird Lowen! How *are* you? It's been too long." His handshake was politician firm, his nails recently manicured.

"Hello, Roy," I said. "What brings you down this way?"

He walked close beside me back up the steps. For a moment I thought he was going to throw an old chum arm around my shoulders. "A little business, Baird. I took a chance on stopping by. I've got a few things I want to talk over with you." He gave his trousers a quick tug before seating himself. Roy wore an expensive-looking three-piece suit, beige with dark buttons. I wondered if he'd picked the color to complement his thinning, sandy hair. He looked completely at ease, even in a vest on a hot morning, all dressed up as though for the campaign trail. The heat did not seem to affect him. His hairline had receded a bit since I'd last seen him in person, and he'd gained a few pounds, but Roy looked fine nonetheless, a prosperous Jaycee, gubernatorial material all the way.

"Some ice water?" I said, and gave him no time to decline. "Be just a minute." I unlocked the door and went inside.

There was a pain behind my eyes. I did not want Roy Duncan in my home. I did not want anyone there. Since leaving Hollywood I'd accepted my circumstances—the circumstances that caused me to leave—and I understood that because of them I would spend my time in company with paranoia. The situation was not an ideal one but I had brought it on myself, and would live with it. I became a hermit, or styled myself as one. Visitors fed the terror in me.

I pulled off my fishing clothes and wondered how quickly I would be able to get rid of Roy. A few things to talk over. It did not seem likely that he had come to solicit a campaign contribution. I might have begun to hide when I returned east, but I had not grown mute. From time to time I fumbled a few lazy steps toward becoming a writer of prose rather than film. I had managed to sell a few pieces, and, hermit or not, submitted them above my name. Evidently that name still possessed some marquee value, for my pieces found homes in print, first in film journals, then in magazines of larger substance and reputation. Some of my articles possessed substance of their own, but I doubted they would make me much of a reputation as a writer. I had a few things to say, that was all, some of them about film, others about the ways in which film had come to rule America in the nineties.

The most recent of my pieces, published in the *New Yorker* a month before Roy's visit, offered a possible clue to his presence at my house. "Lights! Cameras! Prescott!" was an article about New Spirit's television productions. Prescott owned and operated his own cable network and offered hours of sermons and song every Sunday, along with occasional evening-long evangelical entertainment extravaganzas. He produced records that ranged from traditional gospel to righteous rap to comforting country and made Christian music videos to promote them. New Spirit had established an early and ambitious site on the Internet and its traffic there grew larger every day. There was a line of New Spirit software and CD-ROMs, a publishing division that had pushed several of Betty Prescott's books onto national bestseller lists, Betty Prescott greeting cards and party decorations, a college, real estate developments for Christian families, even a clothing label.

But it was television, and television's love of Frederick Prescott, that had made New Spirit's first national bones. What caught my eye, and what I tried to catch in my article, was the degree to which Prescott and his line producers, directors, camera operators, and on-screen talent made subtle use of sophisticated film techniques in their programs. They knew what they were doing and were technically the best crew of all the electronic evangelical shows, and the heart of their effectiveness—beyond Frederick Prescott's vast and admitted gifts as a preacher and on-screen presence—was their knowledge of contemporary cinema. Prescott's team was *good:* There were Spielberg swoops in the sermons, Tarantino crosscutting behind the credits, even a perfect moment of Kubrick coldness when the camera tracked toward the facade of an abortion clinic. I nailed them all.

Technique is one thing, and on technique I had them cold. I was on shakier ground in the latter section of the piece, where my spleen took over for my brain. I suggested that the tools of fiction on film were the perfect tools for the fiction that was faith, and it may have been that my words were too harsh. My editor thought so, but stood by what I had written, although my suspicion was that her support stemmed from my name's publicity value more than any insights my words carried. Certainly I had no illusions: My reputation as a director sold the article as much as my prose or my arguments, even though it was four years since I'd last been on a set. My ego was gratified by the attention, and when I wrote the piece I was not too troubled by my slaps at the faithful. I was not by a long shot religious, and had never really owned any faith to lose. Indeed, I'd taken an earlier slap—twenty years ago in our high school newspaper—at the Prescotts' presence on our campus. That piece had angered Roy, and I was sure the new one had not pleased him, although neither Roy nor Ellen's name was on any of the hate mail I received after the *New Yorker* came out. Some of those letters were not signed, but I doubted the Duncans would send anonymous mail to their old friend Baird, for what it was worth.

None of which did much to explain what Roy Duncan was doing here, on my front porch, waiting for me to bring him a glass of water. I could not imagine that my *New Yorker* piece had prompted his visit. It wasn't that good an article, finally, different from dozens of others only in that it carried my name and a hint here and there of reminiscence, for I had grown up in Samson, North Carolina, home of Frederick Prescott and New Spirit. My article caught some attention in my hometown.

Prescott himself devoted a few minutes of airtime to me. He claimed he remembered me from high school, and he was not a man to lie. He talked of my film career and the sordidness of my films, in particular *Moonstalk,* the movie that ended my career even while it did substantial business. Then the reverend grinned at the camera and turned his attention to larger targets, and as he did so, his crew set to work. For the rest of the program every technique I had mentioned in the article was exaggerated, repeated, satirized, mocked. I chuckled even as I watched myself being one-upped on Sunday evening television.

I was not chuckling now. I pulled on jeans and a faded workshirt. I did not really want to know why Roy was here. I heard from him once or twice each year. He and Ellen always sent a Christmas card. It arrived well in advance of the holiday, specially designed and printed for the Duncan Family. Sometimes there was a photograph mounted within, their names in red ink beneath it. Every other year or so there was a campaign flyer or charity solicitation which I allowed, like the cards, to pass without reply. Twice the Duncans had sent out printed newsletters, chatty sheets filled with talk of Roy's career and Ellen's volunteer work, New Spirit, their three tikes. Their word.

I took a breath. I would know soon enough what Roy wanted from me, and then he would be gone. I walked back through the kitchen, got Roy's water and returned to the porch.

He sat with hands folded together, head bowed.

"Praying?" I said. Roy looked up quickly. He seemed startled and that made me feel a little better.

"You caught me," he said with a grin that revealed perfect teeth. He glanced out over my wide lawn and waved a hand. "It's so beautiful here. Tranquil. I can see why you came back. A man can think here, find peace. Puts you close to God."

"It does that," I said. I hooked my right leg over a straight-backed chair and sat facing him.

Roy turned his attention to me. "You know, you're looking very good, Baird." He pursed his lips, an unfortunate tic that transformed his face from babyfat to pudgy. *"Bear,"* Roy said. His laugh was hearty, a constituent-pleaser. "Anyone call you *Bear* anymore?"

"Hardly anyone, Roy Rogers."

"You remembered."

"It was an effort."

"Nicknames," he said softly, and shifted to look outward again. He sipped some water.

"What sort of business, Roy?"

"Legislative. Just looking over some things."

"This isn't your district. We have our own representative."

"A good man, too. But I'm here on committee work, Baird. Oiling some wheels, greasing some levers, finding out what'll fly, what won't. You know."

"Sure."

"And to be frank, I wanted to see you. It's been a while."

"See me about what?"

"Oh . . . personal things. Old times. Just a talk, Bear."

"Why me?" I decided I would let Roy call me Bear five more times. I would keep careful count.

"Because of how far back we go, Bear. You know us both. Myself and Ellen. I need to talk to somebody who knows us both, who has known us a long time."

"Lots of people know both of you. Talk to Freddy Prescott."

"It's you, Baird. Just accept it. Try, anyway." His voice rose a little and then dropped. "It has to be you, Baird."

"Then get on with it."

"It's just that—" He took some water. "It's hard to start."

"Trouble in the marriage," I said, an easy divination.

"Nothing like that! Oh, no." He laughed again. "I didn't give *that* impression, did I? No, not at *all.* In fact—" He leaned close to pat my knee. "In fact, old chip, Ellen is expecting again."

"Another tike."

"You *do* read the newsletters," he said with a happy nod. "I can't tell you how much that will please Ellen. We have such great fun putting those things together."

He was coasting, an old buddy visiting an old buddy. I put my palms on my knees and wished he would call me Bear four times, fast. "Roy, you're not here to chat. Get on with it."

Roy put down his glass and eased back in the chair. The seat creaked beneath him. For a moment he said nothing. His breathing made a rhythmic nasal whistle, surprisingly loud. He kept his mouth tightly closed, his lips pressed together until at last he began to talk. "It is Ellen, but there is nothing wrong with our marriage. We have the best marriage of anyone I know. Everyone agrees. Ellen loves the kids, she's a great mom, she keeps a fine house." He patted the bulge beneath his vest. "She's a terrific cook, absolutely sensational, as I guess you can tell. I'm headed for a diet before the campaign heats up. But that gal can even make low-cal dishes a treat."

I thought of Ellen. We'd been a steady item throughout our junior year in high school, and it was the first real romance for either of us. Ellen had a killer smile and startling jade eyes. She was a popular girl, cheerful and intelligent. I loved her more than I could say, and after we stopped dating we tried to remain friends. It didn't work out. I watched as she and Roy found each other, and I felt some pain as their relationship deepened and defined itself. But not too much, I convinced myself, for she was not the same girl. With Roy, with the after-school church group that Roy led her to, she became someone else. It may have been inevitable.

Camelot babies, we arrived at adolescence a decade after Camelot collapsed. Had we been just a few years older we would have had the War and the Movement, the Beatles and *2001,* the psychedelic Sixties to fuel our focus. Some world. Instead, we got Disco and the aftermath of defeat, *Star Wars,* Ford and Carter, gasoline lines and the on-ramp to the Reagan revolution. Some world. Born sooner, Ellen might have made a fine flower child, for at one time she had a sweet sense of the karmic and the cosmic and was determined to find a place for herself and her spirit within that cosmos. She wanted to know who she was, and she could not stop looking for some key to that lock. What she finally found was something like religion, and along with Roy and a fair number of our classmates she took to it as though to evangelism born. Their path was hastened by the most expert guidance of Frederick and Betty Prescott, newly arrived in Samson to establish a church and a teen worship program. Ellen let herself be guided. We tried to get back together once, and I could still remember those green eyes flashing as she ruled the evening with apostolic arguments. My ears were deaf to them, for at that point in my life I knew that whatever it was I wanted out of this world or any other world it was not likely to be provided by Jesus. I had some anger toward God, and little use for those who followed Him. So we went our separate ways at the same school, and from a distance I watched Ellen grow daily more committed to the glories of the gospel. It was a devotion which took her far away from me and what I wanted, and brought her to Roy Duncan. He and I were several universes apart, but Ellen moved as though tugged by gravity into his orbit, taken and remade by his force.

I looked at him. Close to two decades had passed, but my memories of Ellen were memories I returned to often. I saw her as her spirit was swallowed by Roy's, and as he gave both their spirits over to New Spirit. She disappeared, as though she had never been. I persuaded myself that my pain faded quickly: It was just a high school romance and she was *his girl now.* Nothing more. But of course there was more and a bit of it came back to me. She had been a spectacular young woman. I could not imagine Ellen poring over cookbooks in search of terrific low-cal meals.

"You inviting me to dinner, Roy?"

"I got carried away," he said softly. "I love her so much. We have such a fine life. We often have you in our thoughts, you know. You always did have talent. We hoped you would put it to good use. You could make films that would help people, Baird." He smiled. "But then you don't make films anymore, do you?"

"No."

"Lately you've been putting your talent to other uses."

It was my turn to be pleased. "You *did* read my article!"

My irony was wasted. "Yes. Quite a few people did. But I don't want to get into that." He drew a breath and it was obvious that he did very much want to get into it. "You disappointed a lot of people, Baird. Old friends of yours. It hurt Ellen." Roy drummed his fingers on the arms of the chair. "That's past. That's not it."

"What, then?"

But he would not let go. My words must have been thorns. "You stirred things up in Samson, old chip."

"Good."

"You know you were unfair to the reverend."

"I know how some people could see it that way."

"They did."

"Good."

He nodded. His pupils were narrow. "You must be very proud," Roy said.

"I have my days."

We fell silent and I watched him change, saw what I was certain other adversaries had seen. The muscles beneath his cheeks grew tense; there was a tightening of skin across his forehead. His shoulders rose. "I am truly sorry for you, Baird."

"Save that."

"The reverend—"

"Get on with it."

"All right." His shoulders held firm. "I'll get on with it. All right."

"Good."

"It is Ellen," Roy said. He loosened his necktie and unfastened the top two buttons of his vest. "There is a problem and it is a serious one." He looked at me. "You're going to help us solve it."

"Am I? Me?"

"Yes," Roy said. "No one else can."

My curiosity was more than piqued, but my patience was just about gone. "What are you talking about?"

He blinked his eyes rapidly, as though against rising tears which he did not wish to show. "This isn't easy for me. Asking for help."

"Asking for help? Or asking for help from *me?*"

"Both."

"Then just tell me, Roy. Get it over with so we can get *this* over with."

The sharpness in my tone annoyed him and anger replaced the tears in his eyes. He was no longer blinking as he spoke. "Just you take your time, Baird. Don't take that tone with *me.* You listen to what I have to say."

"Roy, I *am* listening. You just haven't said anything yet."

"No? Then listen." He took a breath and placed his palms on his knees, leaning toward me. "Ellen got a package in the mail two days ago. There was no return address. When she opened it there were . . . there were . . ." He coughed and his shoulders gave up a shudder.

"What?"

Roy nodded and did not take his eyes from me. "There were photographs, more than a dozen of them. Awful things, wicked things." Another shudder shook him. "Pictures of Ellen doing those things. Ellen doing those things on film."

It was all he had in him. He began to weep silently, he did not sob, turning his head swiftly from me to focus on the tips of his shiny shoes. Teardrops spattered those shoes. I did not move, nor offer comfort of any kind. I was too astonished. Ellen? Doing wicked things on film? *Ellen?*

After a moment and another cough Roy began to regain his composure, another impressive performance. He wiped his eyes with a handkerchief and folded it neatly before putting it away. He pressed his palms together and bowed his head, no tears falling now. I could not make out the words he whispered. Soon his shoulders stopped trembling and his breathing grew more regular. He sat up straight and faced me once more, and once more his gaze was strong and clear.

"I apologize, Baird, although I guess there's no real need to. But it does that to me when I think about it. You should have seen Ellen. I've never seen anything like it. She's a strong woman and she's strong enough to handle this. She *will* handle it, *we* will. Get through it and beyond it. But that day. She was *wailing,* Baird, angry and heartbroken all at once. It broke my heart to see it, and there was nothing I could do for her. And that was the worst."

"What has this got to do with me?"

"She told me to come see you, Baird. She told me that even through her tears. Come see you and get you to *take care of this.*"

That surprised me as much as anything he had said. The bitterness of our breakup had kept Ellen and I from speaking more than half a dozen times over the years. There may have been a part of me that hoped she thought well of Baird Lowen from time to time, but I also doubted if that was the case. I could not imagine that she approved of the movies I'd made. I was a name on the Duncans' Christmas mailing list, a classmate from the old days, nothing more than that.

But now that she needed help, *real* help, she sent her husband to fetch me. I put myself on guard against fatuousness, but a certain satisfaction spread through me as I sat facing Roy. I may have sat straighter and looked down at him a bit. Her husband couldn't help her but her old beau could.

"Why are you smiling?" Roy's voice was sharp and held something I had not heard from him before. It was a dangerous voice; it knew how to command. Under different circumstances I could have been frightened of him.

Not now. I widened my smile. "Why, Roy, I'm smiling at *you*. At this story you're telling me. It's been my experience, old *chip*, that women have affairs because they're not getting what they need from their husbands." It was a cruel remark and intended as one. I let it sink in. "But what I *don't* understand is why you're *here*."

"I told you. Ellen sent me. You're going to help us get out of this. There was a letter. It said the pictures would be published if I didn't get out of politics. That hurt Ellen more than anything, I think. She kept saying, 'I'm sorry, I'm sorry.' She wouldn't stop. I told her not to do that to herself, that it wasn't her fault."

The day I lifted a finger to save Roy Duncan's career was the day I would pray with Frederick Prescott, but I held that comment in reserve. I wanted to sting him one more time, deeply. "Most cuckolds wouldn't be that magnanimous, Roy," I said.

A muscle in his jaw went tight. Drops of perspiration, drawn downward, left tracks across his temples. "Watch yourself, Baird," he whispered, and I heard that edge again and felt that flicker of fear. I did not like it.

"Don't give me orders," I said. "And don't waste any more

time expecting *me* to save your ass from your wife's . . . indiscretion. Ellen doesn't mean that much to me anymore, and you never did."

"You've got it wrong, Baird. It's not like that at all."

"Tell me what it's like, Roy. Go ahead." My words carried the weight of a dare.

His voice was even now, no tension at all, nothing but simple facts that he reeled off. "There was no affair. No adultery. Ellen wouldn't do that and neither would I. Ellen wasn't even my wife when those pictures were taken. We weren't even dating then. She was just a scared kid being taken advantage of by someone who should have known better."

I did not move. I stared straight at those beads of moisture on his pink skin. If I'd possessed Superman heat vision they would have boiled.

"Go on," I said. My voice sounded hoarse.

"It was in high school, *Bear.* It was in high school the pictures were taken. I thought you would have figured. I thought for a while you might have taken them somehow. It was in high school. Ellen wouldn't do anything like that after she married me. We have too much together. But before—"

He spread his hands wide, palms toward me. He did not look away. I could tell he was finished with looking away. "Baird, the pictures are of Ellen and you."

CHAPTER 3

I STARED AT MY RIGHT hand. I could see the blue veins pulsing beneath the skin. My hands did not shake at all. Eventually I turned my attention back to Roy Duncan.

He did not look away or try to stare me down. He sat impassive, the upper hand his. It was my move.

"Just one problem," I said quickly. "I don't remember doing anything wicked with Ellen."

"Don't, Baird. Don't even try. The hard part for me is over now so don't even try. I'll slap you down and squash you flat."

"I'm as serious as I can be, old chip."

"You're denying it."

"Wickedness? Of course I deny it."

"That you had sexual relations with Ellen."

"Roy, I gather you have photographic proof so I'd be a little foolish to deny that, wouldn't I?" He may have winced a little. "But nothing evil, Roy, nothing filthy."

Roy stood up and walked slowly to the far end of the porch. He raised his arms over his head until his fingertips rested against the lip of the overhang. With his back to me he said, "I knew you'd taken advantage of her. She told me, but she didn't have to because I know the kind of man you are, Baird. Were even then. But she told me. Before we were even very serious, because she wanted me to know. Before we got too serious—in case I wanted to stop seeing her because of it."

"Advantage?"

"She was sixteen."

"So was I."

"No excuse. She was a *girl.* You took her because you could, because you knew she didn't have the strength to stand up to your pressure. Or did you call it *technique?*"

"Ellen told you this?"

"She told me. She told me and she cried a little bit, but only a little because she's a strong woman. Was even then. She told me, she told me she would not be able to give her bride's night gift. You stole it from her. You did, Baird. I think about it sometimes, Ellen before she found me. Doing what you told her to do. Those things. Taking the devil's pleasure from *you.*" His voice was thick.

Roy spun suddenly and walked toward me, his steps heavy. He stopped short and balled his clean hands into tight fists. "How do you live with yourself?" he said. He rocked gently back and forth. His jacket drew tight over his shoulders. "She cried when I proposed, you know. In spite of how strong she is, in spite of what *you* did to her." He looked as though he would spit on me. Then he moved.

I came up fast from the chair, inside his first swing, which was a clumsy right. His knuckles brushed my shoulders and I was surprised to find there was some force behind the blow. I grabbed Roy's left arm, spun him around, slammed him back against the house. He bounced out toward me and I slammed him back once more. His hands darted up to cover his face, the first rule of politics being keep the pretty face clean. I brushed his hands out of my way and crossed his cheeks twice with an open palm. The slaps rang through the still morning.

I was not paying attention. As I drew back to slap once more, Roy pounded a fist into my stomach. The air went out of me. He gave me another good one and a knee before backing off. I did not try to rise. It was better to wait, and remind myself not to underestimate him again.

"Just stay there, Baird," Roy said. He stood a few feet away. He was breathing hard but grinning. "Stay there. I've got more to say. I married Ellen and I forgave her, but I have waited twenty years to do that to you, and I have more if you want it. It's my right. And privilege."

I looked up at him. My breath was coming back. He did not move, and for a moment I saw the scene from another's perspective, my director's eye coming back unbidden, as though I were standing on the lawn below, watching. Roy looked like a child who'd just won a fight, and I looked like a child who'd lost. The vision passed and I grew from childhood to adolescence. I could feel Ellen's fingers stroking the back of my neck as she'd done so many times, at movies, or dances, or as we made love. I could hear old songs, *our* song. A scent, hers, came back. Buoyed by memory, I stood up.

"Leave."

Roy did not reply. He reached slowly into his jacket and withdrew an envelope. He tossed it to me and turned away. I carried it to the far end of the porch, sat down and opened it.

There were eight photographs. They wore their age well, the images still clear. I knew immediately where and when the pictures were taken. My parents owned a few acres on a lake thirty miles west of Samson. In the center of the property they built a summer home. Ellen and I went there occasionally, on weekends with my family and on afternoons when we had the place to ourselves. Most of the time we spent walking in the woods. We had a few picnics, talked, sometimes fished. We made love there only twice, and I do not know if we made love a total of a dozen times during our entire romance. It made Ellen nervous and she felt some guilt about it, so there may have been something to what Roy said about me. But I did not really believe that, for I cared too much for Ellen to pressure her. As I recalled, we both vowed more than once to keep ourselves and our drives under control, and when we failed in our resolve we failed together.

I recalled without difficulty the Saturday the pictures were taken. Ellen and I were experimenting with various coital positions, some of them quite exotic. We had not yet learned the deep pleasures more easily available from the familiar standards. So we spent an entire early spring Saturday at the lakehouse, making love inexhaustibly in a considerable variety of configurations. But it was love each time, our sixteen-year-old attempt at it, and that was what Roy could never comprehend. I looked through the pictures two or three times and tried to view them as Roy might. Ellen and I were doing the sorts of things nice boys and girls did not do, not even in the mid-seventies, not good middle-class children like ourselves, things which were even illegal in this state not so many years ago.

I felt a sudden and unexpected stab of sorrow for Ellen, for I knew that the pleasure she derived from our lovemaking far outweighed her guilt and confusion, at least for a time. But when the guilt and the fears won, when she turned from me, she turned that furnace down and I assume its light went out. How else had she lived with Roy all these years? How had she lived missing not the athletics, not the geometry of position, but the passion, the surrender to the senses? Not the calisthenics but the touching. I could not imagine Roy and Ellen touching. I thought of the old joke: If they had four children they must have done it four times. I stood up, walked back to Roy and handed him the pictures.

"You keep these. I have memories."

His shoulders drew up and I braced myself. He was stronger than I would have guessed, and in far better shape, but he would not surprise me again. I hoped he would take another swing.

"There's a sickness in you, Baird. A little germ of sickness and poison. I can smell it."

"Please. Tell me what you want, then get the hell out of here."

Roy did not move. The knees of his trousers were soiled. His jacket was wrinkled. "Find out who took those pictures. Find out who's trying to ruin my life."

I laughed. "Me? For God's sake, Roy."

"You find out."

"Forget it. Get somebody else. Send some of your storm troopers. Get your Godsquad to do it."

"Don't be ridiculous. Nobody else is going to know about these pictures. You already do."

"That's right. I was there."

"These pictures are your fault, Baird. It's your responsibility to deal with them. That's simple enough, even for you."

"It's simple, yes."

"Good."

"No, Roy. Let me put it another way. *No.* Now, leave."

"You claim you loved her."

"I did."

"Then you owe her. You did this to her. Now spare her this shame."

"I don't think it's her shame you're worried about, is it, *Governor?* Now, listen—"

"I'm listening just fine, Baird. You're the one who's not paying attention. You're going to come to Samson and take care of this and whoever sent these pictures."

"I'm not coming, Roy, get that. Why me, anyway? Just what do you think I could do?"

"You have a head start. You know Ellen. You know this was done by someone we went to school with, someone who knew you."

"How do I know that?"

Roy reached into his jacket once more and took out a piece of paper, carefully folded. He gave it to me and did not look away as I opened and read it. Its message was neatly printed in the center of the page:

I got these pictures out the other day. I've had them quite a while but they get more interesting all the time. I hate to think of other people missing all this fun. So I'm thinking about sharing them. And I need to decide before the reunion.

Unless you don't want me to. If that's the case then you have two steps. First, think about what they're worth to you and if the price is right get the money together.

Second, Don't be governor. Don't even run. Or for anything else, ever again. Simple.

Withdraw your name from discussions. In the papers, on tv, at the reunion. Everywhere you say you're out of it and are staying out.

Otherwise, what can I promise?

Get in touch. You can figure where to find me.

An old school friend

P.S. Hi Ellen! Who would ever have thought?

I read the message twice. It offered little. Typeface anonymous, laser-printed, nothing distinctive or idiosyncratic about it. The message itself was more cryptic. But its codes were beyond me. What could I tell from the message? I was no detective. Anyone could have written it.

"Three weeks," Roy said.

"What?"

"The reunion. Three weeks from now."

"Yeah." I'd received an invitation to our class's twentieth high school reunion but I had no intention of attending.

"So you have three weeks," said Roy.

"What's it going to take to get through to you, Roy?"

"You can't." He rubbed his palms together, then laced his fingers behind his neck and stretched. "You'll help me. There are reasons."

"Such as?"

"What you owe Ellen."

"We've been through that."

"It's not enough?"

"No. Not anymore."

"Well, how about some other names, then, old chip?"

I took a breath. "What names?"

Roy smiled. "Billy Toller."

My breath hissed out between clenched teeth. I felt as though he had punched me again. *Billy Toller.* The morning grew hotter. I could feel my shirt clinging to my skin. I did not look at Roy.

How could he know? It was that name, Billy's, which had brought me here in retreat. I had spent more than one moment, upon the approach of strangers, convinced that they had come to say that name to me, whisper it, and with it open me as though it were a knife. Billy Toller.

"You son of a bitch."

"Don't make me mad, Baird. I might have to hit you." His voice carried a load of glee.

"Anything else?"

"Only all of it, Baird. Every bit. Kelsey Stillett of course. And Maurice Devlin, your favorite silent partner. And for kickers I know just where the body is, don't think I don't." He spread his hands wide. "I can show you the details. It's in an envelope, you see, a nice fat envelope addressed to the Arizona attorney general. A friend of mine, by the way." He sat down.

For a moment I thought I would hit him, harder than before, hit him with everything I had, pound him through the wall. I held myself steady and waited for Roy to finish.

His grin was wide now. "Little Kelsey Stillett, child star. You made that awful dirty picture with her. Smut. What was it called?"

"Moonstalk," I said. I'd heard that movie called smut before.

"Ah. *Moonstalk.* Yes. A dirty, dirty film. And didn't some dirty things go on between Kelsey and Billy?"

"All right, Roy. That's enough."

"Is it? I'll see you in Samson, then." He stood up.

I didn't answer.

"Speak up, Baird. Or do I mail the envelope?"

I licked my lips. I was afraid my voice would fail. "Who told you?"

He shook his head. "Not yet. Not until it's over. Then I'll tell you."

"That's no deal."

"I think it is. But maybe this will help. I ran into some of Maurice's associates. You remember Maurice Devlin. Well, it was last year, when we were working the Crack Force. I met a few of his friends. Close friends. I found out some things that helped me then, and I found out some things that are helping me now. You may not care about those pictures of you and Ellen, but maybe you'd like to see some of you and Billy Toller."

"You're bluffing."

"I can make it easy for you to find out I'm not."

I was not ready to take that risk. Too many of his details were true.

Roy clapped his hands together, a greedy sound. "You have had some very bad luck with photographers in your life, old Bear," he said.

"It's going to attract some attention."

"What's that?"

"My being in Samson. My looking around."

Roy beamed like a teacher whose most troubled pupil had just aced an exam. "I *knew* you would see the light. The Lord told me so."

"Okay, Roy."

"And sure there'll be some attention. That's good. It shouldn't take more than a day or two for the word to get around. You're still a celebrity in *some* circles. And once the word's out it will get to the person behind this."

"And then maybe that person comes after me."

"Could be, Baird. But you can handle yourself. You're so good with your fists."

I grabbed at something. "What about your friends at New Spirit, Roy? What are they going to think about me being involved with you?"

"Nobody at New Spirit needs to know anything about this."

"Wrong. I'll come to Samson but I want some conditions. Maybe I'll want to talk to some people at New Spirit. Maybe one of them can help me."

"No."

"Maybe one of them took the pictures, Roy, have you thought of that? Think about it. Surely you're not the only one of the crew at New Spirit. But you're Freddy Prescott's brightest star and that's bound to make some people jealous."

"Forget it, Baird. I already have an idea who sent these pictures. You come to Samson and you'll get the idea, too."

"Who?"

Roy shook his head. "Wouldn't be fair. It's not Christian to accuse out of turn. You're the one who's got to come up with the proof. So you come and look and maybe you'll come up with the same name, maybe you won't." His grin was more wicked than anything in the pictures. "Some of the old crew's with my opposition, too. Maybe you'll find some other things on your way. Who knows?"

"Okay, Roy, fine. Maybe I'll find out a few things. But you give me the name."

He tilted his head back and sighed. "I'll have to see. Maybe."

"Maybe I'll find some other skeletons. Think about that, Roy. New Spirit skeletons, wouldn't that be something?"

"You stay away from New Spirit."

"Then you give me that name."

"I'll tell you what. You take some time to think about the old days. Make a list of who *you* think might do something like this.

Ellen's got a list, and I do, too. I want you in Samson on Monday. We'll compare notes."

"And if it's New Spirit? If I find something there?"

"There's nothing to find out."

"That's not what you and Ellen thought, was it?"

"New Spirit has no secrets, Baird. Our books are as open as our hearts. Maybe you *should* come by. We could pray for you. You'd be welcome there. Maybe you'd even join us." He smiled at the thought. "Just don't forget why you're in Samson. Find out who took those pictures. Find out who sent them. And shut them up."

"How?"

"Well, you shut Billy Toller up," he said. "Work this one out."

I said nothing.

"You'll come through, Baird. For your old friends. I have every confidence in you."

"I'm touched."

"Otherwise you'll be heading back to Arizona. To stay."

"Think so? I think you're bluffing."

"No bluff, Baird. Try me."

"We'll see."

"Yes we will. Next week. Or in three weeks when we all see you off to your old haunts. You have a deadline."

"All right, Roy. I'll be in Samson on Monday. You get some things ready. I want that name and I want any other names you can think of, anybody who wants you out of politics and who could have taken those pictures."

"Like I said: We'll compare lists."

"We will," I said. "And Ellen and I will. I want to see her Monday. Without you."

"No."

"Then mail your envelope." I could bluff, too. I just wasn't as confident I could pull it off.

"Call me at my office Monday," he said, and handed me a

business card. "Call me before you do anything else. We'll see about Ellen."

"Still not willing to let her make up her own mind?"

"All right, Baird. Let it go."

"I'll see you Monday, Roy. In Samson. Now get out of here."

"There are a few more things."

"They'll keep. I've had enough of you."

He opened his mouth, then looked into my eyes and closed it, nodding. He moved to the steps leading down from the porch.

"Roy," I said before he could get too far. "I've changed my mind. How about leaving those pictures? I'll want to go over them."

He handed the pictures back to me. Then he hurried down the steps. I did not move but as he reached his car I said, "Tell Ellen I'll be thinking of her."

"You can imagine I'll tell her that."

"And one more thing." I held the photographs high. "I wouldn't be too hasty about getting in touch with Arizona. Not while I've got these. You know?"

"I know. But I know something else, Baird. You don't finish this, what you're holding is only worth something for another three weeks. What I'm holding has no time limit—or statute of limitations."

"So you say." I wagged the photographs at him.

Roy blinked his eyes. "Thank you for the water, Baird. The hospitality. Now I'm going to leave you alone so you can think. You've got a lot of that to do this weekend, I'd imagine."

Roy Duncan stood still for another moment. "Do go to church on Sunday, Bear. You have great need of it."

Then he got into his car and drove away, raising dust the length of my driveway.

CHAPTER 4

I WENT INTO THE KITCHEN and poured myself a tall dark drink and carried it back onto the porch. I sat at the far end and rocked my chair back on its hind legs, propping myself with bare feet against one of the roof supports. I sipped my drink and spent a few moments replaying in my mind the conversation with Roy Duncan.

He was convinced he had me penned, and there was a chance he did. He knew all the names and seemed to know how they all came together. I had caught the confidence in his look, and could imagine the gleam of greedy joy that passed over him upon learning of my connection with Billy Toller's death. Which version had he heard, and how close to the truth was it? And who had he heard it from?

By the time I finished my drink my thoughts were filled with Billy and Kelsey and Maurice and the strange afternoon and evening of Billy's death. I did not want to think of those things—it was not yet time. Those thoughts always made me crazy and I could not afford that now. I went and got the bottle of bourbon and returned to my seat. I picked up the envelope filled with photographs of Ellen and me. I would spend some time with those pictures.

I took another swallow. For a few minutes I sat still, looking out over my land, watching, chasing Billy from all my thoughts. After a while it felt like I was getting some perspective. I did not think this was the sort of thing which would be used against me twice. This was my opportunity. *Billy Toller.* It was here. This was what I had been hiding from. Or waiting for. I would have to move against it or trade this farm for a cell in Arizona. Fine, I could handle that; it allowed no qualification, it was not a good either/or. I had no intention of returning to Arizona. I was to become a free man whether I wanted to be or not. The only free will I had immediately before me was the choice of action I would take.

Call it an adventure, I told myself, an enforced adventure. Track down a blackmailer and save your own skin at the same time. It was a challenge I would have to learn to live with, and rise to.

The temperature peaked. There was no hint of breeze. The air was as dead as the air of the desert. I gave myself another drink, and then picked up the pictures.

I spent an hour going through them, as impersonally as I could, trying to see them as artifacts divorced from my past. I was trying to become an investigator, and I was in search of clues. Ellen and I had only made love at the lakehouse on two occasions. The first was a rainy February Sunday when we hoped the drizzle would turn to snow and strand us. The second was a lovely brisk Saturday in early March, when the pictures were taken. I closed my eyes and tried to remember who might have known we would be at the lake that day.

I could think of no one. Furtive young lovers, Ellen and I had taken precautions about our secret spots. We placed a high bounty on our privacy for reasons both romantic and practical. Clandestine trysts had their appeal, not to mention what would happen if our parents learned we were intimate. Ellen lived in holy terror of her mother's disapproval, which could become a rage if she didn't like the way her daughter's hair was combed. We kept things very quiet.

So assume no one knew we went to the lakehouse. Were we followed? It seemed the likeliest possibility. Whoever it was had been very careful. The house stood at the base of a steeply sloped gravel road which, when it rained, was always on the verge of impassability. My father must have had that road rebuilt a dozen times. Cars made noise, groaning and complaining as they made their way down that road. Branches and debris constantly clotted the ruts. That Saturday, after love finally exhausted us, Ellen had to gun the engine while I pushed the car through a couple of muddy spots on our way out. The road would give an incautious follower away.

A follower, then, who had parked elsewhere and walked in. Why had we not heard anything? The ground that Saturday was suited to stealth. It came back to me—there had been a late snow that week and traces of it still sparkled in shaded spots. Had Ellen made a wet snowball and thrown it at me? The melt soaked the ground cover silent. There were several paths to the lakehouse, and each offered hiding places. Ellen and I had other things on our minds. We were not looking for voyeurs.

The photographs were taken from the front of the house, easy shots through sliding glass doors. We were cautious of our privacy, but confident we had achieved it there: The curtains were pulled back. I was beginning to lose my objectivity as the bourbon worked its spell and the memories returned.

That Saturday had been warm for March, temperature up near sixty. All of the remaining snow would be gone by sundown. But it was cool enough. Ellen and I had spent days on our plan, and central to the excursion was the delight of lovemaking before an open fire. We heard its crackle as we schemed.

I built the fire and the room grew warm, then hot. I pulled back the curtains and opened the sliding door. At first Ellen was shy, fearful that someone might see us. But birds sang and breezes shook the trees and I reassured her. Her inhibitions melted with rising passion. The photographs offered testament to the heights our fever attained.

I put the pictures back into the envelope. How could I even hope for detachment? Even with the pictures put away I could still taste that Saturday afternoon, smell Ellen's sweet scent, savor the cycle of depletion and renewal that drove us. It was a heady memory and a very tender one. We were so young. I would have wagered that I was invulnerable to the sorts of nostalgia that swept through me then. I had always believed that nostalgia was a dishonest emotion, not emotion at all; but I felt it then, it all ran through me. The time I spent in love with Ellen came back so fully and so easily because in so many ways I had never fully moved beyond those times. My best motion pictures were about adolescence; my biggest success had been with adolescent audiences. My manner of dealing with Billy Toller's death and the conditions it placed upon my life—there was no more adolescent gesture than running away.

So I sat and drank and thought of Ellen and Billy and Roy and Maurice and Kelsey and the ways that my life had led me to each of them and then away and now back again. I thought of the films I had made, films thick with my peculiar sensibility, a sixteen-year-old's imitation of genius, love stories by a man who had known many women but had only been in love once. I was nearly drunk and I deceived myself into believing that I had other motives for letting Roy Duncan have his victory over me.

I wanted to see Ellen again. Why else that surge when I thought she wanted me for her champion? I wanted to take a look at her. I wanted to find out who had taken those pictures, had taken their own look, and with a camera violated something which I myself had put before a dozen cameras, in a dozen different alterations and rearrangements, using actors and the techniques of cinema to work my way through.

After a while I went into the house.

The original owner of that house had been an eccentric who'd put windows of different sizes in every room, and now the house was owned by another eccentric who had for three years kept a wary eye on each of those windows. A weary motion picture director who had possessed at least the good sense and then the clout to insist upon a piece of the gross, and then enjoyed the luck or talent to make films that were profitable, and one film that was close to a terrific success. I was not profligate and I had money enough for six lives. So when I was forced—by myself— to retire, I retired here, to this house, and set myself up in business as a slow writer.

I kept my office neat and so found what I was looking for in less than a minute. The walls of my office were lined with books, thousands of them. I suppose I have not thrown away or parted with a book since childhood, and they all surrounded me now, offering surprisingly less comfort each year.

I fetched my high school yearbooks.

For a time I sat at my wide desk and turned the slick pages, trying to concentrate on the small photographs, squinting at crabbed and faded handwriting. I came across a picture of Ellen and stared at it, seeking some connection between this perfectly combed and made-up girl—she looked in the yearbook photo as though she were a singer in a church choir, which was precisely the image her mother preferred for her—and the woman of the same age in the pictures Roy had left with me. There seemed no connection at all between the yearbook's captured sweet face and the feral, *wild* face in the other photographs. Ellen in the yearbook was pure and innocent, just as Roy said. Maybe he was right. Maybe I had forced her into something she was not yet ready for. Maybe that was why I lost her.

But I had been ready. I knew that despite all the women I had known I still had never wanted anyone as much as I wanted Ellen that year. I discovered that I still could lose my breath upon recalling the intensity of my need. That sweet clot of nostalgia broke free once more and raced through me as I looked at the yearbook. What a fine, lovely girl she had been. I hoped that I had been all right for her. Perhaps I would ask her when I saw her in Samson; maybe I would see something in her eyes.

I turned the page.

I glanced at other photographs, read half-remembered messages, wondered how I could have forgotten so many names. We all looked clean-scrubbed and apprehensive. What lay ahead? Part of what lay ahead for some of us could be found in the pages of that book. There was a photograph of a young Frederick and Betty Prescott surrounded by their followers. Their presence, and their presence in that book, had angered me, and I wrote a piece for the school newspaper about it that had in turn angered Roy and Ellen, by then an item, as well as the Prescotts themselves. They tried to pray for me, but I was deaf to them, and rude. They did not change my mind or reach my soul, and I had little affect on them.

But I saw little else of the future in the faces of those children. I looked at Ellen's face again, at Roy's, at the faces of old friends, at my own. My face was empty and unconcerned. So were the others, with a few exceptions. I wondered which pair of eyes had peered through a viewfinder at Ellen and me, which hands had then held those pictures for twenty years. Roy was right—it had to be one of them. I had a suspicion he knew which one, really knew, and I would be interested to see whose names he offered on Monday. Until then I would make lists of my own.

So I passed an hour over the yearbooks and I thought of all the images, still and motion picture, I had hovered over in my life. For a moment I saw myself as a crouched figure, dark, manipulative and frightened, hunched over only images of life. That was past. I took a final glance at the yearbooks, riffled their pages and put them back on the shelf. Ellen was in them, and I could look at them whenever I wanted; I knew where they were. I had a few names on a piece of paper and that was a start. I put my list, and the photographs, and the notes away. I did not want to see them for a while.

It was after five. I went to my bedroom and changed into shorts and running shoes.

When I first bought my farm one of my goals was to push myself into the best condition of my life. I wanted to be ready if a situation—a visitor—called on me to defend myself. I had for a while some reason to expect such a situation. I purchased a pistol and practiced with it until I was confident of my proficiency, but I did not want to count on the pistol alone. I wanted to be able to run, to throw a punch if necessary. I worked hard at hacking brush, chopping wood, breaking ground. Sweat poured off, muscles built up. I ran every day on one of several tracks I'd beat out through the woods. One of the tracks was a mile long, another just over two. I was near the shape and stamina of an athlete.

And pudgy Roy Duncan knocked me on my ass and laughed at me.

I took the two miler at a slow and steady pace, doing it twice, burning off the alcohol and the tension.

I was drenched by the time I took the final turn up the hill to my home. I put on speed, forced a sprint. My chest bucked and heaved. I reached the top of the hill and collapsed at the foot of a massive oak. Eventually I dragged myself to my feet and went inside. I stood for a long time under the shower, alternating between steam and ice until my head felt clear. I dried quickly and pulled on fresh clothes. I poured another drink and took a swallow. I carried the drink with me as I walked out into my yard, refreshing it more than once as the edge of afternoon faded away slowly. I did not eat; I was not hungry. I watched the sun sink.

The night grew brilliant. The moon and stars gave me all the light I needed. I walked on the beach once with Ellen. We had gone there in separate parties, kids' groups isolated by gender and chaperoned as though composed of potential defectors. I could smell the ocean and feel Ellen's small hand in mine. We were sixteen years old and that was more than half my life ago but I could not chase away the memory. Our shoes got soaked in the surf. Ellen's skin tasted of salt, her hair smelled of shampoo. I loved Ellen then and told her so.

Maybe I had been wrong; I knew I had been wrong. I had loved others since Ellen, in love for an hour or a week. Once in college for nearly a month. But Ellen Jennings was the only love with whom I'd planned a future. We had it mapped so very well. College and early marriage, then the long slow business of creating our careers. Ellen had a vague desire to enter the world of finance; even then I could think of nothing but movies movies movies. We were ready, talking in high school, to spend a decade getting me established as a director. Ellen could support us as she climbed the West Coast corporations, as far from her mother as she could get. I recalled the eagerness with which we'd anticipated shared poverty, small rooms, struggles. Then Ellen made her decision for God and I found my way alone.

I wondered what it would be like to see Ellen again. And others in Samson, hardly thought of since graduation. How had they changed? How many of them were still in Samson? How many had prospered, how many withered? Would I remember them? They of course would all remember me, and there were days when I thought that was the accomplishment I'd sought all along. I'd begun making a name for myself just a couple of years out of college.

Those wild years after college. Planned as a struggle alongside Ellen, they turned out differently for me on my own. I took what I could from college, but academia is no place to become a filmmaker, so I spent some time after school putting myself through the paces in the production of industrial film and slide programs, training shows and benefits explanation packages.

At twenty-two I left that and passed a year freelancing as a cameraman in New York, where I learned some tricks and put on paper some cynical scripts. One of them got picked up and made—not by me—and if there was a worse horror movie—a worse movie!—in all the eighties than *Undead Heart* I do not think I want to know what it was. But I made a few thousand for the script and got myself to California. There I sold a couple more screenplays, got to sit on the set on one of them, picked up some second unit work and when I was twenty-five directed my first feature and within a month my second. They were little exploitation films, barely released before migrating to cable and video, shot in hardly more than a week apiece, but they were better than *Undead Heart.*

My third movie had some luck; *Foreshadows* found an audience against every odd, and turned a better than reasonable profit. It brought me to the attention of a better or at least better-heeled class of producer. I got some television work, and though I did not intend to make my living in *that* medium, I spent a season or two there, and came out of it with a reputation for dependability, budget control and lack of temperament, or at least lack of petulance. I sought no creative control, only work.

No one was more surprised than me when I won an Emmy and was nominated for another. That statue was my lever back into the world of film, and within a month of winning I got my first studio feature. Directing only, no script, I held my demands low and accepted a comfortable percentage of the profits. It then proceeded to make enough money at the till that they had no choice but to share some of it with me. *Infinities* was a space epic, a child of Lucas though not totally derivative, and it came very close to a fifty-million-dollar domestic gross and paid for my determination to work only from my own scripts thereafter.

I put my next picture together on paper at my desk and then got the deal and the picture made, the love story, the one nobody cares for these days; it earned me an Oscar nomination. *Hold Me* was terribly popular for a time, beyond anything I'd expected, and its success made me wonder if I'd missed my intention to capture something of the desperation of young love and had made only another gooey and gossamer picture with no glimpse of anything beyond pretty images. I never have been sure myself, though most critics will give a quick answer.

I bought a Brooks Brothers tux for the Oscars as a way of standing out among the Armanis, wrote an acceptance speech I never got to use, smiled as my points brought in more money. My business manager told me I owned parts of four shopping malls, two marinas and a basketball team. Which team? I hardly had time to ask—the next film hit even bigger, and the two after that held their own. With my career as secure as any career can be in an industry built upon a fault, I took a season off to write the movie I most wanted to make. I took the time to write *Moonstalk*.

The title snapped me back. The moon was higher over my yard, spreading shadows. The ice had long since melted in my drink, but I took a long swallow. It was all right warm. *Moonstalk*. I did not want those memories now, but they were there for me and I could not escape them. I wanted to spend a night free of Roy Duncan and New Spirit, Ellen and memories, *Moonstalk* and blackmail, murder, memory and more memory. I would live full-time with those thoughts soon enough. I squeezed my eyes shut but I could not get free. The coming days, Samson, Ellen and the rest, loomed in the hot evening like a polar berg, inescapable and terrifying, offering irresistible attraction. My course was set—how could I hope to get away?

Moonstalk would not go away. It never had, not for more than a few minutes over the past three years. Now I resigned myself to it; I would not fight anymore. I drifted back to those days, that movie, the work, to the weeks of planning and location, pleasure and strain and violence, to the end of my career.

CHAPTER 5

WE WERE SHOOTING IN ARIZONA, getting a good amount of work done every day, some days three and four setups, marching through my script, catching on film that odd and frightening story of the abducted child who seduces and turns the tables on her kidnappers, and then is herself seduced and must turn the tables on the minister who claims to be her rescuer. We were ahead of schedule and pleasantly under budget. I was bringing an exceptional performance out of Kelsey Stillett, or she was giving me one. We worked well together. We understood each other's intentions, and before the first week's filming was finished we found ourselves approaching that all but telepathic rapport that happens only in the rarest of collaborations between director and actor.

She was far more professional than comments from her previous directors had led me to believe. Kelsey was giving me everything she had, and, as I expected, she had quite a bit. She knew as well as anyone that this was her big chance if not her last chance. At least it was her big chance to extend the life of her career. She could no longer play girls—children—she had blossomed early. She did not have the looks of an ingenue.

Kelsey Stillett had made her name in half a dozen low-budget street pictures, first cousins to the horror films I had made. She was the tough kid, smartmouthed and canny, and she convinced her peers to the tune of comfortable grosses on every release. Though still comfortable, her returns had begun to diminish.

The studios had gotten hold of her, worked their unimaginative magic, and with money and overproduction transformed her into their image of a street kid. Which of course was as far removed from what her peers paid to see as was Brentwood from the real mean streets, at least before O. J. But it wasn't studio mismanagement that took the heat, it was Kelsey. She hadn't missed badly yet, but she would unless she took a risk.

Moonstalk was her risk, and it was mine as well. Like more than one director of my generation I wanted it all. Movies was all the work I knew, and close to all of the art, and it was movies I wanted to make. It was my bad fortune to arrive in the Industry during the years of the Takeover (Round One), with rule by conglomerate and committee, and my voice was less than effective against that of the corporate chorus. Cinematic decisions were being made by oil company financial officers. I had accountants from remote offices visit more than one of my sets and look over the shoulders of my own accountants. These recent years of the Merger (doubtless Round One) are nothing more than the logical outcome of what happened to Hollywood over the past two decades and became endemic when the Actor was President.

It did not help my case that I was a director who wrote his own scripts. The boardroom and corner office types had all seen too many projects inflated by directors' egos into fools' dreams, holes down which tens of millions disappeared. Of course those holes were open, then as now, if it was *their* hole. Find a semiliterate script with lots of gunplay, a bankable star, a director who was willing to be a hired hand and make the same movie he and a dozen others had made a dozen times before, and you could be the emperor of a bottomless pit into which money flowed like Niagara. The rule of the day, raised to an art by now, was simplicity, similarity, product, marketing, licensing, tie-ins and sequels. And plenty of explosions. If vision was thought of, it was as an afterthought, nothing more, easily edited out in postproduction.

I would not let go of my visions and for that matter insisted on holding postproduction control as well. So, like more than one other, I decided to swim as an independent and in those waters put together my own deals.

The problem was that no one was interested.

At least not in *Moonstalk* as I had written it. I knocked on every door in town; my agent knocked until she refused to knock any more for that particular script, and there were smiles, a lunch or a drink, several drinks, offers to finance anything else—another science fiction movie, another romance, repetition they would pay for gladly, even *Moonstalk* if I would tone down the script or better yet let them bring in a script doctor. Make the movie *gentle,* they said, a small gentle picture might be just the thing for the market right now.

I did not want to make a small picture and I did not want to make a gentle picture. I wanted to make *Moonstalk,* to make *my* movie the way I'd seen it and the way I'd written it. *Moonstalk* broke new ground, and it was likely to be difficult and controversial ground. I wanted to have my say about the way this country treated girls and their sexuality: I thought I had a few things to say. And I chose my subject in part precisely because it would more than tweak public propriety. I wanted to thumb a nose as well as send a message.

But the studios had their accepted and acceptable methods and patterns to guide them in the presentation of Kelsey and girls her age, and those methods and patterns were based solidly on last year's successes. *Moonstalk* was next year's model.

It was a film that could have been made cheaply, but for once I wanted to spend some money, and had budgeted the picture at twenty million dollars. Not a fortune, even then, but more of a fortune than any studio was willing to offer. I found some money here and there, and kept those pledges in mind, but did not even come close to the sum I needed.

And then I turned to Maurice Devlin.

I met Maurice through a mutual acquaintance, a screenwriter named Will who had seen better years. Now my screenwriter friend moved on the periphery of Hollywood, taking small work on the edge, running into some scrapes, playing pal to some dangerous types. He knew people I had heard of. I mentioned my problem to him one day—we were pitching the same producer—and he offered to introduce me to Maurice.

For a moment I almost passed. I was nearly ready to abandon *Moonstalk*. The conversation with Will almost made me give it up. I had a name, I had a reputation, I had plenty of lucrative work if I would just accept it. This was a crazy crusade. It had already cost me time; I had lost a couple of interesting projects to other directors. But they weren't me, and their projects weren't *Moonstalk*. Now here I was with Will. Maybe I saw something of myself in him—he had been very good, but hadn't been good enough, and was now almost pathetic in his eagerness for work that he knew he could no longer do. We were similar, but not the same. I felt myself drifting away from movies for the sake of one movie. Will had killed his career by too much of a taste for the high life, but that was not the only way to go down. You could also want too much. I looked at him and I was ready to let *Moonstalk* go, just give it up and let it join all the other fine films that had never been made and that never would be made. It would be in good company.

But I was also willing to make one more try to get the picture moving. You could give up too easily—I did not need to fail at this. To return to work I could get would mean to return to work I had done. There was a chance that I would come across something in the studio hopper, some piece that would strike real gold and elevate me to the company of Spielberg and his peers of the moment, give me some real clout, and then I could insist upon *Moonstalk*. But that was a distant chance. The odds were far better that I would continue to squeeze out good pictures that were not exceptional. I might make more money, and I might get another nomination. It would not be so bad a life—I could make many movies and let whatever it was I wanted to say for myself go unsaid.

And then there was Kelsey. Her agent was holding her free for a few weeks while I tried to strike a deal. Kelsey was excited, but nervous that I had written the part with her in mind. She had no doubt I could persuade her to shine in the role, but if I waited too long she would move on to other projects, and if there was too much of a delay she would age beyond the part.

So I agreed. I knew Maurice Devlin's name. Everyone did. He was a man of substantial reputation, the *provider*. Maurice had connections: There were those who said he was *connected*, connections legitimate and not so, and he worked his two sides of the road very well, bringing those who wanted into contact with those who had. He dealt in a wide variety of commodities, and his were customers who could afford his prices without negotiation. He had made quite a fortune at his trade, made it in just a few years, and the rumor around town was that he was looking for respectable projects to put some of that fortune into.

The following Sunday afternoon Will and I rode out to Maurice Devlin's home. I drove.

It was a comfortable and unostentatious house set back some distance from the road. We were greeted at the door by a tall and carefully dressed young woman. Will introduced me and she offered a hint of a smile. "Mr. Devlin is expecting you, of course," she said, giving a line from dozens of movies—some of them mine. We followed her into Maurice Devlin's study.

It was his territory. The lines of the study guided visitors' eyes. They saw what Maurice wished them to see, saw it in the order Maurice intended. Saw first, in the center of the room, a rich brown desk secure in its pool of subdued light. Maurice sat behind the desk, but from the doorway I could not make out his face. As we stepped closer my attention was distracted by the walls on either side, dark walls holding paintings by artists whose works I recognized, each frame illuminated by a small lamp. The far wall, behind the desk, was lined with shelves that were filled with books and small *objets*. Maurice Devlin stood up as we approached his desk.

"Mr. Lowen," he said. "A pleasure. I've enjoyed your films." We shook hands.

He was a full two inches over six feet, slim and silvering at the temples. He wore a suit and necktie, rare enough in Hollywood, unheard of on a Sunday afternoon. He wore them well; they were clearly his work clothes, and I was glad that I had put on a tie as well. He motioned me to a seat, then turned to Will.

"Will, I'm grateful," he said. "Suppose you wait at the pool. I've asked Barbara to provide some refreshments I'm sure you will appreciate." I had a sudden discomfort: The master wanted an audience while he fed his pet.

But Will simply nodded, shot a look at me, then turned and left the room.

Maurice sat down and we stared at each other. I held up a thick black folder in which I kept a copy of *Moonstalk*—treatment, script, shooting script—along with its projected budget, locations, other details. I did not say anything. I waited to hear him speak.

It took a while. He was cool and there was no doubt that he knew what I knew. I needed Maurice Devlin more than he needed me.

"I understand that you are seeking some financing," he said at last.

"That's right."

"I have made a few calls. You understand my taking the liberty." He smiled. "When a director of your talent and . . . track record, *reputation*, can't get what he needs from the . . . conventional channels I become a little . . . curious."

"Certainly."

"*Moonstalk*, correct?" He nodded before I could, and drew a deep breath. He gave a quick and accurate synopsis of the plot. "The people with whom I spoke told me that it is a work of considerable audacity and ambition, of vision. That it will be controversial, that there will be ratings problems, but that it is also likely to make quite a picture."

"I think so," I said. I was struck by the nature of the industry. I had a good idea who he had called and was not surprised that they spoke well of *Moonstalk*. People told Maurice Devlin what they thought he wanted to hear. Talk cost nothing, and Maurice knew that, too. The people who praised *Moonstalk* had also declined to underwrite it, but that was all right—if the movie got made I could count on them to try for the distribution rights. I had no doubt of that.

"I was told that you want Kelsey Stillett to play the lead."

"That's right."

"And even with her name you've been unable to arrange financing."

"That's right."

He moved some papers across his desk. He looked quickly at one or two sheets. "They praised you, your work, the script, Mr. Lowen. But they also advised that the project is . . . *risky.*"

"They think it is. I think it's just something they haven't seen before."

"*New* is a word that catches in the throat here."

"It does that."

Maurice nodded again. "She has a reputation for difficulty," he said.

"I don't believe in having difficulty with actors," I said.

"A disciplinarian. I admire that. It is a rare quality in these times. Our standards have become so . . . relaxed."

"My sets aren't. Kelsey's perfect for *Moonstalk*. She'll have to work harder than she ever has, but she will. I'll guarantee her professionalism."

"You're confident."

"I'm asking for a lot of money."

"Well, we have arrived at it, haven't we? All right. You have a figure in mind?"

I opened the folder and withdrew the budget. I had prepared an index specially for Maurice Devlin, enumerating everything I thought he would want to know. Some large figures were underlined. I passed him the pages.

He stared at them for some time. I was looking for twenty million dollars, and I thought that if I could get half of it from Maurice Devlin I could make the movie. I studied his face for some clue to his feelings, but saw nothing.

When he looked up he said, "A substantial amount."

"A reasonable one for this movie," I said. "A sound investment."

"Again: You're confident."

"I know I can make this movie."

"And for this amount I receive what?"

"Sole backer?" I said, and hoped I contained my emotions. Maurice nodded.

I passed him another sheet, one I had prepared almost as a whim. He did not spend much time on it. "You're a generous man, Mr. Lowen."

"I want to make this movie. Kelsey's summer is free, but only for another month. She has other offers. But if I get the go-ahead I can wrap by Labor Day."

"And *Moonstalk* will find its place among next year's top ten grossing pictures."

"It has a shot."

"I feel certain it does."

"Look closely. I control the cut, ratings or not."

"Of course. You're the filmmaker, Mr. Lowen. I'm simply an investor looking for a project."

I nodded.

He took a silver pen from his pocket and made a few notes.

He put the pen away and said, "Start things rolling, Mr. Lowen. Make your film."

I caught my breath. I had not expected this, had not expected anything like this. I was afraid to say anything. I thought that if I spoke it might all fade away. And I felt a tremor of apprehension. It was too easy—what might Maurice Devlin want? Another pet? And if he wanted too much, could I turn away?

"You haven't even seen the treatment," I said, and tried to make it sound nothing like an objection.

"Do I need to? I am correctly informed? You wrote the script?"

"Yes."

"Then I know enough." He put his hands on his desk. "I know your work. I'll trust the talent."

"That's a lot of trust," I said. I tried a smile. It was returned with what seemed like sincerity.

"You have a great deal of talent. May I call you Baird?"

"Please." He knew how to work, he certainly did. I was asking for twenty million dollars, and he was asking for permission to use my first name.

"I don't mean to . . . overwhelm you, Baird. I am well aware that this is hardly standard business. But I am no standard businessman and yours is no standard talent." He spoke slowly in a rich actor's voice, pausing as he waited for the precise word to rise. "Baird Lowen directing might be worth a fraction of this. Directing and writing, a more substantial portion." He gave a slight nod, almost a bow in my direction. "But I have an instinct—Baird Lowen writing, directing, *and* independent?" A quick breath, another smile. "I think you're about to make a great film."

It was what I wanted to hear, for I had allowed from time to time the same thought to pass through. I'd never made anything like *Moonstalk.* But I knew that nobody else could make the movie I wanted to make. I wanted it. And for some reason Maurice Devlin wanted it, too.

"Make this movie, Baird," Maurice said after a moment's silence. "Make your *Moonstalk.*"

I said nothing. I could only nod. It would take a while for the technical details to be worked out, there were contracts to be drawn. That would give me some time to think. I still had a chance to back out, but I knew there was no way I would. I would take Maurice's money and hope I did not have to be reminded where it came from.

"What can I say? Maurice, I'm delighted." I was still stunned.

"A sound investment," Maurice said, and we both smiled. "Shall we step outside?"

It was a beautiful Sunday afternoon. Maurice's home overlooked the Pacific. The view went on and on and it was easy to get lost in it. Maurice and I strolled together about his grounds. We talked about movies. He spoke with a fondness and an expertise about my earlier films. He recalled aspects of them—a shot, a line of dialogue—which I assumed no one outside the business had noticed. That Maurice Devlin was a Baird Lowen aficionado, so to speak, was flattery to which I was hardly immune.

Occasionally as we walked I caught a glimpse of our shadows. There were two or three of them, casually dressed, with weapons well hidden, but they were shadows nonetheless, armed guards shifting position and proximity as we walked. Their eyes never left us. I was suddenly curious—how many enemies did Maurice Devlin have? I wondered if I knew any of their names.

We strolled back to the house and out onto the wide patio beside the pool. Will, still in suit and necktie, lay on a chaise beside the pool. Two young girls—they were teenagers, Kelsey's age or younger—swam laps in the blue water. They looked up and waved at Maurice as we approached. "Nieces," he said to me.

Will heard us and sat up. He squinted against the sunlight. He rubbed his fingers across his lips.

Maurice stood next to the chaise. "Will, I must thank you

again for introducing me to Baird. I do appreciate it." He glanced at a white wrought-iron table nearby. On the table sat a squat ceramic jar, shaded by a large orange umbrella. "Satisfactory?" Maurice asked. His voice was as soothing as medicine. "The token?"

Will looked at me, a pet's glance. He pressed his lips together and tossed his head. He sat a bit straighter, but only a bit. "Very nice, Maurice," he said.

Maurice nodded, smiling slowly. Will looked away. "You are staying the evening, Will?" Will did not answer immediately and Maurice said softly, "My nieces are so hoping you'll stay the night."

I could hear very well. I could hear Will breathing. I could hear the girls at the far end of the pool, although they had stopped swimming as though on command. I could hear the hum of the air-conditioning from the poolhouse.

I did not hear Will say yes but Maurice must have for he clapped his hands together and said, "Wonderful. I'll tell Barbara." He gave Will a pat on the shoulder. Then Maurice walked me to my car. I would, I assumed, receive my evening invitations at a later date.

"A profitable afternoon," he said.

I leaned back against the car, its body warm from the sunlight. "I can get to work right away?"

"Immediately. Please do. I'm not fond of delays. Our attorneys, as they say, will be in touch. But that's paperwork. As far as I'm concerned, Baird, the deal is made."

We shook hands. He grinned and said, "Next year you'll earn applause while we both grow rich."

Maurice was already rich but he was not far from wrong. If *Moonstalk* did well, the money going to him would be dramatic. I would do well also, but that was less important to me. I was thirty-two years old and preparing, for the first time, to make a movie that was only *mine*. Maurice accepted my terms, I accepted his. The details, the papers and the contract work, went smoothly and quickly. I was pleased, more than pleased, as the days and the discussions went by. I could feel the start of *Moonstalk* just ahead. Each day offered its drop to the current of anticipation that was beginning to flow. It was a strong current. But it was one in which I could swim.

Maurice let me find my own way. He intended to stay away from the production. He told me he thought movies were magic and that with *Moonstalk* I might become a master wizard. He had no wish to understand how the tricks were done, he just wanted to be the first to see the finished illusion.

Certainly he had no interest in the day-to-day drudgery of the production. I served as executive producer, and the line talent was all of my selection. Maurice would have a representative on the set, so there would be a watcher with us. An investment counselor, Maurice called him, nothing more. And if the counselor saw something going wrong, threatening the production, he was to call Maurice. That was all. He was under no circumstances and in no way to interfere with the production or with my work as director. Indeed, Maurice paid his salary and expenses: The watcher was not on my budget. He was simply to observe, make regular reports to Maurice, call immediately if catastrophe loomed. I could live with that.

His name was Billy Toller and I met him in Tucson, two weeks before shooting began. Maurice had told me when to expect Billy, and Billy was punctual. He carried a brief note of introduction written in Maurice's careful hand. I welcomed him and we spoke for a minute, no more. I had work to do, and so did Billy.

As we were working out our setups, rehearsing on sets for the first time, preparing for the actual start of filming, I watched Billy as he, of course, watched me. I noticed him more than once giving his help to the crew, getting his hands dirty along with theirs, toting, fetching, cleaning, offering assistance in a variety of ways.

He ate with the crew and joined in Frisbee or football games, fitting in. I gave it some thought and could not decide if he were violating the conditions of his presence, or simply going about them in an especially industrious way. I had no doubt he was listening to every word, every whisper and rumor running through the crew, but things went smoothly and there was little they could say that I would mind him hearing. I did not call Maurice to object: I was not going to start off on *that* foot. Billy always had a camera and he took pictures constantly. Photography was a lifelong hobby, he said, but it was also useful in his work.

Kelsey's arrival in Tucson, a few days after my own, was high local entertainment. The airport was crowded—there had not been one edition of a newspaper and few local newscasts in the past two weeks that had not had something to say about *Moonstalk*—there were autograph hounds by the hundreds and celebrity-watchers and teenagers (some of whom actually squealed) and cameras. Billy Toller was there, snapping pictures as avidly as the rest, a fan himself. How many of these pictures would go to Maurice?

Kelsey was accompanied by her mother. Marie Stillett was in fine form as we got started on *Moonstalk*. Kelsey had come late in Marie's life, she had lost her husband before Kelsey was two; it had been a struggle every step, and Marie's pride in Kelsey's success shone in her every action. She beamed, she carried a scrapbook and folder of clippings and spent her time pasting and arranging. She had a framed blowup of the *People* magazine cover with its STILLETT-OH! headline placed on the wall of Kelsey's trailer and invited members of the crew in to see it. Kelsey bridled a bit at that, but she clearly did not know how to tell her mother to back down. Her mother insisted on babying her, treating Kelsey as a child even as Kelsey undertook a role in which she must grow from child to child-woman to woman in the space of two hours' screen time and barely four days' story time. Marie Stillett had not approved of *Moonstalk* from the beginning and was adamant in her concerns about how much of Kelsey's flesh would be revealed over the course of the movie. She thought I was out to take advantage of her budding daughter and she never missed a moment on the set, hawk-watching me as I positioned Kelsey for shots, her ears picking up each time I offered her daughter a bit of corrective direction. Marie would take in her breath in a sharp and disapproving hiss at those times. I got a hint of embarrassment from Kelsey more than once and wondered if she was bothered more by Marie or by being corrected in front of Marie.

There was not a lot of correcting to do. Kelsey wanted *Moonstalk* as much as I did and we worked together very well. She was a good actress and, I soon learned, a good kid. She had a wit and no trouble laughing. It was not a tense set except for Marie's presence, and we soon learned to live with her. We all knew where we were headed.

Except Marie. At some point in the early days of shooting she embarked upon a different direction of her own. She arrived on the set each morning and, as Kelsey went through makeup, arranged a chair for herself, placed a small folding table beside it, organized her scrapbook materials, sat, worked, drank. She was no messy or obvious drinker, and it took me a day or two to notice that she was drinking at all. But she was a steady drinker. Toward the end of each day Marie became more determined to make her hisses of disapproval heard. She had her ideas about how Kelsey should be lit and photographed, what to do about her hair, how I was misleading her daughter. I was shooting the film in a funny sequence, close indeed to story sequence, to give Kelsey a chance to grow into the part as her character would have to grow into the challenges set before her. She grew tougher and sexier every day, as did her scenes. And Marie began to speak up.

She was always polite, always gave the impression of being genuinely concerned, eager to be helpful. Who knew better what was best for Kelsey than her mother? Her manners were at first

impeccable, her only slightly slurred suggestions completely un-
workable. I let her down as gently as I could, but I was firm, and
more than once Kelsey walked away during one of my conversations with her mother. On another occasion we heard them arguing in Kelsey's trailer. But every time, eventually, Marie would
return to her chair, smile with a certain disdain at me, clip or
paste an item or two and soon begin to look for another area in
which to offer an idea.

It would have been tolerable, if annoying, except for the effect it began to have on Kelsey. After some takes Marie called
Kelsey to her side and spoke to her in a crooning voice, a lullaby
voice that told the same stories over and over. Sometimes she
sang baby songs. I watched out of the corner of my eye, and the
rest of the cast and crew were watching, too. So was Billy Toller,
but this was not a catastrophe worthy of calling Maurice. It was
only sad. But it had some potential for problems, and that began
to reveal itself as Kelsey started cringing whenever her mother
walked near. I wasn't sure what to do about it. It had not affected
Kelsey's performance, and secretly I wondered if it was giving her
more to draw upon.

As we moved deeper into the picture Kelsey moved farther
from her mother. Between takes now Kelsey would scurry off in
the opposite direction, waving a hand and tossing an excuse to
Marie. Marie did not seem to mind. That sweet, simple, loving
woman. She sang on, to herself.

Kelsey began playing with cameras between takes, spending
her free moments snapping shots of the desert scenery, and in
that she was not alone. It was a gorgeous shoot, every setup and
every shot had some beautiful background, and I do not think I
have ever worked a film where there were more cameras present.
Kelsey's was among the busiest. She read books about photography; asked sensible questions of our cinematographer; showed
off some of her work; and formed a camera club composed of
members of the crew. Marie was not invited to join. Billy Toller

was a member of that club. His lens may have been pointed for
Maurice Devlin, but it was also a source of pride for him. He
went through four or five rolls a day. I talked some with Billy
myself—I made it a point to; I had an investment of my own to
protect—and I learned that he knew quite a bit about shooting.
He'd worked for a while as a professional photographer, had
brought himself out of an unfortunate youth by his relationship
with cameras. He and Kelsey had a few things in common. Billy
was thirty-two and had a wife whose picture he often showed.
She was expecting their first child, and Billy planned to photograph the birth. Kelsey thought that was neat.

Despite the distractions, I grew more and more lost in the
rhythms of *Moonstalk*. I was working harder than I'd ever
worked, although I never had a picture go so smoothly. It was
the freedom. When I had to think on my feet I could think about
what I needed, not what would please a studio. The only ac-
countant on location was my own. Studio films are the greedi-
est of art; they will suck you dry. For at the heart of the studio is
a committee, a bureaucratic nucleus, and dealing with its members over budget and schedule and negative cost while trying to
hold onto something like an individual vision is a task on the far
side of the impossible.

Moonstalk was different. *Moonstalk* was *mine*. I was home.

Every home must have its eccentricity and mine was Marie
Stillett. The drinking began to take its toll. Her comments grew
shriller, their presentation louder. A couple of times she shouted.
I was ruining her daughter, she said; I was making her into a slut.
Once she began to walk toward me under full and outraged
steam, but before she was halfway she stumbled and fell. I helped
her up. She was surprisingly light. I assisted her to Kelsey's trailer.
Kelsey was mortified, and I gave her some time off. I glanced at
Billy Toller but his face was expressionless. Was he composing
a report for Maurice?

It didn't matter. Less than an hour later Kelsey returned. She'd gone into the desert for a walk, she'd taken her camera, and when she came back her mood was improved, her abilities and concentration apparently unaffected.

But more days went by, there was no stopping them. Marie worsened. Kelsey needed more time between takes. No one objected. We were a crew of professionals, after all, and we all had come to care for Kelsey. It did not seem to be special treatment, and it was not that much of an inconvenience. We remained ahead of schedule and within budget. I did not see Billy pick up the phone.

We were better than halfway through the film when Marie collapsed. She slumped in her chair and her clippings fell to the ground. One of them blew through the set and out into the desert. Kelsey came back later that day to try to find it, but it was gone.

Marie did not make a sound. All eyes were on Kelsey; she was shining in a key scene. We noticed nothing until the magazine page with a photo of Kelsey blew through the set and spoiled the take. Then a grip called out, our doctor ran and we rushed Marie to a Tucson hospital.

Marie was in bad shape. She would not be back to the set any time soon. Malnourishment had taken its toll: Her body was drained. Her liver was weak as a sick baby's.

Kelsey took it hard. The number of takes per scene climbed dramatically. She struggled with lines she'd aced a dozen times in rehearsal. She tried to make it all come together, but it was no longer there. When we returned to Tucson each night she hurried to her mother's side. Sometimes she stayed at the hospital until morning. I tried to talk to Kelsey, tell her how worried we were about her, remind her in a gentle way of her responsibilities and how her mother would want her to meet those responsibilities, but she became angry and adamant. She was doing the best she could and I had no right to expect any more than that. She wept as we talked about it. It was her fault, she felt, all her fault. She'd tried to get Marie to eat, but had not tried hard enough. It was too easy to do other things, to be the *star*. She'd neglected her mother, ignored her, more than once turned on her. She was harder on herself than anyone could have been.

The work went on. After a week Kelsey began to improve. She began to find her character again, and there were moments when we were putting some exceptional things on film. Kelsey was working through her problems, there in front of the camera, and if you knew the story as I did you could see it resolve itself as she worked. She was finding her way.

She was finding her way back to Marie as well, and between takes she took photographs to cheer her mother. The camera club closed ranks around her, assembling a collage of shots of Marie taken during the course of filming. Marie had it propped in her room where she could look at it. I visited Marie occasionally and her eyes seemed cloudy and unfocused except when looking at that collage.

I held onto my own self-control as well, and sought to deal with the problems rather than worry about them. I heard nothing from Maurice and wondered if Billy had sent any alarms. I did not worry about that either. I was making *Moonstalk*.

Early in the final week of shooting Marie Stillett died. There was no warning and there was no pain. Her heart stopped. She died in the morning while we were in the desert, and they let me know before noon. I was not proud of myself, but I got one more take in before I told Kelsey. I rode with her back to Tucson, and spent the evening with her. We talked quietly for hours. Kelsey came close, but she could not cry. Just sat, and talked, and stared.

I called Maurice. Billy had already spoken to him. I could hardly shoot around Kelsey, she was the center of every scene. Maurice was calm, asked a couple of good questions, told me he trusted my judgment. He asked me to convey his sympathy.

Two days later I attended Marie Stillett's funeral. I don't think

Kelsey had slept since departing Arizona. Her pain left its tracks—her face was a mask, her red eyes were shadowed in deep sockets. She took my hand for a moment after the service. I hated myself for thinking that our makeup staff would have its work cut out for them when filming resumed.

And when we did begin again more than Kelsey's appearance was out of synch. Her performance, her gestures, her movements were all off. She could not walk twenty paces at an even gait. Her hands trembled when she held small objects. She mispronounced simple words. But she pushed herself through take after take, trying to rediscover her character. Nothing worked. We were getting at best only a fraction of the footage we needed.

I would not stop and neither would Kelsey. I feared another interruption. I feared a break would cause her to lose her character completely, to lose herself. I told myself I was worried about Kelsey losing herself, but I was more worried about her screen character. She was *Moonstalk*. She knew she was the film's center and that without her the film had no center. But she was becoming reclusive, losing weight, getting jumpy and jittery. She was still Kelsey; she told me once she knew she had the end of the performance within her. She just did not know how to find it.

And still I heard nothing from Maurice. I had no idea what sorts of penalties Maurice Devlin might impose upon me if we missed deadline and budget, but I feared for the safety of my control of the edit.

We slogged on. We all tried to keep an eye out for Kelsey. She was living alone, and that coasted around the edges of more than one law, to say nothing of common sense. She needed someone with her, but she would accept no companion. She kept to her room in Tucson, or to her trailer when we were not shooting. She'd put her camera away and declined the invitations offered by the other members of the club. She hid.

There were good reasons to hide. The vultures were out.

Within a week of Marie's death the *Enquirer* and its cousins filled themselves with stories of Kelsey's loss. *"On Her Own"* and *"Can Kelsey Cope?"* read the more sedate ones. *"Like Mother, Like Daughter?"* and *"Kelsey's Own Bottle Battle"* were what the real filth came up with.

Kelsey did not have much, but she struggled to give me something every day. I wanted to do my part, and attempted what rewriting I could, but I was in love with my own words and every change scalded me a little. I worked with her, encouraged her. I looked at rushes again and again to determine what must be reshot and what could be salvaged through editing. I knew it was not enough.

On what was to have been the next to last day of shooting Kelsey did not appear at all. I sat in her room for a while, but did not try to talk to her. I could see it was all gone. I did insist on a room service breakfast for her: She couldn't afford another lost ounce. And I at last persuaded her to accept a companion for the day, someone to stay in the sitting room of her suite. I think Kelsey may even have been glad to see Sam Richardson. He was a genial, beefy man, the wardrobe supervisor, an avuncular survivor of thirty years in the industry. He installed himself on the sofa with a fat novel and a thermos of coffee, cracked his book and told me to relax.

I went to the desert, to that last location, and sent everyone home. I wondered how long it would be before I heard from Maurice. I knew my rushes and knew that *Moonstalk* gave every promise of being a wildly uneven film. I stayed at the set and sat for a while, looking for something to do. Why bother? At four I went back to Tucson, sat in the hotel bar and had a couple of drinks. I tried to plan what I would say to Kelsey. The two scenes remaining in *Moonstalk* were brief, a day's work apiece, but they were vital. They held the story together, each a surprise. Without their revelations we would not have any movie at all. I would not have Kelsey hurt herself, but that afternoon I wanted to know if she could do her scenes. I dreaded asking, but I gave myself only one more drink before going to her suite.

Sam was nearly finished with his novel. He smiled when I walked in.

"How is she?" I said.

"Much better this afternoon. Full of herself again. She'll be back—"

"She's not here?"

"I tried, Baird." He spread his hands. "I couldn't stop her. I wouldn't worry. She's just gone to take some pictures with the club. Fresh air will do her good."

"The club? Who was with her?"

"Billy picked her up. They were going to meet the others."

There was a thickness in my throat. "Did they say where they were going to meet?"

"No." Sam's face tightened. "Is something wrong, Baird?"

"No, Sam. I don't think so." I needed no rumors flying. "I just wanted to talk to Kelsey. Probably not a good idea anyway. Let her get some air, have some fun."

"Sure."

I went to my room, called Billy's and got no answer. I tried three other members of the club; they were all in their rooms, getting ready for dinner. None of them had seen Billy. I called the desk but he'd left no messages.

They'd been gone a couple of hours. The light was fading. I sat in the lobby and tried to wait, but could tolerate that for only a minute or so. I looked at my watch too often and rehearsed what I would say to Maurice if anything had happened. I could not rehearse what I would do to Billy. I wanted to be very clear, completely precise. Billy Toller had been no trouble at all through the whole of the shoot, and now on one crucial day he had violated every agreement and broken every rule. I wanted his head.

I would have it but I would not get it in the lobby. I needed distraction, and decided to drive. I would see Billy when I returned, and there were some things I would say to him. They would be back before I was. I would give them plenty of time.

I hurried out of Tucson, driving into the desert. How long would I drive? No—how far? I would drive without slowing to the most important of our locations, the cluster of cabins where the kidnappers held the girl. *Moonstalk*'s heart was in those cabins, its central story there. The cabin set was where Marie had collapsed. We had finished at the cabins just before Marie died. I had not been there since, but I wanted to see them now. Our publicist had had an idea, and arranged to leave the cabins standing, *Moonstalk*'s gift to the deserts of Arizona. My goal became a point of discipline—I would drive to the cabins and take a ten-minute walk. Then I would drive back to Tucson, collect Billy and call Maurice.

The cabins would not be much of a gift, although if the movie was huge they might make a minor tourist attraction. Four shacks stripped of props, but it was something. I thought of the scenes we'd shot there. We'd caught some good moments and some exceptional ones, especially in the first days on location, with Marie sitting there clipping and pasting as Kelsey riveted us with her performance. I recalled the moment, the one scene in the film where Kelsey removed all of her clothes. It was a careful and nearly decorous scene, the set closed to all but essential crew and Marie. When it was finished even Marie complimented me on my handling of it. She was in the hospital three days later. I drove faster, looking for the turnoff that led to the cabins.

When I spotted Billy's car parked in front of them I did not know how to feel. I do not recall thinking as I parked the car next to his, before the largest of the cabins. Lights were on in the cabins. But we had cut the power lines before leaving. When I got out of my car I heard the chug of a portable generator.

Billy had heard my approach. He was trying to untie her, to cover her and dress himself at the same time. Kelsey floated, her head drifting from side to side on a dirty pillow, her hair plastered by sweat to her cheeks, her eyes unfocused. She was naked, tied to a bed, that recognizable bed. *Moonstalk*'s bed. I was for a moment startled—it could not be the same bed, that bed was in storage in Hollywood now. Where had he found such a perfect replica?

Then my surprise faded and I took in a new scene.

Billy's camera was at the foot of the bed on a high tripod. There was a video camera on a matching tripod next to it. I suspected he had moved them more than once. I was sure he had captured every angle, every inch of her. And how he had treated that same flesh. Her breasts were scratched, her thighs abraded, her wrists and ankles rubbed raw by the cords that bound her.

A strange sound, nothing I had ever heard, came up from my throat.

Billy looked at me. "It shouldn't have taken this long," he said simply. "I didn't mean for it to."

I found my voice. "You son of a bitch." I fought the urge to vomit. I stepped closer and Billy stood up straight.

"No, Lowen," he said sharply. "You stay."

I stopped. "Billy—"

"It would have worked. Money, too."

"Maurice will kill you. *I'll* kill you."

"Maurice wouldn't find me. This would kill *him*; he's got more riding here than he should, and there are those who know this can stop the ride." He scratched his bare chest. He was wearing only jeans. I saw his tennis shoes in the corner, white socks folded neatly across them. "Maurice is . . ." He stared at me.

I looked at Kelsey. She turned her head toward me but did not see me. Something like a smile crossed her lips. She hitched her hips. She did not blink.

"What have you got her on?"

"Oh, that's just a potion," said Billy Toller, and then the knife was out and he came at me.

I dodged and danced back through the doorway, outside and away from him, but he took a quick swing and tore my left arm. I watched and moved. I do not know where my speed came from, but something told me exactly when and how to react. We skittered through the shadows outside the cabin. Billy nearly got me and it would have been for good, but he did not. I brought a boot down on his toes, then landed a kick. We came together, jarred each other and the knife fell free. We moved for it together but I got it first, pulled back, got inside, twisted and pushed. Billy received the blade with some surprise; his arms went wide and his back arched. My arm felt as though an electric current moved along it. I pushed again and he gave another quiver. "Oh, yes," he said, and then he died.

I lay on the desert beside him. I could not stop gulping air. I thought I could smell Billy's blood as it soaked into the ground. Finally I stood up. Shadows rose with me. I felt the wind toy with my hair. My arm ached where he had cut me, but it was not a bad cut. When I had caught my breath I went back into the cabin.

I untied Kelsey and held her close. She started to hum a soft baby song, one I had heard before. I stroked her hair and let myself cry a little. Then I got her dressed. She continued to hum, so I let her lie down once more while I gathered the videocassettes and the rolls of film. There was a Polaroid as well, with a neat stack of color pictures. I looked through them. Abuse struck me then as too mild a word, and it still does. I had seen pictures of people fucking before, of course, and pornographic films, but never anything like this. I felt sick again. I stuffed the pictures and the film into the trunk of my car and went back for Kelsey.

I caught a glimpse of myself reflected in a window. My left sleeve was damp with blood. I took off my jacket and improvised a bandage. I put on Billy's jacket. I was not much to look at but I thought I could pull it off.

I drove toward Tucson, Kelsey slumped in the seat beside me. I tried not to think about Billy. I had left him in the desert. I could not help thinking of him, and I tried to name the animals that might feed on him. From time to time I reached over and gave Kelsey's shoulder a squeeze. The first time I did that she moaned, a low and sensuous groan that made me shudder.

Halfway to Tucson I pulled off the road and crouched on the shoulder and vomited. I dug my fingers into the ground as I was seized and shaken and emptied.

By the time I started the car again I had something like a plan. I could not take Kelsey to the cast hotel, could not let her be seen as she was. I found a small, anonymous motel on the edge of the city. Its parking lot was nearly empty. I checked in, paying cash. I took Kelsey to the room and put her on the bed, covered her with a blanket. I looked at my watch and discovered that it was barely ten. I locked the door behind me and went to a pay phone—I had no wish to leave a record in the motel—and called Maurice.

I did not wish to give too many details over the line. I let him know that Billy was dead, that Kelsey needed a doctor, that things were very bad. I told him where we were staying. He said he would take the jet and fly out immediately. I got some things from the car—the motel was in a bad neighborhood and it would not do to have certain items stolen from my trunk.

Kelsey looked up when I came back into the room. Her forehead was damp with sweat. She pushed the blanket away and wrapped her arms around herself and once more made that moan. I started bathwater, very hot, then helped Kelsey to her feet and into the bathroom. I removed her clothes slowly, worried that they might adhere to her cuts. Kelsey did not help me. Her muscles felt as loose and flaccid as an old woman's. I took her arm and supported her and lowered her into the bath.

As she soaked I stripped off my shirt and peeled away the strip of cloth I'd used to bind my arm. The wound looked better in the bathroom's clean light. I bandaged it again. I would live.

I turned my attention to Kelsey. She lay in the tub revealed to me; there was no modesty about her. Her eyes still glowed from the effect of Billy's potion; they were still on fire. She had a cake of soap in her left hand and was running it up her belly over her breasts to her neck and chin and mouth, not pausing at all when she passed it over her bruises and abrasions. She caught my eye. Her legs slipped apart, opening, and she looked at me with the clearest look of all. Her mouth opened, then closed, then opened and she said, "Please."

I dropped to my knees beside the tub. I brushed her hair from her forehead and she caught my right wrist in a grip so tight it scared me. She held my wrist and pulled my hand down to her breasts, across her breasts and down, raising her hips to meet my fingers. I had no power to stop her. She held the hand that had twisted the knife and there was no strength left in that hand; there was no strength left in me at all. I tried to meet her eyes but they were wide and hot with the pleasure she was lost in as she worked herself against my touch, as she grunted and groaned and rose up to collapse finally, water sloshing over the side of the tub as she released my hand. I lowered myself until my forehead rested against the cool porcelain of the tub and wept.

I was weak, I told myself; I had been wounded and had no strength, but I found some strength, too late, and a moment later lifted Kelsey from that tub and carried her, dripping and still soapy, wet and squirming hot against me, to the bed. I stood her beside it and, stronger somehow by the second, fetched a towel and used it roughly on her. I dried her thoroughly, threw back the covers and placed her on the sheets. I covered her with the bedspread. I pressed my fingers to her forehead and after a moment she could not keep her eyes open. Sleeping, she was a child once more. She was a child, and that was another thing I would not forget. I kissed her cheek and she smiled through her sleep, settling deeper under the covers. I stepped away from the bed and sat in a chair, watching her. After I sat down, I did not move.

Maurice was moving. He arrived before four in the morning. He brought a doctor with him, who attended to my arm immediately. As he bandaged my wound I gave Maurice the Polaroids. The rest of the film and the cassettes were in the bottom drawer of the room's dresser. The doctor went to work on Kelsey. She never woke, but made small noises as he touched her. The doctor looked up and nodded. Maurice asked me to accompany him to the cabins.

He'd brought two backup men with him, and they sat in the front of his car as we drove. In the backseat Maurice asked how I was. He was concerned about my arm. After a long silence he offered an apology. Billy had been with him for three years and had never offered any reason to suspect he was in the service of a rival. Maurice had given Billy his honeymoon, and had planned some presents for the baby when it arrived. Now—

It was all obvious to Maurice and he explained it to me. There were people who could make a fortune with the pictures and a larger fortune with the tapes. And, not incidentally, these fortunes would be earned at the simultaneous and severe expense of Maurice Devlin.

"Billy said it would ruin you."

"Billy overestimated many things."

But the pictures would almost certainly ruin *Moonstalk,* and Maurice's investment in *Moonstalk* was substantial. A movie destined to be controversial for its portrayal of a girl's sexuality could not stand up to the sort of sexuality Billy had forced upon Kelsey. Kelsey would be ruined and I would be ruined. I said nothing. The sun was rising as we reached the cabins.

We had had some luck. Billy's body lay undisturbed on the floor of the desert. The haft of the knife stood out from his belly. His eyes were still open, staring. Maurice walked up and stared for a while at the body before stepping away. I took his place. "I killed him," I said.

"He would have killed you."

"Yes."

"I am in your debt."

"No. No, you're not." I dropped to a crouch and reached to touch Billy's face. I could not do it. I grew dizzy and wondered if I would vomit again. "You don't owe me."

"You eliminated a threat, which I appreciate."

I thought of touching Kelsey. I wondered if Maurice would appreciate that.

"Does anyone else know?"

I thought of Sam Richardson and wondered if he was still waiting in Kelsey's suite. I did not wish for Maurice to know Sam's name. "No one."

"You've handled this well, Baird." Maurice motioned me to him and I stood up. "It's under control, mine, from here on."

I nodded, happy to cede it to him. I was too tired to speak. Maurice's men carried the camera equipment from the cabin. They propped the tripods against the side of the car, opened the trunk and took out a tarpaulin. They wrapped Billy in the tarp and loaded him into the trunk. They put the cameras and the tripods in, closed the lid and stood waiting.

"Geoffrey and I will take you back to Tucson. Lee will remain here to deal with the generator and the . . . bed."

"All right."

"How much shooting remains to be done?"

"A few days. Two if we're lucky. Four at the outside."

"Take two off. Sleep."

"And then?"

"Finish the movie."

"I need Kelsey to get it done. She can't—"

"I have an idea what Billy gave her. It is intense and it has some interesting . . . contraindications. But it can be counteracted." He

looked deeply at me and I could not tell how far his gaze pene-
trated. Maurice looked at his watch. "Sleep. Kelsey will be back
in two days. You're not going to lose *Moonstalk* now."

I dozed in the car on our way back to the city. Each time I
came near real sleep I was confronted by Billy Toller in a lake of
blood or by Kelsey squirming beneath my touch.

Maurice dropped me at the hotel, where I went immediately
to Kelsey's suite. Sam was still there, loyal as a good dog,
stretched out on one of the couches, snoring. I shook him
gently and he sat up.

"Jesus Christ, Baird." He looked at the light coming in
through the curtains. He checked his watch. "She never came
back." He touched my shoulder, and I did not wince. "Did you
find her? Is Kelsey okay?"

"She's fine, Sam. Everything is." I drew a breath. "She had a
little trouble last night, that's all. Everything coming on her all
at once—Marie, carrying so much of the movie, the whole thing.
We're going to take a couple of days off. She'll be okay."

"Poor Kelsey."

"Don't tell anyone you were here," I said. "No point giving
people something to talk about. They'll talk enough on their
own."

Sam nodded. "I got a fourteen-year-old daughter," he said. "It
never happened." He picked up his novel. "Just wish I'd brought
a better book."

I passed the word to close the set for two days. I was too tired
to answer questions; I was beyond caring about gossip or rumors.
I did not call the motel to check on Kelsey. My arm hurt. I drew
the curtains in my room, stripped and got into bed and slept
until the following morning. My car was parked outside the
hotel when I awoke.

The day after that I was on location early, and so was most of
the rest of the crew. I shrugged off their questions. We waited
and before too many minutes passed a limousine pulled up and

Kelsey bounded out, hair brushed, eyes sparkling, smile a mile wide. She looked at everybody, grinned their looks away and kissed my cheek. There may or may not have been something extra in her hug. But she was instantly gone, skipping off to wardrobe and makeup.

It was a neat trick and I never asked how it was done. I just wanted to get on with it. I wanted *Moonstalk* finished.

Kelsey was full of life. She blew the first take, but the second and most of the remaining takes were remarkable, equal to the best she'd given all summer. She found her performance inside her and gave it back to me. We finished the movie three days later.

The moment we wrapped, a messenger stepped forth and called for our attention. He gave the address of a restaurant at which a wrap party would be immediately under weigh. It was Maurice's party, a gift to all of us who had worked so hard.

It was a good party. Maurice did not attend, and Kelsey put in only a brief appearance, but there was plenty of food and drink and noise, and we all smiled and laughed. Kelsey sought me out and drew me away from the crowd. Other than professionally we'd hardly spoken since those mad hours less than a week before.

We moved to a balcony overlooking the city and when we were free from listeners she said, "Thank you," and I caught in her tone an echo of that night.

"You okay?" I said.

She bit her lips. "I'm not sure. I think so. I really don't know. I don't remember too much."

"Don't try. Let it go away."

"But I don't know what happened to me, Baird."

"You got tired. Call it that."

She looked up at me, a girl's face with those woman's eyes. "If you say so."

"I do."

"I was okay those last few days? The last scenes?"

"Don't kid me. You know you were."

"Yeah," she said, and grinned a grin that showed me she did not remember those last scenes at all. What potion had Maurice given her? Was she still flying on it?

"You're pretty tough," I said.

"I had some help."

"I don't think you need too much help, Kelsey."

"I needed you."

"No."

She took my hands. "You killed him?"

I said nothing.

"I remember you holding me. You felt so strong."

I squeezed her hands.

"Thank you, Baird."

"Where are you going now?"

She smiled, carefree, a child once more. "I'm going to sleep for a month."

"Me, too."

Kelsey laughed. "Oh, not you, Baird. Too much work. You've got to get *Moonstalk* ready. So we can win."

"Our Oscars."

"Two for you, maybe three. You wrote it. Best picture."

"Best actress."

"I've already got my speech. I'll thank Baird Lowen." Her voice caught. "And Mama."

I tucked a finger under her chin and tilted her face up. We looked at each other for a moment and then I kissed her quickly on the lips. "I'll work hard on it, Kelsey, I promise. You did a hell of a job."

She hugged me tight. "How much *do* I owe you, Baird? I just can't seem to remember."

"Just work for me again sometime."

"Any time," she said, and started to dance away.

"Take care, Kelsey."

"You, too." And then she was gone.

I took a few days to rest and then got to work on *Moonstalk*. I was impatient to have it assembled; I wanted to see what I had done. That was some season of work. Editing a film, cutting it and looking at it from every angle and arrangement, perceptions shifted and colored daily by the cumulative effects of constant concentration, insight deadened by shifts of mood, is a course of discovery filled with new and old lessons. It's also a treasure hunt among the pieces for a nugget of understanding, a flake of truth.

Moonstalk's truth was evident from the first day of editing. It was not an exceptional film; there was nothing on screen to compare with what it had been on paper and in my mind. It was not bad, and I accepted more than one compliment on it from those who stopped by and watched a piece or two, but it was not the work I'd aimed at. The center of the film was empty. My outlaw vision was nothing of the kind, and the mood of the movie was romantic in the way that novels for teenage girls are romantic—sentimental with a taste of syrup to make any difficulty more easily swallowed. *Moonstalk* was a cheat.

But I pushed ahead and put in my hours on it. I was working for more than one reason. Kelsey's performance was stunning. Had I not known of the days and the shots where I'd thought she'd lost her way, I would not have seen them as we cut. There weren't a dozen bad takes of her in the whole mass of film. I loved watching her. The scenes put down after Marie's death offered some moments. Kelsey's loss showed in her eyes, but she made her eyes match those of the character she portrayed. How could I not have seen that as we shot? Anyone who doubted her ability would find in those scenes a glimpse of great talent. She ate herself up for the sake of her performance and ended up with a performance that was close to flawless.

As I worked I looked for some clue to the moment I lost control. It was not that mad night. Very little of *Moonstalk* was shot after that, and those scenes showed no strain.

Looking, I ran some parts over and over, whole days' work, and took in every take. But sitting and watching the film was a dead end, and finally I arrived at a conclusion I could accept. The camera captured no clues. There was nothing on film for me to find. I could not freeze the moment my *Moonstalk* slipped away because there was no such moment. It had not been there from the first. The film I wanted to make had been in me and it was still in me. Part of the answer, and a part that was easy for me to accept, was that I had lost my movie when I touched Maurice's money. How could I make an honest movie about innocence lost and transformed when the film was bought with Devlin dollars? That money, I told myself, ruined me because I could never forget where it had come from. I was reminded of it every day by Billy Toller's presence. I was some outlaw.

Maurice did not wish to see a second of film until it was finished, wholly finished, so I worked with postproduction effects, and titling, and with Susie Brower, who scored the film; there was still a month of winter left when I invited him to view what he had purchased.

We were the only members of the audience. For three minutes under two hours we sat in silence and darkness and stared at *Moonstalk.* Maurice said nothing for a moment after the film had ended and neither did I.

"It will make that hundred million dollars," he said finally.

"I have no doubt," I said, and that was another of my lessons. *Moonstalk* may not have possessed vision, but it had a sensibility, and that was the sensibility of the marketplace. It would sell itself and become a hit.

"The girl is . . . phenomenal."

"Better than I ever dreamed."

Maurice sighed. "To travel through the . . . regions she traveled through and still be able to work so beautifully." He sighed again.

"Every bit of that," I said.

His eyes remained focused on the empty screen. "How do you feel about your film, Baird?" he said. "What do you think of *Moonstalk*?"

It was no moment for a quick answer, but I gave one. "It's going to make a lot of money."

"We understood that ten months ago."

"Yes."

"I want more. I want to know what you think."

I had nothing to offer him. I did not know what he wanted to hear.

"Come to my house on Sunday," Maurice said. "There are a few final details to be dealt with."

He rose and left the screening room. I sat there a while longer.

Sunday afternoon he served me a drink on the patio beside his pool. We were alone and there was no sign of his guards. I had not seen them since the night I killed Billy. Maurice was in good humor, and had welcomed me with a firm grip and a large smile. Now as we sat in the sun he asked me again, "What do you think of *Moonstalk*, Baird?"

I gave my answer without hesitation, but it was an answer I'd considered often since the screening. "It's just a movie," I said.

"Not what you expected?"

"No."

"Is it ever?"

"What?"

"Your work? Is it ever what you expect?"

"That's not what I meant. *Moonstalk*'s nowhere near what I was aiming for."

"You're that certain it's not you who's changed?"

I looked at him. "Yes. I'm that certain."

"Then I admire you."

"Well." I took a swallow of my drink.

"You'll be trying again? New script? Trying for what you want, I mean. A vision, a great film. Colored by your new . . . knowledge."

"Not right away. I'm . . . dry."

"No projects on the horizon?"

"No." There were plenty of offers; I had no interest in any of them.

"Good. I have something for you."

"A picture?" I looked at him.

"Of course. Something I came across on my own. Good young writer, a piece I think you'll handle well."

"No, thanks, Maurice."

"Not the right answer, Baird. You'll start in six weeks."

"Maurice—"

"I've got a copy of the script inside. Take it with you when you go."

"No," I said, loudly.

Maurice shook his head and offered me a patient, almost friendly smile. "This picture is perfect for you just now, Baird. Not too taxing, but not fluff either. A good . . . movie. Unless, of course, you do have something of your own. That would take priority, of course."

"No. But—"

"Fine. I'll be interested to see what you do with this."

"Not interested, Maurice. At all."

"You're directing, Baird."

"No."

He waved a hand, that gesture of dismissal. "I've got people working on the casting, but they'll want your input of course. It'll be a good movie." He waved his hand again, toward the house, a summons. "Meet your star," he said.

Kelsey Stillett emerged from the house and walked across the patio. It took me a moment to recognize her. She was ten years older, fifteen. Her hair was carefully arranged, eyes lined, lips painted, fingers and throat sparkling with new jewelry. She'd gained a sculpted pound or two and the dress she wore showed her figure to good effect. She walked a model's glide across the concrete and sat next to Maurice.

"Hello, Baird," she said. Her voice had deepened. "I'm so looking forward to working with you again." Her eyes glinted shallow in the sunlight.

Maurice took her hand. "I thought you might try to turn me down, Baird. But Kelsey? After all you've been through together?"

I stared at them.

"It's a publicist's dream, of course. The two of you together again. And with a project so different from *Moonstalk.*" Maurice clapped his hands. "You're an appealing team."

"No." I stood up.

Maurice turned to Kelsey. "You'll excuse us? We've some matters to discuss in my study. We'll be back shortly." Kelsey nodded. She touched her fingers to his forearm and their eyes locked. How deep could Maurice see? Then the moment was over. I followed Maurice into the study.

Inside, I said, "What, Maurice? What is it?"

"Just a few things about the new film, Baird." He lifted a script binder from his desk and tried to hand it to me. I wouldn't accept it.

"Tell me what it takes, Maurice? Just tell me how to get you to understand."

"You're the one who has to understand, Baird. That's all." His voice grew sharp. "So understand. You will be directing Kelsey's next film. You know how to handle her. To get the best from her. You will do it again."

"That's not Kelsey," I said.

"We become what we become," said Maurice. "We make our own lives. You've become someone else as well, as a result of Arizona. That's why you don't see how good *Moonstalk* is. You've already moved beyond it."

"I don't need philosophy, Maurice."

"Was that philosophy? I thought it was what *Moonstalk* was about. Your great truth."

"Is it?"

"Perhaps not. But some things must simply be accepted. Because there is no other choice. Do you see?"

"Go on."

"Make me another hundred-million-dollar film. That's all."

"And if I say no?"

"You can't say no."

"Can't I? Why not?"

"There are reasons. Trust me."

"Give them."

"Your refusal, Baird, would force me into a distasteful and painful chore."

"Which is?"

Maurice stepped to a cabinet, swung open a door. Inside sat a television and VCR. He pressed a button and the screen came to life. He touched another button.

The light that morning on the desert was strange, but it was strong enough to catch a clear image of Billy on the ground. I was kneeling beside him, just as I still knelt in my dreams. There was no mistaking it.

"I have the body as well," Maurice said. "With the knife still in place. And your fingerprints, of course." Maurice switched off the set and closed the cabinet.

"You said you owed me a debt."

"You released me from it, Baird."

"You're serious?"

"You give me no choice."

I gazed outside. Kelsey stood at the edge of the patio, her back bare and tanned, her left leg cocked in a sad, sophisticated stance.

I turned back to Maurice. "She came here after the wrap party?"

"Immediately after. She needed rest, which I provided. And comfort."

"You've been so good for her."

"I understand young women."

"She's your star now."

"She's a delight."

"Or you have pictures of her which can be shown?"

"No, Baird. Those are private property." He joined me looking at Kelsey. "I've shown them to her, and helped her understand. I've helped her cope."

I rocked back and forth. "I could drag you in."

"No, Baird. You couldn't."

"You'd have me killed?"

"There's another choice, the smart one. Direct the film."

"No."

"Then I'll offer just one more choice."

"What?"

"Work for no one. Retire. It's the only other option I can offer. I'm sorry it's not more generous, but you have to understand my position. Work for me. Or don't work."

I nodded.

"I understand you, too, Baird," he said, his voice a balm. "Give this some thought, but not too much. Take a couple of days and give me your answer."

He walked with me into the dim hallway that led to the front door. I heard a baby cry and stopped still. Maurice smiled a smile which held some pride. "That's Valerie Toller," he said. "Billy's daughter. She and her mother live here now. Kelsey's wonderful with the baby. I'd let you look in on Valerie but I'm sure you want to get on with it. You have some thinking to do."

Within two weeks I had put my house on the market, bought my farm and made my way east. I was thirty-three years old and my career as a filmmaker had come to an end.

CHAPTER 6

I WAS BACK IN THE moonlight at my farm. I rubbed my eyes. I took the last sip of my drink, swirled it over my gums and swallowed hard. I looked and listened for signs and portents. I heard an owl hoot just seconds after a shooting star crossed the sky. That was a good omen, I decided. I would survive all of this; there would be no danger. I would find out what Roy had on me and who had given it to him. I would remove Roy's heat from me. Maybe I would find something on Maurice, an item I could trade. I would be back at my farm before too many days had passed and perhaps I would be through with hiding.

But there was also a halo around the moon, or so it seemed to me, and I was not certain if that boded well for my efforts, or ill.

I walked slowly back to my house. It was not far, but it was too long a walk on that bright night. It reminded me of the full moon nights of my movie, and of all the lessons I'd learned that summer. More than a few lessons, and they became sharper each day. I learned some things about myself, but along with them I learned that Maurice Devlin and men like him made no empty promises. Ambition and drive could not do battle with power, and that seemed an important lesson. Ambition, *drive*, had been my blood for years, but Maurice had hooked me on fear. I could live with that dependency, for it was not my first, and I had no choice. And I had lived with it, was living with it now, and would for a while longer, its qualities and controls reflected in the other, bigger lesson I had accepted when making *Moonstalk.*

I'd learned that ego was addictive, too.

PART
TWO

CHAPTER 7

THE DRIVE FROM MY FARM to Samson takes an hour and a half by interstate, but I took a slower route, traveling at an easy speed on back roads through farm country. I made the trip early Sunday morning, one day early. There seemed no reason to wait. A couple of times I'd picked up the phone to call Maurice Devlin, but had hesitated, and finally I changed my mind. I might gain something by waiting. I might not have to call Maurice at all.

As I packed, I added my pistol, and removed it, and added it again. Seeing the gun nestled in my luggage made me nervous, and at last I chose to leave it, packing a bottle of Wild Turkey in its place. Clothes and necessities I packed as though setting off for a location shoot: hanging bag and a duffel, shaving kit, briefcase. I carried a camera and my ThinkPad. I jerked open dresser drawers almost hard enough to pull them from their tracks. I slammed doors. I muttered blasphemies to myself as I loaded the car, but said nothing worth listening to. Just angry, aggravated cursing, empty promises of what I'd like to do to Roy Duncan for dragging me back into this.

Finally there was nothing left to pack, and I left. I kept a pocket recorder on the seat beside me as I drove, ready to capture any idea.

I did not have many. The first thing I intended to do was talk with Roy and Ellen. Separately. And I had some phone calls to make. I had managed, after sorting memories and studying yearbooks, to arrive at the names of six or seven others. Starting points. It was not much of a list. I was curious to see how it compared with Ellen's list, or Roy's. I went over my names and tried to develop an order and rehearse a plan by which to approach them. What would I say?

On my list were Ellen's closest high school girlfriend, a couple of guys I'd taken to the lakehouse, Roy's best friend from those days, a couple of longer shots. I had no idea how many of them were still in Samson, or whether the women had acquired husband's names, nor did I try to find out before I left. Roy and Ellen could help there, I felt sure: They were so organized.

I was not organized, and my thoughts crowded each other as I drove. I was annoyed enough—more than enough!—at returning to matters and territories I had abandoned or tried to abandon years ago. And my mood was not helped by the fact that it was Roy Duncan who was dragging me there. I had distrusted him and his wide-eyed embrasure of New Spirit twenty years ago, and I discovered that in the time since then my distrust had grown at a rate comparable to the phenomenal growth of New Spirit.

The closer I came to Samson the angrier I got. This was all a waste of time: I could see no way I could get anywhere with what I had. It was a silly list; it was a silly plan. The pieces would not be put together out of old yearbooks; there was no way. I would have to sit with Ellen and we would need to revisit a good deal of old territory. I was not looking forward to it. It had been too long.

I reached Samson shortly after noon. I took the four-lane loop around the city, heading northeast. The city had grown. From a hundred and fifty thousand people when I graduated high school, Samson now boasted a population nearly twice that. From the loop I could see the center of the city where a couple of buildings passed the twenty-story mark. Big town. I left the freeway just a few miles from New Spirit's headquarters and campus. I spent half an hour looking for a motel as close to New

Spirit as possible without actually being part of the cluster of lodgings that clung like grapes to the campus, offering rooms to the hordes of pilgrims that came by car and RV and chartered tour bus to Prescott's land. I thought that some proximity to New Spirit might serve as a reminder of my other mission here, a spur. For I had decided to look into New Spirit as well. *When in Samson—Visit New Spirit* the billboard said, and if I had to be in Samson at Roy Duncan's behest, I intended to pursue my goals as well as his. I was going to visit New Spirit, all right, and I was going to look for some goods of my own that I might be able to use against them, as Roy was using his against me. I was ready to be a prospector, hoping to uncover a nugget or two about Roy, or the organization, or the reverend himself. Those nuggets might be nothing more than wishful thinking, but I was ready to think wishfully.

I chose a quiet, underoccupied motel. Its swimming pool was clean; it had a coffee shop but no bar. It was far enough from Prescott's headquarters that I did not have to worry about being glad-handed by pilgrims over my morning eggs. My room was pleasant and anonymous. I took a few minutes to settle in. By one-thirty I was ready for lunch. I had a mediocre sandwich in the coffee shop. I went back to my room, filled the plastic bucket with ice from the dripping, groaning machine just down the walk, then got a Coke from the tall machine that stood next to it.

For a while I sat at the table in my room, sipping my soft drink, studying my list of names. Roy did not know I was back in Samson yet, and there was no point in letting him know. I thought I might make a Sunday afternoon call or two. I got the telephone directory and began to match names with numbers.

I found four of my old classmates still listed in the book. Three men—Sandy Akers, whom I'd once taken to the lake, who had been quite interested in Ellen, who held a trivial reason or two from high school to wish no good for Roy Duncan; Chris

Wheeler, my top buddy from grade school, far less than that in later years, who once had earned a threat from me by asking exactly what Ellen and I did with all that privacy beside all that water; and Mitchell Tarr, who at one time had been Roy Duncan's best friend, a fellow Christian and early member of Prescott's then-nascent New Spirit, a loud and dedicated evangelical whose falling-out with Roy had come loudly and bitterly during our senior year. Only one of the women on the list was in the book: Shelby Oakes, Ellen's best friend.

Ladies first, I decided. Shelby and Ellen had been inseparable until Ellen found Roy and religion. We had double-dated a few times. Same last name. Had she never married? Was she divorced and once again living under her maiden name? I dialed her number.

She answered on the fourth ring and gave a breathless hello.

"Shelby?"

"Who's calling?" I could hear her trying to catch her breath.

"An old friend. It's been years. Baird Lowen."

There was a second of silence. "Well, I'll be damned. *Baird!* How are you? *Where* are you?"

"In Samson for a few days. Just thought I'd call and see how you're doing. Did I interrupt anything?"

She laughed. "Just yard work, which I'll be more than happy to put off. Can you stop by for a drink?"

"I'd like that. No trouble?"

"Of course not. Remember the house?"

I glanced down at the directory page. I knew that address. "Your parents' home. You're living with them?"

"They're dead, Baird," she said.

"I'm sorry. I didn't—"

"It's okay. You've been gone. Look—we can talk about this when you get here. There's a lot to talk about. You *really* know Mel Gibson?"

I gave a good laugh and said, "When should I stop by?"

"What's wrong with right now?"

I checked my watch. "Not a thing. Be there by three."

I finished my Coke. Shelby sounded happy to hear from me, but also surprised. Which was itself no surprise, unless she happened to have sent Roy Duncan certain photographs. Had my call sent her a signal that Roy was responding to the pictures? Ellen had told me once that Shelby did not completely approve of me, or of the heat of our romance. But it was hard for me to see Shelby lurking in the underbrush, taking pictures of us. Only one way to find out, I supposed.

Shelby's house stood in a comfortable residential section not far from the high school we'd attended. The houses in the subdivision were attractive and well maintained. They'd been built all at once in the early sixties, one more package to accommodate the success of the World War II generation. The similarities among the houses, which had seemed to me as I grew up there mass-produced and without character, had faded over twenty years. Tall trees climbed where I recalled saplings. Shrubbery had filled out; lawns had grown thick. The original paint—I remembered every house as white, yellow or beige—had been replaced a few times, covered, and the introduction of bolder colors here and pastels there gave the homes some personality. Like many of the homes' original owners, my parents had moved away, but I took a detour to drive by our house. I slowed as I passed it, watching a young man wash his car while his wife and toddler played beneath our now grown apple tree.

Ellen Jennings and I had ridden through these streets, on our way to my house for a cookout, or to hers after a date for some furtive driveway parking. The night of the prom we had our pictures taken on my family's front porch, and on hers. It came back to me with some force. I could feel her beside me as I drove.

Shelby's house was set back from one side of a court. A group of boys lined the court, tossing a baseball around an imaginary horn. I waited until the ball was at rest, then pulled into Shelby's drive, parking behind a small red convertible. Shelby was out the front door before I was halfway up the walk, jogging to me, arms wide. We embraced and I was suddenly happy to see her. I put all thought of Roy Duncan from my mind. Shelby took my arm and guided me around the outside of the house, through a gate in a tall redwood fence and into the backyard. A long swimming pool winked sunlight at me.

Shelby looked wonderful. She'd been an attractive girl, half a foot shorter than me with a quick intelligence and more than a bit of a temper. The years had made her an attractive woman. She wore her blond hair Katie Couric short, barely covering the tops of her ears, parted high on the right. A cowlick posed a question mark over her left eye. It suited her, as did the denim cutoffs and sleeveless top she wore. She steered me to a chair beside a small wrought-iron table. "Beer? Or something stronger."

"Beer's fine," I said. "No glass needed."

"Me either," said Shelby, and stepped into the house. She returned with two frosted St. Pauli Girls, and we clinked bottles. I sipped and let its chill work through me. We smiled at each other.

"So, Baird. Just what does bring you back home?"

She said it effortlessly, without archness, and yet there was something in her choice of words that made me wary for a second. I shrugged. "Some work. A book I'm trying to get started, I think. I don't know. At least I'm trying to convince myself to start."

Her eyebrows rose almost to the level of the cowlick. "No more movies?"

I shook my head. "No plans for any."

Shelby took it no further. "What's the book about?"

"That's what I'm not quite sure of yet," I said. "Maybe soon. Anyway, how have *you* been?"

She showed me a great smile. "Well, I have been just fine,

Baird, I really have. I am working very hard just trying to get things back together."

"What things?"

"You probably wouldn't know about it. I can't quite see you keeping up with your old classmates and all their . . . adventures," she said. Again, I was caught by her words, and wondered if they carried more than one meaning. Her head nodded back and forth as she spoke. I looked more closely at her cornflower eyes and saw that their sparkle came from more than one inner fire. Shelby was a little drunk.

"Not really," I said.

"Well good for you. If you still lived *here* you wouldn't be able to say that. They're all around us, you know, our old chums. They're everywhere."

I said nothing.

Shelby took down half her beer in three long swallows. "I will *tell* you they are everywhere! They are coming so close to running a lot of things." She winked at me. *"Ruining* a lot things, too."

She arched her back and sank a little into the chair. She pulled her knees up until her heels were balanced on the edge of the seat. She hugged her legs, holding her beer with both hands against her shins. She leaned forward until her nose met her knees. Hidden, she said softly, "I have been trying to drink myself out of a certain difficulty, Baird, and I am beginning to think that it will not work."

I put my beer on the table. It made a louder noise than I'd expected. "Maybe I should come back another time," I said. I started to rise.

Shelby looked up so quickly some beer spilled on her legs. "No! Don't leave. Please, Baird. I think I want to talk."

I had a bit of a feeling that I really should be on my way. I had no real wish to hear her problems at the moment, whether or not they might help me with my own. I realized that in just the few minutes I had been there I had come to want something else from her, something unrelated to suspicions and secrets. Shelby had seemed so strong, so healthy when she hurried out to meet me, that I had hoped for a pleasant conversation, a chat. If there had been a chance to catch up on some of the names on my list, fine; and just as fine to learn something about Shelby, for she was on the list, too. But despite the fleeting doubts I'd felt sitting beside her pool, that first glimpse had half convinced me that she was no blackmailer. How could she be? What problems could she have? I did not want to know, but as I looked into her eyes and saw the pain reflected there I knew I would not leave. "What is it, Shell?" I said, surprising us both by using an old nickname.

She stared at me and drew her lips into her mouth, pressing it closed tight. For a moment she resembled a toothless cat. Shelby cocked her head and released her lips. A smile began to form. "You remembered. Another surprise from old Baird. But then I have been surprised to hell and back more times than I care to count in the past few weeks." As she spoke, her eyes came into clearer focus and she moved to sit more erect. She did not seem so drunk as she had a moment ago, and I wondered if it had been an act.

And the suspicions came back, for if it was an act, what was its purpose?

I looked around the yard. The high fence isolated us from the neighbors. I heard children laughing, a distant lawnmower. "How long have you been living here?" I said. I was eager to change the subject, at least for a moment. "What are you doing these days?"

"I've been here almost five years. Since not long after Mom and Dad were killed." She read the look on my face and saved me from asking. "Car wreck. On their way to the beach. Drunk driver from the other lane." It was Shelby's turn to shrug. She waved a hand at the house and yard. "I thought for a while I'd sell it. But I changed my mind. Only child, you know, so it all came to me. Plus a fair bit of money. And it earns a fair bit. The house is paid for. Why not?"

"Are you working?" I said, and instantly regretted it.

"I work, Baird," Shelby said quickly, resentment so obvious and proper that I winced.

"Sorry," I said. "Came out wrong."

"Forget it." She took a swallow, then held her bottle up to the light as though to check the level it contained. "I am a teacher. I teach teenagers all the wonders they can find in books. I teach English, grammar and literature, and I teach my subjects very well. I teach as much as I can about language, about what words can do. That's why I was curious about your book. I am now out of a job."

"For the summer?"

She snorted. "No, not for the *summer.* For a good while at least. *Here,* at least. In Samson. See, Baird, I was caught this past spring teaching books that are not suitable for children."

"Yes?"

"You know, Baird, dirty books, filthy books. I taught high school and I had some special kids. I had a special course. *Absalom, Absalom!, Portrait of the Artist, The Sun Also Rises.*"

"Smut," I said.

"You got it. I fought the thing all spring and up until just last week. They let me know on Friday. I've got the letter, if you're interested. Talk about *writing!* Bureaucrat-ese. I will not be teaching in the city school system this fall. I have been deemed, as a result of community complaint and investigation, an unsuitable and corrupting influence on the minds of Samson's young people. Made the evening news Friday, all the papers yesterday." She pursed her mouth as though to spit. "Not a word about it today. No Sunday editorials, nothing."

"I stopped getting the papers a while ago," I said. "Don't watch much news. Doesn't seem to make too much sense. It's . . . not connected to my life." I stopped before I volunteered too much.

"Your life," Shelby said, and from her tone it occurred to me that I might not have much to volunteer. "That farm down east. Where you hide." Her eyes grew mockingly wide and she placed her fingers over her mouth. "I'm sorry, Baird."

It was my turn to be generous. I shrugged it off. I would find out later what she knew. "Maybe you're right. Or were right. Maybe I'm changing."

"It's hard to change, Baird."

"That it is. You knew about the farm?"

"You may not keep up with us, but everybody here keeps up with you. Our own Steven Spielberg. Who walked away from it."

"Right."

She let it drop. She put down her beer. "I really am sorry about what I said, Baird. It's none of my business. How you lead your life. Just look at mine." She waved a hand again. "And here I am going on and on about it. Pouring out my soul to you when we haven't seen each other in fifteen years."

"Closer to twenty," I said. "Besides, people always told me their troubles, their secrets, remember? That artistic soul of mine, I guess. These soulful eyes."

"Something like that," she said. "Good listener." Her face brightened. "And, of course, everyone wanted you to put them in one of your stories."

"Still do," I said. "Only now they *really* want me to put them in a script. Everybody thinks they can act."

"Not me," she said. "I can't even tell a lie well." I looked for any artifice in her face or tone, and found none. "It's how I got in so much trouble. Hot water. Couldn't keep my mouth shut. Still can't. And now I'm fired. Why I've been drinking today. Why I looked forward to seeing you. I wanted to be tight, talk trivialities and old times. But. Dammit! My job isn't. Wasn't. Trivial."

Anger clouded her features and there were tears just beneath the surface. But she would not let them flow. Her shoulders rose. I lifted my bottle to her. "You," I said, but she gave a sharp shake of her head. "All right. To Twentieth-century Literature, then, to the filthy stuff." I tried to make my voice boom. "To good teachers done out of jobs by people who don't know books."

She touched her bottle to mine, a musical clink, and we drank. "They know books," Shelby said. "They know some books."

"Which ones?"

She closed her eyes and allowed a sigh to escape. "The parents who started it, who brought the pressure, they're quite well-read in certain fields. They read a lot, in certain fields. The Bible of course. I even taught a Bible as literature course, for all the good it did me. But they read other things, too, they do. They read and quote from the works of the Reverend Frederick Prescott and his wife, Betty, and *that* is what got me into so much trouble."

I looked closely at her and leaned forward. "You had trouble with New Spirit?"

"Trouble? You don't have any idea what it's like around here. Samson *is* New Spirit, Baird; it's our biggest industry. Close to, anyway. They swing a *lot* of weight. People who don't know anything about it—yes, I *did* see your article, but you don't *live* here—anyway, people who don't *live* here, live with New Spirit in their backyard every day, can't imagine what it's like."

"I've felt Prescott's wrath," I said when she paused for a breath. "At least over the television."

"Some performance."

"You watched?"

"Lately I rarely miss him. Know your enemy. I watched him this morning. Sunday services. Before I started drinking."

"How was he?"

"Scary. He scares me," Shelby said.

"He's supposed to be, isn't he? Scary? Frightening the sin out of us?"

"He's good at it."

"Best I've ever seen. Country agrees, too. We'll feel him in the presidential race. He's got the influence."

"Baird, we'll feel him in every race in the country. Congress to town councils. He's going to do to the nation what he's done to Samson. And in Samson he gets everything he wants. He got my job."

"City couldn't stop him?" I said.

"He owns this city, Baird. The school board is his."

"NEA?"

"They've been helpful, but not great. And appeals take time. Deck's stacked against me here, Baird."

"Bad deal," I said, but she did not laugh at my joke.

"Prescott owns Samson, Baird. I had some friends who supported me, sure. Said *solidarity* once or twice—how's that for a blast from the past? Such very liberal friends. For a while. For just long enough to ease their consciences. Nobody stands up to Prescott and Company."

"You did."

"Right. And here I am without a job. Why bother?"

"Find another town."

"Samson is my home, Baird. I like it here."

"Even with New—"

"They'll fall. He'll trip. They always have, always will. Bakker. Swaggart. He's so much bigger, he'll fall so much harder."

"Sure." A measure of Frederick Prescott's success flowed from the very fact that he was *not* Jim Bakker or Jimmy Swaggart. He was clean, cleaner than clean, and he had returned a great deal of respectability, in certain corners anyway, to the television pulpit. Of course it did not hurt that he was a better preacher than either one of them, and a far better businessman. Nobody was unassailable, but Frederick Prescott came close. "Maybe you can help him fall," I said. Maybe she had some photos that would help Prescott's boy Roy Duncan fall. Did Shelby have that in her? "Is that what you want?"

She paid no attention. "I am such a good teacher. I *work* at it. But those parents. And their kids! Not my special ones, but the New Spirit kids. Trying to have a discussion with them! 'Miss Oakes'—absolutely no way to get a New Spirit kid to say *Ms.*— 'Miss Oakes, this Faulkner, can't you see what a sinner he was? Hemingway sounds like a communist to me, his books are so godless. This Bellow, Miss Oakes, isn't he a *Jew?*' " Shelby's voice was tart; she was a good mimic. She painted for me a picture of those students, and I could see them all, clean-scrubbed and intent. Shelby laughed a bitter laugh. "Of course, sometimes I don't know how sorry I really am."

"Private schools? Get a job there?"

"There are a few. Mostly, though, Samson's private schools are white Christian academies. I don't think *they'd* want me."

"No."

"Couple of good prep schools. But I don't *want* that. I believe in *public* education, you know? I really do. I want to make it work." She stared at me hard for a moment, then without speaking rose and went into the house, returning with two more beers. "I have my master's. Maybe I'll go for the doctorate, I don't know. Hard for me to get too excited about the professional academic life. I'm a *school*teacher, Baird."

We sat for a time without talking. I wondered if I had found an ally or an adversary. Had it been Shelby behind that camera? Had she held those pictures for all these years? A breeze ruffled her short hair. Shelby turned her face to the sun and I saw the strong pulse in her throat. I had an intuition, and perhaps it rode in on that breeze, beat in rhythm with her pulse. Maybe I was just in the mood for a snap decision, and I made one. *Ally,* I decided. Whoever the pictures had come from, I could not believe that it was Shelby. I would tell her my story, and see what sort of an ally she would be.

But not just yet. I continued to look at her. Gradually I became more aware of her, aware in a way and to a degree I had not expected. Long brown legs, curve of breast against blouse, now familiar curl of blond hair.

Shelby noticed my attention and stared straight at me without blush or coyness. I met her stare and we both smiled. She had lovely teeth. She gestured toward the pool. "Let's cool off," she said.

"No suit," I said, without flirtation or *entendre.*

"Wal-Mart's not far from here," she said, then grinned. "Where the old SkyLine Drive-In was, remember? Food City next door. I need a few things—you'll stay for dinner? You buy a suit while I shop."

I nodded. After a meal and a few more drinks I could tell my story, could bring up Roy and Ellen and the rest of the names on the list. We could swap notes.

"Let me get my pocketbook," Shelby said.

I drove. "A DWI is *all* I need right now," Shelby said as she climbed into the passenger seat. The boys and their baseball toss were gone.

I selected my suit quickly, paid for it, and caught up with Shelby in the supermarket. The interior of Food City was as cold as Siberia, and as we shopped Shelby and I discussed the air-conditioning conspiracy. Air-conditioned air seemed to grow colder every year. Buy groceries and contract pleurisy simultaneously; American efficiency at its best.

We paused at the meat counter. "You haven't gone all tofu and sprout-y from California, have you?" Shelby said.

"Not me," I said. "Last of the steak and potato men."

We bought two thick strips, ingredients for a salad, a nice cabernet. Shelby gave an objection to me paying, but I won by reminding her that she was unemployed.

"So are you," she said.

"Yeah, but I'm rich, remember?"

"Mr. Big-Time Hollywood Moviemaker." Shelby watched the checkout girl pass the food over the scanner. "Maybe I won't go back to teaching. Maybe I won't go back to work. Maybe I'll just get fat."

"It's a consideration," I said. She punched me lightly on the shoulder.

I changed in the guest bedroom. When I walked outside Shelby was standing beside the pool. She wore a black one-piece suit which held her as though tailored. I fought an adolescent urge to whistle. Her figure was superb, and somehow I had not realized how long her perfect legs were. Shelby walked over to me, head high, studying me. "You look healthy."

"I live a pure life."

"You wouldn't believe some of the people I see around, Baird. People we went to school with. The jocks, especially. Big bellies, no wind."

"You keep up with any of the old crew?"

She shook her head. "Not really. Not deliberately, anyway. Some of them." A shrug. "I see them around. You know how it goes. Anybody in particular?"

I nearly said Ellen's name and Roy's, but still they could wait. I put nonchalance in my tone. "I don't know. Mitch Tarr? Chris Wheeler?"

She spun on me. "Don't you mention Chris Wheeler's name in *this* house. He's one of *them.* New Spirit's Head Coach. *Doctor* Wheeler now that he has his Ph.D." She slapped a hand against her hip. "And a very active member of the Samson School Board."

"Oh," I said.

"Yeah: Oh."

"Shelby, I'm sorry."

She said nothing for a long second. "No, Baird, forget it. You didn't know, couldn't." She squinted at the pool. "Funny, though, I thought you were going to mention Ellen."

"No," I said. Not yet.

We stepped closer to the water. Shelby stretched her hands high overhead as though reaching for something.

She relaxed, lowered her arms, looked at me and smiled. It was the warmest smile yet. The anger and tension were gone. "It's nice to have you here today, Baird. Nice to have someone to talk with. To see someone from the old days. Who knows me. Who'll listen. Everyone else—" She laughed, no bitterness now. "When it was going on . . . when I was being let go, I did hear from some of the old crew. The ones who are in New Spirit. Who are in New Spirit very tight. You know who I'm talking about."

"Yes," I said. "I do." Another opportunity, and another opportunity I would allow to pass. Sunlight struck the water and cast up sharp reflections. I felt warm, and I did not want to talk about Ellen or Roy. I wanted just to pass a pleasant afternoon with this woman, and if the afternoon became an evening I would have to see how it turned out. It had been a while since I had spent an evening with a woman. I'd grown curious, yet I hoped I could be satisfied with a swim and a meal, if that was all she offered. Even as I hoped, I knew the hope was a cheat. I wanted Shelby; I had, as the song said, been lonely so long. My pulse was rising.

Shelby must have sensed something, for she said, "Look, Baird!", and pointed high at the sky.

I started and looked up. Shelby's hands caught me in the small of the back and I tumbled forward, arms flailing, legs buckling. I grabbed her left arm as I went over. Shelby resisted for a fraction of a second, for just that instant we were in balanced poise, and then she fell into the water with me.

We laughed like children, splashing each other, going for quick dunks, clutching at ankles. Slowly we settled down, and finally we spent close to half an hour doing laps the length of the pool. We could traverse its length in a few strokes, then turn and repeat the process. It was mindless. We did not speak. There was no competition, just shared exercise, hard pushing effort, more and more energy in each lap.

At last we rested, side by side, elbows hooked over the lip of the pool, legs floating out. I brushed my toes against her ankles and she brushed hers against mine. We looked at each other as our breathing slowed.

"I liked your movies, Baird. I liked them a lot."

"Thanks."

"You should make more."

I took a deep breath. "It's just so crazy out there, Shelby. It really is another world. Alien, you know? It doesn't matter what you do, you can't win; somebody else has more power and walks all over your work. I just got sick of that. It didn't make any sense to stay."

"I can't imagine anyone walking all over you," Shelby said. "Nobody ever could. You always did things your way. You had so much ambition. I figured it would protect you." Her eyes were kind.

"It didn't," I said. What would Shelby think of Maurice Devlin?

She gave a toss of her head, drops of water making a quick halo, quickly gone. "You really were good. Outstanding. *Moonstalk*. Pure entertainment, Baird. You're a terrific storyteller."

It was a compliment I'd heard before, and I'd learned to make people think I could accept it gracefully. I was the fool for thinking *Moonstalk* had ever been more than just storytelling, or the bigger fool for not making of that movie what it could have been. "Those movies'll be around. Late shows. Video."

Shelby dragged her fingertips down my shoulder and I turned toward her. "It's just a shame to waste all that potential. This is the teacher in me talking, I guess, but your work really was something special. There's a great film inside you somewhere, Baird. I'd hate to see you not make it."

I managed a grin. "You must be inspiring with a chalkboard, *Miss* Oakes."

She shoved my head under the water.

We spent an hour catching the last of the sun, baking ourselves on matching chaises, occasionally talking, more often drifting at the edge of dozing. As the sun began to set we fetched our shirts from the house. "Beer or something stronger?" Shelby asked.

"Stronger."

She made a pitcher of Bloody Marys, heavy on the horseradish and Tabasco. We toasted each other and sipped, then snorted and honked at the drinks' bite. We worked our way through the pitcher and she made another. We grew giggly and flirtatious. I was becoming drunk; she was becoming drunk. It was fun. My tension drained away.

At seven, Shelby stood—not too steadily—stripped off her shirt, made a running dive into the pool. I followed her and we raced through several fast, sobering laps before climbing out. She pulled her suit taut over her rear. I could not stop staring at those legs. She lit the gas grill, tossed a salad, popped potatoes into the microwave. I helped her set the table beside the pool. I opened the wine and we had a glass. I was glad there was a high fence around the yard.

It was nearly dark by the time our meal was ready. We ate facing each other. The swimming and the alcohol had made us ravenous, and we bent over our plates in near silence, concentrating our efforts on the good American backyard fare, cooked just right. We drained the bottle of wine, and when we talked it was with some degree of astonishment: How was it we managed to remain coherent? How could we judge whether or not we truly were coherent? How much would this cost us in the morning?

After clearing the table we returned to the side of the pool, pulling two chairs close enough for us to dangle our toes in the water. The night deepened but we put on no lights. Shelby produced a bottle of brandy and we applied ourselves with some resignation to it. There was to be no stopping now, and we anticipated tomorrow's hangovers, shared other thoughts, caught our conversation as it veered too close to boozy profundities.

At one point Shelby went inside the house. I heard vague rustlings. Soon soft music floated out over the patio. Shelby returned. "Five-disk changer," she said. "I set it to random play. Who knows what we'll hear next?" She crossed her fingers.

We listened to an old, slow Elton John tune. "You never married?" Shelby said as the music ended.

"No. You?"

She shook her head. Her hair was dry. "Close. But no."

I prodded, gently. "No great loves?"

"Now?" She shrugged. "Not for a while."

"Me either. Not for a while."

"Since Ellen?" Shelby said suddenly, softly. "That long?"

It was another opening, the best yet, and it was another opportunity I let pass. "Not quite that bad," I said. "Who knows? Maybe."

"No starlets warming your bed?"

"On the farm?" I laughed loudly. "I sleep alone. Have since before I came back."

She looked at me, and I could not tell if she believed me or not. What I'd said was true: I was not devout, but I had lived as a monk for a long, long time. "I do, too," Shelby said at last.

"Doesn't get any easier, does it? As we get older."

Shelby nodded. "All of a sudden, Baird, thirty is a good distance behind us."

"Yes."

She put her hand in mine, gave a little squeeze, pulled her hand away. We stopped talking.

I closed my eyes. The CDs Shelby had loaded all contained

slow songs. Elton. Billy Joel. Beatles love songs. Old music, from our youth and the years just before and just after. Music from the past quarter century. Some time fell away with each selection. Memories rose. This song played constantly on my first movie set . . . another brought back a splendid April afternoon fly-fishing in the mountains . . . this one was number one when I drove to California for the first time . . . then there came a song that had been popular when we were in college, a song to which I had fucked more than once, a catchy, touching John Lennon song, a love song of a cynical sort. What was the girl's name? I couldn't remember. John Lennon was dead. He had been dead for a while. At some point during the song Shelby began to cry. She made very little noise. Had she also fucked to that tune?

When the last of the songs ended Shelby went into the house and restarted the CD player. The cycle began again, in a different order. Shelby came back and stood beside me, gazing down with deep eyes. She held her brandy snifter and cocked her head at the music. "To the good old songs, Baird. The good old days."

I stood up and touched my glass to hers. We drank and then put the snifters down. Shelby leaned forward and gave me the most tender kiss imaginable, a fleeting wistful pressure upon my lips. Then she turned away.

I watched from behind as she slipped off her shirt. The muscles of her back tightened as she crossed her arms and drew down the straps of her bathing suit. She stepped out of the suit and tossed it aside. I had never seen anything lovelier than her back. She did not look at me, but arched, ran her fingers through her short hair, took a step to reach the side of the pool, dove in. She sliced the water cleanly, and it seemed to me she made no sound.

For a moment I stood still, watching her swim beneath the surface. I gave some thought to this strong and intelligent woman, Shelby. I wondered what she must be thinking now. There were things I should say to her before we moved farther, but I could not say those things. I stepped out of my suit and pushed off the side of the pool. I made a loud splash and feared that I had broken the mood.

But then Shelby came to me, her body glowing against the night. She kissed me and we swam; I kissed her, and soon she welcomed me into her; and there, in the pool, we both found, we both sought and found, a path away from everything that haunted us; and later, in her bed, we found our way to something which surprised, delighted and ultimately drained us.

CHAPTER 8

I WOKE BEFORE SHELBY AND was content for a time simply to watch her sleep. It was a pleasure to see her face at peace, as striking in repose as it had been all night in animation—both passionate and argumentative. We'd talked and made love until past two, wearing each other out and wearing each other down. There would be, she said at one point, no bullshit between us, and her words were only slightly slurred. It was some night, we surrendered more than one secret apiece, but I shared no real secrets with Shelby. My secrets, I told myself at the time, were best told when the sun was up. Looking at her now in the dim light, listening to her little snores, I felt like a traitor. I had to tell her everything, and soon. I tried to think of how I would do it, and to imagine what she would say.

My hangover was milder than I had any reason to expect. I was paying a small price for the evening's excesses. When Shelby stirred and opened her eyes we spent a moment comparing hair of the dog recipes before deciding against them. Our resolve was impressive but our abstinence extended only so far. After brushing our teeth we returned to bed and moved close, taking an hour of experimentation and exercise to complete the cure.

At nine we rose and prepared breakfast, which we ate beside the pool. We shared the paper. No mention of Shelby: Her cause was yesterday's news at best. It did not spoil the mood. I could do that myself. As we settled back with coffee after the breakfast dishes were put away I asked Shelby if she ever heard from Ellen.

She smiled and touched my hand. "You know, Baird, last night. Before our swim. I was thinking about you and Ellen. About that year. Magic time. I thought about Jack."

I remembered. We had double-dated, Ellen and me and Shelby and Jack Winston. He was a good guy who killed himself during his sophomore year at Carolina, one of those burned-out student suicides that make the news a few times a semester. "It's a long time ago, Shelby."

"That it is," she said. "We broke up a year before. But I still think about him. About those times."

"I know." I stroked her hand. "How is Ellen?"

"Okay, I guess. Anyway, I don't see her often." She tilted her face to receive the sun. "Not much at all really since the wedding, and *that's,* what, fifteen years?"

"Something like that."

"Long time. I run into her here and there. She called once or twice the last couple of months. But I didn't want to hear what she had to say. I get those Christmas cards."

"And the newsletters!"

"God, what great prose." She laughed. "Good old Roy," Shelby said, and there was sudden venom in her voice. "Why ask about Ellen?"

"Just curious?" I exaggerated the question and she caught the hint. I took a slow breath.

"I don't think so," Shelby said. She caught her lower lip between her teeth before she spoke again. "Does it have anything to do with last night? I'm not all that vulnerable, Baird. I don't want to seem—"

"You don't."

"But I want to know why you're here. I really do."

"All right," I said. "What is it you want to know?"

"How much is there to tell?"

"A bit."

She took her coffee cup in both hands. "I'm all yours."

"But will you be when I'm through?" I said, and made the mistake of trying a laugh.

"That depends on what I hear."

"Fair enough," I said. "Okay. You know the early part. Ellen and me."

"Hot stuff for back then," she said. "Ellen was the first of us to . . . do it."

I nodded. "And you disapproved."

"I thought you had her going too far, too fast." She graced me with a grin. "But I was pretty much of a prude that year."

"You?" I said with mock surprise.

"Well, I *was.*"

"Well, maybe you were right to be," I said. "Do you remember my parents' lakehouse? Where we had the party that time?" She did not interrupt me while I told the first part of my story.

"And you're here to find out who sent the pictures?"

"Something like that."

"I see." There was no emotion in her voice. "Why help Roy? And don't tell me you're doing this just because of Ellen."

"I'm not," I said, "although I'll help her if I can." I looked at her, but she would not show me what she was thinking. I had begun, though, and I needed to talk, to tell everything. "You said last night you saw *Moonstalk.* "

"I didn't have much choice. Half the girls in my classes were Kelsey Stillett wanna-bes."

"And you said you liked it."

"Your best work."

"Let me tell you a little bit about its circumstances," I said.

Shelby did not take her eyes from me as I spoke, and interrupted me only twice with questions. When after nearly an hour I finished, her eyes were sharply focused.

"You came here yesterday thinking *I* had sent those pictures?"

"Not really," I said. I had talked enough.

Her eyes flared. "Answer me! You thought I was blackmailing Roy."

"No," I said. "Not after I'd been here a few minutes, anyway. You had to be on the list, you can see that. You and Ellen were too close. But after I saw you, talked to you . . . No."

"Not a bad way to find things out, Baird—screwing your suspects."

It was a slap and I felt it. "That's not fair," I said.

"Really?"

"Really," I said, as firmly as she had. "This has nothing to do with last night."

"You didn't tell me all *this* before last night."

"No, I didn't. And now I wish I had." I waited a moment, but Shelby said nothing. "Now you know the story. It's not easy to tell."

"You still should have told me before—"

"Told you how? Told you what?"

"Something, anything . . ."

"*You* try it, Shell. Try saying it." I looked straight at her. "Just try one."

"What?"

"Somebody's blackmailing Roy Duncan with pictures of me and Ellen from twenty years ago. Try that."

"Not easy to say," she admitted.

"No. Or: Roy's blackmailing *me* because he knows I killed a guy who was—"

Shelby held up her hands. "I get the picture," she said, and then began to laugh at her choice of words. I managed to join her, and the tension dwindled a little. "You could at least have said you were in some trouble," Shelby said.

"I thought about it. I wanted to. I couldn't find the words."

"I can imagine," she said. Shelby studied me a moment, drawing her lips in. "The problem is—" she began, and then broke off. "I don't have any idea what to believe. That's the problem."

"What to believe? It's all true," I said. "I couldn't make this up. I'm not *that* good a storyteller."

"No. I mean about me. How do I know you're telling *me* the truth about *me*. I *could* have been there, you know. I knew where the house was, still do. I could have taken the pictures. And I've got reason to want to get New Spirit. How can I believe you really believe me?"

"Fine," I said quickly, with some anger. "Is it you? Did you take the pictures? Send them?"

"No, Baird," Shelby said. "I didn't."

"I believe you, Shelby."

As I watched her I could see her try to accept my words, and I thought I saw her make some progress in that direction. Then a grin began to form at the corners of her mouth; she only fought it for a second. "I've never been a suspect before," she said.

"Not one now."

"No?" Her eyebrows rose.

"Let it go," I said.

"I'll put it aside" was all she said.

"Fair enough."

She poured herself some coffee. "So what do we do now?"

"We?"

She spread her hands wide. "What else am I going to do? You're an old friend who could use my help. Here I am."

I felt a flood of gratitude, and grinned at Shelby. "Thanks."

She wrapped her arms around herself and gave a broad shudder. "This kind of exotica and excitement coming into my life just now? I should thank *you*. Now, where do we start?"

"I've got some names," I said.

"Lowen's List. There's your next movie."

"Cute. But let's start with Ellen. She's pregnant again."

"That's right," Shelby said. "A baby in the governor's mansion. She and Roy lead such a perfect feature story life."

"They're good at it."

"Aren't they, though? That's what she does, you know. Leads that life. Keeps house, works for New Spirit, stays pregnant. It surprised me for a while, earlier, when I'd see a birth announcement or get one of those letters."

"It surprised me, too, Shelby. She wanted more."

"Of course she did. She could have had it, too. Anything she wanted. Any career. She was something. She was my best friend."

"Yes."

"You were good for her, you know, even though I didn't really think so at the time. But you two took some big steps together. She was so young. We all were. You made her happy."

"I tried."

"And then came Roy Duncan," said Shelby.

"He did come along," I said. "Not out of nowhere."

"Oh, no. Roy was always there and he always got his way. Still does. Look at you."

I took that one; I supposed I deserved it. But I did not flinch.

"So what's your next move?" Shelby said at last.

"See Ellen," I said. "Get her side of it."

"And then?"

"Come back here? If you're interested. Take you to dinner?"

She gave it a second's thought. "I'm very interested, Baird. You can show me the list." She gave up a wink. "Do I get to see the pictures?"

I shook my head. "Not my most flattering side."

We left it at that, and did not kiss before I departed.

I was at the motel before noon. I shaved, showered, changed into a light suit. I was ready to talk to Ellen.

I bought a map of Samson in the motel office and looked up the Duncans' address. It was where I'd expected to find it, in the heart of a subdivision not far from the motel. A new development, a large planned community called Spirit City. I got into my car and drove slowly to its edge.

They had been described by the press as Celestial Gates but they were simply twin brick walls, long and low, with mounted and illuminated white block letters. Some of the letters on one of the walls were missing and I wondered how many times each year kids transformed the sign into what it read now: SPIT CITY. I wondered if it had been done by any of Shelby's special students. And I wondered how long it would be allowed to read this way.

It was a strange place. Ground had been broken for Spirit City a dozen years ago, and except for their relative youth the houses themselves were at first glance little different from those in Shelby's neighborhood. Middle-class homes and above, with four or five basic styles. Ranch, Colonial, Split-Level, a few Cape Cods, more than a few of those faux French Provincials that are so popular these days. The roads were immaculate, no potholes or cracks. Each yard had at least two trees. Sidewalks and walkways were bordered by shrubbery and flowers trying to hold their own against the heat. Spirit City was a normal affluent development, its artificiality cheerful and deliberate.

I looked more closely and there were differences to be seen. Every mailbox, and most of the doors and some of the shutters, bore painted or carved crosses. They looked like set dressings for some mad vampire movie. Every two blocks I passed a corner that held no home, but in which had been left trees standing, a tiny park. In the center of each park stood a couple of birdbaths and a white gazebo. I passed five parks.

Roy's home lay near the innermost border of Spirit City. The map showed only two more blocks before development gave way to woodland. The deeper I pushed into Spirit City the larger the homes had grown. I passed more than one house that might enter the market at more than a million dollars. Like more than a few of Prescott's followers, Roy had done all right for himself.

I turned onto a narrow, shaded street. More trees stood tall here; some care had been taken to save them. I counted down

house numbers until I found Roy's. It climbed two-and-a-half
stories and was mock Tudor, sprawling. To its right stood a massive Colonial, to its left thick pines. I pulled up the driveway and
parked beside a big blue minivan that dwarfed my car. The minivan's bumper was papered with bright, large-lettered stickers.
One said, *HE'S* THE REAL THING, another JESUS IS LORD,
another *I* HAVE NEW SPIRIT—DO *YOU?* I did not see Roy's
car. I hoped he was not at home.

As I followed the slate walkway to the front door I tried to cal-
culate how much Roy paid his gardener. I felt sure that in Roy's
world it was a gardener, not a landscape engineer. Certainly I
could not imagine Roy Duncan putting in the hours and the
effort such well-manicured grounds required. It was perfect,
every blade of grass evenly trimmed, every shrub symmetrically
clipped. I wanted to drive a divot or drop a paper cup. I could
not envision Roy Duncan doing the work, but I could certainly
picture him living here. The house and grounds suited him.

They did not suit Ellen, or not the Ellen I recalled. More than
once, at the lakehouse, she had spoken of how she wished it
could all be left alone, of how it must have looked centuries ago,
before America came along, as she put it, and combed and cut
away the land's natural state, replacing it with something less. It
would be wonderful, she thought, to see it all go wild again, to
find its natural form, to see the world grow unfettered, unhin-
dered, uncontrolled. How did she live here?

I turned my back on the lawn and rang the doorbell.

A moment passed before the door opened. I waited for Ellen
and my stomach grew tense, my pulse climbed, my palms damp-
ened. I recalled similar reactions when waiting at the door of
Ellen's parents' home, twenty years ago, the night of our first
date. Ellen's mother had not come to the door that night—she
did not approve of our date or of any of Ellen's dates until Roy
came along—and it was not Ellen who answered my ring now.
The door was opened by an older woman, in her midfifties, elab-

orately coiffed, carefully made-up. Silver hair rose above her forehead like some natural wonder in defiance of gravity. She struck an impression: perfect posture, a small notebook in her left hand, holding it flat against her stomach, shadowed by her ample bosom. I recognized her from newspaper and magazine photographs, and I had seen her on her husband's television program and on shows of her own. The first time I had seen her was two decades ago, when she and her husband established their ministry in Samson and began a youth chapter at my high school. She was Betty Prescott.

"Yes?" she said. "May I help you?" Her voice was warm and welcoming, but there was an element to her blue eyes that made me feel as though I were a specimen fixed beneath a microscope.

"I'd like to see Ellen Duncan, please. Is she home?" *Ellen.* Suddenly I felt loose and relaxed. What was there for me to fear here? I remembered again the night of that first date, shaking hands with Ellen's father. I thought of how that meek and overpowered man had put me at ease. Betty Prescott did not offer her hand.

"Well, she certainly is," said Betty Prescott. "May I say who's calling?"

"An old friend," I said. "Tell her it's Baird Lowen."

She did not move, did nothing to alter my perspective even as glaciers crept across her face. Then she surprised me by saying only, "Wait here. I'll see." She closed the door.

She was back in less than a minute and Ellen was not with her. I felt like an unwanted salesman and wondered if I would be forced to stick my foot in the door.

But Betty Prescott surprised me again, and one of the things she surprised me with was the warmth and width of her smile. "Did you hear Ellen scream? Well, you *should* have, Mr. Lowen, and you really should have called first, too. Ellen was in the kitchen, up to her *elbows* in pie crusts for Friday night, flour *everywhere,* and now *you* show up to see her when the house is a mess and everything's up in the *air*. You should have *heard* her squeal when I told her you were here. It's bad manners not to call first, but where are *my* manners? Won't you come in?" She had spoken all in a rush, and paused to breathe only when she stepped aside to permit me entry into Roy and Ellen's home. The glaciers had retreated—or been put away. I felt certain they had not melted.

"I wanted to surprise Ellen," I said as I stepped inside.

"You certainly did *that,*" she said, taking my elbow in a firm grip and steering me to an immaculate, large living room, done in pastels. Cut irises stood in crystal vases on several tables. Soft yellow draperies were pulled back from the wide windows, held in place by white ties. Twin sofas and matching chairs created an island in the center of the room, an overstuffed fortress surrounding a low, glass-topped coffee table. In the center of the table lay an oversized Bible, white, with *The Roy Duncan Family* in cursive gilt on its cover.

"So Ellen will see me?" I said.

"Well, of *course* Ellen will *see* you, Baird. She just won't see you 'til she's fixed her hair and prettied herself up a little." She gave a small laugh. "Not that Ellen needs much prettying up, you know. She always has been just the loveliest thing. I wish *I* had her complexion. I do. But I make do with what I've got."

She offered the bait, and it would have been impolite of me not to rise to it. "I think you do just fine, Mrs. Prescott," I said, and stretched the honorific to make it the familiar southern *Miz*, which I assumed she preferred. Certainly she was not one for *Ms.*

"Oh, for goodness' sake, call me Betty. We've known each other long enough, even though you probably don't remember me."

"I remember . . . Betty."

She beamed at that, then took for herself a large overstuffed chair. "But you don't think I remember you, do you? Well, you would be wrong, because I do. You were one of the ones who never came to our meetings. Not even the Tuesday Night Cook-out Club, and *never* a Sunday Teen Sermon. Your classmates used to worry a lot about you, Baird, especially Ellen. I think she still does."

"Worry?" I said. "About me?"

"Well, of course she does. Why, I remember when you wrote that thing for the school paper. About how we shouldn't be using the facilities, things like that." I was surprised she remembered, but also suspicious that she really had not: I could envision a New Spirit dossier on me, a Baird Lowen Briefing book.

"I was just making a case," I said. "My case."

"And that just worried Ellen sick. I told her then that you would outgrow that attitude, but I was wrong, wasn't I?" Her look was stern, but her eyes seemed to be smiling at me. "You're still writing things about Frederick and me." The light in her eyes went out. "And you're still giving Ellen things to worry about."

"Am I?" I said, and wondered if it was all going to come out into the open then and there. Would she play that bold a hand?

Whatever hand Betty held she chose to reserve it, nor was any ante raised. "Your thinking, Baird, your attitudes. Those movies you made."

"Some people here are proud of me," I said.

"Some people don't know any better," Betty said, and there was a trace of a snap to her tone. "But *you* know better, Baird, you always have."

"Have I, now?"

"Please don't patronize me, young man." She used weary laughter to turn that very tool on me. "You sullen ones never cease to amaze me. You're always telling us what we're doing wrong, how awful we are. But, you know, Baird, it's always de-scription, never *pre*scription. You'll tear down, but you won't build up. Because you don't know how."

"Don't we?" I said with what I hoped was nonchalance. I had

not wagered on walking into this particular lion's den, and was trying to find my footing.

"And you always do that, too, you sullen ones. You answer your critics with questions. Well, Baird, I have to tell you that's rhetoric, that's strategy, but that's not discussion, that doesn't help *anything.*" She pressed a hand to her bosom and began to laugh, but this was friendlier laughter, and watching her face I gathered that she was aiming it at herself. "Not that I'm helping anything the way I'm carrying on. Would you just *listen* to me?"

"Betty, I have been," I said, and laughed with her.

She gathered her composure. "Well, you're certainly a tolerant young man to do so. You're a guest in this house, and it's not even my house. Me talking to Ellen's guest this way, she'd be ashamed of me. You won't tell her, will you?" I thought she would offer me a conspirator's wink, but she restrained herself.

"Our secret," I said.

"Oh, good. Thank you, Baird," she said, and managed not to sound unctuous. I was being played like a fish, and it was some fisherman's performance she was putting on. "Now, promise me one more thing."

I let her know I was hooked: "Anything."

"You promise me you'll come to my house, or better still to my office, and leave your sullenness at home, and we'll have a *talk,* you and me. No holds barred, and no dodging the tough questions. A *tussle,* to use one of Frederick's words. You think you'd enjoy that?"

"I think I just might," I said. I was netted and in the boat.

"And I *know* I would. Now you just give me a call when you're ready, but don't wait too long because I'm ready *now.* As I guess you noticed." She fished in the pocket of her skirt and, withdrawing a soft leather card case, made a show of presenting me with one of her business cards.

"Betty, I will call you," I said.

"I'll look forward to it. You put together some questions, we'll make it an interview. Then you can write a *real* article."

I did not hear Ellen enter the room. But she came in and stood behind me and in a strong, clear voice that I remembered so well said, "Hello, Baird."

I started, and turned to face her.

Somehow I had not expected her to have changed. As though the newspaper photographs and occasional shots of her on television at one or another of Roy's functions were simply effects for television, not the *real* Ellen Jennings Duncan. I knew what I wanted to see and had been waiting for some time to see. Ellen was such a creature of youth and promise. To call her coltish would be to indulge a cliché, but clichés carry truth as well as familiarity, and she had been a spirited colt, ready to run far and fiercely full out. It was the wildness in her that had attracted me first, the spirit, the anger at the *way things were,* the determination to change those things and then some. She had been glorious, wild and natural, untamed. No one would ever put a bridle on her. I never wanted to.

The Ellen before me now was a pure Thoroughbred, long broken, trained and beautifully groomed, accustomed to the showring. She was showing for me now, no doubt of that. Her hair was not so huge nor her coif so tall as Betty's, but it was equally a crown, fixed in place and moving as of a piece with each turn of her head. There may have been flour on her face twenty minutes ago, but I had known makeup artists in Hollywood who could not have done the job she had done to make her face perfect. Those strong cheekbones I remembered were still there, and her treatment of her eyes, the shades of foundation and highlight, eyeliner and mascara, all conspired to give her a look somewhat beyond her years, more formal perhaps than even her mother would have worn on a social occasion, much less an afternoon visit with an old friend. She looked like a southern governor's wife from another generation, but in some aspects that generation had not left us. I was reminded by her appearance that this was no social call, but a state visit. I rose to greet her.

"Ellen," I said.

She smiled and held out her arms for a hug, but it was not much of one. She touched her cheek to mine, then stepped back to look at me. "You should have called," she said.

"So Betty tells me."

Ellen looked at her friend and, I had no doubt, role model. "Betty, have you been keeping Baird entertained?"

"We've just had the most wonderful talk, haven't we, Baird?" Betty said, and there was more warmth in her voice than in Ellen's. I could get used to the way Betty said my name, teasing an extra syllable from it. I was enjoying being charmed by her.

"We have indeed," I said.

"I'm sure," said Ellen, with a smile that might have convinced Betty Prescott, but I doubted it. I knew where those glaciers had gone. Ellen glanced at the coffee table. "Did you offer Baird anything?" she asked Betty.

Hand to bosom once more Betty shook her head and said, "I do not *know* where my manners are today. Baird, can I get you something? How about some lemonade, iced tea?"

"A glass of lemonade would be fine, Betty."

"I'll get it," Ellen said, and turned to make for the kitchen, but Betty stopped her.

"Ellen, don't you be ridiculous, Baird's *your* guest. I'll get it, I know where everything is." She outmaneuvered Ellen and was gone, leaving us alone in the living room.

The moment was awkward. There was no other word for it. I supposed it had been a while since Ellen had felt awkward, but at this moment she took a step in one direction, then reversed, caught herself, finally stood still and drew a deep breath. Her eyes were still a lovely jade, but they held no fondness or even kindness toward me. I could have been a bug invading her perfect home.

She stepped close and said in a whisper through clenched teeth, "Seen any good *pictures* lately, Baird?"

I had no response to that and so said nothing.

"I could kill you for this," she said, and shot a glance over her shoulder lest Betty hear. "I could, and don't you doubt me."

"Me?" I said, and made no effort to soften my voice. "I didn't—"

"Yes, *you,* and *hush,*" Ellen said. "Now sit down before Betty comes back."

I took my seat without waiting for Ellen to take hers. She stared at me but did not speak again, nor did a muscle in her face move until we heard Betty Prescott's approach. Then with the ease of an actor when the cameras come to life, Ellen was smiling at me as though we were the oldest of good friends.

Betty entered the living room with a tray bearing a pitcher of lemonade, glasses, a small platter of cookies. I rose before Ellen could move, stepped around the sofa, took the tray from Betty and placed it on the coffee table. I could have cut myself on the smile frozen on Ellen's face, but Betty seemed to appreciate the gesture. Ellen filled the glasses and insisted that Betty take one.

"Well, maybe just a sip before I go and leave you two to catch up on old times," Betty said without looking at me. "It's fresh-squeezed, Baird; we made it this morning. You'll like it. The kind your"—she studied me for a moment—"grandmother? used to make."

"Yes," I said after a sip. "Just like hers."

The reverend's wife took the seat to my left. She smoothed her skirt and adjusted her posture until it was steel-rod perfect: A line would hang plumb from the peak of her hair to the small of her back. Ellen sat the same way, but with Betty it seemed natural. With Ellen it was an act of will.

"I enjoyed getting to know Baird a little," Betty said. "He seems to be a nice young man."

"He gives that impression, doesn't he?" Ellen said, but her act failed to mask her contempt. I watched her try to hold herself in check, but she could not. Discomfort showed on her face, and more than a little distaste.

Betty wrinkled her nose. "Now, Ellen, that didn't sound charitable, did it? Just because he wrote those things doesn't mean we can't be hospitable. It's our duty to *welcome* those who disagree with us, to persuade them, not to condemn them." It was as though she was speaking of someone not present.

I decided to remind them I was there. "I'm not so sure, Betty," I said. "Can't condemnation, under the right circumstances, be an act of faith, too?"

Ellen spoke first. "Baird, don't you think it's hypocritical of *you* to talk about faith?"

"Ellen!" Betty's voice had steel in it to match her spine. "Dear! It's never hypocritical for anyone to talk of faith, for in those conversations are the seeds from which true faith can grow." She turned to me. "You'll have to forgive her, Baird; she's as jumpy as a bug, what with Friday and you coming out of the blue and all. But believe me, Baird, our goal *is* to persuade you, nothing more than that."

I was persuaded, at least, of her considerable charm. "I believe you, Betty," I said, and made sure I was looking at Ellen as I said it. "What's happening Friday?"

Betty let out a whoosh of harried breath. "Just the reverend's annual barbecue. He is doing *six* pigs this year, and he thinks that's work. I will *tell* you that *all the trimmings* are where the *real* work is. *You* try to supervise desserts for six hundred. That's what Ellen and I are doing and look at the time!" She bolted from the seat, gulped another swallow of lemonade, put the glass down with a bang. "I've got to run over to the house—Baird, I've worn a path through the woods coming over here to visit Ellen and those darling tikes of hers. I've got to check on the salads, make sure the vegetables committee has their act together. I don't know *how* this one will ever come off on time." She gave me a smile that wrapped itself around me. "But it always does, Baird. This one, too."

She shook my hand, gave Ellen a peck on the cheek, promised to be back as quickly as she could to help with the pies and left through the kitchen.

"Impressive woman," I said when we heard the kitchen door close. I caught a glimpse of Betty moving full steam ahead past the swing set and sandbox in Ellen's backyard.

"You have no idea," Ellen said. I turned to face her. "I'm sorry you met her," she said.

"That's not . . . charitable, Ellen."

"I don't feel a lot of charity for you, Baird, not right now. Why should I? After what's happened, what you've done."

"What *I've* done? I didn't take those pictures; I didn't send them. Somebody else is blackmailing you. And, other than that, the only blackmailer I know is your husband."

"Just you *don't!*" Ellen said. Her voice was shrill and she gripped the arms of her chair. "He has worked so hard, *we* have, and for all of that to be threatened because of *you* . . ."

I had had enough and said so. "You were there, too, Ellen. However you feel about it, whatever you want to tell yourself now, you were there and, as I recall, you enjoyed yourself. And neither one of us took those pictures."

"Don't flatter yourself," she said. "About me enjoying it."

"I could remind you, you know, of some words you used, some things you asked me to do, but I won't. I think you remember."

A flush came to her face and her eyes did not lose their glint.

I looked at her for some trace of my Ellen, but that was a fool's game, and I had no interest in playing the fool for her or her husband. "Don't think I'm enjoying this, either. Ellen, I could have gone forever and never seen you again and that would have been fine. But I'm here and you know why I'm here and we have work to do."

"Some work," she said. I sat silently and watched Ellen bring herself under control. It was no heroic act, but it was impressive. As she composed herself I tried to measure the distance between us. It was a chasm that would not be crossed. I did not know if my end of the bargain meant leaving Ellen, when all was done, the governor's wife on her side of the divide, and settling things so that she and Roy might someday move into an even larger and more important mansion in another district, but that was terrain for another day. This afternoon, for the next forty-five minutes, I sat in a pastel wonderland of a living room with my high school sweetheart and talked about old times.

CHAPTER 9

SHELBY AND I SAT IN silence in a crowded restaurant. Shielded candles danced between us and Shelby played with their light, catching it in her eyes, sending flickering semaphore. I winked at Shelby but it was not much of a wink. The attention she showed me was different from the attention she'd shown that morning. She had had a day to think about me, and about what I had brought into her life, and I do not know if our positions were reversed if my reaction would have differed from hers. I was no bargain, to be sure, enmeshed as I was in circumstance and compromised positions. I carried a level of complication she clearly did not need at this moment, and as we dined I could sense her wrestling with the question of whether or not I was worth the trouble.

I let her wrestle. My mind was elsewhere, and I was no longer in any mood to plead my case. An afternoon with Ellen had cured me of that. My old girlfriend was nothing if not practical— a terrific homemaker—and her preparations had been thorough. We put aside the tensions between us and Ellen produced a list, names and numbers in alphabetical order, neatly printed in an anonymous typeface. She had placed a brief explanatory note after each name, and a longer entry after one name. Most of the names were of people who were innocent, she reminded me in a tone that also reminded me that I was not. In a couple of places on the list there was an afterthought, handwritten, each letter carefully formed in an attractive script that bore no unnecessary flourish. I recognized that handwriting. I had seen it on a hundred notes passed between classes, on silly and sentimental cards given for occasions real or created, on the pages of yearbooks, on five sheets of her teenaged stationery in a letter written to tell me of how she had found a love greater far than that of the flesh.

Ellen's list contained the same names as mine, and she had added four more. "Why Shelby?" I said.

Her smile was almost wistful, and was the first I had seen that was most certainly genuine. "It wasn't Shelby."

I held up the pages. "She's on your list."

"I had to put her on the list. Roy agreed. She knew about us."

"Only because you told her."

"We were like sisters."

"Not anymore?"

Ellen shook her head. "Not for a long time. You can imagine. She's like you, Baird, in a lot of ways. So sure she has the answers, but they're all the wrong answers, from all the wrong places. Bad places."

"I hear New Spirit took her job away. That Chris Wheeler had a hand in it." She had laughed when she saw Wheeler's name on my list, and scratched it out with her pen.

"You heard about that? That's the media. It wasn't anything like they said. It was a question of standards, that's all. It was clear-cut, and she was wrong. That's all it was."

"Maybe she resents you setting her standards for her," I said, and tapped the pages. "Maybe that's reason enough for her."

"She does resent us, no question of that. She's like you. But Shelby didn't take those pictures. And she wouldn't do a thing like this. I know her."

"Still?"

"If I didn't see Shelby for twenty years," Ellen said solemnly, "I would still know her."

I did not press harder. For one thing I agreed with Ellen. For another, I felt a pang of guilt. I had come to Samson suspecting Shelby, and those suspicions were gone. I felt as though I were betraying something by using her with Ellen now, so I moved on.

We took a few minutes with Mitchell Tarr's name: She had written more about Mitch than the others. He had been Roy's best friend. More accurately, Roy had attached himself to Mitch as Mitch's best friend, and there were a few months when they were inseparable, the Righteous Brothers we called them in honor of their endless evangelizing. Roy and Mitch had been among the Prescotts' first converts at our high school; they quickly became the loudest of their front men. Mr. Bones and Mr. Interlocutor, they had a regular routine, an act that was no act, good Christian Brothers out to bring us all to Jesus. They failed with me, and with more than a few others, but they also racked up some converts. Frederick and Betty Prescott's Children's Crusade found plenty of crusaders among my fellow students. The ranks of the Tuesday Night Cookout Club swelled. Then Roy and Mitch had a falling out, and it got heated. High schools were less violent then—the *world* was less violent then than high schools today—but one bloody nose I did remember was the one Mitch Tarr gave Roy Duncan in front of the homeroom we shared. Mitch got suspended for that, and he came back from his three days off a changed boy. He would not talk about Roy and their split, but he talked endlessly about everything else. Including Reverend and Mrs. Frederick Prescott and the Pied Piper tune they were playing that only led to New Spirit, not to salvation. Mitch called his a "more aggressive Christianity," but most of us simply thought he had flipped.

"What *did* drive Mitch and Roy apart?" I said.

Ellen hesitated a second before she answered, as though giving measure to her words. "Jealousy, I think. Frederick and Betty don't play favorites, they love us *all*. But, Baird, even *you* have to recognize how special Roy is. They saw it then. That's one of their gifts. Mitch didn't have Roy's gifts. It made him . . . crazy."

"Crazy enough to do this? You think he knew about us?"

"Of course he did. Just about everybody did, I found out later.
Roy did."

"Really."

"Yes, *really*. And if he hadn't, I would have told him. Because
he deserved that. He deserved more than that—you *know* what
he deserved from me, but I didn't have that to give him."

"Thanks to me," I said.

"Thanks to *you*."

"My pleasure," I said, and hoped she would evict me, but I had
no such luck.

I turned back to the list. "Who else?" I said.

"No one," Ellen said softly.

I looked up at her. "What?"

"I did that list for Roy, Baird. He told me to, and I did it. But
you're going to waste a lot of time, and there are innocent people's names like Shelby's on there, and there's too much chance
of this thing getting away and getting out . . ."

"Ellen—" The look on her face took my words away for a moment. It was just her, *Ellen*, and I knew her.

"I won't have any innocent people hurt or drawn into this,"
she said. "It's not right. There's enough hurt."

"You're saying it's Mitch and Roy knows it?"

"Yes. And you're not to say anything to Roy about this conversation."

"Then why the others? Why the act?"

"He's a *good* man, Baird. He is. But he's been under a lot of
pressure getting ready for the campaign. I think he just wanted
you to do some digging for him. See if you could find anything
else on your way to finding Mitch." Her voice had shed its archness, and there was a weary warmth to it. She had been married
to Roy for a long time.

"I'd have found out it was Mitch? With no trouble?"

She almost smiled, but would not allow herself—or me—that. Not anymore. "Go see him. You'll see."

"All right," I said, and put the lists away. "Thank you, Ellen. This was a decent thing."

But Ellen was gone. Her voice cracked a whip. "Don't talk to me about decency, Baird. Not you. You deal with Mitchell Tarr and you deal with him right now. He's as bad as you are with his carrying on and his AIDS marches and his *caucuses* and the rest. And now this. You deal with him or I will deal with you."

I could say nothing to her except what I had said on those occasions when I encountered her mother. "Yes ma'am." She gave me an ugly look, but there was no time for anything more, for just then we saw Betty Prescott emerge from the trees. "Our chaperone," I said.

"My friend," said Ellen. "We'll talk again, Baird."

"All right." In fact, I planned on it. I had some questions for Ellen, starting with how much Roy had told her about me and Arizona, and what he had told her of the source of his information.

Her voice grew sharp. "He told me he hit you."

"That's right."

"I worry because I do not know if I am sorry about that," Ellen Duncan said, and a moment later Betty joined us.

I drove slowly out of Spirit City, past all the icons and symbols, past all the homes of fearless, faithful families. I did not drive around the trees to view the reverend's home. I would see it another time. I passed two of the small parks, each with a well-kept lawn, each with a central white gazebo. On a whim I pulled to the curb beside one of those parks. I got out of the car and heard children laughing. I glanced around to see if anyone was watching me. The streets were empty, but I saw a woman watering the shrubbery beside her home. She smiled and waved at me.

I waved back, then turned and walked up to the gazebo. It was a fragile structure of thin white lattice. I recalled another one which had stood in the center of my grandmother's yard, years ago. We had drunk lemonade there. Betty Prescott's lemonade was better.

This small building before me, though, was part of Spirit City, a special place, and it served a higher purpose than simply offering shade on a hot day or shelter on a rainy one. This was a piece of Frederick Prescott's vision, a kiosk for Christ. Here problems would not be solved solely through contemplation or reflection, nor, for that matter, would heat be escaped solely through shade. Here, people could open a direct line to God.

Inside the gazebo, whose lattice struck me as nothing so much as a repeating pattern of crosses, there was a single bench, a portrait of Christ laminated in waterproof plastic and a vinyl-covered book which hung like a telephone directory on a chain. I lifted the cover of the book and was not surprised to find that it was a Bible. Christ stared down at me through a layer of film. I sat on the narrow bench.

Spirit City had received quite a bit of attention and publicity when its construction was undertaken, and I supposed I had read somewhere of these . . . comfort stations, but the memory escaped me. I felt displaced. I felt as though I were sitting in the replacement for those bright red fireboxes and squat blue mailboxes that held the corners in other communities. I had a crazy thought. I saw the fine owners of these fine homes running for a gazebo each time their spirits grew troubled. No glass to ax as with a firebox, no scheduled collections as with a mailbox, no coins to fumble with or digits to push as in a phone booth. Just a harbor and a home in which to relax and be comforted beneath the waterproof gaze of the Lord.

That characterless, bland portrait of Jesus, with its deep eyes which might as easily belong to a greeting card child as to a savior, were no comfort to me. I returned to my car under Ellen's angry gaze, not Christ's caring one. Her eyes watched me as I drove. Those eyes had once been my special harbor and home, and I had run to them more than once in the days when they could see no wrong in me. Now under their scrutiny I felt as though I were emerging from an odd and alien place. To have those eyes so filled with revulsion had been a shock. Maybe I needed a shock. The thought lingered after I left the subdivision. A crew of workmen was putting the final touches on the repair of the low brick sign. The missing letters had been replaced and the sign now read SPIRIT CITY, just as it should. Where had I been?

I drove to the motel and spent some time with my list, and Ellen's. I kept coming back to Mitch Tarr's name, and wondered if Ellen were steering me there. He had a camera shop now. He had been active in the photography club in high school, so this fit. And he hated Roy. Why?

Late in the afternoon I drove to Shelby's; on the way I took a page from Ellen's book and sought to build my own smiling, cheerful facade. I would talk only of light things, tell tall tales of Hollywood and movie stars. We would recapture yesterday's mood.

The facade crumbled when she answered the door. Shelby's eyes had changed, too, and for a lunatic moment I thought they might have gotten to her. Invasion of the New Spirit Snatchers. But that wasn't it. *I* was it. That was clear, although it remained unspoken during dinner. We both left food on our plates, to the consternation of our waiter. As we drove home the silence deepened. In her driveway, when I did not immediately turn off the engine, she touched my arm and invited me inside. Did she think I would not come?

"Baird, we need to talk," Shelby said after we seated ourselves on her sofa.

"All right."

"You first," she said, as though conversation had not been her idea. "You saw Ellen?"

"And Betty Prescott."

That brightened her. "No? Really?"

"Big hair and all," I said, and gave a compact account of my afternoon at the Duncans.

"Mitch Tarr," Shelby said when I was done. I was astonished, considering what Ellen had said, but I did not tell her what Ellen had said.

"There are other names on the list."

"Hell, Baird, *I* was on the list."

"Not for long."

She did not respond to that. "You're going to see Mitchell?"

"I thought I'd pay a call tomorrow."

"You'll let me know what you find out?"

"You're interested?"

"I don't deserve that, Baird. Of course I'm interested. I want to help—"

I nodded. "Sorry."

"But I'm not sure we should see each other—"

"Did Ellen call you?" I said before I thought about my words.

"What did you say? You think they *got* to me? You can't be serious!"

"I'm not. I didn't mean that the way it sounded."

"I think you did, Baird. I do think you did. I think this thing is just screwy enough that it's got you thinking wrong. And it makes all of this a lot easier."

"All of what?"

"Someone called today after you left. An old friend out of the blue, like you. I'm going out with him Wednesday night."

"Like me, except he doesn't carry my baggage."

"Self-pity, Baird?"

"No," I said. "None of that in me, or not anymore. Just being honest. Tell me what you thought about today." I had an intuition and wanted to hear her response.

She gave it to me. "I thought about your story. About what

brought you here, what you're caught up in." She leaned toward me and caught my hands in hers. "And I *do* want to help you, believe that. But, Baird, I just don't know if I have this in me right now."

I felt a tenderness rise within me, and under other circumstances I would have put my arms around her and told her it was all right. But just now it was clear she wanted me at arm's length, so there I remained. "It's all right, Shell."

"No," she said with some anguish. "It's *not*. What happened last night doesn't happen with me. It doesn't; it's not something I do lightly. And it wasn't because we were drunk or I was drunk. I knew what we were doing. *We* knew. Because it was right, felt right, *was* right. You felt it, too. I know you did."

"I did, Shell. No doubt of that."

"There might be something here." She touched her heart, touched mine. "Between us, but not under this kind of . . . cloud. What's going on with you. I'm too vulnerable, I can't risk this. I don't think I can risk this. I need to think."

"Sure," I said. "I understand."

"But one of the things I want to think about is you. Understand that. I want to say this right. I think what I really want is just a day off, a day or two to think. I want to see you again, I do, but—"

I pressed a finger to her lips and looked deep into her blue eyes. "Shhh." I nodded and moved my finger to stroke her cheek. "I do understand and you don't have to say anymore. I'm not a bargain right now, but this will be behind me soon, I promise."

"No, Baird," Shelby said. "You don't understand at all. That's what I was thinking today. Because it doesn't matter, what's between you and Roy. Not if this thing between us is worth going after. And that's what I'm not sure about. So I want to think. And if I'm sure, if we do see each other again, then I will be with you whatever it is you're up against. Whatever it is. That's what I want to say, that's what I want you to understand."

And looking at her then I did understand, and saw what an ally this woman could be, were one worthy of her. I wondered if I was, or could be.

Shelby walked me to the door, and reached up to touch my cheek before I left.

Roy Duncan's call woke me at six. "I tried to get you until eleven," he said angrily. "Then Ellen made me go to bed to calm down. You shouldn't have told her where you were staying. I almost drove over to punch you out again. Where were you last night?"

"Don't start on me, Roy." I fumbled for my watch, read it. "Jesus Christ."

My blasphemy did not slow him down a bit. "It's your second day in Samson, Baird. You were supposed to call me when you got here yesterday."

"It's my third day here, Roy, but who's counting? And Ellen was all the Duncan I could handle in one day."

"You watch your mouth, Baird. And don't you go near her again. Not ever, not without asking me first."

"Don't threaten me before breakfast, Roy. You're hard enough to take on a full stomach."

"Just stay away from her."

"Shut up, Roy. What have Ellen and I got to hide from each other? Or are you afraid we'll pick up where we left off?"

"Watch your mouth!"

"I told you: no threats." I could hear how tired I was. I had driven for an aimless hour or two after leaving Shelby, and her words had kept me awake another hour after I returned to the motel. Somebody needed to live up to what she was looking for with those blue eyes. Somebody needed to measure up to the attention she could give.

"I'm just giving fair warning, Bear. Don't forget who you're working for."

"I don't work for you, Roy."

"No? Your decision, but just try me. I'll shut you down, Bear, believe that. I will."

"And I'll take you with me."

"Will you, now? That's the question, isn't it? You haven't thought this through the way I have. I won't have Ellen hurt, and those pictures will hurt her. But she's a strong woman. You know that."

"Stronger than you," I said, and meant it.

"Maybe so. But I'm strong, too, and those pictures could turn another way. I can spin them if I have to. And Ellen will be right beside me while I do. The woman she is now, not the young girl *you* corrupted. And backing every bit of it will be those other pictures. You're so good at corrupting young girls."

I could almost believe he could make it work. I could believe it. God knows his constituency could believe it. "What do you want?"

I heard him breathing heavily, and then there was a moment of emptiness, as though he'd clapped his hand over the receiver. Was he talking to Ellen? Or was she feeding him lines? "You get this thing moving," he said at last. "You get some results, and I want to hear from you before the day is out." He hung up.

I did not stay in bed long. Roy's threats were not all that motivated me to get an early start. I wanted some answers of my own.

CHAPTER 10

MITCHELL TARR OWNED A CAMERA shop which stood on a narrow street in a formerly disreputable section of downtown Samson, a section in the process of being saved. Salvation was coming in the form of small shops, art galleries and artisans' studios, more than one too quaint antique emporium, a few warehouses being converted into town houses—as the lettering on their signs announced—and a few fern-festooned restaurants. There were still traces of the area as I had known it when it was Samson's hot zone: one building lettered with faded red which promised adult entertainment in private booths, a couple of seedy bars, a pool hall and two pawn shops. The seedy spots made me smile almost as much as the reconstruction. I knew these blocks from my late youth, and had assumed that renewal here would have long since taken the form of wrecking balls and razings, and then on cleared ground the erections of shiny and sterile, characterless new structures. So it was pleasant to see familiar buildings made new with fresh paint, hard work and mercantile ambition, pride. But the soapy windows of the adult entertainment parlor gave me a grin as well. The area had been dying in the days I'd come here as a teenager, and editorial prognoses had been uniformly grim. It was the kind of section my mother warned me away from; an area inhabited by bums living in flophouses, winos asleep outside surplus stores.

But the area then was also home to a pair of seamy, decaying motion picture houses, once-fine theaters whose audiences were lost to the suburbs. They showed what they could get, and in their darkness I discovered some gems. The brooding, moody horror film third-billed after a couple of dreary slasher flicks. The subtle and charming foreign picture playing on the hope that its promise of bared European breasts might be enough to lure a few patrons in from the gutter. The small independent films, shot on something less than a shoestring, for which these fleapits were first (and only) run palaces. I saw some good work on those smudged and torn screens, made my way in their flicker through more than one dilemma, found myself drawn to my career.

I drove past my old haunts, hardly recognizing them now. One of the theaters had been divided into shops and stalls and boutiques. MARQUEE MART, its letters proclaimed. A block farther stood its sibling, its marquee announcing its current identity: SAMSON CINEMA FOR THE ARTS. That particular restoration had occurred when I was in Hollywood, and I recalled receiving an invitation to speak at the gala the day the theater reopened. I declined the invitation. My sense of urban ecology was pleased to see these places restored to utility, but my imp of the perverse was annoyed to see community pretension flourish where cheap art once grew. As with so much else, I was of two minds about Samson, North Carolina, my hometown. A nice place to live, I supposed, but you wouldn't want to visit there. I looked for Mitch's store.

I found it and parked a block away. Mitch, and his part of the old downtown, occupied a place somewhere between renewal and razing. His stores and the others on his block needed paint and attention. As I got closer, I could see that two of his neighboring stores needed tenants. Whatever good the resurrection of the old downtown had done, it hadn't done it here. I paced a few steps beyond Mitch's door, then turned and stepped inside. A small tarnished bell over the door gave a ring as I entered. I paused for a moment to allow my eyes to adjust to the soft lighting. I looked closer and saw that two of the three banks of over-head lights were not turned on.

The shop, which was not large, was comfortably crowded, its stock vying for attention. There was no air-conditioning, but an overhead paddle fan spun slowly and the interior of the store was relatively cool. Glass cases lined each wall, the walls themselves covered with Peg-Board holding hooks from which dangled photographic equipment and paraphernalia. Camera cases and tripods, straps, photographers' flak jackets, two racks of oversize paperback how-to books—a healthy inventory of necessary equipment and junk. Where no equipment hung, the space was filled with matted photographs bearing small white price stick-ers. They were good pictures: some still lifes, some portraits, three shots of the same waterfall from different angles during dif-ferent seasons, two nudes, one of a man, the other a woman. I thought of Ellen's words, and could see Mitchell taking pictures of Ellen and me nude.

The display cases themselves were clean and sensibly orga-nized, mostly holding medium-priced cameras and lenses. One shelf was set aside for more expensive gear, another for cheap pocket cameras. There was a rack of used bodies and lenses and a basket of disposable cameras. It was not a huge inventory, but there was enough to make me wonder if Mitch often left his shop deserted. Had the neighborhood, even this section of it, become that safe? I was beginning my second circuit of the store when I heard a rustle and Mitchell Tarr stepped out of the back room.

"Afternoon," he said. "Sorry to keep you waiting. Nature call." He jerked his thumb at the curtained doorway through which he'd just come.

I might not have recognized him. Mitchell Tarr and Roy Dun-can had been Mutt-and-Jeff twins—Mitch tall, Roy not, both clean-cut, square-jawed, resolutely bright-eyed young Chris-tians destined to mature into solid Samson Jaycees, deacons, members of the Chamber of Commerce, prosperous and secure

in their sanctimony. Examples to us all. They were set on that
course long before Frederick and Betty Prescott came to town.
That Mitch would never have opened a shop in this part of
town—he had been born to be a mall merchant, maybe working a franchise, with reasonable rates for family portraits among
his profitable sidelines.

In some other universe that destiny may have worked itself
out, but in our world Mitchell Tarr diverged from his own course
before we graduated. His hair had gotten long during our senior
year, and he may not have had it cut since. His ponytail reached
the small of his back. His brown beard, a serious growth of
beard, spread down over his throat and onto his chest. It bushed
out like the pelt of some animal. He wore jeans with suspenders
over a white short-sleeved shirt. The suspenders were adorned
with a couple of slogan buttons, and one caught my eye: NEW
SPIRIT IS *NO* SPIRIT . . . BEWARE THEIR RIGHTEOUSNESS.

I blinked twice, said "Hey, Mitch," and stepped forward.

I might not have known him, but he had no such trouble. His
brow furrowed before he relaxed and nodded. "Well, Baird
Lowen. I was wondering . . ." He stopped talking.

Wondering what? Had I found my man? His words of wonder seemed to say so. I offered my right hand and he took it.
"How's it going, Mitch?"

He waved a hand at the empty store. "How's it look? Booming, Baird, just booming." He had not taken his eyes from me.
"Baird Lowen. Be damned. When did you get to town?"

"Couple of days ago."

He looked toward the ceiling and his lips moved silently, as
though he were calculating something. "Here on business or
pleasure?"

"Just a little nostalgia for the old hometown," I said.

"Sure." He crossed his thick arms over his chest. "And so you
came to see me." He smiled but showed no teeth.

"I thought I'd say hello."

"Right. Come on, Baird, can't you come up with something better than that? I mean, *really.* After all this time? Come on."

I shrugged and stuck to my line. "I got curious about the old hometown. I thought I'd look up some old friends. Reunion summer, you know."

"Were we friends, Baird?"

We had not been close. I do not think Mitchell Tarr and I exchanged more than a hundred words after our junior year. I did not like him, and he thought he saw through me and told me so. Each of us had our high school ideas, but Mitchell at that time was polishing his imitation of the style and strategy of William F. Buckley, among others, and would at the slightest provocation drown opponents in carefully articulated Latin and dutifully documented quotation. There was no talking with him. He made clear to me his opinion that I was a fraud, and that my weakness was a spiritual weakness as well. I was one of the damned, and he and Roy prayed for me. "That was a long time ago," I said.

"Several lifetimes, Baird. A few lifetimes ago."

"How've those lifetimes treated you, Mitch? How've you been?"

"Good and bad." He licked his lips. "Going to get good real soon, though. We'll talk about that, about how good it's going to get. Won't be so good as your lifetimes, bet on that. Moviemaker. Good man with a camera, Baird. Or with a camera crew, at least. I liked the look of some of your stuff."

"Thanks."

It was Mitch's turn to shrug. "It was all bullshit, don't get me wrong. But I liked the way some of it looked."

"Thanks."

"Oh, don't take offense. You have to know what I mean; you can't pretend you don't. Your movies didn't have any relationship to any reality I know of, Baird. You know that. Hollywood movie star movies. That's all."

"I've heard that said."

"Well, I'm just saying it again. Not that it matters. You've stopped now, anyway."

"I'm taking a break."

"Whatever you say. You can afford it. You made out pretty good."

"I did all right."

"Glad to hear that. I am. I always thought you'd make it."

"Did you?"

"Sure. Never doubted it." He cleared his throat and went on. "You had that gift: We all saw it. A sort of, ah, instinctive feel for plastic, for junk food. You rode the winds pretty good, I would say. Never risking anything, certainly never doing anything to damage your popularity. Your reputation. Don't get me wrong, Baird, it's a good commercial gift. It's good business, and I've done some commercial photography myself." His eyebrows rose. "Truth to tell, commercial photography is how I'm going to make it, too."

"Is that so?"

"It is. I'll tell you about it, if you like."

"I'd like to hear."

"Wouldn't you, though? I can imagine." He shook his head hard, snorted once and then moved away from me. "Stick around and hear me out and maybe I'll tell you, or maybe you can tell me some things." He waved his hands in an odd gesture, tai chi or karate or just Mitch being flaky.

"I'm not going anywhere," I said.

"And getting there fast, I imagine."

"Mitch—" I felt as though I already had my answer, but I was wary of pressing him too soon or too hard. I had no idea what he might say—or what I might learn from him.

"No, Baird. I think I'll have my say. Haven't had too many people to talk to in here today. Or at all. Not like your movies. You drew crowds. And why not? You leave out anything that might challenge someone to think. L, as they say, CD—consolidate the lowest common denominators and you've got the biggest audience. No?"

"It's business," I said.

"*Everything's* business, Baird. That's what *I've* learned. It's *all* business."

"Okay," I said.

"You never were any fun in a debate, Baird," Mitch said. "You agree with everyone so they won't argue with you." His breathing deepened, his shoulders rising higher with each breath drawn. "I've been in some businesses, Baird. Haven't done so well as Baird Lowen, of course, or Roy Duncan. But I've gotten by so far." He bent and arranged some items on a countertop. "You two have a lot in common, you know? Were you aware of that?" He turned to face me. "You two could be twins working in different fields. You're so alike. But you know that or you wouldn't be here, would you?"

"I never thought of myself as much like Roy Duncan."

"No. You wouldn't, any more than he could see how much like you he is." He fumbled for words for a second, then screwed his face into ugly silence.

"Don't stop now," I said. "Not when you're getting so close to saying something."

"There's nothing I can say that you don't already know."

"I doubt that."

Mitch smiled, this time with teeth. "Okay, yeah. I guess I do know a few things, and some of them may be about you. Some aren't. I've seen some things and heard some things you and Roy could no more deal with than fly to the moon."

"Tell me," I said.

"You wouldn't be interested—I'm not talking about *you,* now. And that's all you care about."

"Try me," I said.

"With what?" he said with a harsh laugh. "What do you want to hear? How I spend my days? Right here, doing no *business.*

How I spend my nights? You want to know? You want to know about my hospice work, about trying to help good people die in peace? You want to know about how many homeless we have in Samson, Baird? Can I tell you about that, and about how we collect shoes and blankets for the ones we can't get to a shelter? How we have services for the ones who die with no forwarding, no relatives, no friends? Or what about abused *children,* Baird? You made a movie that pretended to be about that. I've *worked* with them, ministered to them. You want to know about that? Of course you don't. You want to know about security, about keeping the past past and not rocking any boats. You don't want to know what *I* do."

"Sounds like you do a lot," I said.

"I do what I can," he said, but there was anguish rather than pride in his words.

"Samson's saint?"

"Saint?" He raised a fist but did not bring it down on me. "I am just a *man,* and that is what none of you ever understood about this. Not you; you never even *tried.* But Roy and Ellen, and all the others following *him,* like *he's* some saint when he's just a man and not even a good one."

"Prescott."

He showed his exasperation. "Who else? What else is all this about except New Spirit?" The name became an oath he spat from his mouth. "And they call themselves *Christians.*"

"You call yourself one?"

"I do."

I pointed at the PRESCOTT SUCKS button. "Funny way to show it."

There was a hint of lunacy in his laughter and more than a hint in the gleam in his eyes. "This? What? The *words?* That's what I'm talking about. That's one of the things I'm *talking* about. Words—they worry about words, ideas. You remember Shelby Oakes?"

I nodded but said nothing.

"They got her *fired* last week. From the *public* schools, for teaching books that had *words* in them. And they call themselves *Christians*. Shit," he said, and sneered. "Fuck them. I *am* a Christian; can I have a *fucking* a-men?"

"Amen," I said, for I could not say anything else.

"Fucking Aye A-men." Sweat stood out on his brow. "Those bastards. That bastard Prescott."

"You could have been a pillar of his church by now, you know. You could have been Roy Duncan."

"Watch your mouth." His eyes went wide, wild.

I held up my hands, offering peace. "All I meant was you were there before him. Before he came to town."

"I was, yes."

"You had a prayer group."

"I did, yes."

"Roy was a member, so was Ellen."

"That's true."

"And Prescott came and you walked away from it. Why?"

"Because I didn't buy what he was selling, and it made me sick how easily the others did. Simple as that."

"And what was Prescott selling that you didn't buy?"

"Just words, Baird. Like all the other Christians on TV and most of the ones in churches. Just *words*. Not action, not putting your life on the line for your belief, whether it's Bonhoeffer in Nazi Germany or Christ on his cross or King on the mall in Washington or me in the hospice. None of which Prescott and his kind are interested in. Because it *rocks,* Baird, rocks the boat, rocks the world." He took a step back from me. "But he *sells* it as Christianity and people buy it. *You've* bought it. I saw your article, and for you to take that much trouble making stupid points just shows how you've bought *him* as some kind of example of Christianity, when all he is is television."

"I thought that's what I said."

"Yeah, and you thought your movies had something to say, too. You bought it. You bought Prescott's act. Don't you see that? It's not Christianity—it's voodoo, man. Want to see a zombie? Look at New Spirit. Look at an audience at one of your movies. It's the same. They sit there, watching, watching a movie, watching TV, a sermon. They sit and listen to those songs. *Songs.* Not hymns, not the way they sing them. Not even close. But on tune, every note just right; yeah, they sing beautifully on tune, lift *up* your voices! As one lift up and sing, and be saved. Pay to sing and be saved. *Saved!* Born again, brought to Jesus ready for the rapture, yes, ready for it, tickets all bought and punched and *paid for.*" His voice had become a burning rasp, a fiery brand bristling with the heat of his anger.

Mitch clapped his hands together, a boom of a clap, and tossed his head. His ponytail wagged back and forth, acting as a metronome for his words. "*None* of them are Christians, Baird. But they don't see that; they won't find out until their time comes and they see their foolishness."

"But you're not like them."

"Can't you tell? I *was* saved and no one who has not received the grace of salvation can know what that means. I was *saved!* I became a Christian, *with* Christ, and I have remained one through every bit of my life. And I will tell you that 90 percent of that life, my life, would be *condemned* flat out by Frederick Prescott and his *followers,* because it doesn't fit their *image* of what Christianity is. Well, Christ farted and Christ shit and Christ pissed and picked his nose no doubt, and probably ate it from time to time, and so *what.* Are we to condemn good souls, good *people* because they don't dress like New Spirit, and don't live in New Spirit houses, and don't think fucking Frederick Prescott is the greatest fucking man on earth? Because they look a little different or love different or comb their hair another way or have AIDS or vote Democrat or sing off-key or read books that have dirty words in them or *teach* great books that have dirty words in them?" He surprised me with a gentle smile. "Or make bad movies that make big money," he said, his voice becoming soft at last.

"It's funny," I said. "But I remember your prayer group—"

"You never came to my group."

"Doesn't mean I didn't know what was going on."

"Fair enough."

"Anyway, Mitch, I seem to remember *you* wanting to tell everyone what was *right,* what was *moral,* what was *acceptable behavior.*"

He laughed and his laughter was obviously aimed at himself. "That I did," he said, and it seemed an easy admission. "But things happened. I learned things. People change, Baird."

"Roy hasn't changed."

His eyes got distant. "Roy changed, Baird. He just changed a long time ago."

"When Prescott came."

"He bought image, man did he buy image. 'Cause image has all the answers, doesn't leave room for any questions. *Image.* And nobody does it better than Roy and Ellen Duncan and the Prescotts themselves. Names in the papers and the ballot boxes, campaign slogans, society pages, *front* pages and the evening news. They look good on the front page, don't they, Baird? They take a good picture. Especially Ellen, doesn't *she* take a good picture?"

"You'd know more about that than I would," I said, and was ready to say more.

But Mitch's eyes were growing wild again; he was looking around the shop as though for something just beyond the edge of his vision and spoke with only occasional pauses. "They look so natural. At home. In the big money, too. It's a money machine they've got going there, Baird. You ever *seen* Roy's house? Then you know what I mean. Right next door to Prescott's. Some fine neighborhood, Spirit City. It gives me a pain, Baird, as large a pain as I've ever known to think about Roy and them. How he takes them. All the people who fall for Prescott's act on Sundays and Roy's on election day. Who aren't smart enough *not* to fall, who can't help themselves, so Prescott helps himself to what little they have. So he has more. He can talk, Baird, I'll give him that. I won't call it preaching, but he can *talk.* Those people listen and they get caught up, swallowed. Send in ten dollars, send in twenty, send in a hundred dollars and be *saved!* Be delivered to Jesus without ever meeting *him,* just say his name and then say mine louder, his and mine all at once. Jesus Prescott. Say his name but send your money to *me.*"

Mitch jabbed my chest with a thick finger and gave up a loud ugly laugh that came from deep within him. I watched his shoulders tighten and relax, clenching against his shirt, his suspenders stretching. He rubbed his palms down their length and left damp trails on his shirt. I could think of nothing to say, and yet, beause there was pain in his eyes as well as wildness, I made an offering. "It's okay," I said, and reached out a hand.

He swatted it away angrily. He came close and I could feel the heat of his anger in his breath. "You're no better. Don't think you are, don't even *think* you are. Otherwise why would you be here? Who the fuck are you to try and offer me comfort? Just what is it you think you're offering? What have you ever had to offer anybody in the way of comfort, Baird? *Nothing.* Words—nothing. Pictures—*nothing.* Same as always: all mouth working your way out of making a stand for anything. That's why you're here, isn't it? To work your way out of making a stand? You don't make stands, do you? You don't believe in anything, do you? Something's missing inside you, Baird."

"Love of God?" I said, and he took me by the shoulders and shook me once.

"Don't. Not here. I won't tell anyone, not even you, what to believe; not anymore, that's Prescott's trap. But I won't let you talk that way here." He let me go.

"All right," I said. I had a feeling I could listen to him for another hour or another day and still hear no more than his anger—and I had had enough of that. "Tell me what you're after."

"What I'm after." Mitch took a moment to stroke his beard in an oddly calm, almost professorial fashion. "Let me *see*. What I'm after, Baird, has to do with freedom. With *real* freedom. To do Christ's work and mine. That's real freedom, the freedom that can only come when you've accepted the *vision* of Jesus Christ and his teachings. Not somebody's con, somebody's shuck. I have that vision in me. I try to *share*, that's all. I'm after the freedom to share *more*. Not to teach—it's not something that can be taught."

"I thought you taught Roy, once upon a time."

"Once upon a time I thought so, too. In spite of everything, I thought so. Thought I could lay my hands on and make people *see*." He looked at his feet for a moment. "I couldn't. No one can."

"But you were with Roy—"

Mitch looked up and nodded. "I was with Roy and he was with me. Of course he doesn't remember it that way. I wonder sometimes what he *does* remember." He gave a sigh that was almost a groan. "Have you heard the official version? It's some story. How he woke up one night, *he* says, surrounded in school by all those sinners and drugs and . . . sex. How all that was all around him and he knew it was wrong, all those kids being led into darkness, and he wakes up one night and at the foot of his bed is who else but his—*his*—savior, *his* Jesus Christ, there ready to embrace him, humble Roy Duncan."

"The official version."

"The version that *sells*."

"I'd like to hear your version."

"I'm sure you would," Mitch began, but was cut off when the door of the shop opened and a tall young woman in a cool summer dress stepped inside. Mitch looked up sharply, as though startled, and I moved to the far side of the store while he attended to his business. The woman smiled at Mitch and he said hello to her, walked beside her to a film display. The customer took only a moment. She bought a single roll of film, nothing more. Mitch kept his gaze on her as she closed the door, watched until she passed beyond the edge of his front window. "First sale of the day," he said, and would not look at me as he closed his register drawer. "Now, why don't we just get on with it?" he said wearily before I could speak. He faced me.

"All right," I said, and felt only tired as the answers came into the open before me. I was some detective all right.

"How are the mighty fallen," Mitch said to me in a heavy tone.

"Meaning?"

"Meaning that it must be some comedown to go from Mr. Hollywood to what you are now."

"And what's that, Mitch?"

"Roy Duncan's errand boy."

I made no answer.

"That's what you are, isn't it? Come on, Baird, you've got to answer that one before we get on to *business.*"

"I'm here to find out what you want."

"To save Roy's career."

"To get this thing put away. Back where it belongs."

"And where's that?"

"Out of sight, Mitch. It's ancient history; what's it going to take to keep it that way?"

He was not yet ready to deal. "What I don't get is why *you?* That's what surprised me when you walked in. What have *you* got to lose from those pictures? Why are *you* helping Roy?"

"Why not just figure I'm doing this for Ellen? For old times? First love being the deepest and all that. You know."

"First love," Mitch said. "Maybe I can buy that. I'll assume you won't offer any more."

"That's right."

"Or maybe it's Roy. Maybe he has you in some sort of a sling yourself." Mitch smiled, pleased with an intuition whose truth he must have seen on my face.

"Think what you want, Mitch. I just want this thing done. Name your price and I'll pass it along."

He stared at me for a long moment before nodding. "I'll give it some thought, and you tell Roy to think about it, too. I want to hear his offer before I name my price."

"Ten dollars," I said, "twenty dollars, a hundred. Send the right amount and be saved."

"Something like that," he said. "You go talk to Roy. And let me know how to get in touch with you in case I change my mind."

I told him the name of my motel and turned to go.

"Not going to buy anything?" Mitch said before I reached the door. "You'd be my second customer of the day."

"*I'm* not the one buying, Mitch," I said.

"No?" he said.

"You're causing a lot of pain," I said.

"Pain can be instructive, Baird," Mitchell Tarr said, and did not look back at me as I opened the door and stepped outside into the heat of the afternoon.

CHAPTER 11

THERE WAS A BIT OF the day left, but I had nowhere to go. I returned to my motel, drew the draperies tight against the last of the sun and stretched out on the bed. I closed my eyes and thought about Mitchell Tarr. The force of his anger had impressed me, and it made me cautious. And curious. I may have had more questions after I left than I had when I arrived at Mitch's store.

Why now? was the question that sat at the top of my thoughts. Why was he pressuring Roy now? Just to stop the political career? Or something more? It would be interesting to hear the figure he named for his price, and to know if there were riders beyond the money. I could not believe that money was all he was after—and also believe his sincerity, the outrage and hurt, the strength of his faith as he professed it.

And while I had no trouble picturing Mitchell in the bushes near the lakehouse, camera in hand, I wanted to hear from him why he had been there. What had he been after that afternoon?

The questions darted and danced, then danced slower, darted less. I dozed off.

When I sleep during daylight my dreams are vivid, brief and disjointed, often frightening, rarely sexual. In the motel room that afternoon I dreamed of Samson, of Ellen and Roy but not of Mitchell or Shelby, of the Reverend Frederick Prescott but not of his wife. I woke after only a few minutes. My forehead was damp and my mouth tasted foul. I stripped and went into the bathroom and stood under the spray of the shower, alternating its temperature from hot to cold. I held my face into the spray and let it beat against my eyes. When I got out of the shower I toweled off and sat naked on the side of my bed. I could call Roy, see Mitch again, arrive at a price and end this thing.

And what? Go back to my farm and wait until Roy played Archimedes with the Arizona lever again? *Roy Duncan's errand boy.* I had a sudden vision that this could happen again, and I was not going to have that. I would not be leaving Samson until I knew what Roy had on me, and where it had come from, and who else knew. There was research to do, and I had a thought as to where to begin. I went to the desk, picked up a business card, dialed the number it bore. When the receptionist answered I asked for Betty Prescott.

I was kept on hold for a minute or two. Soft gospel music— a gospel *song*—came across the line while I waited. A second song was just beginning when Betty picked up and apologized for the delay. "I'd almost expected to hear from you this morning, Baird," she said. I still liked the way she said my name.

"I didn't want to impose."

"I won't even reply to that, Baird. I'm not one to issue an empty invitation, and you should know that, too. I'm not like you all are out in Hollywood, hollering 'Let's do lunch!' at every person you see and never meaning a word of it."

"You've been to Hollywood?"

"Of course I have," she said. "Now why don't you stop by here . . . I'm tied up early tomorrow morning with several things, but I'm free by eleven. You stop by then and we'll have a light brunch. How does that sound?"

"That sounds just fine."

"Good. We can talk about whatever you're interested in and see if we can't get some of those questions of yours answered. We'll have that *tussle.*" She laughed lightly.

"I'll look forward to it."

"And I will as well, Baird. Bring your notebook. And a camera, too, if you want—it's a hair appointment early in the morning. Get some good color film."

"I'll see you at eleven, Betty."

"I'll be looking forward to that," said Betty Prescott before she broke the connection.

I dressed quickly and realized with a smile that I'd been sitting naked in a hotel room while talking to Frederick Prescott's wife. Another argument against videophones, I thought. I was still smiling when I went out to find some dinner. I picked an unpretentious restaurant not far from the hotel, had a couple of drinks and a forgettable meal, and was back before seven. When I pulled into the lot I saw Roy Duncan parked near my room. He was out of his car before I stopped my engine.

"Here to talk business?" I said. "Or is this a social call?"

"After we're inside."

I reached for my key but could not resist a prod. "Isn't this a little risky for you, Roy? Going into a motel room with a man? Who knows who might be taking pictures of us right now? Mitch Tarr might be out there somewhere clicking away." Roy fought it but could not contain a sudden flash of nervousness. He glanced from side to side. I laughed and opened the door. Roy hurried into the room and the first thing he did was to give the drapery cord a tug, although they were still pulled tight.

"Care for a drink?" I said.

"Some water," Roy said. "With ice." I took the plastic bucket and walked down to the machine, filled the bucket with cubes, came back slowly. I was willing to give Roy plenty of time alone. I had nothing to hide from him. Perhaps he was searching the drawers or going through my luggage. That was fine. My notes and lists, the photographs of Ellen and me, were all in my breast pocket.

He was sitting in a chair when I entered the room. I fixed his water and poured myself a splash of Wild Turkey. "Now," I said, after sitting down on the edge of the bed.

"You saw Mitch today. For some time."

He knew exactly how obedient an errand boy I had been, and that was annoying, but it was no surprise. He made no effort to hide his smugness. "We talked," I said.

"And?" Eagerness chased the smugness away.

I had a sip of my drink. I had wrestled with this over dinner, whether or not to tell Roy immediately. I was curious to know his reaction, and curiosity won the wrestle. "It's Mitch," I said.

"He told you he took the pictures?"

"Yes."

Roy spilled a little water as he raised the plastic motel glass to his lips. He brushed at the droplets and asked, "How'd you get him to talk? What did you say?" There was a beadiness to his eyes I found repugnant.

"That's my business, Roy. All you need to know is that it's Mitch and he wants you to make him an offer."

"No, I really want to know," he said, and there was an insistent whine to his voice. "I have a right to know."

"You're right, Roy," I said. "I looked Mitch right in the eye and I said, 'Say, Mitch, sorry to bother you but Ellen Jennings and I were fucking one afternoon—' "

"You bastard," he said. It was the strongest word I ever heard him speak, but I let it pass, thinking of what Mitch had said about *words*.

"Let it go, Roy. What passed between Mitch and me is our business. Now you tell me what you're offering him."

"*Me?*"

"Who else? It's your ass that's getting bought off the hook."

"He didn't name a price?"

I shook my head. "He wants to hear your offer first. He's a good businessman; you ought to appreciate that."

"He's filth," Roy said. "Doing this. Other . . . things I've heard about. Mitchell Tarr is a madman, Baird. He is seriously disturbed, and I suspect he always has been."

"Even back in the days when you looked up to him?"

"You talked about that?"

"We talked about a lot of things, Roy. Among them your . . . salvation." I snapped my fingers. "But, then, Mitch wasn't there for that, was he?"

"Mitch has no business talking about anybody's salvation."

I had had enough of salvation for one day. "And neither do you, Roy, and I don't really give a damn whether either of you are saved or left behind when the rapture comes, but it's not coming tonight, and probably not tomorrow, so let's talk *business*, shall we? How much?"

He surprised me by asking, "How much do you think he'll settle for?"

I shrugged. "He's pretty broke," I said. "It surprised me. I remembered him as Mr. Capitalist, Mr. Free Enterprise."

"All theory, Baird, wind," Roy said with a short laugh. "Mitch has always been a financial disaster area, getting a little ahead and putting his money into crazy projects, nutty things. He changed."

"Pretty dramatically. He says you haven't changed at all."

"He's said as much to me himself."

"You two have talked?"

"We've tried. A few times over the years."

I had an image and laughed out loud. "Each of you trying to save the other," I said. "Each trying to prove who's more saved, who's closer to—"

"Mitch's difficulty, Baird, is that he's never understood how things are done."

"And how *are* things done, Roy?"

He held up a hand and ticked off points on his fingers. "You see Mitch again tomorrow. You work out a guarantee that this will *end*. Work out how he'll get his money. And get him to agree to a price."

"What price, Roy?"

Again, he asked for advice. "You tell me."

"Like I said, he's broke. But he may want to sting you, too. Come in high. What can you afford?"

"Ten thousand?" Roy said.

"*Please.* He's broke but he's no fool. How much is your name worth?"

Roy gave a patient smile. "*Please.* I'm not going *that* high. Twenty thousand."

I said nothing but my expression spoke for me.

"All right," Roy said at last. "You start low, but go as high as fifty thousand. If he agrees, we'll put it together."

"We?"

"You're in this, too, Baird, no reason why you shouldn't pay. And you've got a lot more money than I do."

"I'm not buying you off any hook, Roy."

"You've got a hook of your own, Baird, and I've got it in you. Remember that. Maybe I'll sell you that hook. Maybe I'll charge you Mitch's price, plus 10 percent for good measure."

"I might even be interested in a proposition like that," I said. "But first I want to know what you've got, and where you got it. So give."

"I don't think so, Baird," said Roy. He stood up and moved to the door. "Not tonight, anyway. I like having you in the dark. You fit there. Finish with Mitch and maybe we'll talk."

"I'll finish with Mitch," I said. "But we're not going to *talk*; we're not going to *negotiate.* You get whatever dirty little package you have on me together and you have it together *tomorrow.* Everything—names, whatever. And the names of anyone who knows. All of it. I'll have a look and we'll see what it's worth."

"We'll see," was all Roy said. He pulled the door shut behind him.

I did a passable of job of putting it all from my mind that evening, with television and Wild Turkey serving as able assistants. Shelby never called. I was asleep by eleven, and I slept nearly nine hours. I felt groggy after waking, lingered in the

shower, took longer than usual shaving. I did not think of Roy
or Mitch. I would see them both later. I had a full morning
ahead. I put on a light suit and knotted my tie carefully. I wanted
to look my best for the reverend's wife.

At ten-thirty I set out toward Betty Prescott's office, driving
slowly through light traffic, taking my time. My route took me
past Roy's neighborhood, and I saluted the still intact SPIRIT
CITY sign. I braked through the long curve around the periphery of the subdivision, passed a mile of wood and pastureland,
also Prescott property, and came at last upon Spirit Center.

It sprawled over hilly acres. I drove parallel to a half mile of
perfect white fence enclosing manicured meadows. It was a picture. Far off, I saw horses and riders on low hills; ahead the land
leveled and held a cluster of brick buildings and tall trees. I entered New Spirit grounds, passing first the campus of Spirit College; opposite the campus Spirit Center was flanked by a grade
school.

Spirit Center was the organizational heart of New Spirit. The
long loop of the main drive created an island of more than an
acre, at the center of which stood Frederick Prescott's church,
its steeple rising even higher than the huge oaks in whose shade
neatly dressed students sat poring over books. That church
seated two thousand and it was full three times each Sunday. I
had been denounced from its pulpit.

I bore to the right, following the loop past an orientation and
visitors' center, and then past a large meeting hall. Blacktop
lanes barely one vehicle wide separated the buildings onto lots;
every third lane was large enough to accommodate trucks and
equipment. Beyond the meeting hall stood the television production studio. At the back end of the loop, directly behind the
church, stood a four-story steel and smoked glass office building. Down the cut-throughs on either side I could see land being
cleared, with new construction already under weigh. Bulldozers,
whose growl I barely heard over my air-conditioning, raised

clouds of red dust. I found a parking space not far from the office building, noticing as I took it that my station wagon was virtually the only vehicle whose bumper was unadorned by New Spirit stickers. When the rapture came would I suffer for my clean chrome? I took my notepad and camera and locked the car.

I passed a colorful map sealed in a glass frame like maps in shopping malls or airports, but I did not need its help to tell me where to find Betty Prescott. I walked to the office building and stepped inside. A brass legend above the revolving door read SPIRIT CENTRAL. Where else would Betty be?

It was cool in the lobby. A middle-aged receptionist sat behind a white modular desk. On the wall behind her hung a portrait of Christ that must have been six feet wide and ten feet tall. To either side of Christ were hung portraits, smaller, but not dramatically so, of Frederick Prescott and Betty. To either side of their portraits were elevators. The lobby ceiling was a story-and-a-half high. Arched, it was a cathedral ceiling in miniature with wide glass panels that let in filtered light. I stepped up to the reception desk.

The receptionist wore a headset that curved around her strong jaw. I waited while she fielded a flurry of calls. "New *Spirit* can you *hold* thank *you* . . . New *Spirit*, I will connect you thank *you* . . ." I smiled at her and she smiled back. A plastic name tag pinned to her blouse told me her name was *Shirley*.

The flurry faded and she said, "Yes, sir?"

"I have an eleven o'clock appointment with Betty Prescott."

She glanced at a folio-sized date book. "Mr. Lowen?"

"That's right."

She pressed a button on her keyboard and said, "Nancy, Mr. Baird Lowen is here to see Mrs. Prescott." She pronounced my name "Lone," and also said "Mizriz," a pronunciation I had not heard since childhood. Shirley touched a finger lightly to her earphone as though to hear more clearly, and nodded after a moment.

"Nancy will be down for you in just a moment," she said, and turned her attention from me as the flurry renewed itself. "New *Spirit* can you *hold* thank *you.*"

I wandered around the spacious lobby. There were four clusters of couches and chairs, but no one else was waiting. Coffee tables bore Bibles as well as colorful magazines. I took a seat and passed the time leafing through magazines. There were four separate titles: *Weekly Worship, From the Mount, Christian Clippings* and *The Prescott Report,* each bearing prominently the stylized colophon of New Spirit/Prescott Publications. *The Prescott Report* was the slimmest of these periodicals, the one with the longest columns of uninterrupted text, the fewest illustrations, the most overtly political content. It was also the one that most interested me. It was a biweekly journal of American Christian opinion, and was so labeled below its masthead. This was Frederick Prescott's personal vehicle, and I had seen a couple of issues before. I looked through it quickly, came across an article denouncing the absence of strong moral values in Hollywood's latest summer offerings, and was midway through the piece when the elevator doors opened and I looked up.

A young woman barely out of her teens stepped out and hurried across the lobby toward me. Her smile was New Spirit wide, easy and natural and full of friendship. "Hi!" she said, and extended her right hand. "Mr. Lowen?"

I stood up and shook hands with her.

"Sorry to keep you waiting, sir. I'm Nancy Hargetay, and I'm a student at Spirit College. I help Mrs. Prescott three mornings a week, and she asked me to offer her apologies; she's running just a few minutes late this morning. She said if you're interested, I could show you around the building."

"I'd like that," I said, and gave a smile of my own.

"All right, then," she said happily. "Let's go."

In the elevator she pressed the button for the second floor. "What are you studying?" I said.

"I'm a junior this fall," she said, "and I *think* I want to be an architect. I want to build churches. Of course, I'll have to get my advanced courses at another school; we're not a university here yet. But I'll have a good foundation for it when I do."

I looked at her, a confident young Christian who knew where she was headed. She was, what? Nineteen? Kelsey would be twenty now. I wondered how she looked. She had not made another movie after *Moonstalk*. I wondered if she was still with Maurice. The elevator doors opened.

The second floor was devoted to Information Services, and I suspected there were corporations whose equipment was not so sophisticated as New Spirit's. "I guess this is sort of our nerve center," Nancy said as we walked past banks of minicomputers and row upon row of cubicles in which men and women sat before colorful screens. "Everything comes through here sooner or later."

"Names and numbers," I said.

"You got it!" She had a nice laugh. "While we're here, are you on our mailing list?"

"Maybe later," I said.

She looked puzzled, but did not press. "Mrs. Prescott was telling me about how it was not that long ago. Big noisy computers. No laser printers." She spoke as though referring to an alien world, which, to her generation, not two decades behind mine, it was. "And when they first got started all they had were typewriters!"

"I was thinking more of monks and quill pens," I said.

Her laughter was generous, and a few of the computer operators looked our way. "You mean the *real* old days, Mr. Lowen." We turned to go. "Are you a Catholic?"

"Not me."

Nancy nodded.

"Not that there's anything wrong with Catholicism," I said as we reentered the elevator.

"Not at *all*," Nancy said, nodding her agreement. "As the reverend says, 'As long as you're *something*.' "

"I'm something," I said.

"So Mrs. Prescott says," Nancy said.

The third floor belonged to New Spirit's administrative offices. I met some of the organization's managers when Nancy led me into an office long enough to shake a few hands and forget a few names. I could have been a visitor to an insurance agency or brokerage firm. No one gave evidence of knowing my name before we were introduced.

"Each floor has its own chapel," Nancy said when we left the office. She opened a wide door on the opposite hall. The door bore a cross where others held nameplates. The chapel itself was softly lit, its windows covered with rich purple draperies. The chapel was unoccupied, and we stepped inside. Three rows of pews faced a long table on which rested two books and a candle.

"People can come here anytime," Nancy said in a soft voice, almost whispering. "For calmness or guidance. To become renewed during the day. You're never more than a few steps from a chapel here. Not that you need a chapel to be close to God."

"No," I said. I thought of Spirit City's gazebos.

"But it's comforting to have them so close." With a step she took us deeper into the chapel. I could see the titles of the books on the table: a Bible and a collection of inspirational thoughts—*Passages, Psalms, and Prayers* by Betty Prescott. I came close to smiling.

"Would you like to pray with me?" Nancy said.

Her eyes were so open and young that it pained me to disappoint her, but I said, "Maybe later."

She nodded solemnly. "I understand." She turned and bowed her head for a moment while I stood by.

Nancy was finishing her prayer when the door to the chapel opened wide and we were joined by Betty Prescott.

Chapter 12

Betty smiled warmly at Nancy. "Don't feel badly, dear; I couldn't get him to pray with me, either."

"Hi, Betty," I said, and nodded in Nancy's direction. "This young lady has given me quite a lovely tour."

"Well, of *course* she has, Baird. That's why I picked her." Betty stepped past me and put an arm around Nancy's shoulder. "We're very proud of Nancy."

"You should be," I said, and watched Nancy blush.

Betty hugged Nancy close, then released her. "You run along now, dear. I'll take over Mr. Lowen."

"It was nice to meet you, sir," Nancy said to me. I shook her hand again. "I hope the Lord gives you a wonderful day."

"And I hope you get to be a wonderful architect," I said. "Good luck with your studies."

Nancy left us and Betty took a moment to straighten the books on the table before we left the chapel. I pulled the door shut behind us and walked beside Betty to the elevator. She pressed the button for the fourth floor. "What a morning," she said. "I am sorry to be late, punctuality is something I *insist* on, but I've been running around like a chicken since six." We went up.

"Quite all right," I said. "If you'd been on time I wouldn't have gotten to meet Nancy."

"No," said Betty, with a smile that let me know she wanted me to know she had planned it all. "You wouldn't."

I chuckled. "Your hair looks nice," I said. She had charmed

me on Monday, and I intended to return the favor today.

Betty pressed her fingers gingerly against her coif. "It ought to," she said, an old country friend. "What it costs me. But it's sort of a trademark by now. But sometimes I wish I could wear wigs. Wouldn't be the same, though."

"Not as natural?" I said, and was pleased with the laugh that won me. Betty wore a business version of the ruffled blouse that was another trademark. Her earrings were tiny gold crosses. We reached the fourth floor.

"You know, when Frederick and I built this building, the size of it sort of scared us. That was three years ago. Now we're just bursting at the seams. I wish we'd built ten stories." She showed a wise smile. "But then this building would've been taller than Frederick's steeple, and we can't have *that.*"

She steered me to the left, past offices and cubicles that bustled with activity. Betty nodded at the people we passed, but we did not pause. "I'm down here," she said. "Frederick's office is at the opposite end. Absolutely equal square footage, though," she said with a chuckle as we reached double doors with a nameplate that read BETTY PRESCOTT. She opened one of the doors and we stepped into an enormous office, wide as the building and windowed on three sides. "Isn't this *profligate!*" Betty said, and took me by the elbow. "As crowded as we are to have all this space for just one person." She gave my elbow the sort of squeeze a favored aunt would give and shared a secret: "I love it, though. So does Frederick."

"Some view," I said.

Betty released my arm and walked me to the west wall. We looked out on construction equipment and workers. "More offices?" I said.

"In the nick of time," said Betty. We watched bulldozers pushing mounds of red earth. "And it already looks like it won't be enough. Frederick and I were talking just this morning about another building." Her laugh was one of wonderment and surprise.

"Another building! Who would have thought?"

We turned from the window and I saw that the office's interior wall was crowded with bookshelves, framed photographs, college degrees and award certificates, bound volumes of magazines, stacks of CDs and videocassettes, mementos and bric-a-brac.

"You've discovered my wall," Betty said with some pride. "Let's take a look at it before we get to work, okay?" There appeared to be a carrel at the far end of the wall and we walked slowly toward it, Betty stopping a couple of times to point out some noteworthy items.

The carrel's narrow entranceway faced the center of the office, and I approached it and took a look inside. The carrel held still more bookshelves, and a sturdy central desk that held a spotless computer flanked on one side by two legal pads and an appointment book and on the other side by a stack of manuscripts, facedown, the pages neatly aligned with the edge of the desk. There was a simple typist's chair, although a good one, and I could see a shelf, shadowed beneath the desk, on which rested a laser printer. I looked at Betty.

She was beaming. "What do you think?"

"It's something," I said.

"Isn't it? I designed it myself. I don't know about you, Baird, but I like to sort of seal myself away when I write. Insulate myself, do you know?"

"I know a little bit about insulating myself," I said.

"Yes," said Betty, studying me. "I understand that about you." She pressed her hands to her hips. "But this is a different kind of insulation. Because I'm sealing out *this* world"—she waved a hand at the office and its trappings—"but not God's world. And I do feel God's presence when I work here, how could I not? I am after all writing to His greater glory." A frown drew briefly at the corners of her mouth. "But I also am always aware that it's *me* writing, glorifying myself in a way, you see? Otherwise I wouldn't have my name on all the jackets or byline the articles, wouldn't be so vain about the jacket photographs and publicity *I* receive." Her hands darted up. "Wouldn't spend so much time on my *hair*. But you know what I'm talking about, I'm sure."

"Oh?"

She raised her chin so that she was looking down at me a little and said, "*A film by Baird Lowen.*"

"I suppose," I said. "Don't spend as much time on my hair, though."

"It's all the same."

"Maybe. Have you always wanted to be a writer?"

Small lines gathered around her eyes when she smiled. I guessed she smiled often. "Has the interview begun?"

"If you like."

"Then in answer to your question: yes, always." She clasped her hands and held them to her bosom. "I wanted so to grow up to be, oh, Frances Parkinson Keyes. Or Pearl S. Buck. Or Louisa May Alcott. I was always writing stories when I was young. I tried to write a novel when I was ten." She chuckled. "I got a hundred pages done. *Typed.*"

"Ever try again? I might read a novel you wrote."

"Not yet. But someday, maybe soon." Her look grew sly. "I have a few ideas. But my dedication and, yes, my marriage drew me into Christian writing, you know, into inspirational writing. At least my readers say I inspire them."

"I can see why they'd say that."

"You've read some of my books?" she said, and I would not have been surprised if she had batted her eyes, but she did not.

"A few." I had cracked some of her volumes as I prepared to write my article. Her style was as sweet as syrup, and most of the lessons she offered were nothing new. But she could turn a phrase in such a way as to seem clever to those who had not read much. And she knew her adjectives. "I liked the biography best. The Leonard book. He was quite a young man."

I'd pressed a button and it was the right one. She gave the full title in a tone close to rapturous: *"David Leonard—The Life and Death of a New Spirit Missionary.* Baird, that is *my* favorite of all my books." Her look became wistful. "And of course it meant so much because of David himself. I wish you could have known him. Frederick has such a following in Colombia, but it is in so many ways such a wicked place. They never did find his killers."

"It was quite a book. How many *have* you written now?"

Her eyes crinkled at me. "Forty-seven," she said.

"Forty-seven!"

"I told you—I love to write. Let me show you."

We stepped away from the carrel and moved to a long shelf that held nothing but the works of Betty Prescott. There were hardcovers and paperbacks, all in mint condition, covers and spines still shiny and reflective, gaily glittering with bright letters. Some carried the imprint of large New York houses, others came from serious religious publishers, but the bulk of them were published by Prescott Press.

There were cookbooks and gardening guides, introductions to prayer, children's books and collections of magazine articles, a response to evolutionists and a volume questioning the wisdom of welfare, guides to parenthood and Christian sexuality, travel books and picture books, gatherings of music, letters to Betty Prescott and her responses, an autobiography. She had a gift for titles. *The Christian Gourmet, The Body God Gave Us, I Walk the Holy Land, My Life for His, The Responsibilities of Puberty, New Spirit—An Old Spirit Restored, America—A Love Poem, Why Fight Freedom?, Persuasive Promises.*

"Impressive," I said after a moment.

Betty's shrug seemed almost modest. "I told you, Baird, I just write and write. That it gets published and sells is wonderful, but I'd write if I never had a word see print. I'm sure you're the same way."

"Not really," I said. I had felt that way about film once. I'd have had a camera in my hands or a script on my desk if there was no chance of anything ever being shown or produced. But those days were gone. "I just write when I have something to say."

"And even when you don't," Betty said, and changed the subject before I could respond to her sting. "You don't mind if I record this, do you? No offense, but I've been misquoted so often I'm a little gun-shy."

"Not at all."

"Let's go over to the desk, then."

Betty Prescott might write in a walled carrel, but her desk in the center of the office was an elegant mahogany campaign table, its trestle legs sturdy and dark. She was by every evidence a clean-desk executive: There was a blotter with penholder, a telephone with a dozen buttons, a Bible, nothing more. Three chairs faced the desk in a crescent and I could imagine the conversations held there, and the control she exerted over them. Betty placed a small recorder in the center of the desk, seated herself and gestured for me to sit facing her. "Go ahead, Baird."

I made a show of glancing at the first two pages of my notebook, and I had spent some time over breakfast formulating some actual questions should she look, but I dropped the pretense almost immediately. "This may be a sort of free-form interview, Betty," I said.

"Somehow I assumed as much," she said, not unpleasantly. Then she gestured at the recorder. "Just check your quotes with me for accuracy."

"I'll be sure to." The first question on my list actually seemed appropriate. "How do you see yourself in New Spirit? Organizationally. Are you Reverend Prescott's assistant? His helpmate? Vice—"

"I am his *wife*," she said with some force. "And in the eyes of God and most of the laws of our country I am his equal. You can discover from the newspapers that Frederick and I are full business partners in quite a few ventures outside New Spirit. Inside the organization—" she paused and I did not speak. "In*side* New Spirit, there is no doubt that Frederick is the center. His energy, his drive and electricity are so responsible for its growth." Betty laughed. "Of course, if Frederick were here now he'd tell you that's a lot of . . . hogwash. He says we're all equals in New Spirit, that the only edge he's got is the size of his voice."

"And the number of people who listen to it," I said.

"Frederick would say they're listening to the—movement, the *groundswell,* the *need.* He gets concerned that there's too much personality and not enough persuasion."

I thought of Mitchell Tarr's words about Prescott's personality and the centrality of that personality to New Spirit. Obviously the Prescotts had heard such criticisms before. I changed my tack and managed to use another of the questions I'd prepared. "If you were me," I said, "what would *you* think my story should be?"

Betty's smile was eloquent and warm. "Well, Baird, if I were you I wouldn't be writing journalism—or what passes for it— at all. You have a gift for telling stories about people; you've just been writing about the wrong ones."

"Who *should* I be writing about?"

"Here's a story just right for you, Baird. It would be a story about someone who just naturally had to feel superior to anything bigger than himself, someone with a lot of talent, someone too bright, perhaps, for his own good." I sat still and she did not stop. "Someone who, I don't know, doesn't let people get too close. And who decides to tell the whole wide world the truth about New Spirit, about how all the smiling, happy, spiritual, *productive* people there are being exploited and manipulated." She sat back in her chair. "And of course the *story* would be how wrong that person found himself to be—how the true message of New Spirit reached him and he embraced it and was in turn embraced."

"Persuaded," I said.

"Exactly," Betty said.

There was a moment of silence. "That's some story," I said at last.

"And it has the virtue of being a story that *could* be true."

"Maybe in your hands, Betty. You're more of a writer than me."

Betty brushed that aside. "I don't know about that. But I've been blessed all my life to see more clearly than most. Certainly I see more clearly than you. It's such a shame, as I said at Ellen's. You're a prodigiously gifted young man. You have such a talent."

I was growing weary of everyone telling me how talented I was, and then telling me how empty were the uses to which I'd put that talent. "Then you should know that talent is its own reward, Betty. It sees what it sees, and if the talent is honest, then what's created could not come out any other way."

"*If* the talent is honest."

"You think I've been dishonest with my . . . gifts."

"I think you're misguided."

"And you don't approve of me." I'd written that question out as well.

"It's not for *me* to approve or disapprove, Baird. You know that much about us. But I can't condone the subjects you deal with, the manner in which you present your themes."

I tapped my pen against my notebook. "You say you're for freedom, but you would deny me—"

"Where? Where have we said we would deny anyone their freedom? Deny them hunger, yes, as much as we are able. Deny them joblessness and ignorance. As much as we are able. Deny them that emptiness of the soul, which is all too common. *Those* are our causes, Baird. *Listen* to what Frederick says in his sermons. *Read* our literature. Come to *church*, learn what we *really* stand for. We aren't seeking to deny you anything."

I thought of Shelby, denied her profession, denied *her* talent, which was the ability to teach young people to seek their own truths. I thought of Mitch again, doing every Christian act and yet denied the respect of the biggest church in town and one of the biggest in the nation. I looked at Betty. "You'd prefer my films hadn't been made."

"I won't deny *that,*" she said, laughing. "I don't like waste and your movies wasted your talent."

"They were *mine,*" I said. "What my talent saw."

"Because your eyes aren't clear."

"They found an audience."

"So does pornography," said Betty. "So do racketeers." I had not heard that word in a decade and then only in old movies. "You can *sell* anything, Baird, especially today, people expect to be *sold.* Our young people can be *sold* so easily. That's all you did—*sold* them something."

I was ready to play some cards and see what they got me. "I heard that same thing said about you and your husband yesterday," I said. "Right here in Samson, in your own backyard. By Mitchell Tarr."

Betty looked as though she'd caught a foul odor. I wondered if she would speak actual ill of Mitch, but her expression became more gentle before she spoke. "I told Roy once that his attitudes toward you were uncharitable."

"You and Roy have talked about me?"

"You've come up in a conversation or two," she said with little air of enigma. "But his attitudes toward Mr. Tarr are, I must admit, even less charitable."

"They were close once."

"I remember all of that. We were *there,* remember, Frederick and me. We used to talk about which of you two was giving us the most trouble. You objecting to our use of school property or Mr. Tarr with what he called his . . . preaching about us."

"No contest, I'm sure."

"No," she said, and almost smiled. "It really wasn't."

17

"He's still preaching about you."

"Yes."

"Just how seriously does New Spirit take Mitch? As opposition?"

"Oh, Baird, I wouldn't think of Mitchell Tarr as . . . *opposition*. I don't know what I'd call him. Rabble-rouser would be the word my father would use."

"What would your husband call him?"

"Why, Frederick would call him to *pray*, Baird," Betty said with all her warmth. "He would call him to the fold." She studied my face for a moment. "It's very sad, your generation, Baird. There are so many like you—talented, hardworking, but pushing yourselves so hard in pursuit only of . . . emptiness. And there are far too many like Mr. Tarr and his followers. Rabble-rousers. Confused. Hating those who are more . . . secure in themselves."

"Followers?"

"He has a . . . *group*. He doesn't call it a church, thankfully, for it is not. A group that gets together to listen to him. He stands up and rants and calls it preaching."

Mitch's preaching was still clear in my ears and I began to laugh softly, could not help myself.

"What is it, Baird?"

"Just such a motley crew, I guess. Our old class."

"Something went wrong somewhere, Baird. With your parents, with us. With the lessons you should have been taught. With the example that should have been set."

"Roy and Ellen seem to have learned your lessons. They turned out all right in your eyes."

"Because they're secure in their own eyes. They know who they are, and they know who they are in the eyes of God. That's not to say they haven't had their troubles, Baird. Everyone has troubles, tests. Why, they're having a trial right now." It was the first time that morning I had seen her eyes grow hard. I did not wilt under that gaze, or even come close. "But they know where to find the strength they need and they are not afraid to call upon that strength."

"No," I said, "they're not."

"And they know that that strength will serve them well, will get them through this trial so that they can continue to lead the life they have earned and pursue the goals they so deserve to achieve."

"Governor and Mrs. Duncan?" I said.

"The Lord—and the voters—willing."

"A lot of people think that could be a dangerous thing, that much New Spirit in office. Embodied in Roy Duncan."

"A lot of people, Baird, have unclear thoughts." She looked at her watch before I could respond. "It's already past noon! Let's have a quick bite, and then I've got to get back to preparing for the barbecue." She spoke into the intercom, letting her staff know she was ready to be served. "I guess our brunch will be a lunch," she said, rising. We moved toward a low table surrounded by comfortably upholstered chairs.

"Thanks for taking this much time with me," I said.

"Oh, Baird, I could talk to you all afternoon. I could *persuade* you, I could. And I would, too, but this barbecue—" She put her hands to her face. "Where are my manners? I meant to invite you the other day and I forgot and now it almost got away from me again. Baird, you *must* come to the reverend's barbecue on Friday. Just us and five or six hundred of our closest followers. But you must come, please?"

"I'll give it some thought," I said.

There was a soft knock at the door followed by the entrance of a woman in a soft gray uniform and white apron. She wheeled in a metal serving cart bearing a coffeepot and several covered platters. We stood by while she arranged our meal on the table. There were small triangular sandwiches, ham biscuits, slices of fresh fruit and cheese, a plate of sugary pastries, two dishes of apple cobbler. When the cart had been removed, Betty poured coffee and served two generous plates.

We talked over food for close to half an hour, but did not come close to our earlier topics. Betty attempted to draw me into a discussion of the welfare system and the ways its structure degraded rather than uplifted life. She made clear without dissembling New Spirit's doctrinal determination and her own personal determination to restore moral value and discipline to America's administrative machinery.

"Through the good elective offices of Roy Duncan?" I said, but Betty did not rise to my bait. I had gotten what I would get from her, and when the meal was finished she rose immediately. Our time together was over.

"You didn't get to take any pictures, Baird," she said as I gathered my camera and notebook.

"Another time."

"I hope so," she said. "I hope we have another time together. Like I said, I can be very persuasive. Let me walk you downstairs." She took me first to a small office, where she produced and signed two of her books. I promised to read them. "And I hope you'll let *me* read your article before you submit it," Betty said.

"If I write it," I said. We stepped into the elevator. "And I'll think about your invitation."

"Oh, wonderful! Frederick will be delighted—he was sorry to miss you this morning, but—" She waved her hands at the helplessness they faced in confronting their schedules. "Are you bringing anyone?"

I thought of Shelby. "I'm not sure."

Betty looked from side to side, as though to protect a secret. "Baird, I'd be happy to introduce you to someone, if you like. Ellen and I know several lovely ladies who'd be delighted to be escorted by you for the evening. This may sound awful, but I would bet that you haven't had too many dates with good Christian women lately."

"Not too many," I said.

"You just let me know," she said as the elevator doors opened. She stepped into the lobby with me.

"Betty, I will. And I'll look forward to Friday."

"Starts at four for activities. Frederick says the barbecue will be ready by seven, but it'll be nearer eight. Always is. Come hungry!"

"I will."

She shook my hand, then backed into the elevator and pressed a button. "And come with your eyes *and* your mind open, Baird. You keep that good mind of yours open and before you know it, why, none of us would be surprised to find *you* working for Roy Duncan."

CHAPTER 13

IT WAS NEARLY ONE BEFORE I finally got away from Spirit Center. I'd taken some time to walk around the campus, giving myself a little tour. I caught a hasty glimpse of Frederick Prescott himself leaving the office building and entering a limousine. I'd looked for Nancy Hargetay but did not find her. The radio in my car said it was ninety-eight degrees, no chance of rain. By the time I drove off New Spirit's grounds I wanted a beer. I stopped at the first convenience store I came to.

They didn't sell beer. "We don't deal in spirits," said a doughy girl at the checkout counter. Above her hung a well-stocked rack of cigarettes. I wanted to ask how a convenience store could turn a profit without trading in spirits, but I was afraid she would begin speaking of New Spirit, in whose spirit they most certainly did trade—I spied a spinner of Prescott Press paperbacks beside the comic book display. I left and drove to a shopping center near my motel. I bought a four-pack of bitter Guinness and a bag of pretzels.

My car was red with construction dust, so I drank the first bottle in a robot car wash whose jetspray pulsed in rhythm to my swallows. The soapy water washed the dirt from my car, but did little for my thoughts. I was having some dirty thoughts. I was wondering just how hard Mitch Tarr's dick was when he crouched in those bushes. I was wondering if he had kept his pants zipped that afternoon. I was wondering how often he had taken those pictures out over the years, and what he had done when he looked at them. I wanted an answer to those questions, and a few more, and headed downtown to get them. The second bottle had nearly lost its chill before I finished it, and the third was too warm to allow more than a couple of swallows. I put it and the unopened fourth in an alley near Mitch's shop, my gift to Samson's derelicts.

Mitch was alone in the shop, his back to the door, removing camera cases from the Peg-Board wall. There were half a dozen cases on the counter. Mitch turned when the bell above the door rang, and he did not seem surprised to see me.

"Baird Lowen," he said. "Just in time. Make the right offer and you'll save me the trouble of sending this stuff back."

I walked to the counter, but said nothing.

"A little inventory reduction," Mitch said. "What you do when distress sales don't work." He spun and pulled down another case and two ornate straps. "Come on. Name a price."

"We'll talk price in a minute," I said, sharply enough that it stopped him. "I was just talking about you, Mitch. With Mrs. Frederick Prescott."

His pupils narrowed but he kept them trained on me. He took two quick breaths before he spoke. "Good old Betty," he said. "I'm sure she had some interesting things to say."

"A lot of people have said interesting things about you lately, Mitch."

"I don't have time for this," Mitch said. He bent and opened a drawer, began pulling out small colored boxes and placing them on the counter. "I got to get all this stuff boxed and out of here tonight, man. Or I'm in a real sling." He looked at me from his crouch. "You know about slings."

The beer made a weight in my stomach. I was no longer in any mood to dance. I slapped my palms down on the counter and stared hard at him. "I know about slings, Mitch. I know about a lot of things."

"Do you?" Mitch grinned at me and winked, an ugly wink. "Then let's talk terms."

"All right. How much do you need?"

"No, no, no," he said, laughing softly. "What I *need* isn't anywhere near what I'll take for what *you* want. You and Roy. And Ellen. Don't kid yourself, Baird."

"Ten thousand dollars," I said. "A down payment. And you give up the negatives. Twenty more when we have them."

He laughed at me again. "I need more than that just for past-due bills. I'm in a *hole,* man, and I'm not looking to make it shallower. I'm looking to climb *out.*"

"Fifty thousand," I said.

Mitch took it as a bid, and he had no interest in bids. "That *your* price, Baird, or *theirs?* Either way, it's not enough. Not close." His face was open. "Tell you what. Take one more shot, give me one more figure. And make it a good number, Baird. I'll either take it or I won't. Fair enough?"

"Why not drop it altogether, Mitch? You want to talk about *fair?* There are innocent—"

"Who? Where? You, Roy, the Prescotts?"

"Ellen."

"Oh, she's so innocent. You saw to that, didn't you? I saw, too, and Roy of course. Ellen innocent on her knees." He smirked and turned his attention to his work.

I had no words. Anything I could say would sound defensive, and I had come to despise defensiveness. "What you're doing is—"

Mitch stood up. "I'm doing what I have to, Baird, as always."

"To stop Roy Duncan. You'd do anything—"

"I'd like to see him stopped," Mitch said.

"But you'd trade that for a fee."

"For the right paycheck."

"Why? You're the one who talked about *commitment.*"

"Know what it's like to *need* money, Baird? No. You wouldn't."

"How much money, Mitch?"

"A lot. But you can afford it, Baird. They can afford it. They've got money rolling in out there, man, you wouldn't believe the money Frederick P. generates. Millions a *week,* Baird, sometimes a million a *day.* Don't tell me Roy couldn't put his hands on—"

"How much? Get to it."

It was Mitch's turn to slap his palms on the countertop, crushing a tangle of camera straps flat. "All. Right. Two hundred and seventy-five thousand dollars. Tell Roy that."

"That's a sum," I said, more to myself than to Mitch.

"That's my *price,*" said Mitch. He stared at me for a moment, then stepped into the back room and returned with a large cardboard box. Looking at me, he swept the merchandise from the counter and into the box, then knelt and added the smaller boxes he'd piled beside the drawer. "I got to ship this out," he said. "And fuck 'em if they don't like the way it's packed."

"That's more than a quarter of a million dollars."

Mitch licked his lips, then spat on the floor. "I *know* what it is, Baird. I know how much it is. So do you; so will Roy. Now, get out of my store and don't come back unless you've got the money."

I stood my ground, but from my vantage point I could not forget how tall he was. "Tell me what we get for the money."

"What you want. What Roy wants."

"Too vague. Let's get it straight right now. You're a businessman. Call it an itemized receipt, a bill. What do we get?"

"Glad you're starting to see this that way, Baird. As *business.*"

"You said that yesterday, Mitch. Business—you, too. This is no *cause,* no crusade. The other, Roy's withdrawal, you might be able to justify that. But you take this money, you agree to this . . . transaction, and the business ends. You named the fig-

ure, you'd better deliver the goods. All of them." My words left
me almost winded. I wondered suddenly how Maurice Devlin
would evaluate my performance.

"Sounds like a threat," Mitch said casually.

"Just talking terms. Businessman to businessman. For—"

Mitch recited in a mocking singsong: "For the sum of two
hundred seventy-five thousand dollars, Mitchell Tarr, *the Third,*
agrees to cease and desist any and all activities that might contribute to the mental, physical or political discomfort of the Roy
Duncan family, including showing photos of Miss Perfect Wifey
being fucked by Baird Lowen." He raised his bushy eyebrows.
"How's that?"

"In perpetuity, Mitch."

"Oh, don't worry—you'll never hear a peep out of me again.
None of you will. I'll be gone, and I'll even throw that in: a guarantee of absence. Get me my money and I'm out of here." He
folded his thick arms over his chest.

"He's not going to leave the campaign, you know. You won't
get that."

Mitch nodded. "Don't know if I ever expected to. And I know
I don't give a shit anymore. I'm getting out of here. Gone. Got
places to . . . go. Let him be governor. Let him be president. Hell,
with Roy's gifts he could be *pope* if he was just Catholic."

"One more thing," I said, and hardly recognized my voice.

"That's not enough for you? What now? Some of my *soul?*
That what Roy wants, too?"

"No. What I have to say now has nothing to do with Roy."

"Ellen, then? Your old squeeze?" Mitch moved his hands to
his hips, raised his jaw just a little, opened himself to me. "Don't
talk to me about your sweet Ellen, Baird. *I* was the one who
saved her, or don't you remember that? Roy does: You press him
on it, or Ellen herself. *I* took her away from you."

"Did you, now?"

"Ask her."

"I will. But now I've got one for you. Why did you take those pictures, Mitch? Who else knows about them?"

"That's two questions."

"Answer them."

He did so without hesitation. "That depends on Roy. On who he's shown them to. I never showed them to anybody. The only ones who knew what went on out there were those of us who were there. And you two made such pretty pictures."

I took a moment to stare at him. "I'll get you your money," I said. "And I'll tell them you're leaving town. It's all over."

"I'd have left anyway, you know," Mitch said. "It's just that with the money I'll do it by daylight in a new car instead of at midnight after torching this place." He made a gesture.

I thought of something Betty Prescott had said and it kept me there for a moment. I wanted nothing left unsaid, no doors left open. "And how are you going to explain this to your . . . followers?"

His laugh was a snort. "What *followers?*"

I told him what Betty had said.

"Right, Baird, see? See how crazy they are? I don't have any *followers.* I tried to explain that to you yesterday. Not followers. Not *leaders;* don't trust anyone who tries to *lead.* Find your *own* way, that's what God wants."

"What was she talking about?"

He shrugged broadly. "Beats me. A few of us get together. Paint some signs, coin some slogans. Spread the word in our own way. Old news, Baird—nothing formal about it, and they won't miss me."

"Who will?"

"Nobody. I'm cutting all ties with Samson. Should have done it a long time ago."

"Yes," I said. "You should have. I'll be in touch." I turned toward the door.

"Baird?" Mitch said. "This shit has to go out *tonight.* The"—

he tried a smile—"the distributor's a pretty good guy; he's hung on a while. How about letting me have fifty to make the shipping charge?"

I gave him the money and left his store.

The heavy beer had me still feeling bloated and I moved slowly through the heat to my car. The bottles of Guinness were still in the alleyway, undiscovered. I started my car and turned the air-conditioning to high. It was three o'clock. I drove aimlessly for a while, passed Shelby's home when I finally set a direction, but her car was gone. I drove to Spirit City and pulled into Roy's drive shortly before four. Ellen answered the door.

"Are you alone?" I said.

She nodded. I felt the heat of her stare: She could give Mitch a lesson in hard looks.

"Let's call Roy," I said. I followed her to the living room. She was wearing a soft summer skirt and a long-sleeved blouse. Her hair was as perfect as her makeup. The house was still too cool. I stood beside Ellen while she dialed Roy's number, waited until he was on the line and then took the telephone from her. "It's Baird," I said.

"I told you to stay away from my house."

"It's done, Roy. Get over here."

"You talked to Mitch again."

"We did business," I said. I made the word as ugly as I could, keeping my eyes on Ellen as I said it. Her posture and gaze told me outright just how far above me she was. You could read the rectitude on her features, even through the makeup. On the wall beyond her shoulder I could see a needlepoint sampler in pink and blue cursive: *Our Home Is God's Home.* "Be here in half an hour."

"I've got a meet—"

"Cancel it. I want to be through with you *now.*" I hung up on him, took a deep breath, faced Ellen. She gestured at the sofa and took her own place in a chair facing it.

"You talked to Mitchell again?"

"I did. We struck a bargain. Give him what he wants and you won't have to worry about him again."

"And you think he can be trusted?" I had never seen anyone sit so straight. I thought of how she used to sprawl, coltish, my girl, legs hooked over mine as we watched TV or talked beneath the stars. "I asked you a question, Baird."

"As I said. Pay him what he wants and he'll leave you alone. *Business.*"

"How much does he want?"

"Let it wait 'til Roy's here." If she was going to style herself the perfect traditional wife, then I would talk my business with the man of the house. "When do the kids get home?"

"After seven. There's a cookout at the camp."

"Minibarbecue?" I said. I thought of Betty's invitation—by Friday night I would be on my farm, fishing. I'd have to taste the reverend's barbecue another time.

"You really have contempt for us and what we believe, don't you, Baird?" She shared a smile from somewhere in the Antarctic. "Or is that a pose, too?"

"You think this is a pose? My being here?"

"I don't understand the contempt."

"I don't have contempt for you, Ellen," I said. And then I spoke softly to whatever was left of my Ellen, somewhere beneath the lacquer and piety: "How could I have contempt for you?"

She pressed her hands together as though to pray, but did not close her eyes nor take them from me.

I had a question. "Do you know why I came back to Samson?"

"You mean you didn't come to help dear old friends out of a mess you helped create?" Sarcasm did not become her.

"No," I said. "I didn't."

"No," she said. "You probably wouldn't."

"So why am I here?"

"Roy told me you . . . he found out something."

"And what was that?"

"He told me you killed someone." I thought I saw her shoulders tremble a little but couldn't be sure.

"That's right," I said, and this time there was no mistaking the small shudder. "How did he find out?"

"I don't know. He wouldn't say."

I could not resist: "Roy keeping secrets from *you?* Just like you do from him."

Ellen would not rise to my baiting.

"Who else has he told?" I said.

"No one. Roy wouldn't—"

"Roy Duncan would do whatever he thinks he has to, Ellen. Expediency—no, *efficiency,* that's his credo, isn't it?"

"Roy would never hurt anyone."

"Roy Duncan, your *husband,* is blackmailing *me,*" I said with some force. "Come on, Ellen, at least be honest with yourself about that. He's *blackmailing* me. He's no different from Mitch."

I thought for a moment she was going to stand. "Don't you dare talk to me about honesty. Not *you.* And Mitchell Tarr isn't fit to walk the same sidewalk as Roy. Any more than you are."

"I'm surprised you feel that way, Ellen. About Mitch. After all, he told me he's the one who saved your soul."

"He said that?" Her cheeks were blazing, and I thought she might curse if she knew how. "Mitchell should know that it was Jesus Christ who saved my soul, who saved *me.* There was a time when he would have known it."

"Back then," I said. "When we were kids. After what we had."

"What we had? What we had was a mistake, Baird, and one that I have to live with."

"A mistake? Is that how you remember it?" I remembered other things: her hands, her lips, her breasts—her soft cries and requests, some words said shyly at first and then more exuberantly, a welcoming inward and a firm clench of newly discovered muscles. Should I slap her now with those memories? I wondered, but before I could decide I heard a car arrive, its door slam. I waited for Roy's entrance.

He came in through the kitchen and his first look was at Ellen. "Are you all right?" he said to her.

I had a flash of pleasure at the exasperation that darted across her features. "Oh, Roy, of course I'm all right."

Roy faced me. "Okay, Baird. Talk. You saw Mitch again."

"We spent some time together," I said. "This afternoon. I spent the morning with Betty Prescott. But you'd already know that."

He nodded. "Not very smart, old chip."

"Don't tell me what's smart, Roy. I'm not your old chip or your little man or your friend. Don't tell me anything. Let me tell you." I gave him the details of the deal I'd struck with Mitchell Tarr. Ellen looked quickly at Roy when I named Mitch's price, but her husband kept his gaze on me, unwavering, unblinking. When I finished, I asked if he would pay.

"Two hundred seventy-five thousand dollars. How soon?"

"Open date," I said. "Are you going to pay?"

"It's steep," he said.

"For the governorship, Roy? And what beyond that? Senator? President, maybe? You think so, anyway; I know you do. So it's a bargain for all that, don't you think? For your name, Roy?"

Ellen did not give him a chance to respond: The ball I had lobbed was all hers and she let me know it. "It's not just Roy's name, Baird, and you know that. It's *mine.* My fault for being weak, yours for taking advantage of me. Only because he's married to *me* does he even have to *think* about any of this. And the reason it's *my* problem is because of *you.* This is your debt, not Roy's. You pay the price."

Before I could say a word of reply Roy had moved close to Ellen and dropped to one knee before her. I could not have named anyone else who could have pulled off such a gesture, but it worked for Roy Duncan. He took her hands in his and kissed her knuckles, suitor and supplicant all in one. "Ellen, any problem you have is mine as well and always will be. This is not your fault, and I won't hear that again. I *love* you, sweetheart. More than ever." He bowed until his forehead rested against her hands. Ellen gazed down at him, and in her look I got a surprise, for I saw the source of some of the steel in his spine. Roy was the one on his knees, not his bride. I waited.

Roy rose at last, and after giving Ellen's hands a final squeeze he turned to face me. He took the time to straighten his suit. "I do think you should contribute something to this, Baird. Don't you agree?"

"No."

"You have the money, don't you?"

"It's not the money. Or can't you write a check this big?"

His smile was the smile of a patrician. Anyone could tell how wealthy he was, and, besides, he had friends who were wealthier. He said nothing.

Ellen came to her feet in a single movement, skirt swirling around her knees. "This was *his* doing," she said, jerking a hand in my direction. "You see that he pays."

Roy put a gentle arm around her shoulders and drew her close. Norman Rockwell could have painted them. He brushed his fingers up and down the back of her blouse and rubbed a cheek against her hair. Holding his wife, he said, "Baird will pay."

"No," I said again.

Roy shrugged and pointed a finger at me, but once more it was Ellen who spoke. "You pay this debt, Baird. You pay this debt you owe me."

"Ellen," I said. "I won't. I may owe you for some things, and then again I may not. But I don't owe you this. No." I took her measure and showed that I could stand up to her gaze. "Besides, it's not all that much. An hour or two of Prescott TV time. I'm sure they'll be happy to divert some funds."

"Baird." Roy moved in front of Ellen as though to protect her. "That's enough. I won't have you speak that way here. It's bad enough having you here at all."

"My being here is your doing, Roy, and I'd suggest you remember that." I stepped up to him. "I came here and did your work. And now we're going to talk about the debt you owe me." I was ready for him, no matter how close he stood he could not move too fast for me.

But he chose only to speak. "I don't owe you a thing, *Bear.*" He smiled. "But I'll make another bargain."

"Tell me."

"Just this. You take care of the . . . obligation to Mitch and I'll turn over the material you're so interested in."

"No deal."

"Exactly what I expected. And that's fine. There's no deal between us. At all."

"Meaning what?"

"I think you know what I mean. I think you're wondering right now just how much I have and who I might show it to. Well, old chip, I have it *all.* Believe that."

"All of what, Roy? Time for some detail to back your play. What have you got and who did you get it from?"

Roy shook his head, a smile pulling his chubby cheeks tight. "Not any of that, Baird. No way. We just might need to do business again some day."

"Roy," I said, pausing to make my words count. "Don't ever call me again. There's no business between us. You call again, you come to *my* house, you say one *word* about anything—"

"And what, old chip?"

I looked at Ellen as I spoke. "And I'll publish *my* set of pictures from the lake . . ."

He made his move without watching me and I evaded him easily, grabbing him hard by the right arm. I heard his sleeve tear, pivoted him around, dug in and buried my fist in his belly. There was more muscle beneath the fat than I'd expected, but I punched deep. Roy went down fast, and I would have put my knee into his chin, but Ellen was all over me, screaming at me, and I turned away to hold her off. I took a backward step, and she gave up on me, knelt beside Roy and held him. "You go to *hell,* Baird Lowen. You get *out* of my house." She was breathing hard and veins pulsed against the skin at her temples.

I looked down at Roy. He was catching his breath, and I was tempted to wait for him to rise so that I could hit him again. I glanced first at Ellen, and took another moment of her hatred, and then spoke quickly. "Keep quiet, Roy, and no problems. *One* word and I print the pictures. Take me down and I take you down with me. And write a piece to go with them that will be some kind of record memoir. Don't think I won't. After all, *I* don't have a reputation to protect." I turned my back on them and moved quickly to the door, stopping only for one last look.

I had no trouble meeting Ellen's stare. I held it until her face became a mask of disgust and she turned away. "Good-bye," I said, "Governor Duncan." I nodded. "Mrs. Duncan."

"Burn in hell," said Ellen as I left her home.

CHAPTER 14

I LOOKED AT MY WATCH as I rang the bell at Shelby's home. Her car was in the drive and it was not yet six, but I supposed her date could have already picked her up. I wasn't sure whether I wanted her to be home or not. I felt tired, but not tense. My mood was sour and getting worse. I had shaken a bit as I left Roy's house, but I knew what that was. My fist had gone into him the way the knife had gone into Billy, that was all. I managed to calm myself without taking a session on my knees in one of Prescott's gazebos. They didn't even tempt me. I was in a mood to do some drinking, but I had a call to pay first. I took a long, quick swing on the loop around town, then doubled back and exited, and slowed to twenty-five as I passed through the old neighborhood. I did not expect to pass this way again, but there was nothing for me to see. I looked at my family's old home, but there was no one in the yard. Finally I drove to Shelby's.

She opened the door looking lovely, made up to go out, wearing a well-cut, short, dark dress. "Baird," she said, some surprise in her tone. "You didn't call—"

Was she afraid her date would arrive and see me? I didn't ask. It didn't matter. "I just stopped to say so long. I'm heading home tomorrow."

Her surprise turned to annoyance. "Like that? So long, Shelby? Don't forget to say thanks for the fuck." I thought she was going to slam the door in my face, but she caught herself and waited.

"I shouldn't have come," I said.

"Today? Or at all."

"Either way, Shelby."

"But then we wouldn't have had our night, would we?"

"No."

"And it was some night, Baird. You can't have forgotten that so quickly."

"I haven't," I said. "I won't."

"Well, I won't, either, and you keep that in mind, hiding out down on your farm. Where it's *safe.*"

"I'd better go."

She shook her head fiercely, but at the same time I saw some of her anger retreat. "Not that easy. At least tell me what happened. I assume you and Roy finished what's between you."

"I'd say we . . . tabled it. For now at least. Maybe for longer."

"Oh . . . *hell.* Come on inside and have a drink anyway. I want to hear, and we may as well try to pretend to end this like we're civilized." She opened the door wide, but stepped through it before me.

We walked to the living room and Shelby poured, at my request, an ounce or two of Wild Turkey over a single ice cube. It would not, I felt, be my last drink of the day. Shelby had white wine.

When we sat down she said, "You're really going home."

It was not a question but I felt obliged to answer it. "I'm all through here."

"And . . . us."

I studied her. "Maybe another time," I said.

"There isn't another time, Baird. This happened now, is happening now. So what are you going to do, walk away from it, from *me,* like you have from everything else?"

I took the bourbon in two harsh swallows. "Probably."

Ellen thought she had shown me contempt, but I saw it for real from Shelby just then. "The oh so cynical Baird Lowen. So tough and impregnable."

"Think so?" I said.

She swirled her wine a bit. "No. I guess not." There was no forgiveness in her tone, and I do not know if I was looking for any. "But sometime you've got to stop running."

"And do what?"

"Why not try seeing what happens. And with whom."

"Meaning you?" I stepped to the bar and filled my glass again, fuller than before.

"Maybe. Why not?"

"No reason. Or lots of reasons. You know most of them." I raised my glass to her and noticed that my hand was less than steady.

She ignored the toast. "I do. And I also know that for all of it we were pretty good together. Not just in bed."

"For a day or two, anyway. But you think we could be better. That it could go somewhere."

"I think it might be worth seeing. I do think that, Baird." I could see what the words cost her, and that surprised me. "I'd like to know where it could go."

I let the air out of my lungs slowly, a long sigh. "I'd like to know, too, but I don't know if I can. Or should. If it's . . . *not* done, then you'd be in it, too."

"I already am, Baird. Don't make decisions on my behalf."

"I wouldn't dream of it."

"Then don't go. Stay in Samson for a while. My dance card's empty after tonight. We could see, don't you think? Just see?"

I shook my head. "Can't say, Shell." Did I slur my words?

"What happened today? Why are you leaving? And don't say there's nothing to keep you here."

"All right. I saw Mitch. I saw Betty Prescott. I just came from Roy and Ellen. It's over."

"How?"

I swallowed half the drink. "Money deal, I can say that. Pay Mitch off. Nobody gets hurt."

She bit her lip. "Nobody?"

"I didn't mean to hurt you."

"But you are."

"Then it's time for me to stop it. So I'll finish this and be gone."

"Poof! Like bad magic."

"Poof," I said. "Bad magician."

"You like that, don't you? Thinking of yourself as something bad, a bad boy outlaw on the lam and laying low. Well, it's bullshit, Baird, and it's time you got pulled into the *real* world. Since you won't pull yourself."

"Won't, or can't?"

"Please! Spare me. That's your decision, Baird, nobody else's."

"Sure, Shelby," I said, and the sound of the words made me laugh. "Sure, Shell, ever sell seashells?" I took the last of the drink, left my glass on the bar, walked over to Shelby. "You look great, and take care," I said. "I hope he's a nice guy."

Shelby stood up. "He is, Baird. Nice and completely uncomplicated. But—nothing special." She put a surprisingly soft finger to my cheek.

"I'm so special," I said, and tried to turn to leave, but she caught me.

"You're special," she said. "And if nothing else, forget the rest of it, you've got no business driving. Please stay, Baird. Have some coffee." She snapped her fingers at an insight. "Or even go to dinner with us." She showed that grin that I'd almost forgotten. "If you promise to behave yourself. Bill won't mind; he's just an old friend—"

"Like me?" I said, and took a step away without seeing if my words had stung her.

"You bastard. Don't leave like this, Baird."

I looked back at her. "You go have fun tonight, Shelby. He's a lucky guy. You look great. I said that already, didn't I? But you do. Listen, you're ever down my way, stop by the farm. I'd like to see you." I turned and stumbled, spoiling my exit.

"Baird, this is stupid—" Any anger in her voice had been replaced by concern. "You've got no business driving."

I made my own voice even and held out a hand. "See? No shakes. I'm fine."

"At least stay in town tonight. Have you checked out?"

"No."

"Then your room's paid for. You might as well use it. Promise me that."

I wanted to be away from her, and it was growing less easy to leave, so I gave in. "Sure. I promise. I'll go home in the morning." I offered a handshake, but she would not let my hand go. I forced my smile and found that it became genuine. "I'll probably have that hangover we missed the other day. I'll have it for both of us."

"Let me call you a cab. Or we'll drop you off."

I shook my head. "I've got to go."

Shelby moved close to me; she raised up on her toes and offered a quick kiss. "You take care," she said. She held my shoulders hard and looked at me. "I'm mad as hell, and I'll probably hate you for a while, but you take care of yourself."

"You, too" was all I could say.

As I drove from her house another car approached and entered her driveway. I slowed to see if I could catch a glimpse of her date, but the angle of my mirror was wrong. I turned a corner and drove on. I didn't have to see him. I knew things about him already. It seemed a cinch to me that no one had pictures of him having high school sex, that he'd never killed anyone in the Arizona desert, that no one had ever blackmailed him, and that made him more gentleman than me. I wanted more bourbon. I stopped at a package store near the motel and bought two pints of Wild Turkey. They fit in the pockets of my jacket. The prospect of drinking alone in my motel room struck me as being nearly as foolish as trying to reach my farm, so I put fifty cents into a newspaper machine and turned the pages until I found the theater listings. I hadn't done this in a long time.

There was a multiplex a few blocks from the motel. I reached the theater in time to catch most of a seven o'clock feature, and took a moment beforehand in the parking lot to arrive at a schedule. I juggled times as I tried to hold the print in focus. When I had my plan, I walked to the ticket office, paid to see a thriller, got popcorn and a large Coke. I took it easy through the movie, the Coke, the popcorn, three long pulls on the bourbon. The movie was not very good. The nine o'clock show was a horror film, and I moved through the rest of the first pint and another Coke as I watched unknown actors move through the same gruesome paces I'd put other unknowns through in my own slasher flick. The director did as well with the material as I had, and I wondered how far she would take her career.

There is a calculus to crap cinema, and its equation can take you to any number of solutions. Mine, as with the director this evening, was to accept from the outset that the script was the script, and would not get any better than it was. So you work your camera crew, and do what you can with the sets, and above all get to know your actors. If you find a glimmer there, or even the hint of a glimmer, you take it for all you can, styling your shots for the best performances, seeking to come as close to a star turn as you can catch from your talent, building as much suspense as gore so the audience cares or almost cares when the actor gets gutted. It is a rare actor who can find something to hold onto while waiting for masked lurkers to impale her, and a director who can make something of that is an even rarer species. I had been of that species and so was the director this night. As the credits rolled I sent her some silent good wishes from another member of the director's alumni, emeritus.

When the last of the credits were gone I returned to the ticket booth for the late show, stood in line a moment and laughed when the girl said, "Again?" I had ten minutes before the curtain and passed the time playing a video game in the lobby. I was aware of the manager's eyes on me. I did nothing untoward; the Wild Turkey bottles, one empty, were well concealed, and I put some more money into the theater's till, buying a large bucket of corn with extra ersatz butter.

I took my seat shortly before eleven, in time for Coming Attractions, and was not surprised to see that three of the five previews dropped the director's name. It's the hot profession these Tarantino days. The main feature started with full THX sound blare, one of the summer's big hits: a hundred-million-dollar special-effects saga that had promised in the heaviest prime-time ad campaign of recent years to take the viewer all the way through the screen.

Eleven o'clock had brought out a bigger crowd than I expected, and they were primed for the movie, or would be soon. The overture had hardly faded before the marijuana came out and scented the air. I felt foolish for worrying about the bourbon bottles in my pocket. I wished I had some dope, but settled for the Turkey. I worked my way through the remaining pint, and let it work its way through me. At one point I held the bottle high in an effort to interrupt the projector's beam, but my arm wasn't long enough. The bottle would not fit in the cup holder built into the chair, and I thought that inconsiderate of the theater's management.

Once the forces of the dark galaxy were defeated and our heroes lionized, I left the empty bottles in the seat next to mine, walked carefully to my car, drove very slowly without too many swerves to the motel, fell down in my room and managed on all fours to make the commode before I was sick. When I staggered from the bathroom I flicked on the television and fell onto the bed. The room spun, but I did not sleep. I spun along with the room through an old Doris Day movie, spun on toward dawn with Burt Reynolds and Catherine Deneuve under Robert Aldrich's sure direction, was still spinning when I learned from the late late or early early news that Samson camera store owner Mitchell Tarr had burned to death while apparently trying to set fire to his place of business.

PART
THREE

CHAPTER 15

SHELBY'S CALL AWOKE ME AT seven-thirty. I had not been asleep long. "Baird?" she said when I answered the phone.

"I got that hangover," I said.

"What the *hell* is going on?" Her voice was a hiss.

"You alone?" I said. "I'll come over."

"No," she said quickly. "Come at nine." I almost asked if that would give Bill time to shower and be on his way, but Shelby did not give me the chance. There was a click, nothing more.

I got out of bed, pulled on the shirt and slacks I'd worn the night before, slipped bare feet into my shoes. I passed on a look into the mirror, made sure I had my key, walked to the restaurant and bought three large black coffees. When I returned to my room I lined the Styrofoam cups on the dresser and removed the lid from the one nearest the bathroom. I stripped, took coffee and Dopp kit and set to work.

It was eight-forty-five before I left my room again and I looked at least presentable. It was already hot. My stomach felt barely more settled than when I awoke: The coffee had not helped. I stopped my car outside the motel office and left the engine and air conditioner running as I changed dollars into quarters and fed them into newspaper machines. I bought two copies of the *Samson Defender,* careful to insure that the desk clerk saw me feed four quarters before opening the vending machine door. Sometime before I dropped off to sleep it had occurred to me that there might be official questions in my future. I wanted to leave a good impression.

I did not look at the newspapers or turn on the car radio as I drove to Shelby's house. Crossing one high bridge I cast a look downtown, toward Mitch's shop, but nothing looked different. There was no smoke in the sky.

Shelby met me at the door. My hands were filled with newspapers, and she did not offer a hug. We walked to the kitchen without speaking. I put the papers in the center of the circular dinette. I read something in Shelby's look. "Not me," I said, and held up my hands. "But I know who it was."

"I can believe you?" she said, and cocked a glance. Her back was against the refrigerator. She said my name and it came out as a dare.

I had no fight in me. "You can hear me out."

"Again? Someone's *dead.*"

"And I know who killed him, or had him killed, and I *know* I hold some of the responsibility myself. So don't tell me. Shelby, I know it all. I've been up with it since I heard. What can you say that I haven't been through?" I wanted to sit down but could not bring myself to ask. *"You* invited me here. Do you want me to go?"

She shook her head. "Sit down. Do you want some coffee?"

"Water," I said. "Lots of ice." I was not sure how much longer I'd be able to keep down the bad restaurant coffee.

She fixed a tall glass. "Bad head?"

I touched my temples. "All-time worst. Probably well deserved."

Shelby poured a mug of coffee and sat opposite me. "Where *did* you go last night?"

I took a sip of water. "Drinking."

"After all you had here! I shouldn't have let you go."

"Shelby, I guarantee you I wish I had stayed." I gave her an outline of my evening. I had turned down the television after the news, found an all-hours radio news station, listened carefully for any crumb of information. There were not many, and only a few more on the morning's local television programs. "When did you hear?" I said.

"Newspaper this morning. I called you as soon as I saw." She reached out for one of the *Defenders*. She was wearing a knee-length housecoat, open at the neck. In high school I might have looked at her neck for hickeys and beard abrasions. I didn't look now. Her business. When Shelby handed me the paper I lost myself in it.

It had been a slow news night: The story made Page One, although below the fold. STOREKEEPER DIES IN POSSIBLE ARSON read the headline. A photo showed the front of Mitch's shop, windows broken out, smoke pouring toward the camera. The story added few details to the reports I'd heard at the motel. The fire was discovered around ten, already burning fiercely. It was under control by eleven, the store a total loss. Mitch's body, badly burned, had been discovered and removed from the scene by midnight, with suspicion of arson officially expressed by the Samson Police Department well before two. Radio and television had alluded to Mitch's "radical" leanings; the *Defender* went farther. Although there was no photograph of Mitch, the word-portrait gave a pretty good picture.

Mitch had evidently been a familiar figure around Samson, a minicelebrity known for his appearances at city council and school board meetings and as a placard painter and sidewalk philosopher. He had never run for office, but had attempted one year to introduce onto the city ballot a resolution calling for a ban on research into space-based weapons. For a few years he had operated a counseling service for Samson's homeless. Mitch Tarr was Samson's street conscience in some ways, or so he saw himself. He had never married. The *Defender* said that Mitch's business had been struggling for years; he'd attempted to block the renovation of his neighborhood, arguing that the higher tax base would ruin the few small businesses still there. Funeral arrangements were pending the completion of the investigation and the location of a relative.

"Mitch told me he didn't have anyone in Samson," I said.

Shelby nodded. "His mother's dead, father's in a rest home. Alzheimer's."

"You know a lot about him."

"I saw him sometimes. With some frequency, actually, during my hearings. Like the paper said, he went to a lot of city meetings."

"On your side?"

"*He* thought so." She pulled her lips into her mouth and released them with a little *pop.* "He spoke his mind, I'll give him that. But—"

"Off the wall."

"More than a little. You saw him. I don't know what I'd call Mitch. Not *radical.* He told me once he thought of calling himself a 'libertarian revolutionary anarchist,' but you know Mitch. Knew Mitch. How he was when you talked about politics."

"Lots of polysyllables."

"You should have heard him speak in my defense. What he thought was my defense, anyway. I felt like a flake by association. That sounds awful." She twisted her coffee cup, grating it against the table.

"Forget it. I talked to him, too, remember? I know what you mean. But Shelby," I said, and waited until she looked at me before I continued, "even with the blackmail Mitch did not deserve this. I know as sure as I'm sitting here that Roy Duncan had Mitch killed. And I'm just as sure that I'll find a way to prove that."

"Mitch sent the pictures?"

I nodded. "What I tried to tell you last night. Didn't do such a good job, I guess. He named a price. I told Roy; Roy told me he'd take care of it. And he did. While I got drunk."

She studied me seriously for a moment. "Take me through it again, Baird. The whole thing, slowly." She touched my hand.

I took a large swallow of water. For the second time in a few days I found myself telling Shelby Oakes the story of my relationship with Roy Duncan. When I finished, she asked if Ellen had really attacked me.

"Tooth and nail," I said.

"Did you think Roy would pay him? Or make you?"

"I wasn't going to pay him, Shelby, and I had my own set of pictures. If Roy showed his of me, I'd show mine of Ellen."

"Of Ellen and you."

"Sure, but if I had to show them I wouldn't have anything to lose and Roy knew that."

"And you'd trust him?"

"I'd trust his sense of . . . efficiency. It's a lot of money, but the prizes he's after are worth a lot of money. I did trust *Mitch*. If he'd gotten his cash it'd have been over."

"You're so sure."

"I—liked him, in a way. He was a flake, but he was *our* flake, you know?"

"He was a blackmailer."

"Wouldn't *you* like to stop Roy Duncan? If you could?"

"Not that way."

"Maybe not. But you're no libertarian revolutionary anarchist."

"I'm not even a registered Democrat," Shelby said. "But none of this tells me why you're so sure Mitch would have settled for the money."

"He *needed* it, Shelby; he was losing everything. And I think he just wanted to go somewhere and start over. Hell, he joked about torching his shop." I finished my water.

"Did you tell Roy that?" Shelby said, and I could only nod. We were silent for a moment. "What now, Baird?"

I had no easy answer, so I gave the difficult one. "I am going to bring Mr. Roy Duncan down myself, and not just to save my own ass." I allowed a grin. "Although that figures in."

"So you're not going back to your farm?"

"Not yet. Not until this is done. I've got this all over *my* hands, now, and I want them washed clean. As clean as I can get them, anyway."

"And you want to see Roy nailed."

"I want to nail him. I'm going to."

"For the satisfaction of it," Shelby said with some sharpness.

"For Mitch, maybe." I ran my hands across my face, pressed fingertips against my eyes. There were no tears there; I felt dry. I looked at Shelby. "I got him killed."

"Well, you'd better start thinking about how you're going to keep from getting yourself killed."

"Me?"

"You think Roy won't? If it *was* Roy."

"It was Roy," I said. "And I don't think he'll do a thing to me right now. He has me where he wants me. Or thinks he has. He can sit still. The police worry me a little. If they should look—"

"*What* would they find, Baird? If they look?"

"I saw Mitch Tarr twice within twenty-four hours. At least one other person saw me with him." I thought of the woman in the summer dress. Would she have filed her film receipt for a New Spirit voucher? It would have caused Roy no effort to send an observer to Mitch's store. He'd sent me there.

"If he sent an *observer,* Baird," Shelby said, "he's probably got *pictures.*" She used a voice I would not often wish to hear.

"It gets better," I said.

"Can't wait," said Shelby, and she went to refill her coffee mug.

"Observers, pictures, whatever," I said. "Roy's not going to have any trouble finding whatever he needs to link me with Mitch. And he's in tight with the police."

"Roy?" Shelby said, and came close to gasping. "Our local

hero? The Drug Detective? They'll listen to any story he has to tell."

"It gets better," I said again, and Shelby's eyebrows went up a bit. "I dropped Mitch's name, *seriously* out of context, Shelby, in a conversation with Betty Prescott."

"I'm going to decide, in a little while, whether I want you to stay any longer," Shelby said calmly.

"Can't say that I blame you."

"What in God's name made you mention—what the hell were you doing talking with Betty Prescott?"

I told her of the interview, of the trap I'd failed to spring.

Shelby wriggled her fingers like a puppet master and her look mocked me. But then it softened and I thought for a moment she would touch me. "Does she know anything?"

"Does she know *everything?*" I said. "That's the only question I've got. And I intend to answer it."

"*And* nail Roy to a tree."

"That, too."

Shelby shook her head. "You've got a pretty full plate, my friend."

"I hope I am your friend," I said.

"Does it matter?" she said in that tone again. "Friend, enemy, lover—things have a way of happening to people around you."

I stood up. "You're right, so I'm going to go."

"Don't."

"You're asking me to stay?"

"Compromised again," Shelby said. "Tell me enough to get me involved, make me—what?—an accessory, then take off?"

"I had to tell you," I said. "I—" My stomach gave a toss and I turned and ran for the bathroom and groaned through long minutes of emptying myself. When I opened the door Shelby handed me a toothbrush.

"The spare from upstairs," she said. "It's okay—you've used

it before." She read my look and flared at me. "And no, no one else has used it, and *no,* if it's any of your business, Bill didn't stay here last night, and no, we *didn't* go to bed, and when he kissed me goodnight, it was on the cheek. All right?"

"Of course it's all right, Shelby," I said. "Maybe more than that." I took the toothbrush and closed the door again. There was a smear of toothpaste on the bristles. I ran cold water on it. I stared at myself in the mirror for a moment, then brushed until my gums ached. When I emerged from the bathroom Shelby was waiting. She guided me to the soft sofa in her living room and pushed me down gently onto its cushions. "You stay here a while," she said, and sat for a moment beside me. "You stretch out here."

"You don't mind being compromised?"

"Well, maybe I don't," she said, and rested a hand on my shoulder. "Not really. Besides, it's a little late for me to start worrying about that." She rose and gestured for me to recline. I kicked off my shoes and shed my jacket: Shelby would not have to repeat this invitation. "I think I'm safe enough," she said. "I may not even be mad anymore. *May* not."

"I just don't want you to get involved if the police look for me."

"Don't worry too much about them," Shelby said. "If Roy—if there's any New Spirit connection to this you'll never hear it from the police." She showed a brief bitter smile. "The reverend is one of Samson's biggest Benevolent Fund supporters. He'll buy out a whole police barbecue and give the plates to the poor."

I put my hands on my stomach. "Don't mention barbecue."

Shelby went to the kitchen and brought back a glass of ginger ale. "Drink it slowly," she said.

"Thanks, Nurse."

"Just trying to be a good host."

"You are that," I said. My stomach settled slowly and I thought of Betty Prescott's invitation. "Let me be a good guest. Doing anything tomorrow night?"

"No."

"Then let's—" I swallowed a belch. "Why don't you come to the Prescotts' barbecue with me?"

She stared at me as though she'd never seen me before. "Tell me you're kidding, Baird."

"*I'm* going." My mind was made up. I would meet Roy on Prescott's territory and see what sort of message that sent. "Wouldn't miss it. Not now."

"Baird, you can't be serious."

"Deadly. Roy's going to be there."

"Everybody *in* New Spirit will be there!"

"The more the merrier. Think they'll be surprised?"

"They'll lynch you."

"The good people of New Spirit? No way. They'll welcome me into the fold. Besides, bad as New Spirit is, I doubt if too many of them are murderers . . . other than Roy. And whoever he had strike the match."

"They'll crumple you up and throw you away," Shelby said.

I tucked my hands behind my head and smiled up at her. "Not me. Not them. Don't you know? They *persuade,* they don't punch."

"Tell Mitch that."

"Mitch is dead. I'll tell Roy."

"I'm not going to be able to talk you out of this, am I?"

"Not a chance."

We studied each other carefully. "I'll let you know," she said at last.

"Fair enough," I said, and winked. "Just don't wait too long—Betty said she could get me a date."

Shelby's eyes widened. "Wouldn't I love to see that."

"Just say the word."

She smiled. "You just get some rest. We'll talk some more this afternoon."

"About what?"

"About how we're going to handle this thing."

"*We,*" I said. "Okay."

"In for an inch," said Shelby Oakes, and favored me with the best smile yet. "Now rest."

She switched off the lamp and drew the curtains midway across the sliding door that opened onto the patio and pool. I started to speak, but Shelby had heard enough. She held a finger to her lips, then left the room.

I lay on the sofa and stared at the ceiling. I heard Shelby rustling in the kitchen for a moment, then she went upstairs. After a moment a shower began to run. I wondered if she would go with me to the barbecue, and wondered if I had been wise to ask her. She'd been joking about being an accessory, but her other words about the police had been less than completely convincing. If they wanted me they would find me at the home of Shelby Oakes. I could see the headlines, but only for a moment. Then I put those thoughts, and other thoughts, from my head. It was not long before I slept.

Shelby woke me at two by opening the curtains and letting the brilliant sunshine in. I lay still for a moment before sitting up. My mouth tasted bitter, so before I spoke I went to the bathroom and brushed my teeth again. When I returned, Shelby was sitting on the sofa. "We'll eat in a minute," she said as I sat down. "Something light, then maybe some time in the sun. I've got to get you in shape for the barbecue."

"You're going?"

She held up a hand. "Don't be too eager, Baird. I haven't made up my mind yet. But you're going, and you'd better be at your best. Now, I've got something to show you." She stepped to the entertainment center and knelt to punch a cassette into the VCR. "I taped the noon news upstairs," she said as she stepped back and used a remote to click the TV to life. "Watch."

Shelby fast-forwarded in fits and starts, and I got a sense of what was going on in Samson. The story had evidently cooled somewhat, for it was not mentioned until after the first commercial, and then only in the wake of a piece on inadequate health-care facilities for the elderly. The story on Mitch was brief, the same quick clip of film of the burning store I'd seen this morning, along with a few words of explanation from the midday anchorperson. Her hair was as perfect as Betty Prescott's, although less elaborate, and her eyes were absolutely without life as she reported that the Samson Police and Fire Departments had closed their investigations with identical findings: Death by misadventure while in the process of committing arson. The shop, according to the anchorperson, was a total loss; the building itself would probably be torn down. In a moment, she promised, there would be a weather report. Shelby clicked off the set and VCR.

"I hope, at least, that Mitch was dead when they torched the place," I said. "At least that much."

"Don't," Shelby said. "Let's eat first. You need something in your stomach." We went into the kitchen for a quick sandwich. When the table was cleared, she went to the window and looked outside. "Too hot for a swim right now. It must be ninety-five out there."

"Too hot for a drive?"

"Where to?" she said, and turned to face me.

"Downtown. And maybe a walk."

"You sure that's smart?"

"Criminal always visits the scene of the crime, doesn't he?"

"What is it you think you'll see?"

"I just want to see, Shelby, that's all. I just want a look."

"And if the police are there? They won't let you close."

I raised a finger of inspiration skyward. I'd seen a Macintosh upstairs, with a laser printer next to it. "Mind if I use your computer?" We went upstairs.

Shelby laughed and rolled her eyes as I set to work. Ten minutes later I'd prepared a business card identifying me as an adjustor for *Phoenix Fire & Casualty*. I added some clip art and a filigree: I listed my office address as Evangelical Way, in the heart of Spirit City.

"You're shameless," Shelby said.

I printed the card. We could stop by Kinko's and have finals prepared while we waited. "Think so?"

She admired my handiwork, then looked at me. "No. Maybe not."

We took her Miata and, after our stop at the copy shop, Shelby drove an unfamiliar route. Neither of us spoke. She came into downtown from the south, below Mitch's shop, a route opposite from the one I'd taken. There were police sawhorses blocking the sidewalk at the shop and bright yellow WARNING tape making Xs over the windows and doors. A uniformed officer stood beside the blackened doorway. There was a car behind us and Shelby did not slow down. She parked two blocks away and put two quarters in the meter. "We've got half an hour," she said.

Shelby held my hand as we walked the two blocks slowly, pausing to gaze into a window, stopping for Cokes from a sidewalk machine. We said little. Her hand felt just right in mine. Our fingers mingled. Shelby's cheeks and forearms soon glistened with perspiration, and I regretted wearing even a light jacket. I did not want to stop to remove it, though. I did not want to let go of her hand, but I did prior to crossing the final street before Mitch's block. I stood straight as a businessman. Shelby walked beside me.

The officer looked bored and hot. He was alone. Whatever investigating had been done was apparently long over. Weren't there ashes to sift, additional evidence to collect? Evidently not.

I walked up to the store, passed the alley where I'd left the Guinnesses. The bottles were empty now, one of them smashed. My fingerprints would be on those bottles, along with those of whomever had drained them, but I guessed that wasn't evidence, either. Not to the Samson police. This case was closed.

I moved quickly, Shelby keeping up with me. I stepped up to the policeman. "Afternoon, officer," I said.

He looked at me, looked longer at Shelby. "Folks," he said. "Help you?"

I reached into my breast pocket and withdrew my wallet, offered a card and waited until he looked at it. I waited a moment longer, not wanting to have to ask for it, and he handed it back. "I talked to downtown," I said. "Word is it's pretty clearly arson."

"And arson fritter," he said with a coarse grunt. "Sorry, ma'am," he said to Shelby after a second. "That was uncalled for."

"Doesn't bother *me*, officer," said Shelby.

"They said I could come by and take a look," I said. "They call you?"

He snorted. "No. And they haven't sent my relief yet, either."

"How long have you been standing here?"

"Three hours."

"In *this* heat?" Shelby said with outraged compassion. "There oughta be a law." She giggled at that.

"Can we go get you something?" I said. "A cold drink or something?"

"Well, I don't want to be—"

"There's a drugstore right over there," Shelby said. "How about a Coke?"

"Well—"

"On us," she said, and leaned a little closer. "On him, really. Let me go get you a Coke."

"Well, okay." He smiled at her.

As Shelby started to turn away I said, "Everybody I know tries to hire her. That's just the most helpful little office gal you've ever seen." She shot me a look that said I would pay for the *gal*.

"Do I need to call downtown again?" I asked the officer. "All I want's a two minute look. Get this thing off my books by tonight. No payout. Company'll like that."

"You're really supposed to have a form," he said, "but they're really supposed to give me some relief every ninety minutes. Just be quick."

"Thanks."

I leaned over one of the sawhorses and looked into the shadowed shop, but there was nothing to see. The display cases lay shattered, charred scraps among piles of ash and rubble that covered the floor. The Peg-Board on the walls had completely burned. I wondered if Mitch had gotten his boxes out in time; I wondered if he had made his shipment. According to the news his body had been discovered in the back room after the fire was out. I wanted to see that room. I glanced down the street and saw Shelby get two Cokes from the sidewalk machine in front of the drugstore. She headed back our way.

I stepped around the sawhorse, leaving Shelby to keep the officer occupied, and walked through damp ash and blackened plaster to the doorway that led to the back of the store. The interior of the shop was thick with an odor I'd never encountered before. It caught in the back of my throat and brought water to my eyes.

I lingered in the back room for three minutes, but there was nothing to see. I stood still in that room and reached out as though to find Mitch's presence, but he was no longer there. There was nothing in that place for me, so I attempted to put something there. I clenched my fists and I made a kind of a vow. Would Betty Prescott or Ellen Jennings Duncan say that I was praying? I did not much care, but I will say that I was devout in my resolve at that moment. I was tired of who I had been for the past few years, and tired of how I'd allowed myself to become that person. I wanted my determination back, and my ambition, and my drive, and my strength, and my *will*, and standing there I could feel them return to me. I did not know where they came from, or by what mysterious or even mystical transport they found their way back to me, but there they were, and they were mine again. I felt myself at home in that charnel room, far more than I had in seclusion on my farm, and from that home I offered a promise that I took to be sacred. I would make Roy Duncan pay for killing Mitch, or for having him killed. It did not matter to me, either way. Roy would pay, I said, making my promise aloud. I would find out; I would extract payment. Then I went back to the front of the store, squinting against the harsh late afternoon sunlight as I emerged. The police officer was in the midst of what from Shelby's expression must have been an endless story.

"Looks clear-cut to me, too," I said to him. "Makes my job a lot easier, and the company's not going to have pay anything, so they'll like *that.*" I grinned at the cop as his sipped his Coke. "In fact," I said, "the only one who comes out of this with any real work to do is my gal here. Hon, you've got a report to type up."

"Lucky me," she said, and added for the officer before we left, "I don't get many breaks, either."

We left him with his Coke and headed for Shelby's car. My shoes left dark footprints on the sidewalk, but I did not care.

"*Gal,*" she said when we were out of police earshot. "*Hon.*"

"You didn't buy *me* a Coke," I said.

"Not likely after that." But she handed me hers for a sip.

"Anything?" Shelby said.

"No. I didn't expect to find anything, Shelby. That's not why I came."

"I know." She took my hand again.

"Let's drive," I said. "Nowhere in particular. Just drive for a while."

We did not return to her house until well after five. We then immediately changed into swimsuits. It was still hot; we had passed one illuminated sign that read 100 degrees, but we went into the pool to work, and pressed ourselves into the labor of laps. The harder I swam the stronger I felt, and my strength seemed to grow with each turn and push-off I made. Finally I pulled away from Shelby, and by the time we stopped to rest I was a lap-and-a-half ahead of her. "I let you win," Shelby said as we climbed from the water. "I thought you needed it."

"Thanks." We sat in our chaises under the big umbrella. "Can I take you to dinner tonight?"

"Sure. Sort of. Let's not go out. Think you're up to solid food?"

I toweled my hair. "Don't worry about me. I can eat a horse. I'm getting in shape for the barbecue."

"We'll cook out again. Chicken, maybe. I'll run to the store in a few minutes. I'm getting ready for the barbecue, too." She stretched out, eyes closed, smiling.

"Thanks, Shelby."

She raised up and looked into my eyes. "This is for me, too, Baird. Every bit of it. I am going to hold my head up very high, very proud, and look those people in the eyes. They took my job and now Roy has killed Mitch, and he's at the heart of what they stand for. I'll be there for me as much as for you."

"It will be interesting," I said. "It will be an evening."

We had a little wine with our chicken but otherwise abstained. Nor did we talk of Mitch or Roy or New Spirit. There was nothing left to say. The evening news took the opportunity to show once more the station's fiery footage, but added nothing to the official version of Mitch's death. At eight o'clock Shelby and I sat close together on the sofa and watched Cary Grant and Grace Kelly in Monaco. We talked about Hitchcock for a few minutes, and as the movie ended Shelby came into my arms for a long kiss. Then she stood up, and I thought we would go to her bedroom, but I was mistaken.

"I'm going to run you back to the motel," she said.

"I can drive."

She shook her head. "I don't want you to have a car tonight."

"Oh—"

"No. Really, Baird. You'll drive around. I know you. You'll go back downtown, do something stupid like ending up at Roy and Ellen's. I want you to go lock yourself up in that room of yours, and go to bed, and get yourself a good night's sleep so you're ready for tomorrow night."

"Shelby, your confidence in me—"

"Is pretty damned strong," she said, her eyes flashing. "Considering what you've put me through. But that's stopped now, and I think you know it. We're in this together from here on, the same team, *us.*" She showed her teacher's training, pointed a finger at me. "Call it a condition, if you wish—I won't go tomorrow unless you do what I say tonight."

"In that case . . . let's go," I said.

I pulled my car deep into her driveway. Shelby took me quickly to the motel. She left the engine running after parking outside my room. I asked her to come in with me.

"I'm tempted, Baird. I'd really love to. But I can't. Not tonight."

I climbed out of the low car and walked around to the driver's side. "Tomorrow, maybe?"

"Full of barbecue?" she said.

"We could wash the grease off each other."

Shelby laughed from deep in her throat, then tilted her face up and I kissed her. "You get some sleep, Baird. Call me tomorrow morning and I'll pick you up." She popped the shift into reverse and I stepped aside like a matador as she sped back. She tossed a wave over her shoulder and was gone.

I went into the motel room, half expecting the message light on my phone to be flashing, but it was not. I had thought Roy might call, and it was one call I was eager to return. But, as

Shelby had reminded me, some rewards were not for tonight. I turned on the television, tuned it to an old movie, stripped and climbed naked into bed. I did not find out if the late news carried a story about the death of Mitchell Tarr. Despite my late morning nap I went to sleep almost immediately, lamp and television still on, and did not wake until nine o'clock the next morning.

CHAPTER 16

SHELBY AND I LEFT HER house at five-thirty, fashionably late for our arrival at the Prescotts'. We'd talked it over and agreed we had no wish to arrive too soon. We wanted an audience. *Witnesses,* said Shelby.

It had been a long, slow day. I had a message at the desk, but only one, from Roy. *So long,* it said, *Be good.* It was signed Roy Rogers. I crumpled the message slip and threw it away.

Shelby and I had breakfast in a good coffee shop, not the one at my motel, then returned to my room long enough for me to gather the clothes I would wear in the evening. We were at her house by noon; a long swim did not relax us. There was tension, a good bit of it sexual; we could both feel it, but Shelby remained aloof. We tried but failed to play chess, getting through no more than a few moves before putting the board and pieces away. We tried to laugh at a soap opera, but could not. I suggested a trip to the library, a slow prowl through old newspapers to read about Mitch Tarr, the Duncans and the Prescotts, but Shelby wasn't interested and I had no wish to be away from her.

Finally Shelby took my hand. "They're going to think it anyway, Baird," she said. "We wouldn't want to disappoint them."

I rose and she came into my arms. After a moment we went up to her bedroom and undressed each other. The afternoon passed no more quickly but we found ourselves in the mood to take our time.

There was a soft breeze blowing when we left for the barbe-

217

cue, but its air was warm. The sky remained cloudless. We took my car. Shelby was wearing a light blue blouse that was close in color to my shirt, a khaki skirt that matched my slacks. She'd given some thought to a scarlet dress, but had passed; we would be yuppie twins tonight. I put my light sports coat in the back seat. Shelby rolled her window down. "Feels like picnic weather," she said.

"Meaning this will be a picnic?"

"It's a barbecue, remember, Baird? Sacrificial lambs." She reached across to stroke the back of my neck. "You could make a movie about this, you know? Spinster schoolteacher's life made wonderful by a visit from a stranger on the run."

"I'm a stranger?"

"Stranger than most," she said, and we laughed together. "We make a good team, you and me. We're going to do fine tonight."

"Talking to me or to yourself?"

"Both of us, Baird. Teenage detectives, high school sleuths."

"Please. Those days are long gone."

"People on a mission, then, and not in the New Spirit sense. What's Roy going to say when he sees us there?"

"I can't wait to hear," I said.

"I can't wait to say hello to Chris Wheeler and anybody else from the school board who's there. Won't they be surprised to see me? I think I'll take the time to speak to each one of them." I drove past the SPIRIT CITY sign, each letter in perfect place. "Slow down," Shelby said.

"Ever been here before?"

"Not like this. Not on my way to the Prescotts'."

She was staring at the houses we passed. There were people on the sidewalks, couples and families, no one alone, groups of people, all in bright summer clothes, all walking slowly and clearly in no hurry, many of them carrying wicker baskets over which were draped colorful cloths, some bearing small coolers or large thermoses. More than one of them waved as we drove by, friendly citizens of a friendly community letting us know we were welcome. They knew where we were going.

I pointed out Roy and Ellen's house to Shelby. "What's it like inside?" she said.

"Very posh," I said. "Picture-perfect. Like Ellen."

"From these humble roots grow great governors' wives," Shelby said.

The stand of trees that rose at the edge of the Duncans' yard went on for more than a quarter of a mile. Betty Prescott had a pleasant little walk to visit her neighbor. I thought of the paths I'd made through the woods near my farm, and hoped I would be there soon, walking them with Shelby. But there was a barbecue to attend first, and some business to complete. Shelby may have sensed something—she leaned close and gave me a quick kiss on the cheek. I took a deep breath as Prescott's home came into view.

Following a gentle curve the forest thinned, giving way at last to neatly mown grass bordering a tall white brick wall. Ivy climbed the wall but iron spikes at its top insured that nothing else did. There were no gargoyles, of course, and there was probably no broken glass set into the mortar at the top of the wall. There were several cars ahead of us, and I slowed down. We drove a good distance before reaching the gate. A gray Cadillac drove through just ahead of us. A young man in white shirt, dark tie and wide smile stood beside the open gate. I stopped the car and he came to my window.

"Your name, sir?" he said.

"This is Reverend Frederick Prescott's house? We were invited to some kind of barbecue thing here tonight," I said, and gave him a smile which nearly matched his own.

"Oh, yes, sir, this is the reverend's house. It's really something, wait 'til you see. Your name?"

I wanted to see how far he would push, how firm he had been instructed to become. "I'm sure looking forward to seeing it. I was invited," I said. There were several cars behind us now, but they waited patiently, without honking. The young man looked at the other cars, then back at me. His smile had not diminished an inch.

"If I could just have your name, sir. I'm sorry but we've had some—there've been some—some people, sir, don't like the reverend, if you can believe that."

"Oh, I can believe that," I said, and his smile began to fade.

"Your name please."

"Baird Lowen," I said. "And this is Shelby Oakes. My date." Shelby smiled and added a cheery, "Hi, there!"

His face grew dark in an instant; there was an intake of air. He stood up straight and glared down at me, making no attempt to hide his displeasure. "I thought that's who you were. I had a feeling. I heard you were coming. I heard you were planning to come here tonight."

"And here I am."

"This is a Christian gathering . . . Mr. Lowen," he said, and then took a step back. "You remember that." He waved me on through. "Park to the left. You'll see." He turned to welcome the car behind me. I waved fingers at his back and drove onto Prescott property.

"Ooh," said Shelby. "I don't think we're in Kansas anymore. This could be fun."

"Toto, too?" I said.

"Toto, too," said Shelby in a more than passable Billie Burke.

The driveway was more of a road, wide enough for two cars; graveled, it gracefully curved in a long arc through tall trees. We caught a couple of glimpses of Prescott's house. Also white brick, it gave an even greater impression of impregnability than his wall. At last we emerged into a large clearing, a good-sized pasture, which the house dominated, and I rolled to a stop so we might better behold the reverend's home.

It was every plantation manor ever built. Three windowed stories with a full attic, immense columns and a broad verandah with varnished slat flooring, breakfast porch to one side of the house, Florida room to the other. I let out a little whistle. "Frederick P. lives pretty well," I said.

"Doesn't he, though? Samson's Graceland. It's even better than on TV." Shelby squeezed my arm. "I'm glad we came. And I've *got* to get a tour of that house."

"Here we go, then," I said, and eased the car forward, following the direction of another of Prescott's young men. He stood at the lip of the parking area and waved us with an orange Day-Glo wand into a lane between rows of parked cars. There must have been two hundred cars there already, I estimated. Departure was likely to be less efficient than arrival, and I took care to seek a spot that seemed unlikely to be blocked, should Shelby and I decide to take our leave early. I pulled in beside a dark blue Lincoln, one of the behemoths, the old spirit of America on wheels.

As Shelby and I climbed out and locked the doors, the young man with the wand approached us. He could have been a clone of the boy at the gate. He wore the same white shirt, and an identical dark necktie. They had the same barber, and, by every brilliant evidence, the same dentist. "Good evening, folks," he said through his grin. "And welcome."

"Howdy," I said, and restrained myself from tucking my thumbs into my belt. Shelby hooked her left arm through the crook of my right elbow as the young man stepped up to us. I could see beyond him another attendant directing traffic, guiding cars away from us. Was this to be a private conference? The young man with us wore a name tag that read *My Name Is ROGER*. I had not noticed a name tag on the gatekeeper's shirt.

"Folks, the party's around back. I can show you the way if you like."

"Just point us in the right direction, Roger," I said. "I'm part Indian."

His laugh was full and far too hearty. He reminded me of Roy

Duncan. "This place is so big being part Indian would help. You sure I can't walk with you? Okay, then. Right over that way." He pointed his wand beyond the mansion's nearest wing. We could see others moving in that direction. The main lawn itself was obscured by a row of well-kept willows. "Just head straight back there and you'll be fine."

"We'll find our way," Shelby said, and gave the gentlest of pressures again. We took a couple of steps.

"Have a nice evening, Mr. Lowen, Miss Oakes," Roger said from behind us.

I turned to look at him, but it was Shelby who spoke. "It's *Ms.* Oakes," she said, and steered me again with her fingers. We walked away.

When Roger was safely behind us I looked at Shelby. She made a face. "I think we were expected," I said in my best Hammer Films manner. "The Master of the Manor must be close at hand." I smelled thick, sweet wood smoke from the barbecue.

"Fasten your seat belts—it's going to be a bumpy ride," said Shelby in a Bette Davis that was even better than her Billie Burke.

I looked at the house. "It must have thirty rooms."

"Or forty. Think we can get a look inside?"

"Think they'd let us back out once they took us in?" I said.

It was nearly six and the worst of the day's heat had passed. There was even something like a breeze rustling the willows' fringe. Along the front of the house stood a dozen tall rosebushes, flowers in miraculous full bloom. Did Betty Prescott have a staff to hold umbrellas over her flowers against the sun's glare? We strolled past the breakfast porch, rounded the house and looked out on the party.

There were perhaps three hundred people, milling in groups of five to twenty, scattered across a sloping lawn that must have gone five acres, every one of its blades recently clipped. To our left rose a high wire fence surrounding twin tennis courts. Two vigorous doubles matches were under weigh. Fifty feet below the

court, people splashed in a long pool; at the far end of the pool
stood two diving boards, one low, the other about ten feet high.
Beyond the pool a large American flag fluttered listlessly at the
top of a silver pole. A wide stage with microphone, piano and
speakers stood next to the flagpole, but there was no one at the
microphone. Workmen busied themselves at the speakers.

The center of attention, the focus of the event, was at the
other side of the lawn, at the crest of a small hill, obscured by
thick, slowly rising smoke. We stepped that way. I was aware of
people watching us. I was used to that. In Hollywood it is an
index of your celebrity to attract attention as you enter a func-
tion or a restaurant, but the index of your value is whether or
not your presence turns the heads of the powerful and the players as well as the commoners and wanna-bes. I had turned a few
heads during my hot seasons, but nothing like tonight. I would
not say that everyone at the party looked our way, but more did
than did not. I did not return their stares nor did Shelby. We held
to our course and the closer we got, the more clearly we could
see through the haze of smoke rising above us a long pit over
which were suspended, on slowly rotating spits, three large pigs.
Nearby stood three metal pig cookers mounted on trailers, their
hinged lids shut. A tall man in white chef's apron basted the pigs
with a long-handled mop. I recognized him immediately as our
host, the Reverend Frederick Prescott.

I stopped still and stared at him, feeling a fleeting hint of an
emotion barely recalled from childhood—that wild skipping of
the heart as when caught in some misbehavior. *You should have
known better than to come here,* an anonymous parental voice
whispered. I chuckled at that voice, for it had nothing to say to
me. I took two deep, smoky breaths. Prescott continued basting
his pigs and after a moment I looked away.

The lawn sloped down a quarter of a mile, a graceful expanse
of thick grass broken by clusters of willows, apple trees and

maples that offered pools of shade for the benches and tables placed beneath their bowers. The lawn ended at the edge of a large pond. Its water was clear, the pond bordered with white sand. There was a small dock with a rowboat tied to it. Three other rowboats, each holding two fishermen, drifted along the pond's far bank.

Shelby prodded me softly with a finger to the small of my back. "Let's get something to drink," she said. We turned and headed back toward the house. The rear of the Prescott's home opened on a brick patio that stretched from porch to porch. It was surrounded by a brick wall, no more than thigh-high, into which was set on both sides cushioned redwood benches. That patio could accommodate a crowd, and there was one here now. Shelby and I stepped up onto the patio, and some of the other guests glanced our way, smiling, then looking away. We smiled back at them. No one spoke to us. Shelby's hand gripped mine tightly.

Betty Prescott was working the patio, arranging platters and trays of appetizers and pitchers of tea and lemonade on long, cloth-draped tables. She looked in our direction, and her face came alive when she spotted us. She scurried toward us immediately, her arms spread wide. "Baird, you *came!* I was so afraid you hadn't taken me seriously." I released Shelby's hand and took both of Betty's; she held my hands between hers and beamed up at me.

"I can't imagine not taking you seriously, Betty."

"Well, you'd be right," she said with a smile. She looked at my date. "And who is this?"

"Betty Prescott, say hello to Shelby Oakes. I'm sure you remember her from the old days."

Betty took Shelby's hand, again between both of hers. "The schoolteacher?"

Shelby nodded. "Former teacher."

"Well . . ." Betty began. "I know. But let's not let that get in the way of right now, shall we? We're just so glad to have you here. I'm so happy Baird brought you." Her voice was as light as a chirping bird's.

"Thank you," Shelby said softly, but after a moment she smiled.

"You know," Betty said without releasing Shelby's hand, "we're so delighted you came because of what it shows. It shows so clearly that people can disagree and still be *friends.*" Betty wore a frilly white summer dress that covered her knees and neck and rustled against its ruffles and, I had no doubt, at least one full petticoat. Her hair had achieved a pinnacle greater than any I'd seen before. I thought of Babel and coughed to cover a laugh.

"It's this smoke, isn't it?" Betty said. "I *told* Frederick when he first dug that pit that it was too close to the house but he didn't listen. He had his spot and he had his heart set on it. But I told him. That smoke's going to make everyone cough all night *long,* I said that first time. And it did. It gets all over the windows every year, and we have to have them cleaned." She placed her small hands on her hips. "I *told* him it was too close." She shook her head, and I could have predicted what she would say next. She said it to Shelby. "But you can't tell a man *any*thing, can you, dear? They just won't listen; I don't think they can. Why, the reverend dug that pit all by him*self,* and expanded it by himself two years ago, and did all that brickwork where the other cookers are." She sighed, gave a cluck of the tongue. "He does his pigs out there every year, and every year people cough and we have to get the windows cleaned. Well . . . come over here, you two, and let's get you something to drink."

We followed her to one of the long tables where a variety of pitchers, coolers, jugs and large jars stood, condensation spreading dark stains across the white tablecloth. Big galvanized tubs filled with ice and water held cans and plastic-bottle soft drinks.

"Now, what would you two care for tonight?" Betty said. "There's just about everything you might want. Hot coffee in that urn over there, although who'd want coffee on a night like this I couldn't say. No alcohol, of course. There's none of that here."

"Didn't expect any, Betty," I said.

"Of course you didn't, Baird. I was making a joke." She smiled and once more held out her hands to me.

Shelby and I had iced tea, sweetened to the edge of becoming syrup. Shelby puckered her lips at me while Betty beamed. I turned to look out over the crowd. More than one face struck me as familiar, but only vaguely so—there was no one I immediately recognized. I tried to spot Roy and Ellen, but if they were present they were out of sight. My eyes followed the smoke to its source, and I found my gaze resting once more on Frederick Prescott.

He was staring at me. Behind him his assistants were opening the cookers. Prescott stood with his long mop handle braced against the ground, holding the mop upright as though it were a musket. His heavy brows darted up and down. He might have been inviting me to join him, but it was an invitation I could for the moment decline. I stared back at him until he finally dipped the mop in sauce and turned to the job of basting the other pigs.

Betty Prescott took Shelby by the elbow. "Shelby, I do hate to impose upon a guest," she said, sweet as the tea she had served us, "but I wonder if you would mind giving me a hand getting some more of these appetizers out here? Frederick tells me the barbecue may be running a little late, but that's no surprise because it always does. And when we've got everything set up, I'll take you on a tour of the house."

Shelby clapped her hands together. "You must have read my mind, Mrs. Prescott. I'm *dying* to see this house."

"It's *Betty*, dear, you remember that." The reverend's wife looked disappointed in me. "Baird, did you neglect to tell Shelby that we're all friends here? First names, *always*. Honestly, dear, you can't expect a man to remember *any*thing, can you? Now, Baird, while we're getting things set up and I'm showing Shelby around, why don't you just step on over and say hello to the reverend? He's so *anxious* to meet you. You go ahead now. Shelby, dear, you just come with me."

Betty and Shelby walked into the house, Betty moving fast and still talking. Shelby shot a delighted, silly grin back at me before she disappeared.

I finished my tea and tossed the paper cup into a trash barrel. I looked toward the barbecue pit. Prescott mopped his pigs furiously. I took a few steps in his direction. Smoke tumbled upward, and I could hear the sauce and the grease as it dripped and sizzled on the coals beneath the spits and in the bottoms of the cookers. Prescott worked his way from cooker to cooker, carrying his mop and a yellow plastic bucket full of dark sauce. He would move, then stop to stand on one of the rectangular brick platforms he had built himself that marked each corner of the pit. Others were paced at intervals in between, as well as before each of the cookers. Stations of the sauce, I supposed, and allowed myself a silent chuckle. Prescott spread his legs wide, as though bracing himself on the bricks. He set for himself a vigorous rhythm while he basted, rocking from foot to foot as he reached and stretched to cover each pig, then moving on as an assistant reclosed the lid of the cooker. Prescott wore a white shirt under his apron; dark circles of perspiration spread from beneath his arms and across his back. There were several lines of script on the apron, surrounded by decorations, but I could make out neither the words nor the illustrations that illuminated them. I would have to step closer to see more clearly. From time to time Prescott interrupted his work and stared in my direction, fixing those dark eyes upon me. I was able to meet his gaze and hold it.

But I was still not ready to meet him and so turned at last back to the refreshment tables. The sweet tea clotted my throat, and I poured myself a cup of lemonade and carried it with me as I walked down the lawn toward the pond. I studied the faces of those I passed, looking for someone I knew. As I walked I shot an occasional look back toward the barbecue pit and more than once caught Prescott following me with his eyes. I thought I saw him nod, a quick nod which could have said, "Take your time, son; there's no hurry. What I have to say will keep." I nodded back.

For a few minutes I was content simply to stroll around the party, among the other guests, entering into no conversations but exchanging a few pleasantries with some of Prescott's people. Pleasantries they were, for no one showed any discourtesy or displeasure at my presence, or even any reaction comparable to what I'd encountered at the gate. Perhaps that had been the only warning I would get, I thought, and tried to recall if my greeter had stood outside the walls of Prescott's compound when making me feel so unwelcome. Surely such rudeness would not be tolerated on hallowed ground.

Everyone with whom I spoke seemed delighted to meet me, and it may have been that after the first two or three introductions I began speaking my name more loudly. I was not proud of that impulse, but neither did I resist it. I wanted some reaction, but found none. Could they all have been warned to show me every charm and with their warmth win me? It seemed more likely that I had little reputation here. Prescott had sermonized over my article, but that was a while ago, and the article had stayed in print for only a week and then gone. As for my other career, it seemed likely that I was little known here. The number of people who read the director's name, even when it appeared above the title, was small, all things considered, and I was at the time of my retirement something less than an Alfred Hitchcock–like household name. Roy and Ellen had reason to react to me, and my assumption was that Frederick and Betty Prescott shared their reason. These others, though, these good people who welcomed me would have to be prodded. It pleased me that I had not yet reached the point where I felt the need to say, "Hello, I'm Baird Lowen. I directed *Moonstalk* and wrote an article critical of your reverend." I lowered my voice, showed my smile, shook hands firmly. But I did wonder how many, if any, of these people knew who Mitchell Tarr had been.

If I felt a lessening of the need to feed my ego, I nonetheless felt a mood building, an anger gathering. Had I ever been so surrounded by sweetness? Had there ever been such a group of deacons and churchwives assembled in one spot proximate to me? I had never seen anything like this barbecue and its attendants and those attending it. Their clothes were creased sharp and clean; their skin was scrubbed, the light of Salvation shone in their eyes. I did not like that part of me that wanted to fart, or stumble and stain my knees and swear too loud. My career might not have offended the middle moral ire so much as Roy had claimed, but I knew that I could offend it here on my own, without need of special effect. But I also wondered to what end?

I stepped close to the tennis courts and watched a spirited doubles match. I could have been standing with spectators at any of the finer country clubs, I thought; there was no difference. What would Mitchell Tarr say if he saw me here? I wondered what he would say to these people, what he had said to them from his sidewalk pulpits. I finished my lemonade and walked to a table midway between the tennis courts and the pool. The table was covered with plates and bowls of snacks and appetizers. Beside the table a girl in a bright yellow dress stood opening bags of small pretzels. Finally someone I knew. I waited until she was alone at the table, approached her and said, "Hello, Nancy."

Nancy Hargetay looked up and recognized me instantly. "Mr. Lowen, how are you tonight?"

I made my smile match hers. "I'm fine. You?"

She poured pretzels into a bowl. "Getting caught up, Mr. Lowen," she said with a shake of her head as she crumpled the empty plastic bag and placed it in a box beneath the table. "Trying to catch up, anyway. I'm on the snacks committee. I think we've got everything under control."

"You seem to," I said, and took a handful of pretzels. "How's school?"

Nancy looked back at me. "Very well, thank you. And how was your visit with Mrs. Prescott?"

"It was a good talk," I said. "I enjoyed it."

"Didn't I tell you you would?"

"You sure did," I said, and grinned again. I wondered if I was flirting with her. I ate the pretzels and looked at her; a pretty college girl, she could have been Kelsey's classmate or, years ago, my own and Shelby's. And Mitch's.

She fiddled with a bag of pretzels but did not open it. Something was bothering her, and after a moment she told me what it was. "We looked at your article in my Civic Responsibilities class yesterday."

The pretzels made my mouth dry and I sipped the lemonade. "What did you think?"

She did not have the chance to answer. "She thought it was wrongheaded and dangerous," a voice from behind me said. I turned in time to see Chris Wheeler smile. "Hello, Lowen."

"Wheeler," I said, for I would have recognized him instantly even if I had not seen his picture in the Spirit College brochure. The years had been good to him—he looked like the football star he had been, with twenty years of care and attention paid to his body. Vanity, thy name had always been Chris Wheeler, and that hadn't changed. "What a nice surprise, Wheeler," I said. I did not call him Coach or Doctor.

Nancy spoke up. "Mr. Lowen, you know Dr. Wheeler? He didn't say anything in class about that."

"No? Not surprised." I did not look at her, did not take my eyes from Chris Wheeler. "We've known each other a long time, Nancy," I said.

Wheeler looked past me, looked at Nancy Hargetay and said, "Has he been bothering you?"

"Of course not, Dr. Wheeler; what do you mean? We met the other day at Spirit Center."

"I see," Wheeler said.

"I'm flattered you taught my article," I said. "You going to show any of my movies? Might make interesting audiovisual aids."

"Not likely," Wheeler said. "You remember what I said about his movies the other day, Nancy? Like his writing . . . he's one of those *humanistic* types; tries to hide his atheism behind fancy words and pictures, builds his arguments out of empty words and thoughts that have no light or truth to them."

"Is that what I do?"

"Lowen, I'll talk to you in a minute. I have a few things to say to Nancy if you don't mind."

I stepped aside and let Wheeler step close to her. A few people approached the table, but most had noticed or sensed that something was going on, and held their distance. They stayed carefully within earshot should voices rise, close enough to watch. I looked at Nancy and thought of her friendly helpfulness at Spirit Center. She was looking at me, her brow wrinkled, confusion evident. She smoothed some wrinkles on her yellow dress, looked at the ground, then back at her teacher. She spoke a bit louder. "But Dr. Wheeler," she was saying, "shouldn't we— aren't we supposed to make him welcome; isn't that what persuasion is all about?"

Wheeler was silent for a moment. "Of course you're right, Nancy." He glanced quickly at me. "But I know Lowen; I know what he's like. I saw him with you and I was concerned. He didn't—"

"He was a perfect gentleman, Dr. Wheeler. I don't know why you would think he wasn't." I saw the effort it took for her to question her good teacher and I was proud of her.

"He thinks that way because it suits him to tell you what I am, Nancy, rather than letting you make up your own mind," I said. "Don't worry about it. I'll see you around. Thanks for the pretzels." I turned and walked away from the table.

"Mr. Lowen," she said, "I'm sorry—"

"You have nothing to apologize for," Wheeler said. "I'll explain this to you later. Lowen, wait."

I did not stop. I'd made half a dozen more steps before he caught me, grabbing my elbow in a stern grip. "Lowen, I said wait."

I turned and stared at him. "All right, Wheeler, I'm waiting. Tell me what I'm waiting for."

He said nothing. A vein pulsed at his temple.

"Hell with this," I said, and broke free from his grip.

"Don't you use foul language *here*. I'll have you evicted from these grounds."

"Will you?" I said, and was aware that we had drawn an audience, a subtle one, people looking at each other but listening to us. "Will you, Wheeler?"

Wheeler. We had always used last names with each other, but at first it had been a special code, an honorific. Wheeler and Lowen: best buddies. At one time there had not been that much difference between us. We were the same height and weight; our birthdays lay just a few weeks apart; we sat close in first grade; we camped in each other's backyards. It was, we agreed as six-year-old blood brothers, the greatest friendship of all time. Chris Wheeler's seventh birthday party remained one of the outstanding social events in my early memory.

By the time we were ten we had drifted apart. He was an outstanding athlete, a true natural who shone at every sport. I made teams but he dominated, and he wore his stardom poorly, or I was jealous of it. Maybe a bit of both. He rubbed his superiority in and I resented it. We had words and then harsh words. Entering junior high school the drift became a rift and a break: He did not want me on his teams and more than once worked his . . . persuasions on coaches who should have known better, but who followed that coach's conviction that a happy star who could win games was more valuable than any approach to egalitarian athletics. In high school we hardly spoke, save for the afternoon when Wheeler made a comment about Ellen and myself, and I came close to punching him. It would have been an interesting fight and I do not know if I could have taken him then any more than I had confidence that I could take him now. I did not think it would come to that here on Prescott's lawn.

"Roy told me you were in town," he was saying, "but I didn't think you'd have the nerve to show up here."

What else had Roy told him? "I've always had plenty of nerve, Wheeler, you know that."

"I know you have a filthy mind. And if you said anything to Nancy or anyone else that's out of line—"

"Grow up, Wheeler," I said, and turned away once more.

He caught my shoulder and spun me to face him. "I'm not through." My hands were clenched but I forced myself to relax. There would be no fight.

"Go ahead," I said.

But before he could say a word Nancy Hargetay hurried to our side. "Dr. Wheeler," she said, "I'm so sorry about this, but you just have to know that he didn't say anything to me that was unchristian at all." There was a tiny tremor in her voice. "Please—"

Wheeler lowered his hands to his sides. I could see his vanity at work: This was *his* scene and it was not one he wished to create for this audience. That was not the winning play he wanted. I watched him swallow, three times, hard. "Lowen," he said softly, and through all the tension between us I could still see the two of us on Wheeler's seventh big day, laughing kids, his grin as he blew out with a single breath every one of his candles. But I saw it the way a paleontologist sees a dinosaur from a chip of bone in a rock: More than ancient history, it was something from another period. Ice ages had come and gone since then.

"Wheeler," I said. There would be no further thaw.

"That's all, Dr. Wheeler," said Nancy Hargetay. "I just didn't want Mr. Lowen to be accused of anything unjustly. We should persuade, not accuse, shouldn't we?"

"Of course we should," he said in an even voice. "You run along. We'll talk about this later."

Dismissed, Nancy Hargetay looked at me for a moment. I could no longer read her expression. It could have been pity for me, it could have been loathing. She was gone from me, and after a moment she was gone in person, walking purposefully to the snack table, returning to her work.

Wheeler and I looked at each other for only another moment. "We'll finish this some other time," he said. "Later."

"Pick the time."

"I will," Wheeler said, turning his back on me. He waved at a group of men standing not far away, then went to join them without looking back.

Something more than curiosity made me look toward the barbecue pit. Prescott was watching me. I gave him a moment's view, then stepped toward the row of Port-O-Lets that flanked a willow grove.

It was hot inside the cramped toilet, and the air was thick with the scent of bad freshener. I urinated, then stood still for a moment after I was finished. I thought of poor Mitch. He would have pissed on the lawn, no doubt of that. He would have marked this territory with his message. I felt an urge to give voice to that message and wished for an instant that I had one of his PRESCOTT SUCKS buttons to pin to the wall of the toilet. I would have done it, too, I fear, but only in that instant, and then that instant was past. The impulse to anger and offend the people here left me. Loud gestures and shocking actions made for adolescent art and childish action, and I wanted no part of either. I had some things to say and I would say them as a grown-up would, man to man, eye to eye, without tempering my words, but also without coloring them solely for offense. That was Mitch's tactic, not mine, although Mitch was never one to hide his scatology behind toilet walls. Mitch was gone.

I stepped out of the toilet and walked in a straight line for the barbecue pit, no hesitation or doubt in my stride. I did not look for Wheeler, but did make one quick scan for Shelby. I did not see her. Was she still inside with Betty Prescott, getting her tour? I wished her well, then locked eyes with Betty's husband, made my way through the crowd and through the smoke up the low hill to where the reverend waited for me.

CHAPTER 17

AS I CAME NEAR TO Frederick Prescott he took an oversize white handkerchief from a back pocket and mopped his face with it. He replaced the handkerchief and took a single step toward me, then stopped to await my approach.

He was a tall man; his size was apparent on television but nearly overpowering in person. He might have been six-four, maybe a quarter of an inch less, and he had a huge solid frame. His black hair was swept up and back, gray thick at the temples, one thick shock of hair gleaming in the late afternoon light. I stood close to him as Prescott stared down at me, a smile creasing his broad face.

"Good evening, sir," he said in a voice thick and rich, richer even than it sounded on television. "Be welcome here."

"Reverend Prescott, I'm Baird Lowen."

Prescott's smile widened and wrinkles spread from around his eyes, marching out almost to the edge of his thick sideburns. "Of course you are, son, of course you are. I know who you are," he said as he took my hand. Frederick Prescott's own hands were huge as hams, wrapping all the way around mine, embracing my fingers and palm in a sturdy, warm grip. I could feel his calluses. "Welcome to you, Baird. Welcome to our home."

"Thank you, Reverend," I said, and realized I could not imagine calling him anything else. "I appreciate the invitation."

"Well, that's fine, that's just fine. We're delighted to have you here with us tonight."

"Well, I'm happy to be here," I said again, somewhat limply. Was I already disarmed?

Prescott took my arm and ushered me back a few steps, out of the thickest hickory smoke. I looked at his apron, which bore in red embroidered letters a quotation: *"And Samuel said, 'See, what was kept is set before you. Eat; because it was kept for you until the hour is appointed, that you might eat with the guests."* Around the words were stitched more traditional apron decorations: a spatula, a smoking grill, a ham, plus a cross and a pair of prayer-clasped hands.

Prescott watched me read. He held the apron out from his massive body in order to give me a better look. "My Betty made this for me some years back. I've always been proud of it. That passage, of course, is First Samuel, Chapter Nine. I'll let you look up the verse."

"I will," I said, and meant it. "Not King James, though."

His heavy eyebrows rose. "Very good, son. No, it's not. We use a newer version; makes the words more open to today's worshippers."

"A nice quotation, either way," I said.

"It speaks for me. Nowhere, Baird, are people closer together than when they dine together at a table in the sight of God." He turned his attention to his barbecue. Two young men in dark trousers and sauce-spattered white shirts, no neckties, shoveled hickory embers from the pit into the fireboxes beneath the pig cookers. They were working too fast and Prescott offered instruction: "That's enough coals!" he shouted at them. *"Don't* burn the pigs up, *smoke* them. Slow and steady boys, like I been telling you all day, *slow* and *steady."* He faced me.

"Reverend, I know you're busy with the barbecue. I just wanted to introduce—"

"Now, son, you don't think you're going to wander off as easy as that, do you? We got some things to talk about, you and me. I've been looking forward to a little conversation with you, and Betty would have my hide if I let you get away. She had some interesting things to say." He ran a hand through his hair. "And I saw you had time for Coach Wheeler. So you can give me a little time. Can't you?"

"Sure," I said. "Can I give you a hand here?"

He shook his head. Prescott's ears stuck out slightly, bearing thick wings of gray hair. His sideburns glistened with sweat. "Can't talk here, Baird," he said. "Too much smoke." He fanned the air in front of his face. "Let's you and me take a walk. Just let me get a couple of things straight over here, make sure these boys don't burn up my pigs while we're gone. Those're *good* boys, Baird, both of them students at the college." Prescott glanced toward heaven and sighed. "But my *heavens* they don't know a thing about barbecue. They grew up eating hamburgers and hot dogs. Which are fine, of course, nothing better, but you don't learn much about cooking from hamburgers and hot dogs. They move too quick. That's why we served them at those Tuesday cookouts when you were a youngster. That and because they were cheap. Betty and I didn't have much, then, but we could afford cookouts. *Cookouts.* Call it that, but it's still not *cooking,* not like cooking pigs. Son, you got to bring a pig along *slowly,* take your time with a pig, you see." Prescott's accent was not so thick as his wife's, but it was there; the South was there in his words and gave grace to his sentences, coming clearly when he stretched a vowel, as soothing in conversation as it must be in prayer. "I'll be right back."

Prescott strode to the edge of the pit and motioned the young men to join him there. How many such men did Prescott have? These two watched him closely as he showed them how properly to baste his pigs. I imagined it was not the first time they'd received this lesson, but they attended to it closely. Their brows were furrowed, their concentration complete; they might have been a pair of repentant sinners receiving salvation.

When Prescott finished speaking he retreated a step and

watched as the young men took turns with the basting mop. Prescott clapped his hands together, shook his big head, used his thick fingers to massage the back of his neck. He took the mop away from them and repeated his lesson, showed the correct amount of sauce to use, the regulation strokes of the mop. The young men hung their heads as though ashamed, but Prescott put down the mop and flung his arms around their shoulders and hugged them close to him and made the boys smile again with a few whispered words. They raised their heads and Prescott released them. He offered a final bit of instruction and they nodded solemnly. They tried again, each with the mop in turn, and the reverend this time chortled his satisfaction. He slapped each on the back, staggering them a bit, then returned to my side, wiping his hands on his handkerchief.

"They'll get it," he said. "Those pigs'll be fine while we talk."

"It smells wonderful," I said.

"Smelling can't compare with tasting. But that's still an hour off at least. Could be two. I'll hear about it from Betty if we don't start feeding these people before eight, but we had a little trouble with the fire this morning, so nothing to be done but wait."

"Smells like it'll be worth the wait."

"Smelling can't compare with tasting, but you're right, it will be worth it, but *you have got* to have patience; you can't hurry a pig, you got to be patient just as you must be with all things in this world."

"Patience is a virtue," I said lamely. "In barbecue, anyway."

"In *all* things, Baird, yes, you're right. Now, let's get us a drink and walk on down by the pond." He set off without another word; he knew where he was going and I could only follow. He took long strides, his posture military perfect, his apron flapping around his knees as he led me to a tub full of soft drinks, stopping to shake people's hands, shout a word of greeting, grin at a follower. He stripped off the apron, folded it neatly and draped it over the back of a chair as I waited. Then he reached into the icy water and drew out two bottled drinks, Dr Peppers, opened them, handed one to me, and we were off again, down the hill toward the edge of the water. "Patience," he said as we walked, "there is something blessed about a patient man. The Lord rewards him, you see. All good things will come to him by the close of his days on earth, because he was patient, all good things will be his."

"I've heard that said." I was taking a step-and-a-half to each of his.

"Now, Baird, you see, I am not a particularly patient man. Never have been. I have a vision and I have a dream. And when you have a vision and you have a dream you can move mountains, but don't you *know* that's long and hard work. I am patient about the work. I try to be a patient man, Baird, but my heavens I know what awaits us when those mountains are moved, and it is hard for me to wait for those old mountains to *just get out of my way.*"

I did not say anything. We neared the pond.

"So sometimes, Baird, my patience just runs a little thin and I get so all fired up like an old-time circuit rider—like my granddaddy, Baird, he was a circuit rider, you see. And I'll get going, and I'll be ranting and raving and bellering about this and that and the other, all of it in the name of the Lord." Prescott did not miss a beat, he did not seem to take a breath as he spoke.

We reached the edge of the pond and Prescott led me out onto the dock. He stood for a moment at its end, staring across the pond at the rowboats, all four of them out now. He stared at the fishermen. He pointed at them and sighed. "Now you look at that, Baird, would you? Over to the right, that boat there. Watch that chunky fellow in the bow of that boat." I looked in the direction Prescott indicated, and watched as the fisherman worked through several casts, working his plug too fast, casting too hard, wiggling his rod, not sticking to any spot for more than two casts. "That's Buddy Jones, Baird, one of my deacons. Now, Buddy is a good and tireless worker in the church and in a campaign, and he is also one of the most important bankers in Samson. He gives everything he has to his church and his family and his bank, and he'll put in more time on the campaign trail than the candidate himself, but would you just watch him fish."

"No patience," I said.

"You got that one right on the nose, Baird. And poor Buddy just doesn't understand why he doesn't catch many, and never any big ones."

"You ever tell him?"

"Now, Baird, it has been my experience that the impatient, when they are good in so many aspects of their lives, manage to ignore my advice on their occasional impatiences. And, son, that is especially true of the impatient fisherman."

I laughed out loud. I had tried to teach people to fish myself.

"You ever go after bass, Baird?"

"No more than three, four times a week."

"Is that *so?*" Prescott winked at me. "Well, that's wonderful, son, nothing better than fishing, is there? I hope you keep your tackle box put up 'til after church on Sundays, though from what I know about you I doubt that's likely. There's more than one kind of fishing, as I'm sure you're aware."

"Well, lately, I've tried not to miss your Sunday show, Reverend," I said, and met his wink with one of my own.

"Hope it's done you some good," he said, "but it's not the same and you know that." He gave his head a thoughtful little jerk. "No, son, it's not the same at all as sitting on a pew in holy worship with your fellows, feeling all those souls in spirit next to you, all around you, joining their voices with your own as you raise up in hymn."

"Well—"

"No *wells* about it, Baird. Except that *you're* not well if you're missing Sunday worship service. And that means every Sunday." He placed a hand on my shoulder and I rose to meet its weight. He looked far into my eyes. "You just give that some thought, won't you, Baird?" He looked back across the pond. "I bet Buddy hasn't caught squat all afternoon. Well—" His voice trailed off and he passed a moment in silence, his eyes closed. I wondered if he prayed for Buddy to catch a lunker. Prescott opened his eyes and waved his hands at the plank floor of the dock. "Let's sit down. And for goodness' sake, son, take off that jacket. Let's sit down and have a talk."

This was what I had been waiting for and I could not wait for our talk to begin. I slipped off my blazer and folded it as neatly as Prescott had folded his apron, placed it beside me on the dock. Prescott lowered himself in a single graceful motion. He was limber and he was in fine condition. I could tell from the way he sat Indian fashion, ankles crossed, spine straight as a righteous rod. I sat opposite him, bracing my back against a piling. I took a sip of my Dr Pepper, and Prescott matched me with a long, gurgling swallow of his own.

"Peaceful here," I said when we'd put our bottles down.

"It is that. I do love this place. For all the trouble it has caused me."

"Hard to maintain?"

"Not that sort of trouble. That's *not* trouble. That's work, son, and isn't hard work a pleasure? Publicity trouble, Baird, *media* trouble. You'd know all about that, the line of work you're in. Papers and those TV people see me and Betty living like this, the swimming pool and the tennis courts, the grounds, everything we have, and those reporters just light onto us like a starved dog on a pork-chop bone."

"Quite a place," I said, wanting to press him. "Hard to blame them."

"It's *mine*, son, mine and Betty's. We share it . . . our home is open to every member of my church, every one of those good people who worship with me each Sunday, and it is open to every member of New Spirit across the *world*. We had a group here last week from Somalia, and week after next we're taking in a bunch of kids from Bosnia for a month, but you won't read that in the papers or see it on the news. But we do that. And I will tell you that not one penny of church money and not one penny of New Spirit money has ever gone into that house or these grounds or this dock we're sitting on." He arched his back, raised his hands high over his head in a long stretch.

"You know, when I married Betty her daddy didn't have any use for me at all, thought I was just a dumb country preacher taking his only child down a dirt road, and he could have been right." Prescott laughed. "But when that good man passed on he left everything he had to Betty, and he had quite a bit. Betty and I have been right smart with all that money. We took care to put it in smart things and we've been pleased to watch it grow. We've been careful and we've paid our fair taxes every year. Not that there's anything fair about taxes these days; they're too high and they get wasted and they get spent on things there's no business our government spending them on, godless and awful things, but that's the law until we get it changed, so we pay it all. So this is all *ours*, fair and square. Now why would those reporters want to attack us for spending *our* money on a fine home and grounds like this?"

"Maybe because it doesn't fit with the image of humility before God," I said, and then felt the confidence to be bolder. "Maybe because you get so defensive about it."

"You think I was being defensive?" he said with a heavy sigh. "Well, maybe I was but that was not my intent, no. And either way, I'm sure you notice that their attacks just bounce off us. Like yours did a few months ago. You noticed that, didn't you? That your words didn't stick. I hope you noticed that; you should have."

"I've kept watching," I said.

But his mind was still on his house. "This is our tenth year here, son. You remember where we lived when we first came to town? No, you wouldn't; you weren't one of our flock back then·

any more than you are now. Well, we lived in the smallest house you've ever seen, with the tiniest church, and not in a good neighborhood; but we made it a good neighborhood by our hard work and the hard work of those who came to follow us. Some of them your classmates, of course, those good kids. Coach Wheeler—*Doctor* Wheeler, I should say, I guess; he got his Ph.D. two years ago—and of course Roy Duncan and his Ellen. Ellen Jennings then, but you know that."

"I do indeed," I said.

"Yes, I'm sure you do." He chuckled and I wondered if his laughter carried weight. "So about ten years ago, eleven maybe, right after Betty's daddy passed on, we were driving out here on a Saturday afternoon and we saw this place. Did you know it used to be a hotel, a resort back in the twenties? Closed down during the depression and didn't amount to much after that. Wonder it didn't come down. But it didn't and we bought it, brought it back. New Spirit was starting to catch fire then, and maybe our timing was off, 'cause we caught some fire for buying this, media fire; but once Betty saw it she had to have it, and here we are and I reckon there's not much chance we'll ever live anywhere else."

"You've done a good job with it."

"We've *worked;* floors were rotten, doors falling off, a mess. But we built *this* out of all that mess, and we bought some more land, and then a bunch more land so that others could build themselves something out here near us. Home, Baird, our *home.* Built by us." He waved a hand at the followers on the lawn. Some of them were looking at us but none came too close. "Son, I guaranteed these people and all the others, I *guaranteed* their children, their teenagers that is, promised them all the summer work they could handle the year we bought this place.

"*Work!* I worked, they worked, we worked together, every day, five days a week, sometime six, ten hours a day. Shoring the foundation, ripping out the floors, stripping the walls. A thousand things, ten thousand things, none of them small jobs. We dredged that pond and enlarged it. We built this dock we're sitting on now.

"And we'd work through the heat of the day, and then we'd come down here to the pond and we'd splash like little children. And then every evening, before we left, Baird, we would all sit there on that hill and we would have us a lesson in the Lord's good words."

I could see them, he made me see them, Prescott and his young workers, workers worshipping on that hill. Had he bought the place a decade earlier, Roy Duncan and Chris Wheeler would have been there with him.

It was as though he read my mind. "And there was more than just the physical labor, son. Roy was doing all the legal work as we bought the land and started setting up the basis for Spirit City. Buddy Jones handled the financing. And Coach Wheeler saw to it that those boys working for us didn't waste their evenings and wear themselves out for the next day; he ran them like one of his football teams in hard training."

He crossed his arms and rested them upon his chest. His voice grew hushed and heavy. "You see, Baird, the point I making here is this: Son, that was a decade ago and every one of those boys that worked for me has grown up to be a good Christian and a productive member of society. Every one of them. No crack, no AIDS, no ... *malfeasance.* Some of them are still on ministries for me all over the world. They learned from the experience. They had to save 70 percent of their wages and tithe 10, and they did. They learned what it meant to be tired every night, but it was such an honest tired. You think about that."

"And they're passing those lessons on, I'm sure," I said, for it was past my turn to speak and I was ready not to be silent. "With what they do. The offices they run for. The places they picket. The people they put in office and the ones they force out of jobs. What they do to school curriculums. What they do to make sure people think their way, *your* way, Reverend, and hide away any thoughts that don't fit your plan or theirs. Passing their lessons on all right, and passing judgment too against anyone who cares or dares to disagree." I stared at him.

Prescott repaid my speech with one of the gentlest smiles I'd ever seen. "Son, I could make a preacher out of you if your thinking was straight."

"Well, why don't you straighten me out?"

He shook his head. "You really don't understand a word I've said, son, I don't think you do. You're out of step, and you just don't get it. We weren't building just a house here, or a subdivision, any more than we were just building a church or a college. Son, we were building the *future* and we were building it *right here.* It took us three years to finish everything and of course we are not finished yet and never will be. But son we *built,* and while we were building I had the clearest sight of all, my vision and my dream, and I saw the mountains I must move. That, Baird, *then,* was when New Spirit was truly begun. Before that it was just a name."

"I'll give you this, Reverend, you've come a ways in ten years."

He nodded vigorously. "Against some odds, too. You think back to what we were up against. Backlash from Bakker and Swaggart, and wouldn't I have loved to get these on either one or both of them." He held fists out before me. "You think that sounds unchristian, you're wrong. I'd have pounded them behind a woodshed or in the middle of town given the chance." A crooked smile appeared. "But of course they didn't give me the chance. Still won't talk to me."

"Probably afraid of being persuaded," I said.

"Probably afraid of finding out just how big I am," he said with some pride. "But it wasn't just them, it was all the rest. Every other candidate in the country calling himself or herself a Christian, and you ask them to quote the Bible and they can't. Ask them to lead a prayer and it's all earthly they're praying for, politics, and not morality at all, just politics and earthly rewards for all their talk of Holy guidance. So I had that to go up against."

"Not *your* version of Heaven on earth," I said, but he missed my sarcasm or ignored it.

"Not at *all.* Not anybody's vision really except their own. Can't just *call* yourself a Christian and *say* you got morality, Baird, even *you* know that. So we *show,* we don't tell, and if we pass judgment, well we pass judgment, and you're not going to get me to apologize for that."

"Didn't think I was trying to, Reverend," I said.

He threw back his head and issued a great laugh. Perspiration stood out on his great forehead but he made no move to mop it. "You know, you probably weren't," he said. "I think you might be just a little like me, son, trying to teach or persuade. Course you're trying to teach the wrong lessons and persuade people to go in the wrong direction."

I returned the grin he showed me. "Now, how would I be doing that? My article?"

He snorted and waved a dismissive hand as though to remind me of what a minor gnat my words had been to him. "Come on, Baird, even you got to admit that article played right into my hands."

I allowed him a gracious nod, a tip of my head. "And your director's, your cameraman's."

"Didn't they do just a *wonderful* job that night? We've got such talent here and we're going to be using it more and more. Son, I'll give you that. I don't know that it had been all that clear to me beforehand just how much you can do with a camera, with *technique.* Been more worried with substance, I guess, wanted to keep my message clean and simple. But you showed me what *technique* can add and I appreciate that. You got to reach the people with the tools they're used to, and movies are such good tools. Why, we might even make some movies of our own before long. We've done everything else, what with the publishing and the network and the computer programs. But *feature films,* now there's something else we could do and do well. And after that night, let me tell you my film and TV people are just chomping at the bit to show me what they can do." He leaned conspiratorially close. "Mind you, I'll keep a tight rein, wouldn't want them to get so caught up in *technique* they forget about *message.*"

"Can't have that," I said.

"Can *not.* That's what happened to you, you know. See, I can recognize and appreciate genuine talent and technique, *ability,* in just about anything, even things that are indecent. And, son, your ability showed through every bit in your movies, especially that last one."

"*Moonstalk,*" I said, and was glad for the rough wood of the piling at my back.

"That's the one. *Moonstalk.*" Prescott squinted at me. "Now you had the chance to make a fine film there, oh, you had a chance to make a picture my momma or daddy could take all their kids to see and come out proud they'd seen it. That poor little girl, kidnapped, being so brave and trying to escape, and that young preacher there could have helped her, too, and shown her the way for her heart to escape even before her body did. Now, that would have been one fine picture for kids if you had just done it right."

"I'm sure you're going to tell me what I did wrong," I said, and sat taller.

"Way you say that, Baird, I feel sure you know already what you did wrong, and I have a feeling you pay for it from time to time."

"I've paid a price or two," I said with an edge. "Have you got another one for me?"

"Not me," he said, "not me."

"Really?"

"You'll pay your prices on your own, Baird."

"For *Moonstalk?*"

"For the *language,* for what it said to young people about

using their bodies to get their way. All that sexiness and smut. It was *foul.* And what you did with that little girl, her running around in those underpants, those men's butts waggling around, and that preacher as you called him—but he wasn't any preacher at all going after her the way he did—and you making it look like *she* was healing him instead of him corrupting her. How can you live with yourself for that? I'd be ashamed to take my wife to see it, much less to have made it."

"Betty saw it," I said.

"So she did. And she was just as sick about it as I was, son. All that language and smut. And the violence, Baird, the blood. Son, why couldn't you have just told a simple little adventure story that made people feel *good* about themselves?"

"Not what I saw, Reverend." I tapped the side of my head. "Not *my* vision, *my* dream."

"You hear that kind of language all the time?"

"It's called realism, Reverend," I said, and smiled. I was talking with Reverend Frederick Prescott about *Moonstalk.* What could be better on a lovely summer afternoon?

The reverend brought his hands together and raised them to his mouth. My shoulder still felt warm where his hand had rested on me. "Realism?" He lowered his big hands to his sides. "That's not realism, Baird, you know better than that. I expected a better answer from you. I really did."

"Just what answer did you expect?" I said. "I'm not interested in holding anything back from you, and I trust you'll extend the same courtesy."

"Don't you just know I will," he said, but his eyes had narrowed and I could not read them. "But what you call realism wasn't."

"What was it, then? You tell me."

His voice sounded weary, probably from too much patience. "It was a little girl movie star up there on that screen saying those filthy things and acting like a tramp in her underpants and that brassiere, smoking cigarettes and drinking whiskey, *fornicating*, because that's what you and all the others like you in Hollywood and the media think the public wants to see. All those fat cats out there leering up at all those little girls who don't know any better than to get caught up in all that . . . sordidness."

There was not an ounce of fat on Maurice Devlin, and I thought how flattered Maurice would be to hear himself referred to as a movie producer. He'd floated far more sordid operations than *Moonstalk*. I wondered what Prescott would say if I told him some of the things my backer had been involved in, but Frederick Prescott possessed a gift for surprise as well as homily, and he offered me a surprise now.

"Pandering, Baird, that's what it was and what it is, and you'll always be able to find an audience for it. Just like you'll always be able to find somebody to foot the bill when the big studios get scared. Now, don't you get scared, son, but I know a few things about that Maurice Devlin who financed your movie. I know some things about him and his type. *Panderers. Procurers.* Men who chase only dollars and don't care how dirty they get or who gets hurt as long as they can see the green." He shook his head in disappointment. "What sort of man is that for a good southern boy like you to be involved with? What sort of thing is *Moonstalk* for you to make? That's nothing a family could see, nothing kids should *ever* see."

"I didn't make the movie for kids."

"But they *went*. You know that and you knew that before you shot the first scene. You knew they'd go. So tell me where is your sense of responsibility? Where's your sense of morals?"

"I'm assuming I'll find out if you keep talking," I said.

"Too easy. I want to know what *you* think."

I gave it to him as honestly as I could, hoping as I spoke that the words I chose would lead him to offer me another nugget of what he knew, and how much. "I tried to make a movie about a girl becoming a woman in a society that takes as much from women as it can. And takes it even when they're girls," I said. "That's what I wanted to say, to *show*. That and how she turned the tables and turned on them exactly what they wanted in the first place. Even the . . . preacher. That's what I set out to show."

"And you think you succeeded?"

"Not for me to say."

"No? Who then? Come *on,* son. You put it out in the open right now and we'll see what we have to talk about. You think you succeeded with that movie?"

"I think I came close here and there," I said, and wondered if he knew what my words cost me, or who else I had said them to. "But, no, I don't think it works all the way. It got away from me. Or I wasn't as good as I thought I was."

"Or maybe you didn't believe your *message* the deeper you got into that thing."

What thing? I wanted to ask, but held that question in reserve for a better moment. "That could be, too."

"*Now* we're getting somewhere," Frederick Prescott said with a tone that told me he thought he was winning our conversation. "And what did you do when your movie didn't turn out the way you wanted? Didn't live up to your *artistic* vision?'

"This time you *can* tell me," I said.

Prescott slapped my knee with a hearty whack. "This time I'll be *glad* to, Baird. Because I *know* what you did. You *quit*. Quit it all because you couldn't have things your way, even though I think you knew right then and there how wrong that way was." He waved a hand in my face. "Don't say anything, son. Not just yet, not 'til you've heard what I'm here to say. The Lord can't abide a quitter, Baird, and neither can I, and I know as sure as we're sitting here that neither can *you*. If you could you wouldn't have made it as far as you did out there, now would you? Not an easy road that one you chose, but you went to the top, all the way.

Riding the wrong horse, but you got there where others wouldn't have made it. Because you have the talent, the *ability,* because you weren't a quitter."

"I retired," I said.

"You're too young to retire, and that's not what you did. You *quit.*" The word was a sneer.

"So you say."

"No, Baird. *You* say it. And then I'll tell you a secret about what you did."

That was an offer I could not pass, so I gave him his due. "I quit," I said.

"Quit what?"

"Hollywood? The movies? My career? My . . . talent?" What did he want to hear and what sort of reward would the right answer win me?

But each of those answers was the right answer, and Prescott was ready to give me my prize, with only one more lesson attached. "Son. Baird. You didn't quit your talent *or* your career for all that you walked away from them. You couldn't do that if you wanted to; it's too much a part of you, who and what you are. What you quit, what drove you away, was the wickedness, the sordidness, the Devlins and all the others like them and all the littler ones that work for them. You *knew* they were wrong, *vile,* and it was your talent, that God-given gift of yours that wouldn't let you work with them anymore. *That's* what you quit, *that's* why you left. Because you were too good for them, and if you'd just stop your sulking down on that farm of yours, your hiding out, and open your eyes and come back to this world that needs talent so bad, you'd see that."

"I'm here," I said, opening my palms to him.

"*In* the world, Baird, not just of it. That's the price we all have to pay. You, too. Can't go through this life just *watching,* and have hopes of any reward in the Hereafter. Doesn't work that way."

"Maybe I want my reward here on earth," I said.

"Who doesn't? Look at this place I built for myself. But your real reward is your gift, Baird, your talent and your ability. And your prize is the chance to do some good with those gifts."

"How do I win that prize?" I said.

"That's what I'm trying to tell you, that's what I want to say. You don't *need* to make filthy movies and you don't need to turn to men like Devlin to get your financing. Set yourself a challenge, son, a real challenge. Get over your little boy sulking and come into the *real* world and *work* yourself hard to put that goodness up on the screen. I *know* you've got it in you; I *know* you could do it—I'd pay for a movie like that myself."

"And buy Betty a ticket, too?" I said.

He laughed. "Son, you're still not *listening* to what I'm saying. Pay to have it *made.* Put up the money for you, son. I'm making you an offer."

I stared at him, and my jaw may have been open, I was not sure. "You're serious?"

"Son, I even *play* serious. But I'm not playing now. I'm serious."

"You want me to direct a movie for you?"

"I want you to direct a movie for *people,* for real people and their children to see. Something to help show the way."

I shook my head. "Not likely."

"But what if—son, *what if* I could persuade you to come make a movie for me?"

"I don't see how that could happen," I said, but in truth I could see all too clearly exactly how it could. I could see Prescott holding another film, one that showed me kneeling beside Billy Toller. Would he use that? If he had it, would this man so eloquent about goodness use that on me? If he had it. If Roy had it all and had shared it with Frederick Prescott, would the reverend use it? I would have to see.

"Son, there's *lots* of ways such a thing could happen. I know lots of things I could tell you, stories we could go over . . . Why, I could persuade you in no time flat," he said, and laughed at his own confidence.

"Reverend," I said, "I'm just not sure we would get along as well on a movie set as we do on this dock. Too much division of authority for either of our tastes."

"Son," he said, "we may just have to make that movie and find out." He laughed again and there was no hint of a threat in his laughter. "But we'll save the persuasion for later. I'd as soon you came to me on your own, taking your own strong steps." He looked at his watch, then up at the gathering sunset. "Besides, I got to get on back and check on my pigs." He uncrossed his ankles and stood up without a hint of a groan. I grabbed my jacket and stood beside him. Across the pond from us there was a loud whoop and we watched as Buddy Jones fought and landed a bass large enough for us to see from the dock. We waved our congratulations at him.

Prescott threw an arm around me and hugged me to his side as we walked from the dock. "Think about what I said and you'll find your way. I know you will; I've got confidence in you." He released me from his embrace long before we reached the barbecue pit. He had other work to do now, and he set to it. A moment later he had regained control of the basting mop and was shouting orders, flinging sauce and, after his shirt got splattered, dispatching one of his assistants to fetch his apron. "You see, Baird?" he said to me through the smoke and over the sizzle. "You got me all excited about working with you and now Betty'll make me change my shirt. Don't make me wait too long for an answer."

"Patience is a virtue, Reverend," I said.

"Isn't it, though?" said Frederick Prescott. "And I do possess it. You believe that, don't you?"

"I do."

He stepped close, heedless of the sauce dripping from the

mop. "Then you better understand me, son. Baird, you had better understand that I *will* make you see this light. Really *see* it. Something tells me you already know that I *can* make you change your ways. But what I want is for *you* to change them." We stared at each other for a moment. "Now, I've got to see just how fouled up these pigs are."

Prescott turned to his brace of young men, donned his apron over his soiled shirt and got back to his pigs. I watched for a moment but there was nothing for me to see. I turned away from the reverend and went toward the house in search of Shelby.

CHAPTER 18

I DID NOT FIND HER and eventually stopped searching. She would be along, Betty would see to that. Dusk was gathering and crews were busy lighting lanterns and turning on spotlights. I took up a place beside the ranked tables on the patio, sampling the fare on various trays and dishes. Someone had prepared a huge bowl of steamed shrimp and I ate a couple, dropping their shells into another bowl, wishing for just one ice-cold beer. A few people talked with me, and I talked with them, but our words were simply cordialities, comments on how good the food was and how eagerly we awaited the barbecue. My informal survey, taken from these conversations and others overheard, told me the vote was split between spitted pigs and pork smoked in cookers. I promised three people I would sample both. I stepped to the edge of the patio and looked out over the party, and was standing there with my back to the house when I felt a soft hand touch my shoulder and then fingers tickle my neck. I knew that touch. I turned and it was Shelby, and I took her into my arms. We kissed, but after one quick smack she pulled back laughing. "PDA," she said, and lowered her eyes.

I tried to hold her close but she resisted, blushing a bit. "PDA?"

"Public Display of *Affection*, Baird," she whispered. "Betty was talking about it—what it's like at their teenage parties. Don't you remember? Didn't you go to even one of their parties when we were kids?"

"You did?"

"A couple," she said. "Not for me."

"No," I said, and bent toward her ear.

Shelby gave a firm shake of her head. "Not here, Baird." Her lips puckered with amusement. "It's so *common,* trashy." Shelby's Betty Prescott was the best impression yet.

I let her go and she gave me a butterfly-fast kiss on the cheek, then stepped back. "Wouldn't want to offend Betty," I said.

"No point to it," said Shelby. She glanced around, then led me from the patio, away from the crowd.

I squeezed her hand as we walked and she squeezed mine. "Later, then."

"Oh, I've got some things planned for later. PDA."

I looked at her.

"*Private* Display of Affection."

"I'll be waiting."

"Patience is—" Shelby began, and did not need to finish. Virtue was not exactly what I saw in her eyes.

"How was Betty?" We strolled by the edge of the pond, headed away from the barbecue pit.

"God, Baird, you wouldn't believe it. That house. They've got *columns* in their *bathrooms.* And a stained glass picture window. There's a chapel in the *house.* And you should see Betty's writing room."

"High tech."

"Better than the computer lab at school. And she *knows* all that stuff."

"Silicon in service of the Lord," I said.

"Oh, yes." She squeezed my hand once more. "I saw you a couple of times from the upstairs windows. You and Prescott."

"We had a talk."

"Bad?"

I shook my head. "Not at all. Not what I expected, but not bad at all. He offered me a job."

"What?"

I gave her a quick version, but did not edit out anything important. "Mitch's name didn't come up. Or Roy and Ellen's, really. This was just Prescott and me. And *Moonstalk.*"

"Jesus."

"Careful," I said.

"Right."

"Saw Chris Wheeler, too, before Prescott."

She released my hand. "*That* bastard?"

"Shelby, you'll get us thrown out."

She was in no mood to be teased. "He helped cost me my job."

"I know," I said.

"And there's every chance Roy will give him a shot at a lot of other jobs once he's governor."

"Maybe we can stop that from happening," I said.

"How?" she said.

"Let's see," I said, and turned us back toward the party. "Betty say anything about me?"

"Only trying to find out if we were engaged or anything. You can imagine. You know Betty; you've had the talks."

"Not about PDA."

"Oh, that's because you're a man. We gals have responsibilities; we have more control than men do. Didn't you know that? Why, Betty hinted pretty broadly that I should get you to marry me and we should start having those children I'm missing out on."

"Just like Ellen," I said. "She probably wants to change your hairstyle, too."

Shelby laughed aloud. "You *do* know her. She says I ought to grow it out and make it more womanly."

"Now that she mentions it—"

Shelby punched my arm.

We walked back up the hill to the patio. The crowd continued to gather; the spaces among the tables were jammed. The food we'd seen earlier, all that plenty, turned out to be nothing more than prelude, for dinner was in the process of being unveiled. Women came bearing platters and bowls and tureens of vegetables and salads and breads. I told Shelby their conversation sounded to me like the buzzing of locusts, and she asked me please to hush. She had come to enjoy herself and not even Chris Wheeler was going to take that away from her.

I spotted Roy Duncan at last, not far from the barbecue pit. Ellen was not with him. I looked at Shelby, she nodded, turned and walked toward the house. Roy stood near the center of a small group of young men, his age and mine, earnest and bright-eyed and radiant with intent and ambition and purpose. They listened to him carefully, and there was about their conversation none of the backslapping and glad-handing I associated with public politics. This was a private-party gathering, and I decided to crash. I could tell from a few words as I approached that this was nothing less than a pep talk and a motivational speech, a seminar in the selling of good Roy Duncan.

"I'd announce formally tomorrow," he was saying, "just like you want, but I've still got a few things to—" Did he sense something? I had positioned myself so that he could not see me, but Roy nonetheless caught himself in midsentence and stood very still for a long second before turning to face me.

"What is it you need before you make your run, Roy?" I said in the manner of a peanut gallery heckler. "I thought you'd have every detail taken care of by now."

He was angry but he was in control. "Baird," he said calmly. His audience parted, and Roy stepped closer to me. "Fellows, I don't know how many of you have met this man, but I am certain you all know his name. Meet Baird Lowen."

One of them, younger than the rest, bounded forward and offered a hand and a toothy grin before he reread the cue and stopped himself. He retreated a step and his eyes joined all the other earnest eyes on me. None of them blinked. I felt invulnerable to their gazes. "Nice to see you guys. Let's get together sometime. Maybe we'll swap names and handshakes *then.*"

"What can we do for you, Baird?" Roy said.

"I just wanted to join in, old chip. That's all. Hear you speak your piece. I'm a registered voter, too, you know." I spread my hands. "I might even have something to add to the conversation."

Roy kept his eyes on me as he addressed the others. He spoke in a tone that reminded us all, and clearly, that we were subordinates. "You'll have to excuse me, fellows, but we'll finish this another time. I've known Baird for a lot of years and I know how he can be—and we don't need that sort of thing just now, do we? This probably wasn't the best place for our talk, anyway. Don't want to miss the party. So what say my house tomorrow? We'll finish this then. Say three o'clock?" No one demurred to Roy Duncan's selection of place and time.

"Am I included, Roy?" I said.

"See how he is, fellows? Just like I said, isn't he? Eager to show off that smart mouth of his." Roy sighed heavily, a lesson I could tell he had learned, but not well, from Frederick Prescott. "I better go. Sounds like he thinks he's got a bone to pick with me, and old Bear doesn't ever let go until he's been kicked in the face." He turned a grin on the other young men. "Tomorrow at three." They nodded, and I followed Roy away from the group. We had to walk a distance before we were alone. I spoke first.

"Campaign talk without Chris Wheeler?" I said. "I'm surprised."

"Why mention Chris?"

"You haven't heard? We had a little chat. Before my talk with the reverend."

"I saw you with him. With the reverend, down on the dock. You wasting his time and him so generous he gave you that time."

"He was more generous than that, Roy, and I suspect you know it."

"I know you shouldn't be here. And you brought Shelby Oakes."

"Had to bring a date," I said. "Betty told me to. I couldn't let Betty down. And, besides, my old steady was unavailable."

"Be sure you say hello to Ellen before you *leave,*" he said with some heat.

"She's here?"

"Of course she's here, Baird. She's head of the *dessert* committee," he said with the gravity one might use to speak of a nobel laureate. "She'll be out as soon as she's sure everything's ready."

"I'll look forward to that."

"Do that," he said. "You're through here, Baird. Go on home."

"And miss the barbecue? No way. I've got to see which pig tastes better. I promised the reverend."

"I mean leave Samson altogether. Get out. As promised."

"I never promised that. Besides, I've gotten a pretty interesting job offer. From the reverend himself."

That rocked him but only a bit. It could not have been a surprise to Roy, but I could imagine it was news he had not wanted me to hear. "Let it go, Baird. Turn him down. You're outgunned. But don't worry. I'll keep all your little secrets quiet, all tucked away. Just make sure you tuck yourself away like you promised. It's *over.*"

"I don't think so, Roy. And remind me to tell you sometime how much confidence I have in you keeping something tucked away."

He gazed blandly at me, but said nothing.

"Thanks, Roy, but I think I'll stick around for a while. Not just for the barbecue. I've got some curiosity, you know."

"You're going to get burned, Baird," Roy said.

"Nice choice of words," I said. "Poor Mitch."

"He was crazy and he got careless."

"I'm not crazy."

"No, Baird, you're not. But you're foolish and that may be even more dangerous."

"Don't be scared, Roy."

"Dangerous for *you*, Baird. Playing with fire."

Before I could answer him we were embraced around the shoulders and hugged close to Frederick Prescott's sides. He smelled of wood smoke and barbecue sauce, but he held us bear hug tight and gave each of us a shake.

"You boys are talking *way* too serious over here away from all the fuss and commotion. I'm not going to have that. People get the impression you're *rude,* and I won't have any rudeness here, you understand?" We got another shake. "So I came down here to tell you both something. You got any business to discuss you save it for later and for someplace else. This is my barbecue, not a meeting room. That goes for politicking, Roy, and for . . . proselytizing, Baird, if you want to call it that." He spun us around forcefully and gave us a nudge in the direction of the other guests. "Now, I believe a man ought to own up to his own hypocrisies above all else, so Roy I'll tell you Baird and I talked a little business ourselves earlier, and you know about what. But that's between him and me and that's all, you understand?" We took a step forward, guided by Prescott's strong hands. "Singing's going to start in a few minutes. People changing out of their swimsuits and tennis clothes, all of us getting together. Those pigs only got a little while longer." He let our shoulders go and looked at his watch. " 'Bout an hour and a half late, no more." He laughed. "That's right on schedule for a party this big, but you can't tell Betty that."

"How many times have you been asked tonight, Reverend?" I said as we headed up the hill. I had a small urge to make Roy see how casual I could be with Prescott.

"Asked what?"

"Cookers versus spits. The big question."

"How many people are there here?" Prescott said with a large laugh. "But that's one question I never answer. People's taste buds answer it for themselves for one thing. For another, I think my pigs turn out just fine either way. Open or in a box *my* fires do just fine, burn just the way I want them to."

"Desert island question, then," I said. "You've only got one pig, how would you cook it?"

"Just between us." He stopped and looked at me. "And I mean that, both of you. This goes no further."

I nodded my agreement before Roy added his own.

"All right then." He glanced over a shoulder as though in search of a spy. "I like to hang a pig on a spit. I like to see them turn, watch the way they look. It's not as easy as using a cooker, and that's another reason."

"*Looks* more biblical, too," I said.

That got me one of Prescott's heroic grins. "You *see,* Roy, that's his movie eye still working, and he's absolutely *right.* That's why I want him. But there *I* go talking business and I won't have that from me, either." He put a hand on each of us. "Now, I mean this, too. You two mingle and you two smile. And I want to see the four of you—Ellen and that Miss Oakes, too—take your dinner together. You be pleasant, and Roy, you introduce Baird all around. I shouldn't have to tell you two this, grown men. Next year I'm going to print a list of rules on the backs of the invitations. No business, no politics. Just barbecue and fellowship. I mean it. I may do it. I just might. Now, go have fun." He clapped his hands together, turned his back to us and walked away.

"You heard the man," I said.

"If that's the way he wants it," Roy said.

"Then that's the way I want it, too. Now let's go find our gals." I winked at him but it did not have much effect. We moved toward the patio, but before we reached it Shelby and Ellen emerged from the throng, Shelby tugging at Ellen's elbow. Shelby waved when she saw us. Ellen looked less than thrilled to see me.

We met midway between the patio and the stage. "We're going to be dinner partners," I announced. "The reverend says so. Roy and Ellen are going to introduce us around."

"Roy—" Ellen said. Sternness did not favor her features and added some years to her appearance.

"It's all right, Ellen," he said, but he didn't convince me or Shelby. "I promised the reverend."

Ellen let out air through her nose, a slow sighing sound. "I'm not hungry," she said.

"Oh, *sure* you are," Shelby said with much cheer. "You just think you're not because you've been so busy with those desserts. Baird, you should *see* what they've got for dessert. You had better save some room. I've never seen so many pies and cakes even in a bakery. Cookies and brownies, too."

"No low-cal, there, old chip," I said, and nudged Roy with an elbow.

"Careful, Baird, there are limits," he said, and slapped me old buddy friendly on the back, but harder than any old buddy would have need to do.

"Boys!" Shelby said. "Ellen and I are not going to put up with this, are we?" I had not seen her enjoy herself so much. "You can *not* get men to stop behaving like boys no matter *what* you do, can you, Ellen?" she said. She was ready, it was clear, to say more, but her performance was interrupted by the start of another.

There was a whistle from the stage and a whine from the microphone as it was adjusted by a middle-aged man with a hairspray pompadour. Twin spotlights pinpointed him. It took a moment for him to get the volume right, but he persisted, and spoke at last in tones unpunctuated by feedback.

"Most of you know me, but for those who don't, I'm Lester Davidson, Reverend Prescott's musical director."

The crowd applauded, but Lester continued speaking over the clapping.

". . . technical problems, but we've got those solved. The reverend says we've only got a few minutes before dinner, so we're going to have a little music to whet our appetites." There was more applause. A crowd was gathering in front of the stage and we moved that way, Shelby pulling Ellen along with us. "And there will be a full concert after dinner. The night is *young*. But for right now, here are these four fellows. Ladies and gentlemen, brothers and sisters!" He caught his breath and held the silence for a moment during which no one spoke. "*His—Dulcet—Tones!*" Lester waved a hand, stepped back and four men in sequined dinner jackets and white slacks and shoes bounded out onto the stage. One of them carried a tambourine, shaking it high over his head. Their sidemen followed them, taking positions at the piano, plugging in a guitar, sitting at the drums, even as His Dulcet Tones broke into a lively a cappella version of "Gonna Walk Dem Golden Stairs." All four Dulcet Tones were white, but there were more than a few blacks in the crowd. White or black, the audience began swaying and clapping together, cheering as though they were rock and roll fans, although older and more neatly dressed.

They were a good quartet. I'd seen them on Prescott's programs, and heard that they were the most popular gospel group in the country. They recorded on the New Spirit label.

"Dem Golden Stairs" done, their band struck up their instruments and the crowd continued clapping in rhythm, this time to "Swing Low, Sweet Chariot." Shelby was swaying, too, but did not clap, and I found myself swaying with her, our hips bumping occasionally. His Dulcet Tones took us up and up until Shelby and even I was clapping along, then they brought us gently as a feather back down, settling us, finally, with a serene, soft rendition of "Dinner on the Ground." People began glancing toward the house, and quite a few of the women walked slowly away from the stage. I saw men moving picnic tables into place and wondered if I should offer to help, but before I could make a move, His Dulcet Tones ended their song in perfect harmony,

bowed deep to a round of applause and yielded the stage to
Frederick Prescott. The reverend positioned himself center stage,
still wearing his apron. With one hand on the microphone, he
raised the other and waited a moment for silence to settle over
the crowd.

"Your attention!" he said, and his voice carried out over the
lawn and could be heard, I imagined, across the pond. The work
stopped, people stood where they were. Everyone listened when
Prescott spoke.

"Let me welcome you all here tonight, to join with us in our
annual celebration of New Spirit, and of your good, hard work.
I'm proud of each and every one of you, and I bid you once
more—*welcome!*" He waited out the applause. "Thank you all
for coming, and I would not miss any opportunity to thank His
Dulcet Tones for entertaining us—" he was interrupted by more
applause "—for entertaining us while I finished up those pigs."

Prescott waved his free hand in the direction of the pit. The
smoke had dwindled somewhat, and we could see his assistants,
joined now by other young men, lifting one of the spits up, heav-
ing it to their shoulders, moving gingerly toward the long line
of serving tables. "What I want to tell you now is that those pigs
are *done!*"

Not even His Dulcet Tones had earned the response that
Prescott's pronouncement received then, and once more he rode
it out until the last of the cheers and applause was gone. "And I
think they are *good!* And I know they are *hot!*" he said, talking
now over the renewed applause, letting it carry his words. "I
know because I have been *standing* there beside that hot fire for
the last sixteen hours. *Myself!*"

He bowed his head for a moment, then spoke more calmly.
"But we don't any of us do anything all by ourselves. How well
we know that. How important a lesson that is to learn. I want
you good people to know I had some mighty *fine* help this year.
Particularly fine. From those good young men up there. From

those good strong young men from New Spirit College. They helped me." He winked that wink of his, signaling a joke on the way. "But of course I helped them, too. Yes, I did. Let me tell you how.

"Those young men. Those fine young men are going to make fine preachers. They're going to be good counselors and teachers. They're going to serve the gospel so very well." He was silent a moment. "And after *today*. After *today*, why, those fine young men can cook *barbecue*, too!"

That earned a laugh and a good one. Prescott stood onstage beaming like an entertainer. "Now, they're taking the first of the pigs off right now; one from the spit, one from the cooker. And I want each and every one of you to be sure to say thanks to those young men when you pass through the line. No need to say thanks when you come back for seconds, though. Wouldn't want their heads to get too swollen.

"And don't just eat *barbecue*. You out there know who you are—the ones who come through every year and put away a pound or two of barbecue, a gallon or so of tea and nothing else. Our ladies have been working *so* hard, all those hush puppies and potato salad; there's some sliced cucumbers over there that are just *wonderful*, and—you know, if I go into all of the good things on these tables there won't be time enough for us to eat. So, please. Take something besides just barbecue. And take all you want. But eat all you take."

He coughed into a fist. "Just a few more things and we'll start the serving lines. I already thanked the fine singing group. What else?" He pulled a sheet of paper from his back pocket, unfolded it, squinted at it for a moment. "A few announcements. Where are Pat and Donna Stephenson? Where are they, folks?" Prescott looked around. "There they are, folks, I think—there, under that tree. Pat, you're not trying to steal a kiss off Donna, are you? A little PDA?" The crowd laughed again; they were enjoying this. "Well, if you are, I reckon it's all right. Because, folks . . .

tomorrow is Pat and Donna Stephenson's *forty-seventh* wedding anniver*sary!* Now how about that; isn't that just wonderful! Let's show them what we think." He released the microphone and led us all in a long moment of applause. "Congratulations, you two. Forty-seven years, now how about that?" He read off a couple of birthdays and a new birth, and we applauded each.

"Now, I want to take a second here to congratulate Buddy Jones. There he is. Now we all know why we're congratulating Buddy, so I'm tempted not even to mention it. Wasn't going to mention it at all. But I will tell you that I overheard him just a couple of minutes ago saying it must have weighed something like seventeen pounds! That fish has been taking hormones since the minute Buddy landed him!" Prescott wagged a finger at Buddy Jones, who blushed red even as he laughed along with the rest of us.

"Anything else? Yes. We have a couple of very special guests here tonight. And I know some of you have already met them. Some of you have known them for years, but I want to introduce them to everyone. Where is Baird Lowen?" He looked around and I held still. Shelby dug her elbow into my side and I raised my hand. Someone nearby gave a shout and Prescott looked our way.

"Now, you may know that Baird was a moviemaker, though I have to hope that none of you are *too* familiar with some of his movies. Some of you know he's a writer, too, and even wrote that 'Lights, Cameras, Prescott!' article about us a little ways back."

There were a few short jeers.

"Who *was* that?" Prescott said sharply. He took the microphone from its stand and stepped to the edge of the stage. "I will not *have* behavior like that in my home. I hope you are *ashamed.* You should be. This man is our *guest.* I had a long talk with him earlier this evening and I want to tell you he has got the makings of a fine young man, a good and solid young man." Prescott allowed his features to relax, and shared a little chuckle with his audience. "He's a little confused, yes, maybe more than a little misguided, but who of *us* is without sin? Who are *we* to boo at a *guest?* Now, I want all of you, and especially those who booed, whoever you are, to go out of your way tonight to speak to Baird, to show him that he is as welcome here as are all of you. *Persuasion.* Can you remember that for me?"

His fixed his followers with a stare before continuing. "And Baird has a young lady with him tonight, a lady named Shelby Oakes. You think about that name. You all know it. You should, for we are responsible here, yes we are, we are responsible for her being out of a job. Think about that. You give that some thought. Now, you all agree with me that she was in the wrong job; that what she was doing was not what we want done in our schools." I looked at Shelby but her face was a mask, her eyes fixed on Prescott. "But that doesn't change the fact that she's now got no *job.* Some of you know how that feels. Not to know where your next paycheck's coming from. So you think about that, and make Miss Oakes welcome here tonight. She showed enough courage to come here and look all of us in the eye, and she disagrees, I'm sure, as much with us as we do with her. So say hello to her, shake her hand. Whatever you feel about their beliefs, she and Baird are our *guests.*"

He rubbed the microphone against his chin and a scratching sound came over the speakers. "That's about it, I guess. Now, how many of you are ready for some *barbecue?*"

A cheer went up, and applause.

"That's good, but I'm afraid you're going to have to wait a little longer." He reached behind himself and untied his apron, removed it. "See this shirt? These stains from the sauce? Well, you know Betty. She's going to make me go all the way up to the house and change this shirt and come all the way back down here. And you're all going to have to wait, just so's I can put on a clean shirt. Now, patience *is* a virtue, but you've already been waiting a *while.* So maybe—"

Another cheer went up as Betty Prescott stepped onto the stage, carrying a microphone of her own. She gave her husband a look of bemused exasperation. "Oh, go ahead and *wear* it," she said. "You want to anyway, and you'd just get the other one dirty, too. Course, *he's* not the one has to wash them, but you can't do anything with men." She and her husband shared their laughing understanding of each other with us.

Prescott fell for a moment into contemplation, facing us but with his eyes elsewhere, not distant but filled with something other than our presence. "Let us pray," he said at last.

"*Oh,* Heavenly Father, bless all who are here in your sight. Having granted us all such a wonderful year since our last gathering, grant us your grace for this evening of fellowship and community. As we would ask you to grant grace to all gatherings in Your Name throughout this world. Bless all our souls.

"And bless those hands and hearts that have done so much to spread your Word, and those voices who have spoken your gospel, and those hearts which have demonstrated your love.

"And we ask especial blessing for any souls who have strayed from your flock or sought to escape your gaze. Let them know that they are welcome back. We pray for them.

"And last, bless this food, and the hands, my own humble hands included, that prepared it. Bless us now, Father. We humbly pray in Your Name. *Amen.*"

"*Amen,*" said the gathering in soft unison. Shelby and I did not add our voices.

"Now, let's eat," said Prescott, and he jumped down from the stage and walked quickly to the serving tables.

CHAPTER 19

WE TURNED WITH THE OTHERS to follow, walking with Roy and Ellen toward the serving lines. Ellen did not look at us. As we walked, both Shelby and I had our hands shaken, our shoulders touched, our backs patted by strangers making us feel welcome. We nodded and smiled. More than one person asked us to eat with them, but Shelby deflected the invitations easily. "We've already been asked," she said, "but thanks so much." Her smile was as pleasant as the smiles of those who had cost her her job.

The lines were long, and Roy gestured for us to stand back for a moment to allow a group of elderly men and women to move to the head of the line. "Just a minute more," he said, and looked around. "Ah: Here they come."

"Who?" I said, turning to follow the direction of Roy's gaze, and saw Chris Wheeler approaching us. At his side was a petite, wide-eyed brunette, hair falling in long curls that touched the shoulders of her white blouse. They stopped directly before us and said hello to Roy and Ellen first. Wheeler took my measure before speaking, and it was clear that while he did not like what he saw, he was going to take the reverend's advice this evening. His smile was something short of hideous, but still more than a distance removed from sincere.

"Baird Lowen, Shelby Oakes," he said finally. "I'd like to introduce my wife, Cynthia."

We shook hands all around and Wheeler's wife said, "I was

so *touched* by what the reverend said about you two." She was holding Shelby's hand and would not let go of it. "And it's so good of *you,* Shelby. I know how tense things got between you and my Chris, so it's just so *good* of you to be here. We're so happy to have you here with us tonight, so glad you could come."

"Thank you, Cynthia," said Shelby, whose eyes were boring holes in Chris Wheeler. "I can at least get a good meal out of what Chris did. And that's important, you know, not knowing where my next paycheck is coming from and all."

"It's Cindy," the coach's wife said, setting Shelby's hand free at last. "Chris says we're all going to eat together. I'm so glad. We'll let bygones be bygones and bury the hatchet." She looked at the line that now stretched back from the serving table and up the hill to the house. "Well, he may have kept the same shirt on, but we're still going to have to wait a good while."

"Be worth it," Wheeler said. "That barbecue."

Roy studied the line. "Not more than thirty minutes," he said. "Chris, you remember the lines at the Tuesday Cookout Club?" " 'One burger at a time, kids,' " he said in Prescott tones. " 'No seconds 'til everybody's served once.' "

Cindy rolled her eyes. "Here we go. Old-time stories."

"Good old times," Roy said.

Unexpectedly, Ellen touched my arm. "I've heard all these stories, and I'm going to wait until the line thins out a little. Walk me down to the pond, Baird?"

I do not know if I was more surprised or if Roy was, but I said, "Sure," and turned to Roy: "Just make sure there's some food left for us when we get back."

"We'll wait for you," Roy said. His look was intended to show Ellen his displeasure, but she was not looking at him. Her eyes were on the pond.

We stepped away from the others and strolled a good distance before Ellen spoke. "It's a terrible thing to tell someone to burn in hell, Baird," she said.

"Worse to burn someone," I said.

She had a little stumble, stopped and looked at me. "What do you mean?"

"Mitch," I said.

She seemed confused for a second. "You don't think *I*—"

"No. I think Roy."

"Oh, no. How could you think that?"

"Ellen, how could I not?"

Her hands made small fists at her side. Her chest rose and fell a few times. When she spoke it was slowly. "Baird. I asked you to walk with me so that I could apologize for Wednesday night, for my words. You see, I *heard* what the reverend said just now, and I listened to his message. But I will not stand here and listen to you say these things about Roy, about my husband."

"All right," I said, and it was an easy acquiescence. My fight was with Roy, and if things turned out as I hoped, I would not have to say these things to Ellen at all. She would know. "Let's take our walk."

We headed for the pond again, Ellen setting our pace. "Now, I hope you will let me say what I wanted to, Baird. About being sorry. I can't wish you well. You have to know that. But what I said was terrible, and I hope you will forgive me."

Prescott would have been proud of her, and I accepted the apology. "It's okay," I said.

We reached the edge of the water and stood side by side without speaking. I wondered if she was thinking of the lake and the time we had spent there. But when she spoke it was not of our time together, but of me and Shelby.

"She cares for you very much, Baird," Ellen said. "I could see it in her eyes. And she said some things to me in the kitchen."

"I care for her," I said. "Very much."

"Do you?" Ellen said, and there was no dare in her voice, or even doubt, just curiosity.

"Yes, Ellen. I do."

"And how much does she know about you. About . . . all this?"

"Everything."

Ellen nodded. "And that's all right with her?"

"I think it's getting to be," I said. "I think it's going to be all right."

"Then you take care of her, Baird. She deserves that."

"Yes she does," I said. "And what about you, Ellen? What do you deserve?"

She folded her hands over her stomach where new life grew. "I have so much," she said. "Roy's a wonderful husband. I know you don't believe that."

"I—"

"No, Baird." She turned toward me. Her eyes held a certain gentleness if not warmth. "There's too much between us for any more lies. I know how you feel about Roy and I know you're wrong about Mitchell. Roy is a good man who is going to be governor of this state and he will do a good job for its people. He's a good father and he is my husband. And so I have something to ask you."

"Tell me."

She took a breath before she spoke. "I do not know *exactly* what it is that Roy knows about you. Your past. I don't want to know, really. But what was there about *our* past, yours and mine, is gone now. Mitchell killed himself and we do not have to worry about that anymore."

I let her have that. I did not object. I would make my objections to her husband.

"Baird, I want you to leave Samson. I will tell Roy that whatever is between you two is finished now. I will have him put it away where no one will find it. I can assure you that he will do that. You won't have to worry about it anymore. You can leave, and I can set about putting *our* lives back in order, back into the order we . . . *deserve*. That's what you can do for me. Will you?"

"Ellen, I can't," I said without hesitation, but with part of me wishing I could grant her request. "I'm sorry."

Her shoulders slumped a bit. "Not even for me, Baird? For what we had together?"

"We did have something, didn't we?"

"Yes," she said, and I will never know if she was saying it to buy my departure from Samson, or because she meant it, but I have my suspicions. "Yes, Baird. It was wrong in so many ways, but we did have something. For that? For what we had, Baird?"

"Ellen," I said, and touched a hand to her arm. "I can't."

She closed her eyes for a moment, and when she opened them again every reserve was in place. "I didn't really think you could," she said. "Or would. I know you, you know."

"You do," I said, and there was nothing left between us.

"Let's go back to the others."

I walked beside her up the hill. We did not speak, and I became aware of the others watching us as we approached. Roy's eyes were particularly sharp, and they darted from Ellen to me and back again. I thought of offering him an ugly grin, but I did not have it in me just then. Shelby took my hand when we reached them, and broke any ice.

"Well, we're wondering if we're ever going to get to eat," she said. If I did not know her better I would have thought she fit right in here. "And I am *ravenous.*" With those words her eyes met mine, her hand squeezed mine and a secret signal was sent between us that let me know she expected a reward for how well she had played her performance tonight. Particularly where Chris Wheeler was concerned: He seemed no worse for wear, and I assumed if Shelby's hatchet was not buried it was at least put away for the duration.

Ellen reminded us who was the rightful leader of our dinner party and said, "Shall we?" ushering us with her hands toward the thinning serving lines.

We took our places and moved briskly toward the tables.

Prescott's service was efficient and before long I had an oversized, compartmented paper plate in my hands. It was a plate designed to accommodate abundance, but there was so much abundance that the plate's compartments soon became crowded. Potato salad and coleslaw came first. Then I took some of the cucumbers Prescott had praised and spooned up some black-eyed peas and also some pintos. There was a tureen of dark collard greens and I took some of those, along with three deviled eggs from the ranks of hundreds (and whoever deviled the second one should seek another dish to bring to the next gathering). I passed on the hush puppies but helped myself to the corn bread. I was unable to resist some creamed onions but managed to avoid a second wave of potato salad. Roy and Ellen moved through the line ahead of Shelby and me; Chris and Cindy followed. They spoke with others and we said hello as well, acknowledging every good wish and invitation to take more food. It was a jovial line, everyone nodding and talking and nibbling, a steady happy hum, people cooing over this dish or that, urging one another to sample this dish or that, teasing over the paucity of some plates, laughing at the gluttony evident upon others. Everyone took plenty, and even the most conservative or finicky soon found themselves struggling with plates beginning to buckle under the stress of the load.

At last we neared the long table on which Prescott's pigs rested. Two pigs remained over the coals, and the carcasses on which the reverend carved were nearly bare. He held up his hands. "Folks! Going to be just a minute here while we get the other pigs off the fire. Just nibble on what you've got on your plates and we'll be moving again in a second." He motioned to his helpers, who carried the stripped carcasses to a waiting table and then followed him to the pit. He gestured and shouted as they lifted the spitted pig and walked it to the carving table. While they fetched the other pig from the covered cooker I ate a deviled egg (the wrong one) and then quickly chewed some cucumbers to clear the egg's taste from my mouth. The Duncans and the Wheelers said nothing to us as we waited, but Shelby was eyeing my plate with a mixture of bemusement and embarrassment. I chewed happily, and after a moment Prescott was working with his tools, sectioning the pigs for carving. The line began to move again.

"Here you go, Roy," he said, cutting a thick slab from the spit-cooked pig and placing it on Roy's plate. "Now, son, you just move on out of the way while I give your pretty wife here a kiss, that is if she doesn't mind getting sauce all over that pretty blouse of hers." Ellen leaned forward and Prescott gave her a quick peck on the cheek. "Now, Ellen, you need more food on your plate than that, eating for two, you know," he said as he served her barbecue.

It was Shelby's turn next and Prescott studied her for a second. "I think some nice shoulder for you, Miss Oakes," he said, and put two slices on her plate. "You let me know how you like that." Shelby thanked him and moved on, and then it was my turn.

"Well, Baird, I have been waiting for you," Prescott said. He studied my plate. I'd left a space in the center for the barbecue, but it was no longer a very large space. "Looks like you didn't miss too many dishes," he said.

"And I'm going to be back for every one I did miss," I said. "Once everybody's served."

Prescott smiled at me. "Don't make promises before you eat, son, but we'll see." Laughing, he set to work with his knife and long fork, slicing and tearing from each pig, lifting thick pieces of meat onto my plate and all but covering the other food there. He must have put half a pound of barbecue on my plate. I thanked him and tried to move on. "Now, just wait a minute, son! That's not all for you! Here comes the surprise. I want you to have a couple of these ribs here." He plopped them on top of the barbecue. "And this—son, this is my special treat. This is pure crackling pork skin, crunchy and dark and good as it can be in spite of what Betty and the doctors say about cholesterol. You just chew on that and be sure you tell me how much you love it." He wagged his knife at me. "Now move on, move on before that plate falls apart and you waste all that food."

I followed Shelby to the table Roy and Ellen had selected for us. Ellen was already seated, and I saw Roy getting a pitcher of iced tea and a stack of plastic cups. Shelby was opposite Ellen, leaving me to face Roy, and Chris Wheeler, who sat at his side. Cindy Wheeler was perched on the other side of me. Ellen took the pitcher from Roy and poured tea for us all. The Duncans and the Wheelers bowed their heads briefly before they ate, and Shelby may even have tipped hers, but I dug in.

The barbecue was as delicious as Prescott had promised. There were dishes of sauce on every table, but Prescott's pork needed no enhancement. It was sweet, tender and smoky. And it held our attention, for there was little conversation at our table; we were all too busy eating. I surprised myself by eating everything on my plate, and astounded Shelby by finishing her meal. She had not left much. At last I sat back, stuffed. I felt peaceful and drowsy, able to forget that I had broken bread with a man who would like to break me. I looked at Roy and became aware of Ellen's eyes on me.

"Baird Lowen," she said, "you had better not be full, not after all the work we put in on desserts." She smiled, and if it was not a genuine smile, it was enough to set the mood for our after-dinner conversation. What business remained between Roy and me could be done later, and the look that Ellen showed her husband insured that he would honor her wishes.

"Just let me catch my second wind, Ellen," I said. "And be sure you let me know which desserts are yours."

"Tell you what," she said. "Shelby, why don't you, Cindy and I go get some desserts for the table?" The ladies rose and left me alone with Roy and Wheeler, but we did not have time to speak, for we saw Frederick Prescott approaching us. He sank to his knees on the grass beside our bench, and I thought for a moment he was going to pray. But he only said, "Now, Baird, just how was it?"

I did not lie. "Everything you promised, Reverend, and more." I gave my stomach a thump. "Incredible meal, incredible."

"Well, that's wonderful to hear. I told you—and I told you there wouldn't be room for seconds."

"Reverend, there won't be room for dinner *tomorrow!*"

He laughed at that, Roy and Wheeler joining in. "Chris, how's that front line looking?"

"Championship this year, Reverend. We all feel it."

"Baird, you know Chris is the best football coach with the best team in our conference?"

"Is he?"

"You ought to see those boys play. He's got a lineup—well, it's the best line I've seen in all the years we've had the college. We're all living for this season."

Coach Wheeler took the compliment as though it were a well-thrown pass. "Reverend," he said, "we're going to give you that championship. I promise."

"May just hold you to that, Chris," said Prescott. He rose to his full height. "Now here come your ladies, and Baird, it looks like you better get ready to eat some more."

Shelby sat down next to me with a paper dish of cobbler and a plate bearing a slice of chocolate cake. "This is Ellen's," she said, and indicated the cobbler. "And the cake is Betty's."

"I made deviled eggs," said Cindy Wheeler to the reverend, but I held my own counsel.

Prescott laid a hand upon my shoulder and gave a squeeze. "Baird, I'll say again that I thank you for coming tonight. I enjoyed our little talk and I think we ought to have another one real soon. You stop by my office and we'll tussle things out." He lifted his hand from me. "And you two stick around here tonight.

Early yet. Gospel sing'll be starting up again in a few minutes, soon's everyone's done eating. Hope you'll stay for it."

I looked at Shelby but she gave me no lead to follow. "We'll see," I said.

"Good, good. And let me see you two in my church this Sunday, too. That'd mean a lot to me, and even more to you two."

"We'll see," I said again.

"All right, then. Roy, Ellen, good to see you. Cindy, always nice. Chris—you give me that championship. Work those boys *hard* at practice tomorrow."

"You just keep some shelf space open for the trophy, Reverend," Wheeler said.

"You know I will. I got to get along, now. Say my howdys to some other folks. All these folks." He let out a satisfied sigh. "It's just *something*, isn't it?" Frederick Prescott said, and then gave a nod of his great head and turned and walked off.

I grinned at Roy and then at Chris. "Dessert?" I said.

Shelby and I shared the cobbler, and cooed our compliments to Ellen. We managed only a bite or two of Betty's cake, which was outstanding, but we could eat no more. Shelby stood up and stroked the back of my neck. "Why don't we take a walk, Baird?" she said, and began gathering our empty plates.

I stood up and looked at our dinner companions, one at a time. "The reverend's right," I said. "This has been just *something*." I picked up my plates. "And now Shelby and I are going to take a walk. If I don't see you again tonight, I'm sure we'll see each other real soon," I said, and looked at Roy as I spoke.

"Stop by before you leave Samson," Roy said. "If you care to."

"We'll see," I said one more time. I looked at Ellen and she looked at me, then began to clear the table.

Shelby and I dropped our trash in a nearby can, and headed up the hill. Before we'd gone twenty feet we heard His Dulcet Tones begin their warm-up. The air, still scented with hickory smoke, began to fill now with music. I put my right arm around

Shelby's shoulders. She leaned against me, hard, and I kissed her hair. "You okay?" I said softly.

"There was a pie," she said, her head against my shoulder, "the biggest cream pie I have ever seen. It had meringue as tall as Betty Prescott's hair. And it was all I could do to keep from taking the whole thing and shoving it in Chris Wheeler's face."

I laughed. She put her arm around my waist and gave me a squeeze. "Take me away from here," she said.

"Wherever you say. Your place?"

Shelby shook her head. "Not after all this . . . holiness." She began to laugh, deep in her throat. It was almost a growl. Her fingers dug suddenly into my side. "After all this, I want something—tawdry. Really."

"Name it," I said.

Shelby caught her breath, and from the corner of my eye I watched her chew her lip for a moment. Then a grin, and it was a lovely, wicked grin, spread across her face. "After all that barbecue there's only one thing to do."

"What's that?"

"Get some beer and go screw in a motel room," she said.

"Let's go." We walked faster.

As we neared the patio we were ambushed by Betty Prescott. She couldn't believe that we were going, and wondered openly if we had not been taught that it was rude to eat and run.

"Betty, you know we'd love to stay. But it's been a long day for both of us. And that meal! It just filled us up. Tell the truth, I might've been able to stay if I hadn't had a piece of somebody's fantastic chocolate cake. But that just topped me off, and if we don't head on right now we might just nod off right here on the ground."

"Baird Lowen, you know very well whose cake that was, and you don't get off the hook that easy. But I'm not going to argue with you. I'll just thank both of you for coming. It's meant so *much* to the reverend and myself to have you two join us here tonight." She held out her hand and I gripped it and then Shelby gripped it. "Now you take Shelby on home; see her to the door and you go on home yourself."

"Thanks, Betty," I said. "See you."

"In church this Sunday, I hope." Betty Prescott took a step back, she would not block our way. "Take care you two."

Shelby and I walked to the car. Roger was nowhere in sight. I steered carefully among the other vehicles toward the driveway. As we approached the gate the young guard stepped up to wave us to a halt. He leaned down until his face was only inches from mine, eerily illuminated by the soft dashboard lights.

"Goodnight Mr. Lowen, Miss Oakes," he said. "Hope you enjoyed yourselves."

"We did," I said. Another car pulled up behind us and he stepped back to let us go. I drove through the gateway and onto the road, accelerated and we were away. We passed Roy and Ellen's house, and we passed the white gazebos in their corner parks. Shelby rubbed my neck as I drove. I said to her, "Next stop: that motel room."

"No."

"Changed your mind?"

"No." Her hand drifted to my chest and then across my stomach. "Oh, no. But let's do this right. Drop me off at my house. Then you get some beer and go to the motel." She leaned close and whispered into my ear. "If you want to make it real exciting you could change the room registration."

"To?" I tightened my grip on the steering wheel.

"Mr. and Mrs. John Smith. Or Joe Smith." Her breath was hot. "I'll meet you there a little later. We need a secret knock so you'll know it's me."

"Interesting," I said.

Her hand floated lower. "Not as interesting as it's going to get."

She would not let me pull into her driveway. "Just drop me

at the curb and you go get whatever rest you can. Because you're going to need it."

"I'll hold you to that," I said.

"Oh, you certainly will," said Shelby, and she got out of the car and came around to the driver's side and leaned as close as Prescott's gateman, and then closer, her face lovely in the dashboard light. She gave me a kiss that I would not forget and then darted away and skipped across her lawn. Shelby waved quickly from her front porch and then went into her house.

I stopped at a 7-Eleven near the motel and bought a six-pack and then hurried back to the motel. I put the beer on the counter beside the bathroom sink, and took a quick look around the room. It was as fine as it was going to be. I turned down the bed, then took the thin plastic ice bucket and walked outside and down the walkway to the machine. I filled the bucket and returned to my room. I'd left the door slightly ajar and a sliver of light showed around its edges. I did not reach the room.

They came out of the shadows, from hiding places among the parked cars. There was no one to see them. They seized my arms and I dropped the bucket, ice cubes scattering. A low voice I did not recognize said, "Don't try to fight; don't even make a sound. You're coming with us. We have some things to say to you."

CHAPTER 20

THERE WERE THREE OF THEM holding me, and a fourth sitting behind the wheel of the green Taurus toward which they steered me. The engine was running. I made one attempt to free my arms, but there was no point to it and I stopped trying. They had a grip on me that I could not break, and I supposed from their look they were football players. Even in the gloomy light of the motel parking lot they had the look of earnest Christian athletes. Each stood over six feet, each had shoulders that seemed a yard wide. I did not recognize any of them. I knew the uniform, though: dark slacks, white shirts. New Spirit clothing, and no attempt to disguise it. Identical haircuts, short and neat. Their posture was good even as they held me.

They pushed me into the backseat of the Taurus. One of them sat on each side of me. I took a last quick look around to see if there were any witnesses, but there was no one. We left the motel.

"All right," I said as we pulled onto the road. "Where to now?" The initial surge of adrenaline was fading. I felt no particular fear, but was sure that it would come. I wondered if they had participated in Mitch Tarr's death, and decided that before the evening was over I would ask them. I did not think they were going to kill me.

"Be quiet, please, Mr. Lowen," said the young athlete on my left. "You have nothing to say to us."

"No? I'm—"

"Be *quiet,*" Mr. Lowen, said the player on my right. "We'll give you a chance to say some words. We're just going someplace private first, where we won't be overheard. We have some things to say, too."

I permitted myself a laugh. "Going parking with four guys on a Friday night," I said. "Who would have thought?"

"Just a quiet place for a quiet conversation, Mr. Lowen. That's all."

"Coach Wheeler have a name for this particular play?" I said. "Split right kidnapping, maybe? Go long abduction?"

"Be quiet," said the boy to my left, more firmly.

"Let him talk," said the driver.

Invited, I fell silent. I had questions but I doubted if they would answer them, just as I doubted that I would be hurt. I felt sure this was just a little scare for Baird Lowen, something Roy and Wheeler had cooked up to hasten me out of town. I sat still and kept my eyes open. It did not take long to tell where we were going.

We passed Spirit City. Prescott's barbecue was still going on, I supposed, gospel singing picking up steam now, His Dulcet Tones making everybody's spirit *move.* I wondered how many people at the barbecue knew where I was just now, or what was in store for me. Perhaps a half mile beyond the main entrance to Spirit Center, the driver took a sharp right onto a dirt construction road. We bounced along the road for a time, then he swerved right again, onto a much narrower path. Trees hugged close on both sides. More than one limb brushed against the side of the car, and rocks skittered off its pan. We rode close to a mile into New Spirit woodland, at last coasting down a steep hill to emerge into a clearing the size of a football field. The driver took the Taurus to the center of the field and stopped it there. I was shoved and dragged out of the car. Four tall young men stood close to me.

I looked around. On a high hill in the distance, visible even

over the tops of the trees, stood New Spirit's famous and un-
mistakable transmission tower. It was the most famous broadcasting tower in the South, perhaps in the entire country, and
Prescott kept it in place despite having long since moved to satellite distribution of his programs. The tower's fame derived not
from its height, but from its adornment: Halfway up the east face
of the tower was suspended an enormous white cross, one hundred feet tall with a fifty-foot crossbar. Red lights winked at various points on the cross.

"You look at that tower," said one of the young men. "You
look at that cross symbolizing for all to see the death and the resurrection of our Lord Jesus Christ."

"How could I miss it?" I said.

"You've missed something, Mr. Lowen."

"What's that?" I wondered if Shelby had gotten to the motel.
I wondered what she would think when she arrived there and I
was missing. Then I felt my first fear—were there other fine
young men waiting to take Shelby? Had there been any waiting
in the bushes at her home? "That's enough," I said. "You've had
your fun—"

"This isn't *play,* Mr. Lowen," said the one who'd driven us
here. "But it is a pleasure to show a nonbeliever what he has
missed."

"You do everything your *coach* tells you to do?"

"We're acting on our own, sir. Serving the Lord."

"By dragging me into the woods? Some service. What would
the reverend say?"

"We wouldn't bother the reverend with this," said the one
who'd sat to my left. "He has higher matters to concern him. And
you will say nothing of this, either. When we're done tonight,
when you have given your prayers, you are going to leave."

"Prayers? You boys may be good athletes, but you haven't
done your homework on me."

"Sir, you have a smart mouth."

"I've been told."

"Watch that mouth, sir. You've done enough foolish things tonight."

"Have I?"

"You should not have attended the reverend's barbecue tonight. It was a mockery."

"Tasted good, though," I said. Prescott's food sat like a stone in my stomach. I had some heartburn.

"It was wrong. Your presence defiled it."

"*Defiled?* Learn that word in minister class?" I looked around, trying to get my bearings. I did not think I could outrun all of them.

"We are studying to preach the gospel, yes."

Another spoke up. "I was called to preach when I was ten. I was called by the Lord himself."

"You've never heard that call," the driver said.

"No. I was out."

"Watch. That. Mouth," said the one who'd sat to my left, and gave me a hard shove that sent me back against the bumper of the Taurus.

The driver moved close before I could speak, and put his hands on his hips. "Mr. Lowen, we have brought you here to pray, and for us to pray for your soul. Sir, we can show you the path to your salvation."

"All of this in one night."

"In just a few minutes, Mr. Lowen. That's why we're here."

"And if I don't listen?"

"You will listen. You will listen while we preach."

How many sermons had I heard since coming to Samson? Since visiting Betty? Or Mitch? I had heard enough. I looked toward the edge of the woods.

"Let us pray," said the driver.

The others came to me and placed their hands on my shoulders, pressing. "Sink to your knees before God," one of them said, and I had no choice but to do so. I knelt and put my hands against the ground, feeling for a rock, for something I might use as a weapon. But the ground was as clean as if it had been swept. I bowed my head and braced my feet. I began to breathe quietly but deeply.

The driver led the prayer. "Oh, Heavenly Father, we have brought you a sinner tonight. A man who has shown sin as an example to others by way of his movies, and who has encouraged young people toward sin. Show him now the proper path," he said as I picked my path. "Show him as we pray in unison—"

I filled my lungs and, as they began to speak as one, I bounded to my feet, pushing off hard and running as fast as I could toward the edge of the woods. I caught them by surprise; I made good distance and got up some speed before they could react. I pushed, thinking of the long sprints at my farm, thinking of Shelby. If I reached the trees I could get back to her.

I almost made it.

Those four young men were without doubt outstanding football players. They came up fast, split apart, my head start no help after the first few seconds. They took after me from four separate directions, pushing their vectors ever closer, offering no path for a breakaway. I kept myself straight ahead, ran toward that forest, ran.

The driver took me down ten yards short of the trees.

The others helped him pull me to my feet. I gasped for breath. They shoved and prodded me back to the center of the clearing. One of them went to the Taurus and switched on the headlights. I shielded my eyes against their brilliance. The four football players stood facing me, their backs to the car. They took a step toward me as one, silhouetted, spooky. Two of them took my arms and held them tight. I strained, but they were still stronger than me.

"What purpose will this serve?" I said. I wondered, now, if they were going to kill me, but I did not ask the question.

"The purpose He gives us. The purpose we accepted when we were called to preach."

"Smiting the foes of the Lord? That's your service?"

"Sometimes it has to be done, Mr. Lowen. Some enemies cannot be persuaded by showing them the wonders that await. More direct methods must be used, but you should know that it is preaching, too. Now, hold him tight," he said.

Then they took grinning turns, beating me and praying for me until I passed out.

PART
FOUR

CHAPTER 21

SHELBY SAT ON THE EDGE of the bed, pressing a cool washcloth to my forehead. I watched with something like wonder as she took shape and came into focus and became Shelby. I tried to speak and I sought to sit up, but I could manage neither.

I felt as though every muscle in my body had been taken, not gently, and separated, and then reassembled with some pieces missing and the rest in the wrong order. I knew as I came more awake that I had never been in pain before that exact moment, there on the bed. Now I knew. I felt as though every nerve lay upon concrete and jagged rock.

Worry drew Shelby's features taut. She pressed the cloth softly over my forehead and touched it delicately to my cheeks. It felt as though she was pounding me with a small hammer. She began to cry.

"Oh, Baird," she said. "What happened to you?"

I closed my eyes for just a second. It seemed that a month passed, and it was a long month, but when I opened my eyes Shelby was still there; she had not moved. She was taking care of me. I ran my tongue around the inside of my mouth. None of my teeth were missing. My mouth had never felt so dry. I took a breath and that hurt, too, a couple of ribs grating, a cough gathering—I did not want to cough. I looked up at Shelby and managed a croak. "D'rink," I said. I was a sick child.

She nodded and took a clear plastic motel cup from the bedside table. She went to the bathroom and I could hear the tap running. When she came back she held the cup to my lips but allowed me only a small sip before withdrawing it. I kept the water in my mouth for a moment before swallowing.

"Can you talk?" Shelby said.

I nodded, but did not speak.

"Baird, what happened?"

I licked my lips. They were cracked and swollen. "I . . . had a litt'le meeting," I said, and then found myself laughing and crying at the same time.

"Baird," Shelby said. "I've got to call a doctor, the police. I have to."

It took hours for me to move my hand the three inches to her wrist. I could not close my fingers. "No," I said, and a vague memory floated up of someone saying the same thing last night. How had I gotten back to the motel? "P'lease. Talk."

"Baird—"

"How long . . ." I couldn't finish the sentence.

Shelby shook her head. "I came last night, like we planned." She brushed my cheek with the fingers of her right hand. "But you weren't here. The door was open. I saw the car, your car. I waited, but you never came back." She took a sip of the water, then held the cup to my lips again. "I didn't know what to do, who to call. I sat down, waited, dozed off, I guess. About three I heard something and there you were, outside the door. I didn't see who brought you."

"I did," I said.

"Do you remember coming inside?"

"No."

She closed her eyes for a moment. "You were . . . barely conscious, not making any sense. I don't think you really knew where you were. I got you inside. And—"

"Anybody . . . see?"

Shelby shook her head again. "No. I don't think so. I got you to the bed. I was going to call the police. But you said—" Shelby gave a quick, harsh laugh. "It was like a goddamned movie script."

"What?"

"You said, 'No cops,' and then you passed out. I've been sitting here beside you."

I did not remember saying anything. I remembered nothing but the feel of their fists and the look of their faces. "Time is it?"

Shelby looked at her watch. "Eight-thirty."

"Day?"

"Saturday. It's Saturday morning, Baird, I've *got* to—"

"No, Shelby."

"You can't *see* yourself. Who *did* this to you?"

"Wheeler's boys," I said with some difficulty. "Football boys."

"But why?"

I tried to smile for Shelby, but when I saw her expression I stopped. "It's all right," I said.

"All *right*? For God's sake, Baird, you've been *beaten!*"

"Yes. For God's sake—"

"It's not funny. You could have been killed. They could have killed you. You might be bleeding inside. Or broken bones. Or— Baird, I *have* to get some help."

I shook my head, which was a mistake. I breathed sharply and squeezed my eyes shut. She couldn't call a doctor or the police. What could I tell the police? That I was beaten by a bunch of holy jocks, Prescott's first team? It would just complicate things, and things were complicated enough already. It was time to begin simplifying. I lay on the bed and thought of how much I wanted to end it, the whole thing, and I wondered how long it would be before I had the strength. I kept my eyes closed and tried to take an inventory of my pains but they melded together, becoming an alloy of aches, constant and deep. They had done a job on me. But I was not dead and I did not think I was dying. No permanent damage. Perhaps these young men were skilled at beating heathens. Maybe this was their favored form of persuasion, their best skill in service of their Lord. Maybe they knew just how many times, and how hard, and in what areas of the anatomy, they could hit in order to wound, and to warn, but still leave sufficient health to heed the lesson they offered.

I accepted the lesson. I had learned something at last. I had thrown away too much by not learning. Before Roy came to my house—was that just a week ago?—I had been willing to waste my time doing nothing, and since coming to Samson I had wasted my time—and maybe Mitch's life—by doing too many things wrong. Lessons learned. Through my pain I made the same resolution and vow I had made at the barbecue. Was that just last night? I would have an end to this. There were people who had lessons of their own to learn from me.

I opened my eyes and looked at Shelby. "Love you," I said.

"Ah, Baird." A tear made its way down her cheek.

"Tell you what." I coughed.

"I'm going to call a doctor."

"No. Tell you what. You be my nurse and that's all I want."

"Baird. Really."

"No. Let me sleep. Stay here and I'll be all right."

"You shouldn't—"

But I had closed my eyes and was sleeping. I did not dream.

I woke before noon and the pain was no better, but I thought that I might be. My thinking was clearer. Shelby helped me into a hot bath. The water felt as though it was eating into my skin. I managed not to scream. I grew accustomed to the heat and lay in that tub without moving, a hot cloth over my face. I stayed in the tub almost half an hour, taking the heat into my bruises and wounds, filling my lungs with steam. I mumbled a list of items to Shelby, and she went out to get them while I soaked. I almost wept when I heard Shelby return.

When I got out of the bath I almost felt better. Shelby had a tube of ointment and she rubbed me with it. I found the strength to put an arm around her. She had brought back Chinese food, and a large Styrofoam cup of egg-drop soup for me. I wrapped a towel around my waist and sat in a chair and drank all the soup. While Shelby ate, I stepped into the bathroom to have a look at myself in the mirror. I had avoided it during my bath.

I could barely look at my reflection now. Stomach and shoulders puffed and purple. Both cheeks swollen. Lips split, hands stiff, knuckles bruised and torn. Maybe I had gotten in a few blows of my own. I intended to find out.

I thought of what I planned to do, and thought of how little I looked like a hero. But I planned my tasks nonetheless, and tried to see if I was ready for them. I closed the bathroom door and stood before the mirror. I stretched my arms out parallel to the floor, slowly extended my fingers and tried to twist at the waist. For a moment I thought I would vomit. I drew a heavy, ragged breath and tried again. I did three slow deep knee-bends against every joint's protest, and thought I might cry out each time. I considered trying to touch my toes but gave that up.

I leaned against the counter for a moment, then stepped to the tub, and despite the bath I had been in half an hour earlier, I turned on the shower. I heard Shelby call me but I did not answer her. I played with the temperature, then reached up against my shoulder's protest to adjust the spray. I undid the towel and stepped into the shower and stood beneath the spray without moving, letting it beat against my bruised body. I hurt a little less, or was better able to handle the pain, with every drop that struck.

The light in the bathroom changed and it was Shelby coming in. "Baird," she said, and drew back the shower curtain to look at me. She looked at me for a time, and I looked at her and let her see me. She did not say anything, but slowly removed her clothes and stepped into the shower with me. She took a washcloth and a small bar of soap and began gently and carefully to wash me, rinsing away the very ointment she had just applied. After a few moments I took the cloth from her, and the soap, and washed Shelby, forcing myself once more to bend and stretch to reach all of her. She moved close and at last we kissed, but cautiously, for my lips were rough and tender.

Shelby helped me from the shower. We dried each other and made our way to the bed, where she lowered me onto my back, and then lowered herself, more slowly and gently than I would have thought possible, onto me. She moved above me in the light of early afternoon. I lay beneath her, flowed at her guidance, let my pain seep away. I watched her, saw the concern and the concentration on her face. When at last I rose up within her, she braced herself against the headboard to keep from tumbling onto me, every muscle for a moment taut; then she settled more gently than a feather against my chest, and I felt no pain but only her wonderful warmth and weight. She covered my swollen face with kisses. It seemed as though we had both come from someplace far away, and that though the journey had been a fearful delight, the homecoming was a wonder.

By two o'clock I was getting dressed, and doing my best to calm Shelby's anger or at least ignore it. "This is crazy," she said. "*You're* crazy for even thinking about something like this." She put her clothes on furiously, thrusting an arm through a sleeve, jerking her legs into her shorts. "And I'm crazy for even thinking about helping you. Dammit, Baird, you don't need a hospital, you need to be committed."

"Shell," I said, "you don't have to come."

"Don't I?" she said with some defiance. "Really?"

"No. I wouldn't ask you to."

"You silly son of a bitch. Do you think you'd have to *ask?*"

"No."

"You're damned right, no." She laced and tied her tennis shoes. "This is the stupidest move yet, and it'll serve you right if you keel over."

"I want to see them," I said. "I want to see them practice ball, and I want them to see me."

"Jesus Christ," said Shelby Oakes.

. . .

The athletic field at New Spirit College was expansive and beautifully maintained. Its centerpiece was the football stadium, concrete bleachers rising high on either side. The New Spirit team was running scrimmage on the field under Chris Wheeler's guidance. Shelby and I stood in the shadows of one of the concourses that lead to the bleachers on the home team side. We had passed a few people on our way to the stadium, but no one we recognized. We had turned a couple of heads, but I felt certain that was more a result of my appearance than any recognition of who we were. Slowly, because I was not ready for Wheeler and his boys to see me yet, we moved from the shadows and turned to climb the stairs and take a seat.

A few people were in the stands, among them Frederick and Betty Prescott, watching their favorite team at work. They did not see us, and I made my step a bit more brisk, over the objections of my muscles, and moved in their direction.

Betty saw us first and started to wave a greeting, then looked more closely and clapped her hands to her face. "Baird!"

Prescott looked up at his wife's exclamation and echoed it. "Baird!"

They rose and hurried down the bleachers to us, reaching my side just as my knees failed. I twisted and sat down harder than I wanted to, Shelby crouching beside me. "I'm all right," I said. "Just a little shaky."

"Baird, what happened to you?" Betty asked.

"Son, you didn't have a wreck last night?" Prescott said.

I shook my head and took the time to remove my dark glasses so that they could see the twin shiners I'd earned. "Just a little run-in," I said.

"Oh, Baird, you look like you've been *beaten*," Betty said. Her surprise and concern was unmistakably genuine, and if she had been on any list of mine I would have removed her from it right then.

"Yes, ma'am," I said.

Betty touched my arm and said to Shelby, "Has he seen a doctor? He shouldn't be up and around."

"*You* try telling him," Shelby said. "I've decided you're absolutely right on this one, Betty. You can't do anything with a man."

Prescott's expression was stern. "You say somebody beat you, son?"

"I reckon my face speaks for itself, Reverend."

"You got any idea who?"

I nodded in the direction of the field. "What I'm here to find out."

"What are you saying, son?"

I would not let him have it that easily. "I'm here to take a look," I said.

"Not those boys, there," Betty said. "Not the *team*."

"Not all of them, anyway. Maybe not any. That's what I'm here to see."

Prescott sat down beside me, maybe harder than I had. "Baird, you cannot be right about this."

"Reverend, I hope I'm not. I do. Because I enjoyed your hospitality last night. We had a good talk and I ate your good food. And Betty, I did enjoy our conversation and I'll remember it. I'll read those books of yours. But I don't know how much you two know about why I'm here or what's going on. So I'll just tell you this.

A friend of mine who I didn't even know was my friend is dead. I could be, but I'm not. I just took a beating, and took it right here on New Spirit property. And since I'm not dead I'm going to stop dancing; and, Betty, you'll pardon me if I put my charm away. I hope you'll keep yours in place. I'm probably not going to be very polite, and you'll pardon me for that, too, because that's your nature. But I'm through with pardons and pleases. You've got some real problems with some of your . . . followers, and I'm not talking about their thinking. I'm talking about people getting killed and beaten within an inch of their lives, and little warnings and big threats. I'm tired of it, and I'm going to put a stop to it; and it may cost me more than I would like, and cost you, too. Those prices will be paid, by me, Reverend, or by you, or maybe by both of us. But some other people are going to pay, too. And now, if you'll pardon me just one more time, I'm going to watch some football and see if any of those people are here."

My sermon had cost me almost all that I had, and I looked at Shelby; but her eyes were on the Prescotts and the expression on her face made me proud, for it said, *I'm with him.* I took her hand and turned my attention to the football field.

"Baird," Prescott began, but I had nothing to say to him, nothing more to say. I leaned forward and focused on the field. Wheeler was looking toward the Prescotts and me and Shelby, but I did not even have the strength to wave at him; and would not have anyway, for that was a gesture and I was weary of *gestures.* Prescott was watching Wheeler. The coach shifted from foot to foot, then turned and blew his whistle to call another play. The team went through its motions and moves, but some of them were off their game and the play fell apart. The boys were wearing helmets, of course, and I could not make out their faces. We were too far away and my eyes were weary.

"Should have brought some binoculars," I said. I shivered a little against the cold, despite the afternoon heat. I felt a dizziness gathering, and closed my eyes for a second until it passed. I felt Shelby's hand in mine, and then Betty's hand on my back. She rubbed my back a bit, and I did not mind that.

"Baird," Prescott said again. I had not heard his voice so soft. "You're wrong about this, and I'll prove it to you. I don't know what happened to you; I know somebody got ahold of you and did a job, but it wasn't those boys down there. Couldn't be them; we don't do things that way."

"No?"

"No, sir, we don't. That's not our way, and you know that's not our way. Beat you up? Right after we fed you? No, Baird, you're wrong, and I'm sorry."

"So who was it, then?" I could not tell if any of the players were watching me, but something had shaken that front line, for they could not get their act to hold together; the rhythm of their routines was broken. I kept my eyes on them to make sure no one left the field. "Some strangers take me out, and preach to me in the shadow of *your* cross, on *your* land, and talk about *your* fine character, but they're not *your* boys? No, of course not."

"There's a simple answer for that, Baird." He rested a hand on my knee, gave a pat. "You should have thought of this yourself. It was somebody trying to make us look bad. Make you think it was our people. People are always trying to put New Spirit and me and Betty in a bad light. You've written some things yourself—"

"Words," I said. "Not fists. Not *fire.*"

"I'm not even going to answer that last. Son, your thinking's not straight. You need a doctor, might ought to be in the hospital."

"No," I said. "I want some answers."

"And I'm trying to give them to you."

"No, Reverend, you're not. You're telling me what you believe, but that's not necessarily what's *true.* Sounds like something you might say about me in one of your sermons, doesn't it? But I mean it. You need to take a hard look at a lot of things. Starting with that football team down there and moving right on to your Roy Duncan."

"Oh, Baird," said Betty Prescott, "what does Roy have to do with this?"

Prescott did not let me answer his wife. "Son, I've had about enough of this kind of talk. It's nobody's secret that there's some bad blood between you and Roy, old blood."

"New blood, too," I said. "On Roy's hands. Mitchell Tarr."

"Shelby!" Betty said sharply. "Get this boy some help."

"Baird's doing fine," Shelby said.

"You, too?" Prescott said.

Shelby nodded. "Listen to Baird, Reverend. You talk a lot about listening. *Listen* to him."

Wheeler's whistle sounded again and I turned my attention back to the field. "Looks like he's giving his boys an early afternoon. Four of them, anyway. Wish I'd had a closer look."

I could almost hear Prescott thinking, and did hear him when he made up his mind. "Coach!" he hollered, rising to his feet and cupping his hands around his mouth. "Coach Wheeler! Hold up those boys! We're coming down."

I needed help to make it down the bleachers, and Prescott was there beside me, supporting me at the elbow with his big hands. We walked to the chain-link fence that ran the length of the field. Wheeler waited there for us, his eyes narrow. "Yes, sir?" he said. His team waited midfield, watching us.

"Coach, call your boys over," Prescott said. "Baird here's a football fan. Wants to meet that championship line of yours."

"I really hate to break their stride—"

"Coach, looked to me you were sending some of them to the showers early. Call them over."

Wheeler held his ground for only a second longer, then turned and waved his team to join us.

They took their time.

"Boys," Prescott said when they were before us. "Take off those helmets and visit a minute. Got somebody here wants to meet you. His name's Baird Lowen, and the young lady with him is Miss Shelby Oakes." He allowed himself a smile, and it was aimed at Shelby. "More probably it's *Ms.* Oakes."

"More probably," she said, but said it smiling.

Helmets off, there was no mistaking them. "Good to meet you boys," I said to the team. "And good to see some of you again."

Prescott turned to me. "Baird—"

"Number twenty-three," I said. "twenty-six and thirty-one." The player whose jersey sported 14 sported himself a whale of a black eye. Odds were it came from hard scrimmage, but there were shorter odds that I liked better. My knuckles gave me a twinge of pride.

Prescott was flustered but only for a moment. "You're standing by your story?"

"Standing right here, Reverend."

He grunted deep in his throat. "Those boys you pointed out. That's Terry MacNamara, Cal Johnson, Tom Evans and Brett Hargetay. Fearsome foursome, they got called in *Sports Illustrated*. Best in the conference."

"You must be very proud of their skills," I said to Wheeler, who did not answer me. I turned to Betty. "Nancy Hargetay's brother?" I said. She nodded.

I looked at the players one at a time, looked at each of them until their eyes dropped and they would not return my stare. "I've seen what I came here for," I said to Prescott, and turned my back on his team.

"Coach Wheeler," Prescott said with no emotion or expression in his voice. "Have those boys, those . . . that *foursome* in my office at five this evening. You be there, too. Now get back to your practice."

"Frederick—" Betty began, but he waved her off, then reached over and squeezed her shoulder by way of apology. "We'll talk about it later, Betty. Right now let's get Baird to a doctor. Jack Latham lives over in Spirit City; we'll go there. He ought to be back from golf by now."

He took my arm again. "Come on, Baird," Frederick Prescott said. "Let's get you looked after."

CHAPTER 22

SHELBY AND I CUDDLED AND cooed in her bed over coffee and the Sunday paper. She made me brew the coffee and fetch the paper, saying, "If you're well enough for the stunt you pulled yesterday, you're well enough to wait on *me.*" I was happy to oblige.

We were up early, well before seven, and I was surprised at how well I felt. True, I had never been stiffer in my life, but the deep ache, the weakness, was diminished. Prescott's doctor had been thorough. A couple of cracked ribs, some pretty serious bruises. But I would heal and I would live. He asked how it happened, but Prescott steered the conversation in other directions.

They were grim, Frederick and Betty Prescott, that afternoon, and unwilling to reopen our conversation. That was fine with me. I did not have the energy. He could think about matters for a while, and get in touch, if he cared to.

I had a sip of coffee and turned the pages of the *Defender.* There was a two-page Sunday social feature on the barbecue. A following page had a picture of Roy Duncan addressing a Saturday evening convention audience. His topic: "God's Law, Man's Legal System—How Can They Be Combined?" The obituary page had a squib about Mitch.

"Feel like Sunday services?" I asked Shelby.

"Sunday servicing more like it," she said with a bawdy laugh. She snapped her fingers. "Hey! I never got that motel sex I asked for."

I looked at her. "Well, just what was that in the shower and—"

She touched a finger to my lips and looked into my eyes. "Love, Baird. That was love," she said softly. Then her grin returned. "I mean, you know—*motel* sex. *Dirty* stuff. Vulgar underwear."

"I've still got that room," I said, although I planned to check out that afternoon and move my things to Shelby's.

"Not there. Someplace . . . else."

"I'll see what I can do," I said.

"Soon, please."

"Promise." Now, I was serious. "Want to go to Sunday services?"

"At Prescott's church? What—"

I shook my head and showed her the brief news item. MEMORIAL SERVICE FOR MITCHELL TARR. It was to be held at one o'clock that afternoon in the conference room of an old downtown hotel not far from the ruins of Mitch's shop.

"Yes," Shelby said. "I'd like to be there."

"I'd like to be there with you," I said.

She nodded solemnly, then pushed the newspapers aside. "And as long as you're with me here now . . ."

We were lying together almost dozing in the afterglow when the telephone rang. Shelby answered it, said a word or two of pleasantry, then handed it to me.

It was Prescott. "How you feeling, son?"

"Better," I said. I was stroking Shelby's shoulder.

"Good. Betty and I are worried about you."

"I appreciated your help yesterday."

"That was nothing."

"How did your meeting go with Wheeler and his . . . boys?"

"Son, that meeting was behind my doors and I guess you'll understand if I keep the details to myself."

"If that's the way you want it."

"It is. For now, anyway. Why I called is to ask if you're feeling up to church this morning."

"Not today, Reverend," I said. "But put in a good word for me, will you?"

"Always, son, always. For Miss Oakes, too. Now, you're sure you can't be there?"

"I'm sure," I said.

"Well, then I want you to tune in my talk show tomorrow night at eight. What I have to say will keep 'til then I reckon, but not much longer. And what I have to say includes some things you need to hear."

"More sermons?"

"More in the nature of lessons, I guess. Some things I'm going to show that concern you. That concern both of us."

I felt a tremor of apprehension, but also of anticipation. What did he have to show? "Care to give a hint?"

He laughed at that. "You know I'd love to, son, but it's Sunday and I've got to run and preach. You tune in tomorrow night. You watch."

"I'll be there," I said.

We hung up.

"Shelby," I said. "You pack your vulgarest—we'll be in a motel room tomorrow night."

We let the rest of the morning drift away and at noon went out for a quick sandwich before Mitch's service. We took both cars. After the service I planned to check out of the motel, and then I had somewhere to drive to. I did not elaborate, and Shelby did not press me.

There were half a dozen people in the conference room when we arrived shortly before one. The hotel was still called the *Bentley*, but it had been in decline even when I was a teenager, and no arts council or condominium developer had yet stepped forward to arrest the slide. The Bentley had been a grand place once, and although the conference room carpet was faded and bore many burns, the walls remained beautifully paneled. Any other elegances were long gone, though. There were twenty cheap metal card chairs, divided into four rows, set before a small dais. On a tall easel in the center of the dais stood a large, striking photograph of Mitch at his most hirsute—beard untrimmed, ponytail unbound and fanned out like a matador's cape over his shoulders. I wondered if he had taken the photo himself, or if it was the work of one of the others in the room.

There were not many of them. The twenty chairs would not come close to being filled. The others had looked up as we entered the room, and I caught one of the two women looking our way. I looked at Shelby. "Know anybody?"

She shook her head. "Introduce ourselves?"

I glanced at my watch. It was one. "I don't think so. Sit in the back?"

She nodded and we stepped over to the fourth row and sat down. The others took seats as though responding to our cue. There were eleven of us altogether, seated in twos and ones. A man of nearly my height took the stage. His suit did not fit well, his cuffs were slightly frayed. He looked at us and nodded, then raised his eyes to look out over us.

"How he loved this room!" he said, and with a sweeping gesture invited us to look at the portrait of Mitch. "How *many* times have I sat where you are seated now, and watched our friend Mitchell on the stage. Or stood behind him, but within his aura, as *he* stood here and tried so hard to spread the truth. Press conferences," he said, "and colloquia, and calls to action. These walls that Mitchell loved in this hotel in this part of the city that he loved, yes loved. These walls bore witness to many of the most noble moments of Mitchell's life. Now they must try to contain our sorrow."

His voice was a drone, but we listened as he went on. "I'm Roger Sherburne. I was Mitchell's attorney and I was his friend.

For a time we were partners. And I've organized the gathering today. By all rights, this should be a press conference itself. I invited them, but I don't see any of Samson's fourth estate. So we'll just talk."

Sherburne looked for a long moment at the photograph, then turned to us once more, a look of chagrin on his face. "Those of you who know me well are not going to believe this. *Mitch* certainly wouldn't believe it. I'm not sure I believe it myself. But . . . I can't say anymore. I don't have anything . . . I don't know *what* to say. I loved him and that was true in so many senses of the word. But I—would someone else, could someone else? Please?"

A woman hurried from her seat and stepped onto the dais. She embraced Sherburne, and held him to her for a moment. Then he left the stage. She faced us, a tall woman in her late thirties, I guessed, with a bit of gray in her brown hair. She put her hands on her hips. "I know what Roger means," she said at last. "I do. Because Mitch was my friend, my mentor and my lover." That brought a couple of glances from the others in the room. "Not in any physical sense, you know that. I was not the way Mitch was bent, to use his phrase. But in the sense that our karmas, that aura of which Roger spoke so beautifully—and you *did*, Roger, Mitch would be proud. But Mitchell's karma embraced mine as a teacher's would, or a gardener's, and cared for mine as would a friend's." She smiled. "Roger, I have no more to say than you, it seems, but isn't that all right? Wouldn't Mitch understand that? Wouldn't he, though?" She held out her arms for us to feel the radiance of her aura, but this pause was even briefer than the one following Sherburne. Another man took the stage.

He was dressed like a cowboy biker and boasted a beard that nearly matched Mitch's own. "What Andrea said is right, but I think you know me well enough, most of you, to know that I am here to play the devil's advocate. Not to say the nice things, but to say the necessary things. Even here at this service—thanks,

Roger—I've got to do what Mitch would want done. As usual without the press, without any recognition of what's going on here. But Mitch would want this said.

"For Mitchell Tarr may have been ignored by the media, but he was not ignored by our government. They took him very seriously indeed, certain branches of it. And that flattered Mitch; it gave him confidence. Because their . . . interest proved to him that he was right. And because he was right, he attracted attention. And because he grew more right every day, and was attracting more attention every day, Mitchell was executed last Wednesday night by operatives of a deep black federal agency. Mitch knew they were watching him, and he would not let that scare him. He was going to expose them and their crimes against all of us.

"But they killed him." He stalked from the stage and sat down heavily, arms crossed over his chest, breathing hard in his leather jacket.

It got worse. We were told by a lovely and delicate older man that Mitchell Tarr had grokked the fullness of the universe and that it was a pleasure to share water with him. One man revealed that Mitchell had contributed hundreds of dollars he could ill-afford toward the development of a revolutionary communications device that operated on principles long suppressed by the United States government. A heavyset adolescent stepped forward to tell of how Mitch had introduced him to science fiction, had opened his bookshelves to him; he wondered if anyone knew what would be done with Mitch's collection. In the midst of one eulogy invoking power pulls and mystical trees, the cowboy biker stood and shouted "My God!" He smacked his forehead with his hand and announced that the delay in releasing Mitch's remains was part of the plot: No clonable cells could be allowed to exist. "My God!" he said, and sat down.

Eventually, no one else rose. Barely forty minutes had gone by. Roger Sherburne at last stood up. "Isn't there anything else?

Wouldn't anyone else care to speak?" He looked at Shelby and me; we were the only ones who had not offered a moment. I had nothing to say, but Shelby suddenly stood up and walked to the front of the room.

"I *liked* Mitch Tarr," she said. "I liked him a *lot.* This world is a poorer place for his passing." She came back to her seat, and took my hand.

"I suppose that's all, then," said Roger Sherburne. "Anyone caring to join us in the lifting of a toast can meet at Hooley's immediately after we leave here. Mitchell loved that bar. His ashes, so you know, are to be released later this week. Those who have suggestions for where they should be scattered can contact me."

"Why not cremate them?" the biker said.

"Dennis!"

"Mitchell would have liked that joke! That's the kind of joke *Mitchell* would have made!"

Shelby and I slipped out of the room.

"Sherburne was Mitch's lover?" I said as we walked through the lobby. Two elderly men slept in tattered chairs while the desk clerk watched television.

"Once upon a time," Shelby said. "A while ago. He wasn't seeing anybody lately, that I knew of. But I really didn't keep up with him. We just crossed paths now and then."

"It was nice, what you said. Good words." We stepped into a brilliant afternoon. It was barely two.

"Well, I *mean.* Somebody had to say that. Just those words."

"I'm glad it was you," I said.

We kissed quickly at her car. I told her I wouldn't be long. What I had in mind was just a short drive after gathering my luggage at the motel. She told me she'd count the minutes, then rolled her eyes.

I packed my bags quickly, loaded them into my car, settled my bill and accepted an unexpected piece of mail along with the desk clerk's hope that I return soon. I tucked the papers in my breast pocket, then headed out of Samson, along a route I'd known since childhood, although the countryside had changed since then. There were strip malls and wood-floored country stores where I'd once bought Cokes and peanuts. Some ponds that I had fished as a teenager were still there, though, and I could see a few teenagers fishing in them.

Then I was at the turnoff, and went down another six-and-a-half miles of blacktop, before stopping to unlock the chain and drive carefully down the dirt drive to the house by the lake. There were more houses here now than when Ellen and I were young, and across the lake there was a condominium community with boat ramps and a golf course. As I grew wealth I offered to buy the place from my father, but he would not sell. He intended to retire there, and he and my mother got down from Michigan once or twice a year. They would be down for Labor Day this year, and I wondered if I would bring Shelby to see them, and if she would come. I parked my car beside the house.

Before going inside I walked down to the edge of the water. Tadpoles darted back and forth, and I could see a few bluegill cruising close to the shore. Ellen and I had fished here as well as fucked. I walked back up the hill among the pine trees, unlocked the house and went inside. The air was musty and close, but I opened no windows. I would not be there long. I walked to the fireplace and sat on the raised hearth and stared at the sliding doors. I did not open the curtains. I knew what I would see: the hill sloping down to the lake, the trees, the woodpile and the bushes from whose cover we had been watched and photographed. That had been some guerrilla operation. I closed my eyes, but could not make Ellen come back to me.

Before long I rose, locked the place, drove slowly back to the blacktop, which I followed, taking random turns, avoiding highways and city limits. I put a tape in and listened to a song I loved, Patty Loveless singing "Nothing but the Wheel" in that startling voice of hers. There was a time, and not long ago, when I might have played the song again, and kept on driving with no set direction. That time was past. I had a place to go now. I came upon a store, a real country store. There was a pay telephone on its wall. I drank a Coke from a glass bottle, and ate a bag of peanuts, and called Shelby Oakes, and heard her say that she wanted me to come, that she wanted to be with me and wanted me to be with her. I drove back to Samson.

CHAPTER 23

SHELBY MADE LAUGHING FACES AT the mirrored ceiling. "My *God,*" she said, and laughed harder. The gaudy room delighted her.

I'd gone to some trouble to find it that morning, and book our reservation for the night, for the evening of Prescott's program. I checked in before returning to Shelby's, and inspected the room and tested the television. It was the largest screen available at any motel in Samson, a sports bar–sized big screen set in a lewd suite lined with mirrors. The motel was called Love-Inn and was itself a find: a neon palace of the flesh, no pretense about its purpose, blazing tacky defiance in the heart of New Spirit country. Spirit Central itself was only a couple of miles away. Shelby laughed harder as she bounced on the water bed and rubbed her fingers over the crimson brocade spread that covered it. She glanced at the red ruffled pillows. "Satin sheets?"

"What else?"

Shelby tossed her head and blew me a kiss. "When you go for motel sex, Baird, you go for *motel* sex."

"It was the TV that sold me. Prescott on the big screen."

"You sure a place like this gets his channel?" Shelby leaned forward and rested her elbows on her knees.

"I asked," I said, and began to laugh myself. "You should have seen her face at the desk. But they get Prescott—and three adult channels, and an in-house hard-core video feed. They've got four hundred films in their library!"

"Any of *your* movies?"

"I didn't ask," I said, and blew her a kiss of my own. "Didn't tell them who I was, either. We're Mr. and Mrs. Smith."

"You're so clever," she said.

"I try."

It was seven-fifteen. We had a bottle of good champagne on ice, and Shelby retreated to the bathroom to prepare for the program. I sat still in an overstuffed chair and listened to her singing in the shower. I felt a twinge in my ribs, and there was a low ache in my muscles, but I was feeling better by the moment. Shelby came out at twenty to eight, wrapped in a red silk robe that covered her from neck to ankles. "Depending on what the reverend says, you may or may not find out what's under this," she said, and kissed my ear. Her fingers tickled the back of my neck.

"Come on," I said, and slipped an arm around her waist, pulled her onto my lap. My fingers found the knot at the robe's belt. "Patience isn't such a great virtue. Let's see."

But she pulled away from me and stood up. "No way. You've got just enough time for a quick shower before the show." She added an extra knot to the belt. "All you need to know for now is that what's under this robe is just *so* appropriate for this room. Now, go!"

I didn't have a silk robe with me so I carried light slacks and a clean shirt into the bathroom. I ran the water as hot as I could stand it, and as cold, and was still standing under the spray when Shelby knocked. "Ten minutes!" she called. I turned off the shower, toweled myself, brushed my teeth. I dressed and looked in the mirror. I took a deep breath or two and then joined Shelby.

She had arranged so that we could recline on the bed and watch Prescott. The lights were turned down and the screen glowed with the final moments of a Christian news broadcast. Shelby looked up at me and patted the bed beside her. "Ready?" she said.

"More than," I said. I lay down on my side of the bed and

made myself comfortable against the pillows.

Shelby held the remote and waved it before me. "Here goes." She thumbed the mute and the room filled with New Spirit sound.

The screen faded to an image of a tranquil country sunset and a young couple walking away from the camera, each holding the hand of a small child. That scene faded forever, maybe the longest fade I'd seen, and when the screen was completely dark there was a drumroll, then a single spot of bright white light, a point, no more, in the center of the screen. The drumroll grew louder—it was thunder—and that point of light began to expand, an image slowly coalescing at its heart. The image was Prescott's broadcasting tower, shown cross-on, that huge cross. Then the cuts began. Fast cuts, jump cuts. New Spirit College . . . Prescott's church with its mighty steeple . . . Frederick and Betty Prescott's home . . . hundreds of happy faces . . . praying hands . . . bowed heads. Horns came up, an overscored horn section that drowned the drums, and the picture became live, a long pan over the evening's audience. Then the director shifted our perspective to that of a high camera from which you could see only a darkened stage. The music reached its crescendo, then stopped suddenly, giving us a beat of purest silence. But only a beat, for a brilliant spotlight came to life and illuminated the heart of the stage, which held a simple podium, and a deep announcer's voice addressed us:

"Live! Tonight from the stage of the Almighty's Auditorium on the campus of New Spirit College, on the grounds of Spirit Center, home of the world's *greatest* crusade for the Lord, the Reverend Frederick Prescott!"

And he walked out of the shadows and into the light.

Applause rose, and rose higher. He was there and he was *theirs,* their Reverend, standing tall and stern, dark suit and white shirt, shoes polished mirror perfect, light glinting from his carefully combed hair. He raised a hand, then raised it higher and the applause dwindled.

"Good evening," he said. "And God bless you."

There was applause again, and this time the director shared it with us by way of a shot from behind Prescott, over his left shoulder, showing us the reverend looking out at his clapping flock.

"Thank you," he said, and raised his hand once more. "My name is Frederick Prescott and I'm a minister for the Lord." He did not allow applause to build again. "I appreciate your hand, folks, but like the man said, this is a live broadcast, and we've got a good piece of ground to cover tonight. I have a lot I want to say."

He stepped to the podium and stood to one side of it, resting his forearm on its surface. "There are some hard truths and some wonderful glories I would share with you this evening; some business we must attend to; some stories you should hear; some people you'll enjoy meeting." He grinned, a friendly country preacher saying hello to worshippers in forty-six countries. "And we've only got ninety minutes. So let's get started."

Prescott moved behind the podium. "You know me, you know I'm going to get in at least one sermon this evening; so why don't I just go ahead and preach?"

Cheers accompanied the applause until Prescott raised his hand.

But as his hand went up his eyes went down, he bowed his head in contemplation and prayer, and when at last he looked up his eyes were squinting as he stared at us.

"To *smite!*" he said, his voice booming through the auditorium and bouncing off the satellite. He made a fist of his upraised hand. "To *beat!* To *chasten* with our blows those who do not share our love of the Lord!" He brought his fist down hard on the podium.

His voice became softer. "You can still find preaching like that, you know. And sometimes you can still find it coming from me. I still stir that hellfire and call up that brimstone once in awhile. Catch me on the right day and you'll find me doing a good job of it. You will.

"And it's a *contagious* sort of preaching. You know that? A good preacher, and I mean a *preacher,* you get a good one going full-out, and his congregation's going to get caught up, and they're going to be swept along with him, and they're going to leave that church or that tent or the side of that mount and they're going to carry with them a love of the Lord. *Yes,* but they'll also be carrying a love and a deep one for the *fire* that their preacher set ablaze in their blood. What a fire that is! How purely it burns, how hot it can be!"

Prescott stared out at us, both hands clenched and held before him. After a moment he opened his hands slowly to show us his palms.

"I've felt that fire. I have. So have you. So, I think, has anyone born into the arms of the Lord. How could you not feel it? *His* fire. *His* flame.

"I understand that fire, you know. I can think back—I've started a few of those fires myself. More than a few," Prescott said, and chuckled as he looked out at his congregation. "When you've got someone in just that right attitude, that state—when they're seeing Jesus and I mean really *seeing* him for the first time—it is such an *easy* fire to light. It is. Doesn't need much tending, you know that? It'll burn of itself once it's kindled. And burn and burn . . ." He shook his head. He stroked his upper lip for a moment, let his gaze drift left-to-right across the auditorium.

"It is a fire born of goodness, but I don't know anymore if it is a *good* fire." Prescott's eyebrows rose and he wagged a finger at us. "Now there are good fires, we all know that. You can start a smaller fire and stop a forest blaze. *Heat* can sterilize and it can cook. Boiling water can run a train, burning gasoline our cars.

"*But!* Those are our fires, the fires we start here on earth, here on this earth the Lord gave us. That fire in the soul, in the blood, in the heart and in the hands, that *Christian* fire!" He leaned forward fast and stared hard. "*That* fire may not be such a good thing," Frederick Prescott said simply.

He held the moment and did not speak. A couple of *amens* came from the congregation, a couple of coughs. "*Because,*" he said at last. "Because of what I just said. That fire doesn't need much tending. But that's not quite true. I thought it was; I did. I've taught it to others, taught it for years. Start that fire, set those Christian flames burning and cleanse the world. Do as Jesus says and burn the sinners out!

"But Jesus didn't say that. *I* did. And others who lived long before me did. And still others are saying it now. On other channels, but you can take my word for that, don't feel like you have to check." The laughter was welcome and Prescott waited it out. He laughed a little himself, and took one of his big handkerchiefs from his pocket and mopped his face. He put the handkerchief on the podium beside a book that was undoubtedly a Bible. "Cleanse the world. The Lord can do that with our help.

"But not by fire. After a fire, what's left? *Ashes.* And we must ask ourselves if that is how we see our duty as Christians. Is that our purpose? To burn, to return ashes to the earth? Is that what we should do? Let's think about that. What *are* we? *Who* are we? You know the answer. We are *His children.*

"And would we let *our* children play with fire?"

Prescott gave his followers a moment to chew upon that question, and his director gave the rest of us a moment's view of that audience lost in thought.

"No," the reverend said. "We would not. We don't. We put the matches up. We keep them clear of the cookstove. We put screens in front of the fireplace. Because children are not ready for the responsibility that fire brings.

"Looking around the world these days I do not know if *we* are ready to handle our Father's fire. I really don't. Waco. Oklahoma City. Bosnia. And I see littler fires but no less tragic on so many of our streets and in our schools and in too many homes. But big or little, there are deadly fires being burned in the name of Jesus everywhere, and signs everywhere that those fires are starting to burn out of control.

"You see, you can't beat the Devil out; but neither, I think now, can you burn the Lord in. You cannot. Abortion parlors," Prescott said, and here his face grew twisted. "You will find no one who hates those vile places more than me. But there are those who call themselves Christians who have set bombs in such places, and used guns to kill, and when the smoke has cleared and the bodies been carried away they claim they were serving some *militant* arm of the Lord.

"Well, the Lord has *two* arms and they are both reached out to embrace, not to smite. I know that; I feel that embrace.

"And in those hands the Lord has a fire that he gives to us, to light ourselves that we might better see, not to be touched to a fuse on a bomb.

"What does it say in the Book?" Prescott lifted his large Bible in one hand. "You know where I'm quoting; you know this chapter and verse. St. Luke. Eleven: thirty-three," he said, "we have read it so many times before. But let us read it now and hear it again.

" 'No man when he hath lighted a candle, putteth *it* in a secret place, neither under a bushel, but on a candlestick, that they which come in may *see* the light.'

"And thirty-four: 'The light of the body is the eye: Therefore when thine eye is single, thy whole body also is full of light; but when *thine eye* is evil, thy body also is full of darkness.'

"You remember thirty-five? You should: 'Take heed that the light which is in thee be not darkness.'

"And how about thirty-six? 'If thy body therefore be full of light, having no part dark, the whole shall be full of light, as when the bright shining of a candle doth give thee light.' "

Shelby touched my shoulder when I gave a soft laugh. "King James version," I said.

Prescott cleared his throat. "Does that speak to you? It does to me. Those are Jesus's words. *That's* preaching. It is.

"But does it speak of fire and does it even speak of heat? No. And if He doesn't, should we? The *light* is the gift, His great gift to us. Fire for light, to help us *see.* Too much heat burns, and that is not ours to do. Not to our fellow men. But there's no such thing as too much light. Not in this dark world.

"And in that light, with that light in *us,* we can find our way. Saying as it says in that same chapter of Luke, its second verse, 'Our Father . . .' "

The congregation joined him in the prayer, the picture fading as they said *Amen* with one voice.

A commercial began, showing us the campus of New Spirit College, earnest students bent over books, Prescott himself in classroom discussion groups. The announcer told us of the unequaled educational and spiritual resources the institution offered. I looked at Shelby.

"Feel the heat?" she said. "See the light?"

"Lots of talk of fire," I said, "but it was Mitch who got burned."

Shelby touched my temple and gave it a soft stroke of her fingers.

"Some sermon," Shelby said. I moved close to her, but she smiled and pushed me back. "I want to hear what else Prescott has to say before I let *you* whisper in my ear, Mr. Lowen."

The commercial droned on for another moment, closing with footage of the football team making a pledge to the flag. I saw the faces of my companions from Friday night. They did not look as tough to me as they had.

Then the screen faded briefly blank, and when the picture returned it was Prescott, but the setting had changed. He was in a comfortable paneled room behind a desk, surrounded by bookshelves and photos of himself and Betty. A man's study, a good place for a talk.

"Welcome back. You know, that's a good school you were just looking at. Of course I have to think that. Betty makes me."

Prescott grinned at us. "But it *is* a good school, and we're all proud of it. Gets stronger every year. In the classes and in the church. And on the field. Not too many schools our size field a football team as good as ours. Coach Chris Wheeler tells me he's got the makings of a championship season, got four men on his line who he'd put up against anybody anywhere in any conference.

"Which makes the film you're about to see all the more special."

Shelby's hand found mine and clutched it tight as footage began to roll.

"You know who these fellows are," Prescott said from location. My football friends, all four of them stood flanking him, two to a side, clean-scrubbed in bright daylight. Hargetay's black eye had barely faded: This was fresh film. "Terry MacNamara, Cal Johnson, Tom Evans and Brett Hargetay, the brightest stars in Spirit football!" The boys nodded in turn as their names were announced. "Champions, every one of them. Got written up in *Sports Illustrated,* got a shelf full of trophies and a wall full of ribbons. Our *Superstars.*

"But it's not football that makes them superstars. It's what's inside them: their dedication to the Lord, and to helping spread the Lord's message. And they're *real* dedicated boys. That's why we're here today."

The camera dollied back, revealing their location. Jets taxied behind them. They were at the Samson airport. My heartbeat rose.

"You see, these boys, our superstars, got concerned that they might be taking more satisfaction from knocking people down in the middle of a field than from saving someone from the fall. Being a superstar can do that to you. It can turn your head. But not *these* boys' heads. They've been thinking, and praying, and, yes, talking with me. And do you know what? They're going on from us in just a few minutes in one of those airplanes. Going on from New Spirit College and from football to play a tougher game on a far rougher field."

Prescott's face was solemn as he stepped in front of the boys, camera dropping to shoot up at him and keep them in his shadow. "There is a little village in Somalia," the reverend said. "Its name doesn't matter. It's like hundreds of others. Too much disease, too little hope. Too much war, too little food. Too much hate, too little love. Little babies, sick, starving, no muscles on their bones.

"Well, we know four big boys with plenty of muscle, don't we? And don't we know how proud we are of four boys like these who would give up their senior year, their last year of eligibility, the peaks of their careers, their best chance at a conference championship—giving up all that glory here to go share *His* glory there!"

Prescott turned and fixed the boys in his gaze. "And they're in a hurry to go. So much of one they can't even take any more time here with us. They've got a plane to catch, so run on, boys, run on and God bless you over there; may the good Lord watch over you and the work you're going to do, the might hardships and challenges you're going to face."

The boys turned and marched, but did not run, offscreen, and the film ended with a shot of their backs as they moved down the long airport corridor.

The next shot came back to Prescott at his desk. "You know, Coach Chris Wheeler would have been there to see those fine young men on their way, but he's got a line to rebuild. And he'll do it, too. We got a lot of fresh young talent coming up and I'm sure Coach Wheeler will make the most of it. Because he was as thrilled as I was at what those four boys have done with their lives."

Prescott stared at us for a moment. "Be right back," he said.

Another commercial came on. Shelby hit the mute button. "Africa," she said.

"The Dark Continent. Nice." I laughed.

"Out of sight, out of mind," Shelby said with a snort. She turned quickly, moving to her knees to stare down at me. "And that's all? Those poor boys miss their senior season? Chris doesn't get his championship? Some punishment."

"I think it is," I said. "I think it's just *fine*. Fitting. What more do you want? They didn't burn Mitch."

"You're so sure?"

I nodded. "Shelby, I am. I'd say the boys and I are even. I may even have come out ahead."

She did not break her gaze. "Don't you settle this too easy," she said.

"Don't worry about that. Shelby, I know what I'm after and I'm going to get it." I raised up and took her by the shoulders but did not draw her to me.

"You think so."

"I do." The robe was cool beneath my fingers. I gave Shelby a quizzical look. "What *have* you got on under this thing?"

Shelby pulled free of my grasp and moved far back on her side of the bed, her hands making a shield over the knotted belt. "Shame on you, Baird. Asking a question like that when the reverend's on TV."

"It's a commercial right now," I said. "And one of the reasons I picked this room was to see what you'd wear under your robe. In a place like this."

"Well, I gave that some thought," Shelby said. "And I think you'll like what you find. But not until after the show."

The commercial break was drawing to a close, and Shelby cut

the sound back on. "What's he going to do next? Any ideas?"

"Not a one," I said.

"*I* have one."

"What?"

"I'll bet you," Shelby said, "his next guest is Roy Duncan."

"Taken," I said, precisely as the commercial ended and the program resumed.

But the screen held neither Prescott nor Roy Duncan. We were given a shot of the moon, the fullest moon I'd ever seen, glowing orange and ruling a cloudless night. Then the director smash cut to a young girl running through the desert, running in torn underpants through the desert night beneath a full moon.

Prescott was showing *Moonstalk.*

CHAPTER 24

THEY'D FADED AND FILTERED THE shots of Kelsey, of course, and imposed digital screens over her breasts. But it was certainly Kelsey, and there was no doubt at all it was *Moonstalk*. The clip ended as Kelsey collapsed against a boulder, shuddering and gasping for breath. The screen went dark, and when the picture returned Prescott was again behind his desk.

"Surprise you?" he said. "Make you think you had the wrong network? You don't. You're right where you want to be, right here with me. *I* wanted you to see that. It's from a movie I want to talk about a little bit. It has something to do with tonight's show."

Shelby moved from her side of the bed then, to curl tight against me.

"What you just saw comes from a movie called *Moonstalk*. Some of you may remember that title, but I have to say I hope none of you paid good money to see it. Lot of people did, though. Lot of people paid their good money to see *Moonstalk*."

Shelby said, "Oh, shit," very softly, and squeezed my arm. I watched the television.

"Movie's about two hours long. That's not a lot of time, now, is it? I've preached sermons go on longer than that, and some of you have sat right there and slept through them.

"But I always get to the point, and my point is this. For two hours *Moonstalk* showed that poor little sixteen-year-old girl you just saw, showed her strutting around in her drawers, showed her body, showed her smoking cigarettes, drinking liquor, smoking *dope,* cursing, being *used* in sin by men two and three times her age, showed her fornicating, fornicating with a *preacher* among others." There were groans of disbelief from his audience.

"That little girl's name is Kelsey Stillett and she was a pretty big star. What Hollywood calls *bankable.* She made money and her films made money. Because the kids went to see her. Went to see her doing all those things, all that wickedness. But do we blame her?" he said.

"No, we do not. Of course we do not. She was a *child.* But there was an adult in charge of that movie. He wrote it for her and he directed her, told her to do and say those things. And his name is Baird Lowen."

Shelby's fingers dug at my arm, a brief pressure.

"You know that name, too. Wrote that clever *New Yorker* article about us couple of months ago. You know he's from right here in Samson? He is. Went to the very high school Betty and I started our first teen outreach ministry at. He did. But he didn't listen to Betty and me. He grew up and made *Moonstalk.*

"Maybe grew up's the wrong expression. But maybe not. Because *Moonstalk*'s the last movie he made. Bought himself a farm down east and left Hollywood behind. And I'm going to tell you why that is."

"Baird—" Shelby's voice, barely a whisper, said nothing more than my name. Prescott did not give her time.

"I know Baird Lowen," Prescott said. "I think I know him pretty well. He might call me his friend. I know that I would call him my friend. And because he is my friend, I care about what happens to him. I want to see him redeem himself, overcome the mistakes he's made, put his God-given talent to higher purposes. No more *Moonstalk*s."

Prescott laced his fingers together and studied them. "I had Baird to my barbecue the other night at my place. We sat and talked, Baird and me; we got to know each other. I told him about myself and New Spirit; he told me about himself and he told me about *Moonstalk.* And from listening to him and his talk of . . . *realism,* that's what he called it . . . I could tell that he was troubled by what he had done, by what that film said to its audiences. And it was that trouble, that trouble inside him, that's had him down on his farm doing nothing instead of doing the *good* work the Lord gave him that talent to do."

I turned my head toward Shelby, who was watching me rather than the screen.

"From listening to his talk," Prescott said, "I decided I would have to do something. Do something positive. Do something that will set an example of affirmation to offset the example set by Mr. Lowen's school of realism."

He leaned back in his chair and placed his hands on its arms. "And I asked myself, what can I do? And that's always such a good question. What can *I* do? That's the big one, you know, the one we each must ask. What *can* I do?

"And God gave me the answer. And it's kind of funny and maybe more than that. Because that article Baird wrote was called "Lights! Cameras! Prescott!", and that was the answer God gave me."

Frederick Prescott stood up. He had never looked taller, never seemed more substantial. "And that's what God said to me. Not in those words, but that's what He said.

"And *that*—that is why New Spirit is going to make its own movies!"

He held his hands wide. "Movies that *affirm* life, not degrade it. Because I don't think a *Moonstalk* can compete with that kind of picture, do you? How about it? Do you think I'm right? Can we do better than people like Baird Lowen?"

As one, his audience *affirmed.* Prescott rode the applause. He smiled on through. And when the clapping ended, Prescott brought his own hands together. His broad face was bright with joy. "Now, that's *intent,* but intent has a ways to go before it becomes *achievement.*

"You see, it's one thing to decide to make a movie, to tell everybody you're going to make a movie, but it's another thing to *get it done.* Well, I'm going to get it done. And I'm going to get it done right soon. And that's why, right now, I'd like you to meet somebody. Somebody very special."

Prescott spread his arms wide and said, "Ladies and gentlemen, please make welcome the star of Spirit Films' first production, *Miss Kelsey Stillett!*"

"That son of a bitch!" I shouted, and applauded along with his people. As the curtains parted for Kelsey to make her entrance I began to laugh, heavy rolling laughter coming up from deep within me, no weight on me at all to hold it down.

Kelsey came onto the set. She looked demure and a bit shy, but wholly in control of herself in a dress that was a few years too old for her. She would be twenty now but she looked a decade older. The dress itself was blue, but the lace collar was white and frilly. I wondered who had picked it. Her hair, that boyish cut I had stroked, was now a lustrous blond, piled high and mightily curled. Her stalk was gone, and gone was the model's glide I'd seen at Maurice's home. She simply walked to Prescott's side gracefully, as conscious of her posture as any New Spirit woman. She could be at home with Betty Prescott or Ellen Jennings Duncan any day of the week. The crowd loved her, its roar went on and on. Kelsey bowed twice before Prescott ushered her to the seat nearest his desk.

"Welcome to New Spirit," he said.

"Thank you, Reverend," said Kelsey Stillett. "I'm very proud to be here." Her voice held none of its old edges.

"Now, Kelsey, before we talk about our new movie, let's talk a little bit about you. About the things that have affected your life, and how those things ultimately brought you to Jesus."

"All right," said Kelsey.

"You saw that footage from *Moonstalk*. That was a big picture, wasn't it?"

"Oh, yes. It was quite a hit."

"And how did it feel to star in such a big picture?"

Kelsey dimpled. She did it well. "I'll be honest. A lot of it was real nice. You know. The people you get to meet, the places you get to go. The fan letters. But I wasn't really happy."

"Why not, Kelsey?"

"Well . . . I never thought *Moonstalk* set a good example . . . I mean, I had to do things in that picture that just weren't *me*. You always do, but these were—" She searched for a word.

"Sinful?" Prescott said.

"Yes. That's right." Kelsey looked down for a moment, but then raised her head. "Things I knew were wrong."

"But you gave a good performance."

"I was proud of that." She laughed a little. "I thought I was going to win an Oscar, and I *did* get a nomination. My only one."

"So far," Prescott said, laughing.

"Let's hope," said Kelsey. She began to relax a bit, becoming more at ease in Prescott's presence. "But you know, Reverend, when I see some of *Moonstalk* now, even just a minute, well, I feel a little sick. I think about my mama, you know. I wonder how she would feel if she saw how that movie came out."

"But she passed away while you were making *Moonstalk*, didn't she?"

"Yes she did. Jesus called her while we were on location." Prescott handed her a tissue and Kelsey twisted it in her hands. Her nails were manicured and painted pink.

"And when she died you were left alone. With nobody."

"Just my friends on the set. They were so nice. They helped so much. They did."

"You didn't miss much work."

"No, sir. A lot of people were depending on me. I couldn't let them down."

"Your mama dead and you didn't want to let anybody down," Prescott said with obvious admiration.

"I had a job to do."

"Of course you did. But it couldn't have been easy. With *any* job at a time like that. But having to do what that script called for. The swearing. The smoking. The nudity. The sex."

"It was . . . rough," she said. "But my director helped. Baird Lowen made it as easy for me as he could. You need to know that he never forced me to do anything. He always told me *why* my character was doing these things. And he helped me through my scenes. He got me through it."

It was generous of her, and I had no doubt sincere, and it spread a certain warmth through me, and a certain pride as well.

"But that's just my point," Prescott was saying. "You and I have talked about Baird. It doesn't matter that *Moonstalk* wasn't absolute trash. In fact, it might be worse that it's not. Most people, young people, aren't going to be misled by absolute trash. But something like *Moonstalk,* kids go see it and it's like Hollywood holding up a big green light saying, 'Go ahead! Do whatever you want to!' And that's not right. And that's why we're going to make a *good* movie starring this fine young Christian actress."

"I'm so excited about it. I can't wait."

"And I'm sure we all can't wait to see you in it. It's been a while since you've had a good movie."

"Yes, sir. I've been sort of wandering. From bad movie to bad movie, from party to party." She lowered her eyes again. Her voice was barely audible. "Men . . . drugs." I thought of Maurice Devlin. I had seen Kelsey at his house and I had left her there.

"But no more," Prescott said.

"No more," Kelsey said, and looked up. "I found what I *really* needed."

"And what did you find?"

She looked straight into the camera. "I found Jesus."

"*Amen,*" said Prescott, and his audience joined him.

"And with the help of Jesus—well, here I am."

"Kelsey, tell us how you found Jesus."

She nodded. "It was a bad time, just a few months ago. I'd been with someone, but he got tired of me and I was on my own. My pictures weren't doing well. The scripts got worse and worse. *Moonstalk* was sinful, but at least Baird could tell me why his characters did what they did. These films—" She shuddered.

"And that one night you told me about."

Kelsey smoothed the folds of her dress and folded her hands in her lap. "I was out walking the Strip. Sunset Strip. I'd done some cocaine; I was high and getting off on being recognized, feeding my vanity and my pride. I walked and walked even though the neighborhood was getting worse and worse. I came around a corner and there was this awful, filthy theater. And it was showing *Moonstalk.*" She took a deep breath. "I bought a ticket. I wanted to see. You know?"

"I do," said Prescott.

"And I went inside. I had to look at four different seats before I found one clean enough to sit in. It was . . . pretty disgusting. The place was filled with drunks and dirty old men. One of them tried to . . . touch me, but I moved to another seat, and he was too drunk or stoned even to follow me. So I sat there and watched myself on the screen."

She took a gulp of air. "But I was watching the men, too. Watching the way *they* watched *me* on that screen. Watching what they did when I . . . did things."

"It's all right, Kelsey," Prescott said. "You're with friends now. You're with *family.*"

She composed herself. "I watched the movie twice. Then I got up—it's funny because I remember being very calm when I got up and walked out of the theater. It was very late and the area was bad, but I didn't care. I just kept walking until I came to an alley." Kelsey smiled briefly. "It was full of wine bottles and crack vials and needles but there was no one in it but me, and I just fell to my knees and got sick. I vomited up every poison I had in my body, then. I was crying for the first time since mama left me and when I looked up, there He was."

"Jesus?"

"Yes, sir. It was Jesus Christ, and he put his hand on my forehead and my sickness just went away. Mama was with him and she gave me the best hug I've ever had." Her face was radiant, that light shone so brightly from within her. "They told me everything was going to be all right."

"And what did you do the very next morning?"

"I fired my agent, and got rid of all the . . . trappings of my old life. I got myself a little apartment. And I prayed and I waited."

"What were you waiting for?"

"I wasn't sure."

"And what happened?"

"At first it was about what I expected. A lot of calls from the same old people. The same awful offers. But they finally got the picture. And then one day the phone rang and it was something different."

"What was it?"

"It was Mr. Roy Duncan," she said, "and he was in Los Angeles and had gotten my phone number and wanted to talk to me."

That was the last piece I needed. I would be talking with Mr. Roy Duncan very soon. But first I would hear Kelsey out. I looked at Shelby but her face was blank.

"He had a copy of a script he wanted me to read. He wondered if he could bring it by. He told me who he was working for."

"The Lord."

A spark of the Kelsey I had known showed through. "Yes, sir. But also for you."

Prescott laughed and nodded.

"I'd been watching you a lot. So Mr. Duncan and I talked. I told him about my problems, and he seemed so understanding. He left me the script, and made me promise to keep it very quiet."

"And what did you think?"

"Reverend, it's just the most wonderful movie I've ever read. I can't wait to *see* it!"

"It won't be long before *everybody* gets to see it," Prescott said to generous applause. "We've still got a few things to take care of before the cameras can roll. We're building a big new sound-stage. We're putting together a staff and crew. And we're still looking for just the right director for this job. And you never know. Might be able to get Baird Lowen out of retirement for this one. Wouldn't that be something?"

"It would be wonderful," said Kelsey.

Prescott spread his hands. "We've got a good script, if I do say so myself. I'm pretty close to the writer. Kelsey, why don't you tell the folks who wrote this movie?"

"Betty Prescott," said Kelsey.

Prescott nodded and grinned through one more round. "Every word of it. Nine drafts—I know, she made me read every one. Tell them the name of this good Christian movie we're going to make."

"It's called *The Brightest Light,*" said Kelsey Stillett.

"Betty's going to join us after this next break, and I hope you'll all stick around for some more good talk with this fine young woman."

A commercial began.

Shelby was smiling. "Kelsey Stillett."

"America's sweetheart. Soon to be, anyway. Count on it."

"This was what it was all about."

"Looks like," I said. "It's some feather in Prescott's cap. His people love a redemption better than a barbecue. You can't imagine the publicity he'll get. Kelsey'll be on the cover of *Peo-*

ple next week, count on that, too. No way this can miss."

"And you don't have to worry anymore."

"I doubt I ever did. They're not going to jeopardize this, but they're no fools. If any of them knew the whole story, Roy too, they'd never have hired her. They don't want that much . . . *reality*. Now, packaged like this, she's got just enough dirt on her to be their new favorite lost sheep welcomed back to the fold. That son of a bitch."

"Prescott?"

"No—more power to Prescott. He works his fields; I work mine. This one's as good as any I've ever seen." I thought of an old joke. "Good career move for Kelsey, too. Not Prescott. Roy Duncan." I rose from the bed, pulled on socks and shoes.

"Baird—"

"I'll be back." I took my jacket from the closet.

"Where are you going?"

"Mitch is still dead," I said. "I have a call to make. Let me know if Prescott says any more about me."

"You sure you should?"

I took her in my arms. "Absolutely sure. You wait here, Shelby. I'll be back. I want to see what's under that robe."

Chapter 25

Roy duncan did not invite me into his house, which was fine with me. I had no wish to go inside. Nor did I particularly want Ellen to hear what I had to say. Roy could tell her himself.

His face was tight as he stepped outside, pulling the door closed behind him. "Ellen's watching the reverend, Baird. I don't want to disturb her."

"Neither do I, Roy."

"You were watching."

"Good guess, *old chip*. Watching as you just got screwed by your boss."

"Well—"

"Right. So let's get to it. Did you negotiate with Kelsey? Or was it Maurice?"

He did not even try to evade the question. "It was Kelsey and her new agent. I took the time to meet Devlin. He told me a few things about Kelsey. She told me more." Roy shivered and tried to stare me down, but he could not. "Disgusting things. And Billy Toller."

"And me?"

"And you."

"So there was never any—you never had *anything*."

"I put some things together. Had some luck. Made a guess that paid off."

"It's going to pay off all right. Soon. And you'll just have to

336

wait, because you can't do anything to ruin Prescott's new venture, can you?"

"Let it go, Baird. Let's just call it quits."

I shook my head. "I'm enjoying holding the trump for a change. I've still got my set of *your* pictures, remember? I could just send those pictures out and see what happens."

"Then I'd talk. Maybe I was guessing, but I was right. And maybe Maurice would talk, too."

"Go ahead. All I have to do is go on TV with the reverend and own up to all my sins and ask Jesus's forgiveness. Want to bet I couldn't get away with it?"

Roy said nothing.

"You push me, Roy, and for good measure maybe *I* can come up with some pictures of Kelsey just in time to sink that movie of Prescott's."

"You would do that," he said.

"You know I would," I said, and bet that he was venal enough to believe my lie.

I won the bet. "What do you want, Baird?"

"I want to know why you had Mitch killed."

"You can't prove that."

"I can start trying to."

"Mitch burned in an accident, Baird. He got sloppy. He was out of his league." Roy coughed into a hand.

"Mitch *died,* Roy, and you had a hand in killing him."

"Prove it."

"Some of the pictures can be in the *Defender*'s office tonight, Roy. The *Times* will take longer. Who hired out the job?"

For a moment I thought he would sag to his knees. "There's no way to connect me to Mitch," he said. "I didn't do the hiring."

"Who did?"

"Chris."

I stared at him. I could believe it, but I also knew that Wheeler moved to Roy's tugs at the string. "Be telling me the truth, Roy. Don't be doing anything else."

"It was *Chris,*" he said, and it was nearly a sob.

"You gave the order?"

Roy nodded at last, but I wanted to hear him say it. I gave him a tap on the shoulder with a stiff finger. "I told him how . . . who to hire. I knew from the courts . . ."

"What did you boys pay?"

"A hundred thousand."

"Jesus Christ, Roy, you were a third of the way there to what Mitch wanted. Where'd the money come from?"

"Don't ask me."

"Where?"

"Athletic building fund. Here and there. Chris crunched the numbers. None of this leads back to me."

"But it will. I don't have any illusions about why you're telling me. You're telling me because you're scared I'll hurt you. Maybe you're right to be scared. Maybe I will hurt you."

"Baird, please."

Suddenly I wished that Roy would call me *Bear* and beg. It was something I badly wanted to hear, something I wanted him to do. I stepped back from him and planted my feet. Then I heard a little scrape, and glanced up at the house, and saw, in a high window, Ellen Jennings Duncan watching us. I could not see her eyes, nor did she move when I spotted her. I turned back to Roy. "You deserve to die," I said. "Because, Roy, you have *got* to know what's waiting for you after you're gone."

He had a little spirit left, for he sneered at me. "That's between me and my Lord, Baird. You have no right—"

"I've got a good right, Roy," I said quickly, and crouched, and cocked my arm back to throw the hardest punch of my life. But I did not have to, for Roy Duncan squealed his fear and dropped to his knees on the perfect lawn while his wife watched. "You stay there and pray a while, Roy," I said, and threw a glance at Ellen, but she did not move. I left them.

And because I was close I took the road to Spirit Center, and arrived as the show was breaking up. Everyone from the audience was talking about Kelsey, and I could not help wondering if any of them recognized me. I smiled at those I passed, and used my smile to talk my way past the guards outside the auditorium. They were young men who knew my name, for I told them who I was. They told me where I could find Miss Stillett and Reverend and Mrs. Prescott. I made my way backstage.

But before I could find Prescott I heard my name being called. It was Nancy Hargetay, and she smiled at me, then looked more closely at my still swollen features. "A little accident," I said. "Nothing to worry about."

She was nervous, and drew me to a relatively quiet corner.

"You must be very proud of your brother," I said to her.

Nancy shook her head. "I just want a minute to say something I have to say." She would not meet my eyes. "I rented your movie last night."

"*Moonstalk?*"

"Yes . . . and the reverend's right, but Mr. Lowen he's also wrong. Because that happened to me with a preacher when I was twelve. Not like Kelsey in the movie, not wanting it like that. But having him, having him . . ."

Her shoulders were shaking and her voice broke. I put a hand under her chin and lifted her face. "Nancy? Have you ever told anyone?"

She shook her head. "I wouldn't even let myself think about it. But when I saw . . ."

"You talk to somebody about this right away," I said. "You talk to the reverend and Betty. They'll help you, get you help."

"I couldn't."

"You could and you will. Promise me that. You haven't done anything wrong. Talk to them—"

But she turned and hurried away from me, eyes downcast once more. I watched until she was out of sight. I felt I should go after her, but I did not.

Prescott's back was to me, and he and Kelsey were surrounded by fans. I was worried about Nancy, and I was in a hurry to return to Shelby; but if I had to be patient to get a word in with Kelsey, then I would be patient.

It did not take as long as I had feared. The crowd diminished, and stragglers were ushered along by Prescott's helpers. Finally, Prescott and Kelsey were speaking to the last of the crowd, an older couple. I let them have their turn, then moved quickly behind Kelsey and tapped her shoulder as softly as I could.

She did not look like Kelsey anymore, but she looked wonderful. I could tell from her eyes, I had no doubt, that every word of faith she'd spoken this evening was true. Those eyes were clear but they filled with tears when she saw me and softly spoke my name. Her hands fluttered to her cheeks before she opened her arms and we embraced. "Oh, Baird," she said.

"This Is Your Life," I whispered to her, and made her laugh.

Kelsey held the hug for a long moment before releasing me. When she did, it was slowly, her fingers tracing their way down my arms. She said my name again.

Prescott waited until Kelsey and I had broken our embrace before he spoke. "I *thought* that would get you out tonight," he said.

I joined his laughter. "I dropped by to wish good luck to a very dear old friend."

Kelsey began to cry. "I'm so *happy*," she said.

"Then that's all that matters," I said, and bent to kiss her cheek. "You're doing great. Just don't let this man make you do anything you don't want to."

It was a risk, but it made her laugh again. "Thank you, Baird.

There's a reception. I have to—can you come?"

"You run along," I said. "I'll see you again."

"Kelsey, you wait right here, and we'll be going in a minute," Prescott said. "Baird, you sure you won't come? Well, at least let me walk you to the door." He laid a heavy arm across my shoulders, but I simply stood straight. "You going to direct my picture?" he said.

"I'm on vacation."

"Not retired?"

"Just a vacation, I think."

"Four years' worth?"

"Work hard, play hard," I said.

"You ready to stop playing?"

"Just about."

"Then come direct this movie."

"I don't think so," I said. "But who knows. You've got a lot to do before you have to decide."

"Don't I know it," Prescott said.

"Do you?" I said.

He looked hard at me. "Son, I'm sorry about the football players—"

"It's more than that, and I think you know it."

"Maybe. Maybe I don't want to know."

"I think you do. Because I think that's the kind of man you are. So let me ask you to do two things."

"All right," he said heavily.

"First, have Betty talk to Nancy Hargetay. She'll understand when she does."

"And the other?"

"Go talk to Chris Wheeler. Take a look at the books. Ask him about Mitch Tarr. Ask him about a hundred thousand dollars. Ask him about Roy."

"Now, wait—"

"Done waiting, Reverend. I'm just asking you to look. Nothing more. Now, I've got to run. I've got somebody waiting for me."

"Miss Oakes," he said, and winked, but behind the wink his face remained grave.

"Somebody's got to take care of her. Since you threw her out of work."

Prescott sighed. "Another thing for me to think about."

"You should."

"No doubt," he said. "No doubt."

"Take care of Kelsey, will you?" I found myself saying. "Keep an eye on her."

"She'll be staying with Betty and me, so . . . She'll be in good hands."

"That she will," I said to Frederick Prescott, and meant it.

The television had been turned off and the lights in the suite had been softened. I put my key on the dresser and began removing my clothes. Shelby watched me. "I've got some stories," I said to her.

She nodded. "They'll keep," she said. "I just want you, now. No excess baggage."

I walked to the bed and sank onto it beside her. I reached for her belt, ready to discover the wonders she had hidden beneath her robe. I untied the knot and uncovered only Shelby, nothing more. It was all I wanted.

EPILOGUE

CHAPTER 26

WE WERE DOWN AT THE lowest of my three ponds, going after bass. It was early August, a cloudless afternoon, and each of us used the tools we most enjoyed. I was working slowly with a graphite fly rod, eight feet long and weighing less than three ounces. I had a light fly tied to the end of nine feet of leader and a tippet that was lighter than gossamer, itself tied to a yellow fly line that I worked in careful slow arcs before letting my fly settle to the surface of the water. Prescott used a heavy spinning rod. He was chunking dark plastic worms and dragging them across the bottom of the pond. Neither of us was having much luck.

His arrival that afternoon had been a surprise. He had not called in advance, and I had not heard from him since Shelby and I left Samson in late June. She spent the summer with me and watched as I slowly got back to work.

I was working when I heard his car. It was a black Lincoln, more than a few years old, but immaculately maintained. I called to Shelby when Prescott climbed out. "Baird!" he said. "You home?" I stepped out onto the porch. Prescott hugged Shelby and slapped me on the back, then said that he was in the area and just took a chance on stopping by. We sat in the shade and drank iced tea for an hour. The afternoon melted away. I finally asked if he would be interested in wetting a line with me. His grin came as no surprise: He had old clothes and tackle in his trunk. I got my gear together as he changed. Shelby said she would wait for us, but not to expect her to clean any fish.

When we reached the pond, Prescott and I separated, working our ways in opposite directions. He moved counterclockwise while I went with the hours. I changed flies several times, and caught Prescott watching me work my delicate equipment, raising bluegill but little else. He patiently tossed worms and retrieved them. The sun moved lower in the sky. We met at the far side of the pond.

He did not speak while I made two casts. "Roy Duncan told me how pretty your place is."

"How is old Roy?" He had announced his candidacy at the high school reunion. He was doing well at the polls.

"Well, Baird, he's going to be governor." I reeled in my line and used clippers to cut off the fly. I tied on another one. "Maybe," I said.

"Looks good."

"Did you look into what I asked you to?"

"I did. And didn't find any trace of Roy."

"What about Wheeler?"

Prescott turned the crank on his reel. "Son. Chris Wheeler died around dawn this morning. Crashed his car into a bridge. Burned. It will be on the news tonight." He would say no more.

"Convenient," I said, but he did not dignify that. "And Roy gets to be governor," I said. "Simple as that."

"You haven't heard me out yet, Baird," Prescott said. "I get the impression Roy's done some things he shouldn't. Maybe I've heard a few things. But I want you to look at me." His face was set and stern. "I've got something with Roy now I didn't have before."

I finished tying on my fly. "What's that?"

"A leash," said Prescott as I let the line shoot, depositing the fly near a little stump that stuck a few inches out of the water. "I've got him on a leash now, and he'll do right or I'll jerk him up short."

I said nothing. I wasn't worried. Prescott might hold the leash, but I owned Roy Duncan's collar, and no one knew it but me.

The afternoon of the day he died, Mitchell Tarr mailed a letter to me at my motel. Nothing had ever surprised me as much. I must have read it twenty times, at the motel and, later, at the lakehouse. It was a good letter.

> Dear Baird,
>
> I guess this will be over tonight, and I will have my money or I will not. I don't trust Roy and I know you do not either. So let me offer something.
>
> Roy was with me all those years ago when those photos were taken. That's what made this such a shuck. Because he was beside me, we had followed you, and we wanted to be alone, too. Roy and I were close.
>
> We didn't last much after that, and Roy went on to Ellen. But I loved him and he would pretend that never existed, but I am writing this because of something you said. First love and all that.
>
> I am HIV positive, and I want the money to work with a clinic. So it will go to good things. (And fifty thousand will go to Roy's opponent the minute I get paid, just to make some more of his hair come out. Maybe he will have a stroke.)
>
> I am not afraid of dying, but I am afraid of dying with my work undone.
>
> You should be, too. You can be better than you are.
> Mitch

"Now, do you know something else I should know?" Prescott asked.

I did not answer immediately because the bass came up like a freight train, its huge mouth wide open as it sucked in the fly.

My patience held, and I set the hook at just the right moment. Then I held the rod tight and let the fish take some line. I coerced it with some gentle pressure into one spectacular leap, and then I brought it in, removed the fly from its jaw, held it up for Prescott to see before I turned it loose.

Prescott reeled in all the way. He was done. "I'd like to fish here again sometime," he said.

"Any time. Bring Betty. We'll have a picnic."

There were clouds coming up fast, pushed by a strong breeze. I broke down my rod and we hurried up the hill.

"You working, Baird?"

"I'm working *on* something. We'll see where it goes."

"I hired Luke Blair for *The Brightest Light.* Kelsey and Betty like him."

"He's a good man," I said.

"This a movie you're writing?"

I nodded. "Back to my old tricks. A little older and maybe a little wiser."

"That's a dangerous combination, Baird."

"And nobody's got me on a leash."

We walked in silence, and I thought of my July flight to California and my meeting with Maurice Devlin. He seemed pleased to see me, and was even more pleased with the treatment I brought along. This time he read it, and when he finished he offered me full financing, and a full balancing of our books. I was polishing the script when Prescott arrived. Maurice was amused by Kelsey's new career, and even allowed that he missed her sometimes. I did not stay with him long, but was there long enough to see him tease Valerie Toller as she splashed in the small pool he had built for her. I promised him the script by October. We would begin shooting next May.

Prescott placed his tackle in the Lincoln's trunk, and I fetched his clothes from the house. He felt like driving in his fishing clothes. "Got to change when I get home. Got a widow to comfort."

Shelby did not come out to say good-bye, and I think the reverend understood that. I had asked her to marry me, or at least accompany me back to California for the shoot, to stay with me. She was not certain, for as June receded further and further into the past, some things weighed upon her. Once, she cursed me for the time I had shown her. More often, she held me close, and told me she loved me. Call us a couple of cripples, learning how to walk.

"What's your movie called?" Prescott said as he got into his car.

"*One Soul,*" I said.

"Nothing for me in it? I'm getting to like this film business."

I shook my head. "About a man who's killed so others can get power."

Prescott sighed. "You naming names, son?"

"Just telling a story," I said.

"Well, I guess I'll look forward to seeing it."

"I guess you will," I said, and before he left I asked, "How's Nancy Hargetay?"

"That was a good thing you did, and maybe some good, the only good, that came out of that *Moonstalk* of yours. She's getting better. Betty's helping. And Kelsey—that girl's got a gift for helping."

"She does," I said.

We shook hands without further words, and Prescott left my house.

I stood in the driveway for a long time and thought of what I had to do. At some point before election day I would have to pay a call on Roy Duncan. I thought of working with Maurice Devlin again, and thought of all of Shelby's fears about that.

Thunder rumbled and I laughed a little. I checked the car

windows and closed the door of my shed. For a few minutes I simply stood in my yard and watched the tops of the trees swaying in the wind. The first big drops of rain caught me unprepared and I had to run to my front porch. But I took the steps slowly, and lingered there a moment before going into the house where Shelby waited warily for me.